Kokio

A Novel Based on the Life of Neill James

Stephen Preston Banks

Tellectual Press
tellectual.com

Tellectual
Press

To Janet & Tony, with gratitude and affection~ Steve

Tellectual Press

tellectual.com

Valley, WA

Print ISBN: 978-1-942897-08-8

Tellectual Press is an imprint of Tellectual LLC.

Table of Contents

Praise for *Kokio*

"*Kokio* is a wonderful contribution to the increasingly popular genre of biographical novels. Rather than dramatizing the story of a famous figure like Virginia Woolf, Friedrich Nietzsche, Sylvia Plath, or Marilyn Monroe, as so many skillful biographical novelists have done, Stephen Banks pictures the unfamiliar life of Neill James, a spectacular woman who was an under-cover intelligence agent, travel writer, novelist, and adventurer. Kokio testifies to the value and power of the biographical novel, which, in this instance, does the important cultural and historical work of resurrecting a nearly lost life."

—**Michael Lackey**, author of
The American Biographical Novel and *Truthful Fictions: Conversations with American Biographical Novelists*

"Stephen Banks refers to *Kokio*, based on the life of Neill James–intelligence agent, intrepid adventurer, writer and, above all, a woman adept at recreating herself–as a novel based on a life, but that's an understatement. He's accomplished far more. After ten years of intensive research, Banks has succeeded in creating a character so believable, so true to life, she jumps off the page of this masterful page-turner of a book."

—**Diana Anhalt**, author of
Second Skin and *Because There Is No Return*

"Neill James had the rare luck and the rare talent to invent–and re-vent–her life as she lived it. Her "inventions" often disguised secrets; some trivial, others not. Stephen Banks has done a masterful job of reconstructing and revealing that life, weaving it together with a strand of fiction that Neill, doubtless, would appreciate."

—**Richard Spence**, author of
Secret Agent 666: Aleister Crowley, British Intelligence and the Occult

Il n'y a pas un être humain capable de dire ce qu'il est avec certitude.

—Léon Bloy, *L'Ame de Napoleon*

Native Hawaiians used the kokio, one of the showiest of native flowers, as an invisibility aid.

—Lavonne Leong, "The First Hawaiians: Native Plants"

Prologue

Look back upon the ages of time past
Eternal, before we were born, and see
That they have been nothing to us, nothing at all.

—Lucretius, *De Rerum Natura*, Book III, *tr.* Ronald Melville

She had just finished her bachelor's degree at the finest women's college in the South. She was a mediocre student, vainly handsome, a bold and accomplished athlete, and a first-rate stenographer with a professional certificate to prove it. She told people her parents were wealthy plantation owners and her father owned the first Buick in Mississippi. A century later her descendants would report that her father had gone bust and the family back then was dirt poor.

It was 1918, and she landed a job in Washington, D.C. at the Department of War. She was then merely sixteen years old, or nineteen, or perhaps twenty-three—it would depend on which of her stories you believed. Her name was Nell Neill James, but by then she insisted on being called Neill James.

Before the end of 1918 she would be assigned as secretary to the base commander of Fort Vancouver in Washington State. Within the following year she would be reassigned and have the same job title at Fort George Wright in Spokane. How she achieved those senior positions so early in her work life is not revealed in the records. In the three years following demobilization, she would operate a clothing boutique in Portland, Oregon, sell ice across Oahu while living at Waikiki Beach, and then join the U.S. Department of State as a clerk in the embassy at Tokyo, Japan.

In Japan the State Department put her up at the Imperial Hotel and later settled her in a house, alone but for her maid and cook. She went, or was sent, on a wintertime sojourn to Mukden, Harbin, Manchuria, Mongolia and Korea, traveling behind the lines of the Sino-Japanese War. In her first book she called the trip "a holiday." Upon returning to Tokyo she wrote directly to the Secretary of State to complain about her pay: Her clerk's wages couldn't cover her housing expenses and wardrobe, and she demanded a raise. Secretary Kellogg asked Ambassador McVeigh in a hand-written note if he might find less costly lodging for her. The Ambassador filed the note in her personnel folder.

While in Hawaii she passed her free time sunbathing and surfboarding and told everyone she was half-Native Hawaiian. In Japan she told colleagues she was seven years younger than census documents would show it. Later, in Berlin, she claimed to be part Japanese. At age twenty-five or twenty-nine or thirty-two, depending on which of her stories you believe, she convinced a German customs official that she was eighteen. So she claimed in her first book. Her age on half of her passports was wrong, some off by four years, some by seven.

She wrote feature articles about her marriage to a Scottish lord with six names and managed to get the articles published in newspapers in Portland, Oregon and New Haven, Connecticut. She included details about her wedding at New York City's fashionable Riverside Church and told of the groom's aristocratic family back in Scotland. On March 13, 1937, the day of the purported nuptials, Riverside Church was closed for a civic event. Neither the Scottish lord nor his families can be found in the genealogies and biographical sources. The new husband, she had written, was a graduate of Carnegie Mellon University. That institution, however, has no record of his ever enrolling there. She claimed she attended the University of Chicago in 1919, but officials there can find no evidence of her matriculation. No record exists, either, for the marriage.

By the time she was entering middle-age, Neill James had circled the globe at least twice; summited most of the highest peaks in the continental U.S., Hawaii, Japan, Europe and Mexico; conducted studies of Lapland's Sami, Hokkaido's Ainu and the Otomí of Mexico's highlands; and published four travel books and one novel with the top publishing house in the English-speaking world. She shared her editor with Ernest Hemingway, F. Scott Fitzgerald, Thomas Wolfe, Ring Lardner, Erskine Caldwell and Marjorie Kinnan Rawlings. She took charge of the publicity for her books, broadcasting on WOR New York as The Petticoat Vagabond–traveler, author and lecturer. She did similar broadcasts in wartime Japan, Korea and China. She corresponded with her editor, Maxwell Perkins, on letterhead stationary of luxurious hotels where she had never lodged.

She stayed four months in Mexico City's American-British Cowdray Hospital to recover from near-fatal injuries she sustained in a fall descending from the summit of Volcán Popocatéptl. She grew impatient with the medical staff at Cowdray, left against doctors' advice, and took over her rehabilitation at a remote hot springs resort near Toluca. The Paricutín volcano had just begun its violent birth from a corn field in far Colima. She hitched a ride with three women touring Mexico in the future Princess Titi Von Furstenberg's chauffer driven phaeton. Overnight at the foot of Paricutín, the log hut Neill was sleeping in collapsed under the weight of volcanic debris, and her legs and shoulder once again were crushed. She was the only one seriously injured.

The four women were chauffered back across Mexico to the Cowdray Hospital. An old friend arrived from San Francisco to visit the convalescing travel writer and spoke of a quiet place on the shore of a spectacular lake in the Jalisco Sierra where Neill might recover from her injuries. When Neill could travel they went to the tiny fishing village of Ajijic and settled in at the casita of the Heuers, émigré German brother and sister, who saw them through the first few weeks. The friend left for home; Neill remained at Ajijic for the next fifty years, ever after walking with a limp. There she established a women's millinery cooperative, created two public libraries, was said to have brought in electricity and telephone lines, and bought, sold or gave away dozens of houses. She would tell people Amelia Earhart was her dear friend and Ernest Hemingway, George Bernard Shaw, and Tennessee Williams had come to see her.

After settling in Mexico she stopped writing, although for the rest of her life she would sign gift copies of her books "The Authoress Neill James," making a little circle for the dot over the *i*.

I

Damon Byrd James

> To survive, she had to be alert, adroit, and bold, and she had had to wrap
> herself in a legend from the very start.
>
> —Nina Berberova,
> *Moura: The Dangerous Life of the Baroness Budberg*

I was not long into my teens when my mother first told me I had an ancestor who was a famous author. In her later years she would tell that to me again and again, for she dearly loved to reminisce about our distinguished relatives, despite her growing forgetfulness. That first time, however, she also showed me a crackled photograph of an intense young woman with darkly seductive eyes and a nest of thick black hair encircling her head. There was something of a challenge in the girl's expression, and she conveyed considerable self-regard. She seemed to be both inviting me to admire her proud beauty and simultaneously challenging me to defend my admiration, and I recall feeling uneasy. My mother said she was the daughter of my great-grandfather's half-brother, which I then reckoned made her one of those obscurely titled distant relations I had yet to settle in the family pantheon.

Mother said to me, "Now Damon, you remember stories about Byrd Cullen James? He was your great-granpapa, and he was the inspiration for your middle name. Well, his father, John Culpepper, married three times, and Byrd Cullen's mother, Margaret, was John Culpepper's third wife. John Culpepper's second wife was Lucinda, and she gave birth to six children, one of whom was Charles Campbell James. That was the author Nellie James's father."

I must admit I had difficulty making the connections. Adding to my confusion, Mother told me little was now known about the girl in the photograph named Nellie or about the Charles Campbell James line of the family, the Mississippi branch, except for the few stories that survived the five generations from John Culpepper James to my father. The tales said that that other line of Jameses hadn't done so well as our people here in South Carolina, at least counting down from the era of Charles Campbell James. They were mostly Baptists, and we remained Episcopalians. They stayed in agriculture, crop farming, while we went mostly into the professions—banking, medicine, the law, and publishing. But the story that Mother told most often was that Nellie James had been a world traveler and a well-known author who was orphaned as a young girl, who never married or even cared much for men—Mother had a delicacy about such matters—and had faded, perhaps like that old photograph, into obscurity. The family lore said she had died in Mexico.

Many years after my mother's first mention of Nellie James, long after I completed my studies at The Citadel and had taken over as publisher here in Charlottesville and improved the family enterprise, and after my parents both had passed, I came across the photograph among my mother's effects. Like any businessman who believed he had arrived, I then felt in need of a constructive pastime, and as there was no member of the James clan who declared for the post of designated genealogist, I determined to take up the mantle, charging myself with learning what is possible to discover about my ancestors, including the Charles Campbell James line. And so I also acquired a legitimate goad to look further into the life of the young woman in the photograph.

Following my retirement, I eventually left off my work on the clan genealogy and pursued an irresistible urge to learn about and tell the story of my third-cousin, or great-aunt once removed, Miss Nell Neill James. This is so because the more I learned, the more intriguing her character became to me. I have ever since been collecting stories, visiting graveyards, interviewing any person with a connection to her life, and searching through remote and often stale archives. The story never will be complete, but now I can at least tell the saga of her growing-up years. I have learned as well about her late years in Mexico and her struggles and legacy there.

Nell Neill's mother's name was Willie Anna Wood, and she was born into a respectable Mississippi family in that pivotal year of 1861. The Wood family had been successful cotton planters. Willie was the second of ten children, seven girls and three boys. She became Willie Anna James when on November 18, 1884 she married a high-spirited Gore Springs farmer and Grenada County politician full of promises named Charles Campbell James.

That branch of the James clan had come to Mississippi in the early nineteenth century, starting from North Carolina, where our forebears had landed from Europe. Two generations before Charles was born, his direct ancestors had split off and migrated westward to Warren County Tennessee, then down to Autauga County on the Alabama River. Like so many before and after them, the James clan spread west and south like the edge of dawn on the new continent. They moved briefly back to Tennessee in the early 1830's and by 1833 had gone south and homesteaded at Horse

Pen Creek in the Mississippi Territory, near what today is named Gore Springs. There they stayed for the next half century, until Nell Neill's generation of James children arrived and began scattering like feral chickens across the state and even beyond. Many of their descendants, however, are in the Gore Springs area today, either returned from afar or as progeny of those who remained close to the local soil.

Charley, as Nell Neill's father was commonly called, was born into a farming family in 1857. His father, the John Culpepper James of my mother's stories, was a prosperous landowner and prominent citizen before the Civil War, but family records say he lost much of his wealth in the War. Later, Charley supplemented his diminishing farm income by working for the County. Soon the gradient began changing so severely that the farm earnings would become the supplement to Charlie's government pay.

Nell Neill seemed to have forgotten everything of her own childhood before her sister Jane was born. In her books she never mentioned her early days in Gore Springs or her mother, and her father figured only in the stories she occasionally told acquaintances about his grand Buick touring car and the imagined family plantations. The last of Nell's generation, Jane, came along eight years after her, and Jane's birth was probably related by more than mere propinquity to Willie's death shortly afterward. The story must begin, then, at Jane's birth in the summer of 1903, rather than at Nell Neill's, which the few reliable records say occurred on January 3, 1895. My rendition of Nell Neill's childhood and family life depends largely on the diaries faithfully kept by her maternal aunt, Mattie, which was how Matilda Wood was called.

Willie Anna James would have the baby at home, just as she had done with the previous eight children, one every two years or so, going back to the first, in 1886. It was the usual way then for rural families, and most American families in the early Industrial Age were rural. Willie had lost the second child, the infant Elma, in 1888, just eleven months after an easy birth. All those earlier deliveries had been uncomplicated. This time, though, Willie was troubled.

The baby wasn't positioned right, not breech but nearly so, and Willie lay upstairs on the James's high pine bed and struggled in agony for forty hours before Charley saddled the roan mare and rode to the Four Corners to fetch the doctor. The other women in attendance—Willie's older sister Mattie and the elderly neighbor Hannagrace Griffin, who had trained as a nurse during what she always called The War of Northern Aggression—stayed by her like doulas, insisting that she frequently change position and wrapping her in warm towels. They gave her a tea of chase-devil and told her old family stories to calm her and distract her from the awful pain of the baby's urgings. Eventually the three women succeeded in their efforts to bring the infant into the world, and when Charley and Doctor Denison arrived all that was left to do was decide on a name and register the birth in Grenada. The doctor said Willie would be just fine in a day or two.

It was July 23, 1903, and the only other person present that day to witness the birth of Jane Elizabeth James was eight year old Nell Neill. This fact—that Jane was born under the awestruck gaze of her older sister Nellie, while the other six siblings were out of the house—might partially account for the lifelong special bond between the two, evident in all the letters and travels and gifts they shared, far more intimate and trusting and constant than the ties either of them had kept with any of the others in the James clan of Gore Springs, apparently including their parents. For the rest of her long life Jane repeatedly claimed she had been a motherless child, and she never spoke of her father.

When Jane was born, her brother Damon Donald, with whom I share given names, already was seventeen and working on the county road gang. He found time also to continue helping each evening with the farm work. Sue Aileen would turn fourteen in a few days, but just then she was too easily distressed by matters of sex and reproduction to want to be present. The other children, ages twelve, ten, six, and almost five, had been sent away under the reluctant surveillance of Sue Aileen for a few days at Grandmother Wood's plantation. Only Nell Neill demanded to be present for the birth. Charley knew his willful daughter well enough to anticipate there would be a long and intense struggle with her unless he relented. Perhaps he reckoned that she could be a comfort to her mother. Nell was, he would reason, more resourceful and independent than the other children, and she seemed uncommonly interested in how nature works in all its wonders. He told his friends Nell was his clever house cat.

A few days passed and the infant was thriving, but Willie still was unable to leave her bed. She had trouble holding down food and was listless and weak. For a time Nell Neill brought meals of broth and soft bread to her and helped Aunt Mattie care for infant Jane, who had been named after another aunt on the mother's side. It was suspected that Aunt Mattie was the wet-nurse. By the morning of the fourth day, Charley could see that Willie Anna was not improving, so he brought Dr. Denison out to examine her. There were whispered consultations among the adults, and the five children at Momma Wood's estate were told they would have to stay on for a bit longer.

The days turned into weeks, the young ones returned to prepare for school, but Willie failed to improve. Charley had business around the county, examining agricultural properties and disbursing the new state and federal funds, but he came home to the farm almost every evening, turning his buggy up the long, red-dirt driveway just before sunset, past the windbreak of spruce-pine and dogwood and stopping at the well pump. The hunting dogs greeted him with bowed heads and wagging rumps. Donald already would have been out in the cooling fields supervising the help, or servicing machinery in the sheds, and the two next younger kids, Elwyn Edward and Sue Aileen, would be looking forward to relief from their bedside care and babysitting responsibilities. They liked going out to greet their father and taking charge of the livery and grooming chores.

Often during those weeks when all the children were back home and Willie lay abed, an aunt or cousin would bring over a chicken casserole or cheese grits and fish and some butter tarts, as supper for the whole family. But there was no pleasant talk and laughter as there would be ordinarily, no singing, no buzz of activity: The house was hushed, and always there was a dark awareness of Willie declining upstairs, barely registering her raspy breaths and growing more ashen and thinner it seemed by the hour.

She continued to ebb, sometimes lying motionless as if she were in a coma. She became cadaverously thin and eventually refused all food. After two months with no sign of improvement in her condition, Dr. Denison took Charley aside and told him it did not look favorable for Willie. "I shall do what I can to keep her comfortable," he said, "but there is not much more I can do for her."

"Please see that she doesn't suffer unnecessarily."

It was early autumn when Willie died. The red maple and tulip trees already had turned to amber and gold. The sweetgum fruits had passed, and swirling fog rose in the hollows each morning. Though she had wearily clung to life, Willie seemed toward the end to have given up, as if the weight of returning to the care for so many children and a sprawling household bore her down so that she could not rise from her bed. The funeral was well attended, as Willie had so many brothers and sisters, now all adults with children of their own, and Charley was the ninth child of his father's ten.

Nell Neill told Charley she would help with the meal following the service. "But then," she said, "I want to leave. I want to go live with Auntie Mattie."

"All you children will stay right here after the burial, and nobody is going to live with Aunt Mattie."

"She asked me to join her, Daddy, and you can't take care of us all anyway."

"No she didn't." Charlie well knew his scheming daughter. "We'll find a way, Nellie, don't you worry." He was well known for his gentle durancy. "Now just get along and make yourself ready for your Mamma's funeral." Charley would have spoken slowly in quiet, somber tones.

"I can't guarantee I will be here tomorrow, Daddy."

"I can guarantee that you will, Nellie. I will be needing you here."

And she did stay at home, she did continue going to the four-square, white clapboard school near the crossroads in Gore Springs, and she continued to help with work around the farm, as all the children uncomplainingly would do. But she sometimes went off alone into the sweet-smelling pine woods below the pastures and sat by the creek for hours, watching birds and hunting bugs and salamanders and dreaming of a getaway. When Charlie upbraided her for skipping out on her chores, she would say she had been secretly doing schoolwork or had been in prayer and lost track of time.

A few years later, when she again was sent to Momma Wood's plantation, Nell would see the Gypsy families encamped in the shade at a water hole's edge, and she would long to travel with them. She was lodging again at her grandmother's home because Charley had been voted out of office as County Agent. After Willie passed away, Charley had found it difficult to bring his usual energy and focus to his government responsibilities while tending to the children and farm. The citizens of Grenada County needed an Agent who could devote more dedicated attention to the proper management of their agricultural needs, and so Charley became unemployed. His drinking had increased noticeably, too, and that didn't enhance his opportunity for future work in Grenada County.

Out of office, Charlie fretted about the family and struggled to keep the farm running—Damon Donald couldn't be expected to assume full responsibility for managing the field hands and sharecroppers on his own, even with the increased help of Elwyn. Ailene was just entering high school and wasn't grown up enough to take over all the household supervision. Charley knew he could find work at the lumber mill down in Hattiesburg, and after Ailene finished school in a few years, she could manage the household and the four youngest children could rejoin the family.

He later would rent a sprawling apartment above a grain store in Hattiesburg, and he hoped eventually to have a house again. Meanwhile he was just lucky that his mother-in-law consented to take in the young ones once more.

Charlie delayed going to Hattiesburg for nearly a year while he settled up the farm. He was delayed also because of another grievous death. Ever after, he would wonder from time to time if his decision not to move immediately to Hattiesburg somehow contributed to Tom's accident. Maybe if he had left right away Tom would still be telling jokes and playing tricks.

Two years older than Neill–around this time she began insisting that she be called by her second name only–Tom was the mischievous, happy-go-lucky child. He also had a knack for getting into difficulty because of his persistent curiosity about how things work. They occasionally found him stuck in a culvert or pinned by the hand to a shear block in the barn or stranded high in a tree, where he might have been inspecting a kite's aerie or a white-tailed hornet nest. He frequently was seen sporting a new bandage or brace.

But on that bright afternoon in 1905, barely six months after his father had lost his job, Tom got too close to the chain and transfer gear of the manure spreader. He could have been trying to extract a turd ball from the tines. Perhaps he just wanted to know how all the parts were related. But it was still hitched up, and the horse moved forward and Tom's sleeve must have been caught in the chain before the horse bolted. He did not suffer long, but there was not much of him left intact.

The other children were not permitted to see the remains, nor did they attend the service. In those days, public mourning was thought to be unseemly. Tom was buried next to his mother and other Wood descendants at the big church cemetery in Grenada. Charley said Willie would have wanted it that way, instead of burying him at the James family graveyard off the Cadaretta-Conley Road. Charley was heartbroken, of course, but he had the other seven children to think about. Donald would stay a while in Grenada and Gore Springs, but the others would need supervision and housekeeping. He would take the two next older ones, Ailene and Elwyn, to Hattiesburg with him, where he thought he could soon move up from yard man to office worker. The other four–Nell Neill, John Cullen, young Willie Anna, and the baby–would stay on at Momma Wood's home for at least a year. Charley hoped the arrangement could last until Ailene finished high school, nearly three years off.

Neill didn't like the arrangement. "I don't want to live at Momma Wood's place, Daddy. Her house is too big and clean, and we always have to be quiet. She says I am too noisy and full of myself. Anyway, I'm eleven now and old enough to be with Ailene and Elwyn, I'm not one of the little kids anymore."

"You won't be eleven until next January. I know it's difficult for you Nellie, but your grandma is being very generous to help us out in our time of need. Give it all the patience and strength you have for this one year, Nell, and we'll see later about next year."

"How about if I came down to Hattiesburg next summer? I could be a help to you there, and really, Daddy, I want to stay close to Ailene."

"We'll see, we'll see."

"It would give Momma Wood a respite from my noise and troublesomeness," she said with a hint of a smirk and a sidelong flash of her dark eyes.

"That might turn out to be a good idea. But right now Momma Wood needs your help caring for Jane. All I can promise is to consider it next year."

"All well if I don't take sick. There's bad air at Momma Wood's, Daddy, real bad."

"Next year, Nell."

"Will you think also about Christmas, Daddy? We should all spend Christmas together, and I don't want it to be at the plantation."

"We'll see. One thing at a time," Charley replied wearily.

The decline in Charlie's luck and fortunes might have been a source of intentional distance that developed between the Mississippi line of the James clan and ours here in South Carolina. My people descended from successful plantation owners, community leaders, bankers and physicians, and even my grandfather Guy Aven James, who moved to Gore Springs early in his life, turned handsome profits with his landholdings. But it wasn't until the most recent generations that Charlie's reputation achieved something of a makeover, and that was partly because of the imaginative storytelling and self-elevation by his daughter Nell Neill, who otherwise scarcely mentioned him.

In time, Sue Ailene dutifully finished school, and she took over the James household in Hattiesburg the summer of 1907. Neill and her younger siblings John Cullen, Willie Anna and Jane, left Momma Wood's plantation and rejoined their father, Ailene, Donald, and Elwyn. Donald by that time had taken a job working in the lumber mill, too.

Neill enrolled in the local schools and soon distinguished herself as an athlete, social whirlwind, and theatrical performer. She was a handsome girl with thick hair and dark, penetrating eyes that could convey confidence or arrogance with equal ease. She played softball and tennis in the Hattiesburg parks circuits and excelled at basketball in high school. She soon began inviting the most popular girls and the ones from the best families to the ramshackle upstairs apartment. She used fresh honeysuckle to mask the creosote and urine smells and covered over the worn spots in the linoleum with rugs borrowed from Momma Wood, and she served lemonade in summer and hot tea in winter. Not a few boys who were dizzy with infatuation followed her home, but Neill brushed them off. She was more interested in being close to the best girls in town. She was an undistinguished student, but she showed enthusiasm for her commercial business courses and was fascinated by current events and journalism.

Entertaining and dressing properly, however, were difficult because always there was insufficient money. Before Neill entered her junior year at high school, Charlie had suffered a green chain accident at the mill that put him out of work and made it painful for him even to rise from a chair. He was despairing and began drinking hard every day, and the rest of the household became dependent for income on those children who had jobs but still lived together in the apartment. That mainly meant Aileen and Neill, because the older boys had already gone out on their own and could contribute only occasional donations.

Charlie died in quiet despair on October 16, 1911. Sue Ailene took over the family like a brigade commander under fire, and the remaining children who were then living together rallied around her leadership. In contrast to Neill, Ailene was blue-eyed and red-headed. Although she was short for her age and was teased for being scrawny, she had a bearing and gaze that conveyed much strength of will and self-confidence. Her look also carried the tired warmth the children often had seen in their mother's face in earlier years.

Neill thought that after she graduated from high school she would move on, travel to New Orleans, maybe work in a bank or become a reporter for the *Picayune.* But she had no money, not even enough for bus fare to the Gulf, and given the household situation it looked doubtful that she ever would. After commencement, the high school commercial arts teacher helped her secure a job in the paste-up shop of a Hattiesburg advertising company. Neill was to assist the artist and in her slack time keep the balance sheets and open mail. Within a month, however, she was composing ads and developing new accounts on her own. Neill confided to Aunt Mattie that she learned the business so fast she already knew more about advertising and selling than her boss.

She soon began offering schemes for vastly improving the business, but the owner, Mr. Broadus Knight, found her ideas impractical and risky. He told his Young Men's Business Club associates that his new employee was "a bit too rambunctious."

Neill stayed on through the winter, walking to her job at Knight Advertising & Engraving six days a week and contributing to the family bank account. She saved nothing, though, and soon accumulated a sizable debt for the clothing she had been buying for herself at Rubinstein's Hub department store. A business woman has to be properly dressed for her job, Neill frequently said in response to her older sister's chastisements. Eventually, at Sue Ailene's insistence, Neill devised a plan to pay off her debt, and she stuck to it. But by the spring of 1914 she had become restless and was thinking of ways to resolve all her dissatisfactions. She would find her rightful station in society. By pinching her pennies she could save enough to travel away from Hattiesburg and Gore Springs and Grenada, and she would prepare herself for a professional career, perhaps in advertising or public information work. She would find adventure and see the world, free as the Gypsies at Momma Wood's estate.

A chance event disrupted that daydream. In April, Kittie Holcomb, a close high school friend and daughter of State Representative, later to be U.S. Representative, Wallace Holcomb of Hattiesburg, returned home from a year's internship in Washington D.C. Kittie excitedly told Neill about her good fortune.

"I'm just in heaven," she gushed. "My future is sealed, and I'm sure to meet one of those Oxford boys, and the only thing lacking to make it perfect will be you, Neill. Oh, I so want you to come with me."

"What on earth are you talking about?"

"I'm going to the girls' college come August." She brandished in Neill's face the acceptance notice from the vice president of the Columbus campus. The founding legislation had named the postbellum school The Industrial Institute and College for the Education of White Girls of the State of Mississippi. It was one of the oldest and finest women's liberal arts colleges in the South, and some people deigned to compare it favorably with

Mount Holyoke and Smith Colleges in Massachusetts. Eventually the school came to admit Negro girls, and in 1982 the U.S. Supreme Court ordered the institution, by then called Mississippi University for Women, to admit males too. But in 1914 only White girls whose families could pay the living expenses were admitted. On the other hand, the population of Mississippi was so small and rural that any smart White girl whose family could pay the room and board was almost certain to be let in.

Neill wanted to be happy for Kittie, but she could not imagine just then how it would be possible for her to join in her friend's dream of a perfect future. Although the college was tuition-free, it still cost dearly for lodging and meals, books, laboratory supplies, proper clothing and social expenses. And it was forbidden then to attend the college while holding down a job. Almost immediately, though, Neill began to think of the possibilities. She reasoned that going to college would be a respectable way to leave Hattiesburg. And she might gain the training and credentials she would need for her future jobs. If she went to the girls' college she would be surrounded by lovely young women and easily could make connections with families of the right sort. Surely there must be a way to fund it.

"I think I just might look into that, Kittie," she said. "My grandmother Wood has always favored education for girls, and for a time I was practically one of her own children."

But when Neill told Sue Ailene of her plan to ask Momma Wood to support her college education, her sister was firm in opposing the idea: "Momma Wood declared she would have nothing further to do with us after Daddy's unfortunate last years. She believes she has paid any debt that might be owed to the children of her deceased daughter. Besides, she is an old woman, seventy-six now, and her financial affairs are no longer in her hands."

"I'm confident," Neill responded, "that Aunt Mattie would help me gain Momma Wood's favor. She has always been committed to my education."

"I never heard mention of your education from her. Besides, all of our mother's living sisters share in the overseeing of the trust. Even if you were to impose on Aunt Mattie, there are too many aunties to get through and too many cousins to share with. No, you'll have to find some other source."

Neill, however, seemed to have the natural luck of a house cat. Within days of Ailene dismissing Neill's plan, Damon Donald paid a visit, and at supper he announced a plan of his own for the household.

"We need to do something to better our future," he declared, "as a family, or what's left of our family." Donald eyed Neill as if the future of the clan rested upon her agreement to his idea. "There needs to be a way to get the younger kids a better chance in life than I've had and you, Ailene, have had so far, and that way must be through education. I have thought up a method to get all four of the young ones still living here a good college education. I will get the log rolling, but everyone will have to do their part and cooperate."

He proposed that he pay all the expenses for Neill to attend college, and he reminded Neill that he was thrifty and had had steady work as a machine operator at the mill for half a decade. She could attend any college she wished, but it must be a reputable one, and the arrangement was only on condition that she finish her bachelor's degree and return to Hattiesburg to execute her duty by funding the next younger sibling's college of choice.

"That way, eventually Nellie and Cullen and Bill and Janie all will get a fine education and have greater chances for success in life," he concluded. By that time young Willie's siblings affectionately called her Bill.

Neill cringed whenever they called her Nellie, but she stifled her irritation, for she instantly recognized her immense good fortune. "Why Donald, that's overly kind of you to think of helping me with my education, and I think it's a powerful good plan. I wonder if you might go so far as to think it would be possible to pay for a place like the girls' college in Columbus? I mean, if I could be accepted. There are no tuition costs, and it's the finest college for girls in the South."

"If you can get in there Nell, I'll find a way to pay for it. And you won't have to work while you're there. But my offer isn't just for your education. You must promise to do your duty afterward and come home and pay for the rest of Cullen's schooling."

"Oh y'all can count on me. When I make up my mind to do something, I won't be turned aside."

Neill immediately started a campaign to gain admission to the Industrial Institute and College of Mississippi. She gathered letters of recommendation from her teachers and tradesmen she knew in Hattiesburg, including Frank Rubinstein of the department store. She lobbied some of the city's political leadership she had met through her job to gain their endorsements for her application. Representative Wallace Holcomb wrote a letter in her behalf, and Mr. Broadus Knight enthusiastically wrote her a note of appreciation. All these letters she appended to her papers when she applied to the college. In due course a notice arrived saying that she was admitted provisionally. Her acceptance was contingent upon receipt of proper assurance that her room, board and all other expenses would be paid in full and on time. Damon Donald and an officer of the Hattiesburg Trustmark Bank wrote a letter explaining how Neill's education would be financed.

When Neill arrived at the Columbus campus in August of 1914, she was the last girl to sign in at the reception desk. At the start of the term, each student wrote into a register her name, date and time of arrival, date of birth, home address, year in school, and persons responsible for her welfare and payments. For the first two years Neill signed the register as Nell James and gave her birth date as January 3, 1895. From the start of her third year she signed in as Neill James and subtracted two years from her age. She always was among the last to arrive back on campus and always listed herself as the person responsible for her own welfare and payments.

From the start Neill wrote enthusiastic letters from Columbus to her sisters. Her letters and her college scrapbook–the only surviving personal documents of hers from those years–tell a vivid story of her coming into adulthood at the women's college. Much of that story is confirmed in her roommate's diary of the era, which somehow came into Neill's possession in mid-life and was rescued by a neighbor in Mexico after Neill's death. I am indebted to the anonymous neighbor for the gift of that diary, for it has informed much of my understanding of Neill's early intimate affairs.

She described the neocolonial and antebellum instructional buildings and the massive red-brick Civil War infirmary that had been transformed into dormitories. She wrote about the ancient oak and magnolia trees and broad lawns, the winding brick walkways that passed through gardens and under arbors to the Chancellor's yellow clapboard cottage, and the quaint shops and cafes nestled along Fifth Street near College Avenue. President William Howard Taft, she wrote, had once delivered a campaign speech on the steps of Poindexter Hall. Her letters told how she would sit by a window and read philosophy for hours in Fant Hall, the ancient block that housed the library and was then the social center of the campus. Many years later, after Neill had settled in Mexico, Fant would be renamed Welty Hall in honor of the school's most famous alumna, Miss Eudora Welty. Neill's academic transcript indicates, however, that she never took a philosophy course.

She lived in Shattuck Hall and was assigned to share Room 27 with Mae Foster, a tall and slender ash-blond from Jackson. To Neill, Mae Foster's blue eyes seemed to burn like gas lamps, and from the moment they met at the orientation session Neill felt something inside her grow warm and stirred up. She didn't understand her response to Mae, but she knew she wanted something of Mae, wanted to be like her somehow, to be with her, to be seen with her. The attraction was mutual and they became inseparable, but for two years they never spoke more of their feelings than to acknowledge their "Shattuck girls loyalty" to one another. They always appeared together for meals at the gleaming Shattuck Hall dining room, where a fusty dress code and proper manners were enforced. Suppers were always formal, served on linen tablecloths, with fresh flowers and tall candles and never a salmagundi. Neill and Mae would sit side-by-side and share private gossip or intimately criticize the other girls' appearance. After the meal the table groups would compete for bawdiest rendition of their class songs, each uniquely created as a satire on the administration's rules of comportment.

Singing was required of most of the students, including Neill. It was routine for the first year girls to sing popular and traditional songs to older students gathered on Serenade Walk. In short order, Neill and Mae introduced songs of suffrage, including their favorite, "She Walketh Veiled and Sleeping":

She Walketh Veiled and Sleeping
    For She Knoweth Not Her Power;
    She Obeyeth but the Pleading
    Of Her Heart, and the High Leading
    Of Her Soul, Unto This Hour.

Slow Advancing, Halting, Creeping,
    Comes the Woman to the Hour!—
    She Walketh Veiled and Sleeping,
    For she knoweth not her power.

In spite of the popularity of protest songs among the young singers, the administrators preferred ballads and riverboat ditties and forbade any further rebellious singing. The choice of songs for the teas at the Chancellor's cottage was strictly controlled. Specially invited students would troupe down Serenade Walk to the cottage and sing on the piazza until the Chancellor opened the front door and invited them in for tea. They would gather around the seated executive like medieval entertainers at the knees of their queen and perform light operetta and chorale selections.

Neill and Mae never were invited to the Chancellor's teas. They considered the shunning a planned punishment that happily had the opposite of its intended effect, since they had become critics of the elites who cozied up to faculty and administrators, and they loathed the executive teas. They saw themselves as different from the other girls, and their self-regard as exceptional was confirmed by their unpopularity among the campus academic elite.

Through the mild months Neill played tennis and learned to golf from some of her more privileged friends. Winters she played indoor sports and practiced archery. She made her strongest effort in basketball, continuing the success she had earned in high school. In her third year she starred on the junior varsity squad. A team photograph shows the junior players arranged in a V. Although not the team captain, Neill is the one holding the ball at the center of the photo. She was a first-string forward on the varsity during her senior year.

She enjoyed the camaraderie and quick-witted repartee that occurred in the locker room and on the court. She learned things from the talk of the other basketball players that she had only guessed at or fantasized about before. She learned how girls avoided pregnancy and how they had lost their virginity. She heard the girls talk about sexual experiences, some advocating either men or women as partners or both, some declaring no interest in either sex. She learned about women loving other women, not only as friends but romantically, and shortly she began to feel not so different and ashamed.

It probably wasn't merely coincidental that when she was approaching puberty she had chosen to go by her middle name. Neill is after all ambiguous, semantically fitting, but for one L, to either a boy or a girl, and unlike her sister Willie, who always objected to being called Bill, she was the one who insisted on being called by her boyish name. Like her brother Tom, she had a keen interest in all things mechanical. She loved roughhousing and competitive sports, and she often challenged her siblings to games of quickness, daring, or strength. She frequently wandered alone. But she also loved fine clothing and flowers and all the animals of nature, and she enjoyed equal popularity in Hattiesburg among boys and girls. In her young years she was a clutch of antipodes. Her ambivalence about sex, however, became resolved at college, and what I learned from the diaries of her roommate at Shattuck Hall tells how it happened.

———

At night in her bed by the open window of Room 27, Neill puzzled over some of the locker room revelations, but she also felt relief and confirmation, as she began to recognize her own feelings of attraction to both men and women, but especially to Mae Foster. As she listened to the breeze in the magnolias just outside, she wondered if Mae felt something similar. She contemplated broaching the subject but fretted about possible rejection. Maybe she should share her feelings with one of the team girls. But then, she wasn't much attracted to any of them and they might get the wrong idea about who was the person of Neill's interest. She couldn't talk with Kittie about such things, that was obvious. Kittie was one of the girls who sang at the Chancellor's teas, and she was always mooning about the laurel tree legend. The custom said if a College girl sat under a certain laurel on the Institute's campus at the same time that a boy at the University up in Oxford was sitting under a laurel tree on his campus, and a blossom dropped on each of them, they were destined to become husband and wife.

Maybe, Neill thought, she should write to Ailene about her epiphany. But surely her pious sisters just wouldn't understand, and such a revelation would be most disturbing to them. After weeks of silent struggle and yearning before dropping off to sleep each night, she decided she had to take her chance directly with Mae. It would be just a small chance, and she could feel her way through the conversation and turn it around any time she detected resistance or suspicion. She could say the girls had caused her confusion.

"If y'all are still awake," she whispered, "I have something that's been on my mind I'd like to talk about."

"What's the matter, Neill?" Mae's voice was sleepy.

"It's really nothing wrong, it's just what the girls on the team have been talking about that I'm pondering."

"Those girls have been talking about me?"

"Not about you. Nobody in particular. Just that, well, they sometimes get to talking about friendships and some of them say they prefer the company of other girls to boys."

"Course that's natural when it's only all girls like it is here. I'll bet the boys up in Oxford prefer spending their time with other boys."

"I mean they aren't discussing mere friendship. It's more like, I suppose it's like being in love. That's what some of the girls have said."

Mae paused a long time before saying anything and when she did there was a detectable tone of interest. "Well?"

"Well, I was just wondering, you know, wondering if it's possible, if it's really done and such."

"You mean you're wondering how it's done?"

Neill's pulse quickened. "How it's done, yes, how it happens, how it gets started."

She heard Mae rustle in her bed. "So you've been thinking on this for a while, have you?"

"Don't you ever think about such things as this?"

"I do, but I was afraid to bring it up, afraid you would make fun of me or ask to change rooms."

"I have been fearful, too, and that's been part of my puzzlement. When they talked like that, I always thought about you."

There was a long pause and Neill felt her heart pounding with excitement. She had made her declaration, for the first time in her life. She heard another rustling sound and then her top sheet was being raised and she felt the silky softness of Mae's naked body as she slid into Neill's bed.

"I've been thinking of you, too," Mae whispered, and she kissed Neill on the lips. They enfolded each other and began an expectant, joyous exploration of their bodies and passions. Mae's diary recorded with satisfaction and gratitude Neill's description of her response. Neill had told her she felt like she was "drifting aloft, up into the highest branches, floating among the treetops and beyond, rising up and up and then hovering on a cloud somewhere in an immense sky."

———

After that long, sleepless first night together they felt bereaved whenever they had to be apart. It was an agony of suspicion and imagined loss just for Neill to be away for basketball or for Mae to be gone to her cookery class. They tried not to be seen loitering around in wait for each other, but their yearning to be together all the time was a source of painful self-denial. They struggled to refrain from touching each other in public, and they often left the dining room or social gatherings at the earliest time good manners would permit, so they could be alone together in their room.

The other girls at the women's college were not scandalized by the obvious attachment of Neill and Mae. As it was not an unprecedented event for an undergraduate to fall in love with a classmate, a silent acceptance ensued that was disturbed only when Neill became too aggressive when sheltering Mae against would-be rivals or when there was a rumor of a lovers' quarrel. Spats did occur, almost always when Mae complained to Neill about flirtations. Neill was as much enamored of her new self-revelation as she was with Mae, and she played at seduction as if she were learning a new sport. She wondered how others would feel in her arms. She adored the response she could elicit when she gazed at another girl a few moments too long. At socials, she sometimes paid more attention to a stranger than to Mae. Whenever Mae would object, Neill would deny it. "She was waving at me, and I thought she maybe wanted to interrupt us," she would say. Mae always seemed to forgive, and they lived through the winter of 1917 in a tense intimacy.

Their anxious bliss, however, was short-lived. One Monday during the spring of her third year Neill came back to Room 27 after a class and found an envelope on her bed. It was a letter from Mae explaining that over the weekend she had decided to leave college. She said she had to return home to care for her mother, who was suffering ill health and in severe financial trouble. She asked Neill not to contact her, promising to write or phone when she was settled at home in Jackson.

It seems that Neill really grieved over Mae's absence. She lost her appetite and all interest in classes and sports and other friendships. She barely slept. There wouldn't be a new roommate until September, so she stayed alone in Room 27 whenever she was not required to be elsewhere. She often wept for hours on end. After a couple of weeks of grieving and hearing nothing from Mae, however, Neill began to suspect that she might have been jilted. Maybe Mae had grown weary of their affair or felt guilty about it. Maybe she was returning to someone she had left back in Jackson. After all, at the beginning she had been the experienced one. It was clear she couldn't have been sincere in her affections, or she would not have been able to just leave like this. Neill's sadness turned to anger, and her anger was fed by the knowledge that there was little she could do to verify her suspicions and less she could do to exact revenge.

She threw her angry energy into school work and sports. She ate ravenously, began riding horses at the polo club and played golf almost every day the weather would permit it. She went to bed exhausted each night and slept forgetfully. It wasn't long before she began to realize her life would have to go on and, as she told herself, "there are more fish out there in the sea for anybody interested in catching them." Kittie Holcomb had noticed the changes in Neill since she had lost her roommate and repeatedly tried to comfort her. Neill liked Kittie well enough and appreciated her kindnesses, and soon the two of them were going off to

Oxford on weekends to attend dances and stage plays and football games with smartly dressed young men from the state university.

"I'll get your life turned around, Neill," Kittie brightly proclaimed.

"You don't know what you're taking on, Holcomb, but I'll go along for the ride anyway," Neill replied.

Still, her declaration had been made, and she was changed after being with Mae, so changed that she could not imagine retaking her place in the James family as before. She became estranged from her past, silent to her relatives and supporters in Hattiesburg. She stopped writing, except to notify Ailene and Jane that she would be spending winter holidays at the college.

Neill's life on campus that winter returned to a routine of steady work and the fulfillment of ambitions. She concentrated on her courses and achieved middling grades, struggling mainly in French and math, both of which she barely passed. She enjoyed her business and industrial arts courses and did well in them; she already had completed a professional certification in stenography, with highest marks on record. As a senior she campaigned furiously for a position on the Honors Council and at the eleventh hour managed to discredit her main rival, thus winning election to that prestigious committee. She later claimed that she was nearly expelled from the college for interfering with the campaign and thereby earned the sobriquet "Rebel." That story has never been confirmed and appears to have been part of her self-made publicity for her first book. It also might have contained more than a grain of her self-identity at the time.

At age twenty-three, Neill was graduated with her Bachelor of Arts degree from a first-rate women's college. The world beckoned to her like a lover beyond an open door, and she boldly stepped through. But she could not go back to Hattiesburg. Instead of returning home she followed Kittie Holcomb to Washington D. C., where Kittie's uncle, a general in the War Department, had settled them in jobs and a place to live. Neill told her family in a postcard note she was going to the nation's capital for a government job, but that was all.

It would be a long time before any of her siblings could forgive her for reneging on her agreement with them. It would not be long, however, before she would find herself in an entirely new and strange world of secret orders, duplicity, violence and enchantment.

Damon Donald joined the army and was never heard from again.

II

Kittie Holcomb

> Be sure
> Not to look back
>
> Attempt the art
> Of metamorphosis
>
> —W.G. Sebald, "Memo"

My uncle was a gentleman and a kind, wise man. He was head of civilian staffing for the War Department during the First World War, and he was a Brigadier General, and immediately upon the heels of my graduation from The W, I became one of his close civilian aides in the Personnel Improvement Bureau. Well, I was so young it was like wearing oversized shoes, and I looked it—even now, at this age, people always tell me I look much younger than I am—but I was game back then and capable and well succeeded in my job, all the way through to the end of my government tenure. And as I had been his intern for the four summers of college, Uncle Bradford—the General—had become well acquainted with my abilities and I became well acquainted with how things are done in Washington.

He was my mother's Maryland brother—they had different fathers—and therefore not an authentic Southerner, but nonetheless he was well-connected and influential, and we enjoyed a mutually beneficial arrangement insofar as that he procured employment for me and many of my friends and college classmates, while in the process I procured for him a supply of well-schooled and well-spoken young ladies to comprise the raw material for his department.

Naturally I became immensely popular among the girls from Columbus, but it was a role of considerable importance and I took it most seriously, as I have also in all my volunteer activities since the wartime. I lived in those early years with the General and my auntie at their Georgetown residence, despite the fact that Daddy was still a Member of Congress—we thought it might lead to gossip had I been living at my parents' townhouse at Dupont Circle—and in that way I became much more efficient and better informed about the inner operations of the Department. All my government work occurred before I came out in Richmond, long before I settled in New York with my late husband, both of us refugees from Mississippi, though Rudy had gone off to college in Boston, and all that was ages before my charities work began. And even though I'm not a native New Yorker—I've never mastered that awful Yankee dialect and that's probably because I never cared to, though people say I sound now like I might come from maybe Virginia—well, in spite of those little obstacles I have achieved a lot for the university and hospitals. I must say, over that long time my experiences in D.C. proved to be very helpful to my personal growth and insight.

Even before I arrived at the Bureau following my graduation, I was granted my security clearance and was given a special job in what would become in time the Military Intelligence Service's Negative Branch. My assignment was to keep surveillance over many of the ordinary girls we hired for intelligence work—because of my experience and my popularity and natural amiability, and I suppose an inner sense of decorum, I was chosen over dozens of others who would've been joy-jumpy happy for such a delicate assignment. And so it happened that my dear friend going back to our high school days, Miss Neill James, was one of those girls I monitored. Oh we had our ups and downs in school and college, she could be a scant bit forward for my parents' taste, and she lived in that dreadful flat and sometimes she had to borrow my clothes for social affairs—dances and teas and such, not so much in college—but we never competed for the affections of boys, and I let her take the spotlight in sports and never felt compelled to call her up on her outlandish stories and her occasional back-alley speech.

I arranged for her entry into the public service as I had for the others, but despite her ho-hummy way of describing it in that first book of hers, she was particularly frantic to get out of her family situation back in Hattiesburg, and she came to me and practically begged for an introduction to D.C. even before I had the chance to recruit her. Miss James well fit the bill for military intelligence—that was no surprise because all through college I had been watching her grow up and change from how she was in high school, when we were such close friends, and so I knew what we would get. At The W she went crazy sort of, fell in love with her roommate, and some of us more sophisticated girls had surmised about that even though she tried to keep it secret, the affair, but she really could lie cleverly and cover up without blinking an eyelash, and I don't think she had to learn that from scratch, and that proved to be a valuable asset. Oh, I also knew she was daring and had a quick imagination and was a marvelous stenographer, almost like she was doing something athletic, certainly the best steno among our graduating class at The W, so I knew she would be easy for Uncle Bradford to place.

We needed them for intelligence work, stenographers, and as I had concluded about her personal life, some of which I personally disapproved I assure you, and her reputation at college, too—many of the girls found her overly pushy, or maybe overly competitive and willful and without sufficient cause to be all that self-confident, and still I shielded her from such criticism—she could be as well entrusted to keep secrets as a bulldoggy parish priest. So I had the opportunity—and the official requirement, of course—to monitor her closely for a few years at the beginning, as long as she was a civilian War Department employee and a short while afterwards, because that was my job. It furthermore was a continuation of my watchfulness toward Miss James over the previous eight years and some, but I also kept track of her because to me she was an important piece of my own history, even while she would pass me by as a friend.

Since those early days I have often thought about how she got her start in world travel and what they call the great game, and I guess in some ways she was typical of girls who became intelligence agents in the period between the Wars. She wrote about this part of her life in that first book, but her version was a very convenient telling of events, and of course it covered over all the important episodes, as it must have done. I'm sure she had riskier adventures after she became a contractor in military intelligence, and she properly covered over those too, but my records end at about the time she left the United States, which was barely a year after Army demobilized her.

Much of what I can disclose about her work life is based on my recollections of the official dossier I kept compiled on her, as well as some old diaries of my own that I kept all these years, and that has forced me to recreate some conversations as I expect they would have taken place and according to personal information I received from many of her contacts. Some things, of course, can't be divulged, but it's surprising how much people will tell you about situations they're supposed to be keeping hush-hush, if only they recognize you as superior to them in some way or you just approach them with the right air of authority. Or if enough time has passed.

So Neill James arrived in Washington D.C. on the twenty-second of June 1918, two weeks after our graduation ceremonies and only a few days after my return from Mississippi. As she described it, when she stepped down onto the platform at the Pennsylvania Station, she was not thinking on the importance of her destination at such a historic time or on the challenges of a new job, because after all that would be unlike her, but instead she thought about her appearance and commented on her sense of intimidation, which was meant I'm sure partly to gain sympathy, for our

Miss James was not intimidated by much. Here in her first book she wrote: "An odd, sinking feeling gripped my heart when the train puffed into Washington and halted. I felt far, far smaller than my 120 pounds in the enormity of the great curving dome, the largest building I had ever seen, with hordes of travelers milling about. I didn't like it."

Naturally she didn't like the strangeness and regretted leaving the South, but she surely was excited by the possibilities and was full up with high-hopes optimism. It was as if she was asking her readers to take their pick and thereby to decide for her how to respond, or possibly she was trying to have it both ways, which would have been just like her. Once, when we still were at The W—we were seniors, as I recall—she told me, "Kittie, I want it all, everything life has to offer, and I have forever."

In that passage from her book, she portrayed her situation in wartime Washington as the plight of a poor, lonely adventurer facing an alien and scary-bad city, when in fact General Keynes had already secured her a job, and I had reserved a room for her in a boarding house on K Street as temporary lodging and even had paid the deposit. No, she wasn't destitute or abandoned: In her purse she carried the last two hundred dollars her elder brother Damon Donald had sent for her college expenses, which anyone would declare was a considerable sum for her in 1918.

On that first day, she checked in at Mrs. McGibbon's boarding house and immediately went out to report for duty at the War Department, with her letter of introduction and her Civil Service examination report clutched to her breast, and she appeared half an hour early at our reception room in the suite on Fifteenth and M Streets Northwest. Those high-ceilinged hallways leading to the reception area were crowded just then with desks and chairs piled on top of one another, file cabinets and bins of charts and maps and pallets of typewriters and stacks of packing boxes, just all kinds of mish-mashy office paraphernalia we needed to complete our move-in.

A secretary led her into an elegant, quiet office, where a tall, thin man with a pencil-line moustache introduced himself as Mr. Taylor, and I can just imagine her checking his nameplate on the desk: Lt. Col. Henry A. Taylor. He would be in mufti, a wool suit in spite of the early June humidity, and he would briskly ask her to be seated while he briefed her about her new employer. All the time he was talking he would pace around the office with his hands hooked behind his back, and he would examine her carefully from all angles. That was Colonel Taylor's routine way of meeting them. I now confess to eavesdropping, but it was because Neill was one of my girls just entering the inner sanctum.

"You can see there are lots of changes going on here, Miss James," he began. "The entire Personnel Improvement Bureau was just moved here from E Northwest, we're growing so fast we had to get larger quarters, and leadership changes are happening even as I speak." His accent and his bearing suggested to her an East Coast aristocracy and Ivy League background.

"It all sounds very exciting," she enthused.

"There will be much more excitement for you in days to come. But first we need to finalize your security clearance so you can do the job we want you to do. Our new Director, General Churchill, has plans to move us out of the War College and onto the General Staff, reporting directly to General March, who himself was appointed as Chief of Staff just a month ago. General March has a direct line to Secretary Baker."

The importance of all this probably would have escaped her at the time, she was so new, but she would try to memorize the names and titles anyway, and I must say she did have a knack for such things, though she sometimes would overestimate it.

"Soon our mission will encompass both domestic and international operations," Colonel Taylor went on, "and we will have primary responsibility for identifying traitors, enemy agents and other suspicious persons and subversive groups. Navy has the rest. Your work will be essential to the national war effort and will contribute significantly to the morale and wellbeing of American citizens. It's important work, but to do it properly you must be able to gather information without revealing who you are or what you are doing. Are you willing and able to do that?

"Yes, Sir, I can. And I have never felt a need to tell what I'm about, as long as it's in the cause of serving my family or my country." She hoped that was the answer he wanted.

"Would you lie in the cause of serving your country?"

"Certainly I suppose I would."

"Are you willing to risk your own safety among people of criminal backgrounds or among anti-Americans, in the cause of serving your country?"

"Well, I thought I was going to be a stenographer. I didn't know I was being hired for spying, Sir. This is all a bit of a surprise, not a disappointment of course but something entirely new to me. But if that's where I'm going, I'm all for it, Sir."

"We use the term *intelligence,* not spying. We are the Military Intelligence Section, Miss James, and soon we will be a Division. You are being brought in precisely because you are a professional stenographer, and your skills will be put to strategically important uses. We are recruiting young ladies who are college graduates and also are expert stenographers, thousands, much like you. It's as if you know a very useful foreign language that the enemy and most military intelligence personnel never have learned.

"There are many critical roles for stenographic experts in military intelligence, Miss James," he continued. "At MI we have specialized departments, each responsible for a particular kind of work. All have stenographers. All MI departments have numbers. We here are MI-4, and we are tasked with investigating possible cases of subversion or disloyalty by civilians. Two Branches are proposed for the new Division when we come under the Chief of Staff, a Positive Branch and a Negative Branch. We are Negative. Positive units gather information abroad about foreign entities. That is all I can tell you for now, I'm afraid, until you are cleared for your job. In the meantime, I will have you meet Sergeant James Henry, and he will give you some work to do until you are fully qualified. It should be only for a week or two." He sat down at his desk and began to examine some papers, and she knew she had been dismissed.

"*Negative* intelligence. Now I wonder what that ever could be like," she mused out loud, as she left Colonel Taylor's suite. I'm sure she also wondered if she could be stepping into a hall of mirrors, where even people's names might not be true. She would be likely to think, maybe Sergeant James Henry borrowed his name from the writer—she never had the patience to read big novels but she surely had heard of him, and she always said she hoped there was a family connection with those famous Yankee Jameses.

She spent the rest of June and July reading employment applications for civilian jobs in various federal agencies, and she was to notify Sergeant Henry whenever she spotted an applicant who wrote inconsistent answers on the forms or revealed a suspicious personal background. Sergeant Henry, who was a recent Ivy graduate, as many on the staff were, including my Rudy, my first and only Harvard boy—though at just that time I was, I believe, yet unaware of his eyes following me whenever we passed in the hallways—in any case, Henry was to Neill James a puzzling and aloof sophisticate. He never let on whether her detective work was valuable or useless, but he always smiled, thanked her, and said, "Very good. Please proceed."

Her temporary assignment quickly became little more than fuddy-dull clerical work, and she grew restless for something more interesting to do. I stayed out of sight on the job, hiding like a suspicious parent behind the curtain, and met her only at the rare social gathering organized by the Section, for by then we were drifting apart as friends.

Each morning she would leave Mrs. McGibbon's ancient, dingy-dark boarding house for work before seven o'clock, walk west along K Street to Mount Vernon Square and then head up Massachusetts Avenue toward Dupont Circle. At Huyler's she would duck in for coffee and a breakfast sweet roll, and the dear thing would often save part of her donut or bear claw to eat as she ambled along the cobbled sidewalk to her office on M Street, not an itty-bitty care in the world about what anybody would think. Shortly after the July 4th holiday celebrations, she stopped as usual at Huyler's, but on this occasion she encountered two of our classmates from The W, and it so happened that they too had taken government employment, but not through me, and so they didn't work for my uncle but for other agencies. They told her there was another Mississippi girl in the city, someone who had just started work at Treasury, but they didn't say who.

They talked about joining forces and Neill said she might could do that. And so Miss Neill James, Miss Elizabeth Scott, and Miss Mary Ruland agreed to live together in an apartment that these two and the additional young woman had found on Mass Ave just the previous day. Now, in that book of hers, the two were called Irene and Ignatz, and I've always wondered why she chose Ignatz for Mary, since I've never come across a Miss Ignatz anything anywhere, or for that matter a Mr. Ignatz anything, either. But I could understand why Neill was eager to leave the boarding house, with its danky rooms and smells of boiled cabbage and mildew and her feelings of isolation there.

Unfortunately, when I had looked for a place for her, not much was available. Elizabeth Irene and Mary Ignatz had quickly reached the limit of their tolerance for vermin where they had been living, and so it would be a convenient and pleasant arrangement in that there would be four girls from Mississippi, all civilian federal employees, to share the rent and board in a much improved residence. Neill promised them she would add her name to the lease and join them at the end of the month.

Over the following few weeks they exchanged postcards and letters as they planned their relocation, but the planning wasn't complicated for Neill, as she had little else but her clothes and cosmetics, a few books and her personal linens to move the twenty or so blocks to the brick walkup on Mass Ave. She hired a taxi, and when she directed the driver to carry her boxes up to the apartment, the old Negro cabbie insisted on leaving them in the hallway. She probably high-hatted him and just turned and opened the front door and stepped into a sunny, modern living room. From somewhere in the apartment a voice she might have recognized called out, "Welcome home. I'll be right there."

I got the roommates' version of the story much later, when I debriefed them after Neill's reassignment. It's the only version I have, but it rings true in all its details, especially when you compare it with what she wrote in her book.

———

Even before the person behind the voice entered the living room, Neill knew it was Mae Foster. Her heart was thump-thumping as Miss Foster strolled in from the kitchen, wiping her hands on a tea towel. I was surprised when I learned of this turn of events, because like the other girls in my group I had guessed their affair in Columbus and the breakup, and I assumed that it was over and done for. Neill never confided in me about such things those last months at The W, I think because she thought I wasn't worldly enough to accept her that way, but she had no idea. I tried to let her know and often said to her that she thinks she knows me but doesn't know me at all, but then she always changed the subject on me.

Anyway, Mae Foster always had been very open to me. This is her recollection of the beginning of their new living arrangement. She wasn't surprised on seeing Neill James standing there. An expression of anxious tenderness came upon her face. She stopped a few feet from Neill and gazed at her, and she felt as if she were a grown-up child looking at some elder who had once abused her. "I'm sorry," she said evenly.

"Now, you tell me what you have to be sorry about," Neill snapped.

"We didn't tell you I was the fourth girl. I was afraid you wouldn't come if you knew."

"Why would I do a silly thing like that?" After a silence she continued. "That all you're sorry about?"

"I couldn't go back to Columbus, Neill. It was true that Mother needed me more than you did, and you and I were moving down such different tracks."

"So now here we are with our two tracks joined up again. How peculiar."

"Mother passed in March, Neill, and Elizabeth suggested that I come up to Washington to look for work. And I already knew you and Kittie were coming up after graduation. So it's a fact that this is not entirely a coincidence."

"I certainly am sorry for your loss. But why wouldn't you call me or even send a postcard? Fourteen months, good God, and I am *still* bereft."

"You don't look bereft, Neill, and you never let on that my absence would cause you any heartache, not while we were together and not after I had to leave for home." Mae looked serenely down at Neill. "And I believe I asked you to wait until I had my affairs straightened out before anything else."

"You only told me not to write or call."

"You assumed the worst, and you couldn't imagine how divided and bereft *I* was then. I had no means of paying my expenses and I was needed at home. I was both embarrassed and called to duty."

"Why didn't you stay and let me help? I would've paid for your keep. We could maybe have figured out some way to care for your mother, figured out something together, if we could have just talked."

"Would you have accepted that support from me, Neill, if it had been the reverse? I also might ask why you didn't wait for me to finish up settling my duties at home before you went off having a good time."

Neill fell silent and turned toward the bay windows. She gazed down at the tree-lined avenue and sunny park catty-corner across. "You look none the worse for wear," she said, "though you do seem a trifle sad."

"I'll take that as a compliment and a sign of your sympathy."

"I have missed you fiercely."

The living arrangement was settled without any discussion of Neill and Mae resuming their relationship from Shattuck Hall. It was as if all four already knew how it would be, and so Elizabeth Irene volunteered to take the front room with its Murphy bed, leaving the small bedroom for Mary Ignatz and a larger one beyond the kitchen for the other two. Immediately the four women fell into a smoothly coordinated routine for meals, sharing the one small bathroom, and getting off to their government jobs by seven-thirty each morning.

Neill was the coordinator, and she organized their domestic schedules and posted cooking and cleaning assignments on a sheet she taped to the wall near the kitchen sink, and she updated it weekly. She saw it as her duty to scold anybody who fell behind.

For the first few months it was all peaceful at home. The four often would be going out together in the evening, sometimes to a theatre or dance hall, occasionally to a nightclub in their neighborhood. On weekends Neill and Mae would be walking for hours around the city, learning the landmarks and tarrying in museums and stores. Neill was worked up by the culture of the East, and she wanted to take it all in, to absorb it into herself, as she had a painful urge to be on the go, to see new places, and as always it seemed impossible for her to tire her body out.

When Mae became exhausted from walking the city all day, Neill would leave her at the apartment and set out for the Army's tennis club and find somebody to play a few sets with under the lights, or she sometimes would go dancing with one of the Army officers and return long after midnight. Other evenings she would simply say over her shoulder, "I'll be back tomorrow" and stride off to the Union Station and take a train to Baltimore or Philadelphia.

Sometimes she would slip into the lobby of some fancy-ritzy hotel and snatch a sample of the house stationery, and later her sisters would receive a letter from her under the hotel's letterhead, which probably was the beginning of a habit of friendly deception that became an abiding trait, although now that I think on it, I saw her do the same thing in Columbus and Jackson. Military intelligence did not have to persuade her or train her about the worth of creating impressions.

By October the broad sidewalks of Mass Ave and M Street were strewn with fallen leaves, frost was on the roofs of taxis idling at the curbs like docked riverboats, and we Mississippi girls had already bought woolen winter coats. As the nights grew longer and colder, Mary Ignatz and Elizabeth Irene began hearing angry voices behind the door of the large bedroom, Mae Foster's always accusatory and imploring, Neill's defensive and contemptuous. The dear things quarreled often now, and even though each morning they would make up, by the next evening there was a new grievance and a new outbreak of fighting.

Mae would complain that she was crushed whenever Neill entered a room and looked around in search of admirers, and then Neill teased too much, as she could gush about some attractive young woman they had met or make little jokes in front of others about Mae's height or what she called

Mae's pathetic loyalty. I heard her say that, and I know sometimes Neill would strike up a conversation with a passing person while Mae was still talking to her, as if Mae had ceased to exist, which to most well-bred girls would be a discourtesy to even a casual acquaintance, let alone an intimate. For her part, Neill had grown tired of Mae's predictability, tired of her generosity and her attachment, so steady and dutiful, she said, and as usual Neill was longing for change, but Mae would have to be the one to demand it, for Neill always found it necessary to hold herself blameless.

She was ready for a change at work by October as well. Her clearance had come through in July and she immediately had been assigned to the offices of Wrisley Brown, the new head of Negative Branch. She claimed she didn't even have time to say goodbye to Sergeant Henry or me. Brown's people sent her to Camp Devens for a week of field training, where she quickly learned the basics of information gathering and coding and reporting, how to protect a covert identity, how to administer pay for services and other operational regulations. She was given a thick file of information about the Military Intelligence Division, for by August the Service had become a staff Division under Major General Marlboro Churchill, just as Colonel Taylor had predicted.

She also was given a package of records to read that introduced her to the current political and military situations of interest to MID. So she read about the landing of Allied troops and American sailors in Murmansk, whose purpose was supposed to be to protect the huge stores of armaments sent for Russia to use against the Germans. But the papers said the real purpose was to aid a new counterrevolution in Moscow.

Neill learned about the rise of Dzerzhinsky's Cheka in Russia and the socialist and anarchist leaders in America's labor movement, and the spread of radical anti-American political and religious groups across the country. There were long lists naming suspicious churches, civic associations, social organizations and political clubs. At first she didn't like the political angle as much as I did, but she shortly got used to it and eventually got hooked like a mudcat on international intrigues.

Her new job put her in the Division's public affairs office, where she sometimes wrote press releases and ghost-wrote speeches for military officers, and as she was an able first-draft PR writer, she favorably impressed her boss with her inventions of catchy phrases and clever arguments, nothing awfully serious. Her stenography skills also were noted as especially advanced, and despite her stubborn Mississippi accent, she nonetheless had a keen ear for dialects of all kinds and an uncommon ability to transcribe sounds of any language, even if she had never heard it before and couldn't imitate it. But because it came so easily to her, the public affairs and steno work quickly grew monotonous, and soon Neill again was asking for more exciting work.

So she was given an additional assignment to read and evaluate reports from field agents of the old American Protective League. The APL was a national posse of patriotic private citizens–businessmen, service workers, bankers, even laborers–who spied on suspicious individuals and organized groups of all kinds. Thousands of reports flowed in at our M Street offices each week from field sections across the country, and Neill was to aggregate the pertinent ones by threat category and compose a summary sheet for her military supervisors. She promptly demonstrated an aptness for sorting the relevant away from the trivial and spotting the reasoned cases as apart from the hysterical or biased.

It wasn't long before she also demonstrated her unusual talent for deception, which depended naturally on a flair for the theatrical, another talent she seemed to have even in high school. Her boss, Army Captain Vernon Shaw, planned to expand the investigative capability of the D.C. office and saw an opportunity for gathering intelligence by placing undercover agents at meetings of targeted groups, just as units in the field had been doing all along. Captain Shaw, a fervent atheist from Vermont, with a bushy, rust-colored mustache and watery blue eyes, and an officer most of us much admired–though I disagreed with his religious views and such, but after all, we have the principle of separating church and state in this nation, so that didn't much matter then–well, Captain Shaw wanted to investigate the American Theosophical Society. He saw it as low-risk surveillance, and since he was short of military agents and personally disapproved of APL operatives, he decided to take a chance on assigning his inexperienced but energetic and willing and flamboyant civilian aide.

Captain Shaw asked Neill to attend a recruitment seminar posing as a potential enrollee, which would be her first domestic NOC assignment. That's what we called any work under false identity that didn't give an agent cover as an official government employee–it was a not official cover, so she wouldn't have the usual protections. Neill pounced on the chance for such an adventure, and for three weeks in late October and early November she attended the Society's "Seminar of Pure Thought" series, held Tuesday nights at the Hall of Labor auditorium near Foggy Bottom. I recall everyone around the section was just waiting to see how her NOC assignment would work out.

Neill always loved to hobnob with elegant people, especially from the better-off classes, so she was pleased to see that nearly half the seminarians–"visitors" was what the Society's regulars called the potential recruits–the newcomers, that is, who trooped into the granite hall on those frosty evenings were women, many dressed in fashionable outfits and wearing expensive overcoats. The Theosophists at the dais were serious looking people, bespectacled and formally dressed, and they spoke like professors to the audience of nearly two hundred visitors. They lectured about the glories of pursuing Truth above all else, the universality of humanity, and the rights of all creatures, including most animals. Neill reported after the first night that she felt right at home.

Every night after the lecture the audience was invited to form so-called discussion teams, and a Society member would join each team to facilitate its discussion of pure thoughts. Time to time throughout the evening the visitors were told where they could find tables with application forms so they might apply for membership, if that appealed to them. After an hour or so of exploring the recruits' ideas and uncertainties, the facilitators would lead their teams into the salon, where snacks and beverages were served, while the Society officers debated among themselves about ongoing developments in the international organization of Theosophy.

Neill was fascinated, as you might expect, but she carefully kept track of the political talk, too, and she reported the proceedings in great detail. She had nearly filled two large notebooks with her stenographic notes when, late on the last evening of her surveillance, one of the Society officers who had been standing guard at the entrance doors tapped her on the shoulder and said, "What are you writing there?" He wore a nametag on his lapel that said Arthur Crowe–MARSHALL.

Neill turned her best smile towards the Marshall and held her notebook to her breast with both hands. Now, she was a flirtatious young woman, and she knew how to flatter with her eyes and smile and her Mississippi accent. Most of us from Dixie were trying to learn how to whisht-up our dialect and acquire a more widely acceptable form of speech, but Neill cultivated an ability to retain hers, which she saw as an asset.

"Why, I'm just trying to take it all in," she said. "There's so much of value, and it's all so new to me, I feel I can't get enough."

Marshall Crowe grasped Neill's elbow. "But what is that language you're writing? Wouldn't be a code of some sort, would it?" In spite of his nonchalance, Marshall Crowe was not smiling, and his question didn't sound like casual conversation. To Neill it sounded more like an accusation, and she felt her pulse race up while she tried to keep that calm, sweet expression.

"Why that's just my stenography. It is a kind of code, I suppose. A kind of speed writing? I work as a secretary, and stenography is a most handy skill for a secretary."

"Oh, I see. And who is your employer, may I ask?"

"I work for the federal government, my first year, starting out at the lowest rung y'all might say. One of the meek who are destined to climb one step at a time."

"How interesting. What a coincidence. I also work for the government. Maybe our paths already have crossed. What agency?" He still held Neill firmly by the elbow and stared sternly at her face.

"My now, wouldn't that be a coincidence indeed? But it's such a vast and varied thing, our government. You Sir have the demeanor of a man who must be very high up on the ladder. And if you are in the government, I would venture a guess that you must be one of Mr. Wilson's noble knights at the Labor Department." Neill described herself as thrusting her chin forward pugnaciously and continuing to smile up at him.

Crowe shot an appraising glance around the salon. "It's a shame our battles go on within our own government and our own agency. We're always fighting for the working person, man or woman, while the political people look the other way and those hoodlums at the absurdly named Justice Department try to intimidate and deport honest workers for the benefit of corporate bosses."

"I wouldn't know much about that, I'm just a secretary in a personnel office at Treasury, very humdrum. But I do know y'all have the reputation of a chicken on a june-bug when it comes to saving child workers and keeping the mines safe."

He asked Neill if she would like to join him at the buffet table for some coffee and a pumpkin muffin. She told him her name was Mae Foster, and when the evening was over he invited her out to dinner. Here she used her slip-slidey deftness and said she would think on it and contact him later.

In her analysis report for Captain Shaw she said the American Theosophical Society in the East, as this branch was called, appeared to be a no threat to the war effort or the American way of life. She wrote that they were mainly concerned about internal jurisdictional disputes and about who could use the title of Theosophist and about the philosophical problems invited by their credo, especially the principle on animal rights. Their main political issue, she said, was deciding how to push for women's equality in the workplace and equal voting rights, and I'm the first to say that she tried to make her report sound neutral about those matters, but I know she personally agreed with most of the Theosophists' ideas, especially about equality for women. She beat the drum on that for years at college. Now she found it more convenient than the Theosophists to keep quiet about such sentiments.

A person might have to wonder about the depth of her commitment to our cause, but Captain Shaw was happy with the report and her detailed field notes. He either failed to detect Neill's sympathies with her target or he softened his own resistance and began to backtrack on his assessment of Theosophists. In any case, he was so greatly pleased by her NOC work that he next assigned her to work undercover as a would-be journalist, attending public speeches by union leaders, the IWW and leftist political groups. He suggested that she also might attend meetings at night of other religious sects and philosophical societies.

Soon Neill was devoting all her work time to her undercover assignments. It was clear she felt a surge of excitement each time her presence was challenged and she successfully told her cover story, and she began to relish each morning's envious comments by her MID co-workers. They often kidded her about being a star of the illegitimate theatre, and the analysts called her our secret weapon. We were supposed to be working in the shadows, but she loved the bright lights, even if it had to be just inside our offices.

Two events caused a ground-shaker change to Neill's blossoming career. Mae came home late from work one night, long after dinner was over, and she told her housemates she had been detained at her clerking job in her payroll unit at Treasury. Along with several other payroll clerks, she was being investigated because some money had gone missing from her office, and by that time she had already been interrogated both by Secret Service agents and city police officers, plus she had been hauled off to the Justice Department for further interrogation.

More than a decade later Neill described in her first book that very same incident, but she placed herself in the role of the accused, like the starlet of the show and totally in character for her. She closed the episode in her book with a racy story about a congressman's assault on her, a scene someone must have thought would sell more copies. She wrote that the mystery of the missing payroll voucher and money was never solved and was eventually forgotten, and then she used the incident as the reason for her move westward, as if she just wanted to get away from bad feelings about being accused of a crime.

But the actual case wasn't so easily wrapped up for Mae Foster. The questionings and surveillance of her and others in her office went on for nearly two weeks, and none of the suspects confessed or pointed a finger. I don't know if a thief ever was found or charged, but Mae and two of her coworkers were given the choice of being fired outright or accepting reassignment out of Washington D.C. So with that, Mae laid her distress at the feet of her three companions at home. Mary and Elizabeth later described the situation to me the same way, so I believe it actually went like this.

May flapped her long hands and said, "I am beside myself with confusion and anguish."

Mary and Elizabeth tried to comfort her by saying that the real culprit soon would be found out, and her job and reputation would be unharmed or, at worst, bruised and restored. Elizabeth asked Mae if anything odd had happened recently to her that might have implicated her.

Mae thought for a long moment and said, "I can't think of anything. The only thing out of the ordinary was some man named Crowe—Andrew or Arthur, something like that—came to see me at work. He said he was looking for Mae Foster but when he saw me he clearly was disappointed. He looked highly suspicious."

Mary said it didn't sound like anything important and for Mae to not worry about that.

Neill's face had gone stony-cold, and she was not so sympathetic. "You have got yourself a real sour pickle here, and you don't have much time to figure out what to do."

"I don't see as I have any choice, Neill."

"By accepting their terms you'll be admitting that you did something wrong, and you'll be making it easy on them. You should go plead for the mercy and intervention of our junior Senator. And don't ever mention that Crowe fellow's visit."

"But I'm not guilty of any wrongdoing."

"I'm not saying you are, darling. But you don't have to convince me. And all I'm saying is your choices are either to leave or to get political protection and fight this thing. If you don't your only other choice is to be fired, and there will be no second chance to patch up your reputation."

"Maybe I should see Mr. Williams. He's a kindly man."

"John Sharp Williams is not known for doing other than sleeping at his desk. Senator Harrison, on the contrary, has long been a vigorous voice in the House and now is our Strong Man in the Senate. Besides, the important thing is he was personally endorsed by President Wilson just last year. No, Pat Harrison's your man."

Mae, however, couldn't imagine taking her problem into the halls of power in Washington. The prospect of approaching a U.S. Senator overwhelmed her, so in a panic and without further consultation with Neill or the other housemates, she told her boss the next morning that she would accept reassignment, and within twenty-four hours she received orders to report the following Monday to the Chief of Personnel at the Treasury Department regional office in Boston.

In the meantime, Neill had decided to take a few days off from work, for after all, what did she care that Mae was neck-deep in trouble? She was away in Richmond, lounging like a pasha's girlfriend at the Palm Court swimming pool in the Jefferson Hotel when Mae placed a farewell note on her pillow. Then Mae lifted her two suitcases and kicked the door shut on her way out of Neill's life. This would be the second time Mae left in the midst of great personal distress, and I thought this time it was for good, and it seems it was, although Mae's name would come in handy again and again.

The other event that altered Neill's career prospects and put her on the move for the next goodness knows how many years also involved a crime. The difference here was that Neill was caught in the act and Captain Shaw and the agency were put to the test. Decades later Vernon Shaw's second book, *Memoir of an Unhappy Warrior*, included a detailed and complicated description of the episode. He wrote:

> In my request to Mr. Wrisley Brown I restated the history of competing interests within our theater of responsibility. I described the operational fact that there were overlapping jurisdictions, intense rivalries and much confusion among counter-espionage agencies since the end of the war. The Office of Naval Intelligence contested the Military Intelligence Division for domestic counter-espionage. Justice's Bureau of Investigation had argued that it should be the lead agency on any matter involving national civilian security. I pointed out how vigorously Mr. Brown himself had fought to preserve the mandate for negative intelligence previously granted to the War Department and, by extension, to MID. Clearly it was a problem, I said, that although APL agents worked for various units in the War Department, they were assigned to and funded by the Justice Department. Adding to the confusion and competition, other agencies also were conducting undercover investigations–the military's Corps of Intelligence

Police, the Office of the Secret Service and agents of the Labor Department, plus many and various state and municipal law enforcement organizations.

None of these units, however, devoted much effort to coordinating their activities with the others. So that when my new protégée Miss Neill James was assigned to gather intelligence at an IWW rally in a warehouse on the Baltimore docks, Justice's Bureau of Intelligence knew nothing of her presence and went forward with a plan they had secretly created to raid the meeting. Mr. Brown always requested detailed narrative descriptions of cases held for his decisions, so I composed for him the following depiction of events.

IWW organizers had been notably successful in outflanking the ineffective American Federation of Labor and organizing dock workers on both the east and west coasts of the United States. On the unseasonably mild afternoon of Wednesday, January 15, 1919, Miss James had been granted permission as a sympathetic journalist to attend the meeting and take notes on the speeches. She was standing in a crush of workers near the front of the hall, calmly writing quotes from the keynote speech being delivered by the Negro orator Mr. Ben Fletcher, who had come down that day from Philadelphia. She had retrieved copies of the IWW "Principles and Platform" and Fletcher's article "Growth of IWW in Baltimore," reprinted from a 1917 issue of Solidarity, *and had placed them in her handbag.*

Before Fletcher could finish his speech, three men in dockworker clothing jumped out of the crowd and onto the stage and restrained him. At the same time dozens of other men in the audience pulled off their coveralls and wool jackets and pinned metal badges on the lapels of suits they had worn underneath. One of the assailants/agents grabbed the microphone and told the two hundred union men looking around in astonishment that the doors were being locked and nobody should attempt to leave. He said they all were going to be interviewed by agents of the United States Department of Justice and anybody who was a noncitizen or socialist sympathizer, or was suspected of any crime, would be detained. A roar of protest rose up from the crowd, but dozens more government agents had been let in a side door, and they surrounded the gathered dock workers. Immediately Miss James made for the side door, hoping for an escape. When she was almost there an agent's hand grabbed her wrist and pulled her aside. According to her report, the following exchange took place.

"Excuse us, Ma'am, but the speaker said nobody is to leave until interviewed."

"It's all right, Sir, I'm not a sympathizer. I'm just a news reporter from the Montgomery Sentinel. *Here, I have my credentials."*

"What is a reporter from Gaithersburg doing way up here, Miss Foster?" [Miss James had used the cover name of Mae Foster.] *And I'm surprised that the* County Sentinel *is back to publishing again."*

Miss James reported that she tried to control the color of her cheeks and neck, though she could feel the heat pressing out against her skin. She reflexively clutched at her hand bag. They had to shout to be heard over the yelling of the impounded dock workers.

"Why Sir, my editor, who is as new at this as I am, thought that covering the presence of a right famous Negro labor executive from Philadelphia would interest the readership in Montgomery County. On account of the Negro college over in Bowie?" She tried to engage his eyes with her most winsome expression. Her story was a long shot but the only idea that came to her mind. Naturally she could not reveal her true identity, lest she lose her cover for future assignments at labor gatherings.

The agent had just arrived from New York and had no idea how far Bowie was from Gaithersburg or even whether there was a college there. But he had taken notice of her hand bag. "Let's see what you have here, Miss Foster. He opened her bag and pulled out Fletcher's article and the several copies of Solidarity. *He pocketed the papers and held onto her bag.*

"Suppose you just come with me to the table over here, and you can be the first interviewee."

Neill James was later arrested, along with twenty other people, mostly undocumented immigrants and known Socialists or members of the Communist Party of America. She was charged with being in possession of seditious literature and lying to a government officer, Section 553a, UCFR 40 and Section 1001a, UCFR 18. The reviewing official–a senior Justice agent called the Hearing Administrator–released her on her own recognizance the next morning and told her she had to appear for a preliminary hearing in two weeks. Given the rivalry among intelligence agencies and the recent postwar requirements to stand down from surveillance of civilians, MID could not provide witness to her clandestine assignment: It would have been a public admission not only that Negative Branch infiltrated labor meetings but also of our failure in this investigation. Our employee Miss Neill James had become "neutralized" as an agent.

Captain Shaw's memoir recalled that he conferred with his superiors about what to do with his "talented, daring young stenographer," as he was avid to retain her services for MID in spite of the general staff reductions and the shrinking of MID's counter-intelligence role following the Armistice. Colonel Masteller, who had recently taken over from Wrisley Brown as head of Negative Branch and who always struck me as a most astute and decisive executive, reviewed the memoranda about the case and decided Neill should be moved, quietly and quickly. He would ask General Churchill to intervene with the hearing administrator from Justice, and meanwhile, his assistant, Lt. Colonel Alexander Coxe, would arrange the transfer.

A stranger's hanky-panky proved lucky for Neill, and in that I must confess I agree with what she says in her book about her natural luck–she always seemed to land on her feet such that some of the worst fixes she might get into turned out in the end to favor her. So, the previous autumn, just before dawn on October the sixteenth, police in the state of Washington, supposedly acting on a bellhop's tip, had raided Room 422 of the downtown Spokane Davenport Hotel. There they discovered a woman in bed and in the arms of a man who was reported to be "not her husband." It wasn't that she was shamelessly wanton, but Clementina Rogers was lonely and a long way from home, as she had come to Spokane from Oklahoma a year earlier with her husband, who was serving as head counsel for the Spokane area's IWW offices, and the husband, a lawyer and all, was often absent on business, and then again when he was with her he was still away at work in his mind.

Clementina Rogers quickly saw the good sense in the arresting officers' suggestion that she share with them something useful about the activities and plans of the Northwest IWW, and so she spilled the beans and told them the IWW men were mobilizing for a massive walkout of shipyard workers in Seattle. The strike, she said, was to take place in four to six weeks, and the police calculated it would involve as many as forty thousand workers.

Now, as Neill's good fortune would have it, the Seattle shipyard strike occurred exactly one week after the day she was arrested in Baltimore, and by that time Colonel Coxe already was considering suggestions that she safely and usefully could be put to work in Washington State. Rumblings of serious troubles in the Pacific Northwest had been trickling in at M Street since the early fall of 1918 from agents in Butte, Spokane, Seattle, and Portland. For decades the mines, timber operations, shipyards, and transportation centers there had been hotbeds of labor unrest and union organizing, especially by the IWW, and now the strike made it all the more reasonable and urgent that her transfer should be completed.

Coxe assigned her to Fort Vancouver Barracks, between Portland and Seattle–though her primary supervisor would continue to be Captain Shaw–and she was given a cover job as the replacement for the Fort

Commander's personal secretary, so it wasn't actually not-official cover. Colonel Coxe must have hoped nobody would question the odd fact that a young woman with barely one year of experience in the government had become secretary to the Fort's highest ranking officer, for that seemed to be the biggest threat to her cover assignment. I was opposed to that part, but nobody wanted to listen to me.

Before leaving the East Neill made up a story about Negative Branch receiving a requisition from Western Section for eleven additional clerks, and by mere happenstance the requisition had come in just at the moment she was telling a colleague that she would like to go as far away as she could. Naturally, Neill would have submitted an application for the transfer, and as I recall, this is the version of the story she wrote in her first book, and it was the excuse she offered to Elizabeth and Mary one night several weeks after her arrest, as she began packing for her train trip westward.

Her roommates understood, up to the limits of what they had been told by Neill: Since the loss of Mae and the stressful events at Neill's job—which she of course couldn't tell them about in any detail because of military secrecy rules—and the beastly weather, surely she must be fed up with Washington D.C. They also reasonably understood that Neill needed a new adventure, a change of scene, as that was her nature and had been for as long as they'd known her. They would have no difficulty finding another girl to share the apartment with them, and two days later Neill was gone.

In the spring of 1919 Neill had a stand-in, a much older woman who for nearly twenty years quietly had run the Commanding Officer's desk at Fort Vancouver Barracks. She pretended she was training her own replacement ahead of retirement, and she continued doing all the office tasks while Neill took her title as Secretary to the C.O. Neill told me she knew she could actually do the base secretary's job but our work would take up all her time. She never lacked confidence in her abilities, from the basketball courts to her social climbing to her Negative Branch assignments, and in making all that seem acceptable to everyone who might matter, but sometimes I wonder if I was one of the ones who mattered, because she had ceased caring whether I believed her or not, it seemed, or at least she had ceased trying to be charming to me. But she was at bottom partly right, because in fact she was almost constantly on special assignment as ordered by Captain Shaw from M Street and his superiors. She handed in her reports directly to Mr. F.B. Stansbury at MID's San Francisco office for analysis, though I eventually got an official look at them.

The Seattle General Strike had occurred in February and by the time Neill arrived in the West and General Churchill had returned from the European peace negotiations, MID was in full operational mode again. General Churchill wanted to renew pressure on the radicals and IWW, in part because the Justice Department's Bureau of Investigation had become a powerful competitor in the counter-intelligence business, and that was just about the time a terror campaign of mail bombings started in April, first barely missing the Seattle mayor and then successfully hitting the home of a former U.S. Senator from Georgia. Other bombs had been discovered by the postal service, and on May Day a bomber blew himself to smithereens at the doorstep of Attorney General Palmer's home, and June would see seven more bombings. The Bureau was growing by fearsome leaps and bounds, and we were kept hurly-burly busy at the M Street offices to maintain our mission intact.

Neill went to work checking on the mill workers. She never produced much intelligence of value, perhaps because the men were all Four-L unionists, well paid and orderly, or maybe it was because Neill's cover left her open to suspicion of being too close to the Army, even though she was a civilian. But there's more to this little story, for her real function, at a deeper layer of secrecy, was to make sure the military interviewers were properly identifying IWW sympathizers and eliminating them from the Loyal Legion of Loggers and Lumbermen, which was a major investment by the Army's Spruce Production Division.

The Four-L union was an arrangement between workers and timber executives, designed and financed by the Army under Colonel Brice Disque, with the aim of neutralizing the appeal of the IWW, thereby so to avoid costly strikes in the lumber industry and build up the spruce production workforce in the Northwest that was needed for the war effort and beyond. By the time Neill was in Vancouver the military was funding the mill and constructing bases and war materials solely from the mill's output and eventually it would be for our aircraft and other allies' planes, too. We were practically running the Four-L union and the timber industry, and the Wobblies were mostly subdued.

Now, I said Neill was always restless, and so she took advantage of the warming weather and the nearby Cascade mountain range to get out and about. She tagged along with an Army mountaineering team on maneuvers at Mount Adams and got her first taste of climbing above 10,000 feet, which she found to be magical, and every chance to climb after that first one was irresistible, and she would go mushy-gushy about her mountain climbing adventures. Through the summer of 1919 she hiked in the Cascades and the Olympic Range, but she also went swimming in the region's lakes and at beaches along Puget Sound, played tennis at the Fort club and rode horses in the coastal valley. Sometimes she was alone on her outings, but more often she was in the company of nurses from the Fort hospital or cavalry guard officers, and on more than one occasion Captain Shaw had to warn her against compromising her effectiveness by becoming too chummy with post personnel or union people. You would think she had no work to do, and I had a hard time keeping track of her, plus I had other duties and other girls to keep watch over.

Neill, as usual, began to sense she was idling in a backwater assignment, and she repeatedly sent complaints in her letters to Shaw, saying not much exciting was happening to her, she was kept busy sending bland reports to San Francisco, and all seemed to be running as MID had wanted it to run under the Four-L union, so there was no action or real need for her. She said she was hemmed in. Now, Neill hated idleness, but here it seemed to me that she most likely felt confined and restrained, like an imprisoned drifter. She was sent to Seattle several times during that year to meet with groups of civilian informers, who mostly worked for the fragmenting American Protective League, but those details offered no new challenges to her, and so she continued to complain.

By early winter it became apparent that policy in Washington D.C. had changed and M Street's undercover work was being closed down. Lt. Colonel Coxe went west to discuss the new restrictions with Stansbury, and they met for a confab in a Portland hotel. I got the story of the meeting from Colonel Coxe's report.

After reviewing routine business and sorting through logistical matters, Colonel Coxe got to his main purpose. He said that Justice was moving ahead with mass arrests under Hoover at their General Intelligence Division and yet we were still giving them our raw file information. The difficulty for us was that the American voters and our civilian leadership had said loud, clear, and often that they want the military out of counter-intelligence, which meant for us a return to the restrictions of a year earlier. There were to be no active investigations, no duplication with any other agencies, per order of Secretary Baker, but at the same time, the American public wanted to see the end of radical rebel groups, the bombers and Bolsheviki seditionists.

Stansbury hum-hummed his agreement with the summation.

General Churchill had a plan, however, to overcome that contradiction, Coxe said. While our agents must cease any and all nonmilitary investigations and undercover work, we were permitted to mobilize patriotic groups whose members might serve as informal agents off the books. He said it had already begun in Central Division, and Colonel Johnston was having excellent results there, funding it by his miscellaneous operating expenses budget line. Stansbury might consider creating one from the spruce mill's earnings if he could get past Disque. He said he brought a list of twenty-seven such useful organizations, indicating those that the M Street staff found to be well organized and thriving in the Western Department.

Stansbury examined the list, hum-hummed some more and scratched his chin. Then he identified the American Legion posts as the most active, by far the largest and growing rapidly, what with the demobilization.

Colonel Coxe told him, "We want to move swiftly, especially in Spokane and Portland and of course down the coast. Does this plan present you with any severe obstacles to success?"

"I have almost no personnel. There's nobody I can spare for the Northwest assignments."

"Shaw's girl, the Mississippi stenographer, she's underutilized and restless and she's right here in Vancouver. Shaw says she can do anything, and her loyalty is unquestionable. She proved it by holding the line when the Bureau arrested her last year. Sounds like she could organize the Legion posts up here. Why don't you give her a chance at it?"

They all had taken up on Neill's version of her talents and maybe had grown tired of her griping and grumbling, but in any case a week later Neill arrived at Fort George Wright. It was a modest compound, scarcely a thousand acres set on a high bluff overlooking the Spokane River and Indian Gulch and, further east, the prosperous city of Spokane. Neill was assigned quarters in a plummy two-storey red brick house with white porch railings that easily might could have been in Columbus, Mississippi, if it weren't for the snow that covered the ground and lay fresh on the pine trees. She again was given cover as personal secretary to the Fort's Commanding Officer and again had the stand-in arrangement.

She went right to work shaping the American Legion posts of northern Idaho and eastern Washington into counter-propaganda machines and conduits of information about radicals. She created local magazines and press kits, trained members how to screen candidates for intelligence gathering and cultivated friendships with local business and political leaders. I have to admit that she had the skills for that sort of assignment, for she had been used to tending to the details of publicity work and journalistic writing, which she excelled in while at The W.

MID continued to shrink, however, and by mid-1921 General Pershing had become Army Chief of Staff. His first acts were to change MID's name to G-2 and to disband the Negative Branch, and soon the demobilization reached even the most valued civilian agents. I was lucky enough to be retained in G-2, undoubtedly because Uncle Bradford spoke well for me. I was permitted to continue my surveillance over a few of the more important girls in the field. Neill was vexed but she cooperated.

She received her discharge letter hand-delivered by the Fort Wright civilian personnel officer. She said he told her, "We regret, Miss James, that there is no funding for transport back to your post of entry on duty. We hope you will find suitable new employment wherever you wish to go from here."

That she was required to leave her rooms at the officer's quarters immediately stunned her, but ever on the offensive, Neill straightaway phoned the wife of a Spokane banker she had befriended. Neill asked the woman to recommend a local boarding house for young business women. The executive's wife was Mrs. Beverly Jeanne Wheatley, and Neill knew she was a marooned and lonely Alabama socialite, so Neill probably had asked the question with a strategy in mind. Mrs. Wheatley invited Neill to lodge at her home until she might find suitable new employment.

Grateful for her nine-lives luck and Mrs. Wheatley's perhaps not-so-unexpected kindness, Neill didn't waste a moment in moving the short distance from the Fort to the grand house in Spokane's poshish Browne's Addition. She wired Shaw the next morning:

HAVE BEEN AXED NO EXIT BONUS STOP NEED WORK PLEASE ADVISE STOP YOURS NEILL.

Forty-eight hours later she received a telegram from M Street.

GO TO PORTLAND OREG FIND ANY TOLERABLE EMPLOY SEE STANSBURY SEWARD HOTEL 27 TH STOP WORK FORTHCOMING STOP SHAW.

Neill's first job in Portland was with a railroad shipping office, and the day after she was hired, she asked for a week's leave so she could familiarize herself with the city. Her new boss reluctantly approved her delayed start, as she probably already had charmed him, and he might also have assumed that she had some personal business to take care of. Her personal business was to meet with Stansbury at the upper-crusty Seward Hotel and then redirect her career, only this time it would have to be as a contract agent for MID.

Stansbury told Neill she would have to provide her own cover as a businesswoman, all NOC of course. As new benefits she would have more flexibility because her G-2 work could be done mostly in her off hours, and her compensation would be higher than her old government salary. Neill watched her money carefully, always knew exactly what she had and what everything she wanted would cost, that part she freely admitted, but she always seemed to have insufficient income for the style in which she wanted to live, the same as at college, though I have to say she never to my knowledge borrowed money–clothes yes, but not cash. Nonetheless, the contract was a boon to her bank account, and she rather enjoyed the game of deception and impersonation. So she returned to work, now as a contractor, and G-2 continued almost as before but without traceable employees doing negative intelligence, which we weren't supposed to be doing. Part of that for me was keeping track of the girls' finances and mail, and it was an easy task in those days.

I should say another boon to Neill's bank account had occurred earlier that year. Her late father's will stipulated that when the youngest child reached eighteen, each of the surviving children would receive an equal portion of his remaining estate. The youngest, Neill's sister Jane, turned eighteen on July 23, 1921, and the probate began immediately. It wouldn't be much, but I imagine Neill highly valued the possibilities. It was as if she had been looking towards that event for some time before, as she seemed to focus on Jane, occasionally sending a post card to her or a note to the others still at home in Hattiesburg or Grenada to check on Jane's well-being, and as Jane's birthday neared Neill initiated an exchange of letters with her. The first letter was written on Seward Hotel stationery.

Dear Janey,

I have moved from the dreadful cold and darkness of Spokane. I now live in Portland, a temperate, green and grey city, as gentle rains fall some three hundred days a year around here. I have bought a pair of waterproof Wellingtons and get around just like a native Oregonian. On the rare clear days I can see Mt. Hood, a jagged snow-capped peak over 11,000 feet high, from the front window of my apartment on the South Hill. Soon I shall climb Mt. Hood with a group of my friends from the Mazama Mountaineering Club. I do hope they can keep up with me.

My work at the railway firm has been an education. I had to learn a new language, the special vocabulary of the railroads, which is as different from the vocabulary of the Army as chalk from cheese. I sometimes am required to work on Sunday–please don't be alarmed, Oregonians think nothing of working at their jobs or repairing their plumbing or tilling their fields on Sundays, even though many attend church as well. Oregonians are an independent lot and I rather admire and enjoy that. I think you too would enjoy the society here.

Please tell everyone at home that I am well and busy. Of course I think of them all of the time, but especially of you, Janey, as you prepare to go on for business school. I encourage you to pursue your studies, but do remember also to play sometimes, and please write back to me soon.

Love, Neill

I'm not sure whether Neill had suddenly become lonely for contact with her family, or maybe she'd felt a special identification with Jane as the younger sister approached adulthood. But there also is the possibility, and to me it is much more likely, that she wanted to remind the family that she deserved a full share of the inheritance and didn't want her college expenses deducted from it.

Now, fortunately for her, Neill's clandestine work required her to circulate among all levels of Portland's society, from wage laborers to heads of the largest businesses to City Councilmen and officials in the Mayor's office. She spent some nights at union meetings, others in the bars of the finest hotels and private clubs.

Well, one night at a gathering of city financiers in the Benson Hotel's Oak Room lounge, Neill met by happenstance Helen Gravely, who was then an unemployed salesgirl out looking for opportunities and trying to lure potential backers for a business she wanted to start. We knew about Gravely because she posed a potential threat of compromise to some of our contract employees, what with her repeated and insistent attempts at liaisons, almost as if she knew what we were up to, though to my knowledge we never found any solid evidence against her.

Helen Gravely and Neill immediately saw many things in each other, things like a competitive challenge, a sort of seductive glamour–in her first book Neill crudely described Helen as "a stunning blonde"–economic opportunities, a social openness and vulnerability. Helen had an idea to start a fancy-schmancy lady's clothing shop, and Neill couldn't resist the prospect of being intimately involved every day with both this enticing woman and endless racks of fine clothes. Within weeks of their meeting they had cobbled together all of their savings and borrowed an additional thousand dollars to open "The Lovejoy Ave Atelier," which, as their slogan said, was "offering high fashion for today's fashionable woman." Because Helen Gravely appeared to have found her mark, I was instructed to keep closer watch on events.

Helen was a decade older than Neill, had been married and had three young children. Nonetheless, she and Neill jumped into a romantic affair and struggled to arrange a life together in Portland. Neill convinced Helen they should split the shifts at the shop, in that Neill would take the early mornings and occasional late-late hours while Helen worked afternoons when Neill would be secretly working for G-2. She couldn't and didn't tell Helen about her G-2 assignments, nor could Helen bring Neill home to stay, and so consequently they had after-work dates as often as they could arrange, dallying at Neill's rooms or at one of the hotels where they dined together.

The atelier did not make a profit, and the two partners quarreled about finances and advertising and inventory balances, but still they managed to keep the shop open after the first quarter of business, and they continued their part-time affair in the evenings. By the end of spring Neill received the disbursement from her father's estate. Her share was four thousand, enough to buy a modest house or a new Cadillac sedan outright, if she had wanted to, and even though she used some of the money to pay debts weighing on the boutique, she kept most of it for herself, splurged for clothes and bought a full-length fur coat at Meier & Frank, in case, she said, she had to return to Spokane. Neill wrote to Jane that "Daddy has finally given us the lives he always wanted for us. Now, with your share, you can have the education that I was unable to give you."

Almost immediately she began reducing the hours she spent working at night for G-2, and I began to worry for her. Sometimes when her paymaster, 1st Lt. W.D. Long, asked about her availability for an assignment, she would say she didn't want to overexpose herself, or she would tell him her business associates were becoming suspicious about her absences.

Helen was suspicious about a lot of things. Apparently Neill often ordered the wrong merchandise or too much of it and squandered money on lushy-luxe decorations for the shop and for ads in high priced magazines in faraway cities. And so the business continued to flounder. By June, Helen decided she had to confront Neill about her choices, which she did one evening at one of their favorite hotels.

Neill later described it for me in what was to be our last conversation.

They sat side by side, she said, on a velvet covered settee before the stone fireplace in the Benson's Oak Room. Helen told her the shop was going under, and they needed to take action immediately.

"Now, now, now. I know we're in the red, but we still have reserves," Neill said.

"We're not in the red, Sweetie, we're dead in the water. Our reserves won't cover this month's rent, let alone the oversized inventory on order for the summer season." Neill described Helen's expression as "icy."

"Helen, I'm not in a position to contribute more cash to the business. I have a very uncertain future to consider."

"Well, the business has no future at all, as it is. The reason we're in this situation is your recklessness. Yes, you have contributed twice as much capital as I have, but you've put us in the poorhouse, and I don't see how that's going to change. It's time we ended the arrangement."

"So, y'all just want to sell off everything and split the remains. And is that it for us?"

"No. I want to keep it going but I want sole responsibility. This has nothing to do with our friendship, it's just business. I want you to turn it over to me. After all, my name is on the line, not yours. I've taken all the legal risks here."

"Well it seems that I've taken some risks here, too, since we have no contracts for the money I paid into this shop in the first place."

"That's right, Neill, there are no contracts. But if you just leave the business, I will consider your investment to satisfy payment for your part in the losses, and I will take responsibility for the debts we have and the risk of any future financial troubles."

"Fine how d'you do this is. Well I'll just keep my samples and get out of your hair."

Neill said she rose, fetched her raincoat and umbrella and walked out through the lobby's revolving door. She didn't look back and pretended not to hear when Helen called after her, pleading for her to stay.

For the next few months Neill lived mainly on her savings from the inheritance and only occasionally took temporary jobs as a stenographer in organizations Lt. Long would assign her to investigate. There was a fuel cartel and a religious sect called Heaven's Soldiers Society and a private college seeking to establish an ROTC unit–but most of her time was free, and she avidly devoted herself to mountain climbing in the Cascades and horseback riding with the Portland Hunt Club, and she steered clear of the Lovejoy Ave Atelier and shopped only at downtown department stores.

It was a pleasant life for Neill, but she knew her savings couldn't sustain her for long, even in Portland. She eventually would have to find a career position or else greatly increase her commitment to G-2, and she worried over it constantly, she said, but as she deliberated over those alternatives, her fate was decided for her by the national scandal involving Lt. Long.

Long, a youthful anti-radical, sent a letter all on his own in October to every county sheriff in Oregon to alert them about threats to the nation. He wrote, in part:

> The Intelligence Service of the Army has for its primary purpose the surveillance of organizations or elements hostile or potentially hostile to the Government of this country, or who seek to over-throw the Government by violence.
>
> Among organizations falling under the above heads are radical groups such as the I.W.W., World War Veterans, Union of Russian Workers, Communist Party, Communist Labor Party, One Big Union, Workers International Industrial Union, Anarchists, Bolsheviki, and such semi-radical organizations as the Socialists, Non-Partisan League, Big Four Brotherhood, and the American Federation of Labor.

Unfortunately for the patriotic but witless Lt. Long, for nearly a year a G-2 policy had been firmly in place forbidding any investigative activities or surveillance of civilian organizations, and it had come directly from Col. Heintzelman, the new head of G-2. Within days Long's letter made it into the newspapers, and editorial writers across the country sharply criticized it, as a flood of protests inundated the White House, accusing President Harding and Secretary of War Weeks of spying on good Americans. The AF of L was bitterly stung by the letter and did everything it could to raise the noise level of the protests.

Even before Lt. Long's blunder shut down the network, Neill knew it was time for her to make a move. She was restless, her romance had ended, and her savings were running out. As had become her usual practice, she turned to her connections for help, and so she telephoned me in Washington D.C. We talked over her predicament and considered some of her options. She asked about Captain Shaw, and I told her he was now working for Naval Intelligence. When she finally reached Shaw, who had been given the naval rank of Lieutenant Commander, he told her to look up a Naval Officer in Seattle named William Anderson. He said Anderson was reliable and might have something for her, and by the time she sees him he would have received Shaw's recommendation. Shaw wished Neill luck in whatever life would bring her way.

That was the last information I received from Vernon Shaw and my contacts in Portland. I never learned what happened to Helen Gravely after Neill left, and, other than what I've read in Shaw's and Neill's books or heard on The W's grapevine, that was the last reliable information I had about Neill's story.

After her second book was published and she got on the radio in New York as The Petticoat Vagabond, I decided to go and pay her a visit, just for old times' sake and to congratulate her, because she really was becoming known in the City. She had an apartment on Northeast 83rd, but when I told the doorman who I wanted to see, he would not let me in. Neill never answered my letters or returned my calls and eventually I stopped trying.

III

Geraldine Sartain

> Perhaps this very absence of memory and future was the cause of my
> happiness–a kind of crazy happiness ungrounded in reason: wild,
> gratuitous, inexhaustible in its emptiness.
>
> —Jorge Semprun, *Literature or Life*

When Neill left me in Hawaii I thought I would never see her again. That
was her instinct and need, to just turn away and go on to other adventures.
And even before the moment I knew for certain it would be my destiny, I
had a sense that her compulsive need always would be stronger than any
attraction my love could offer her. But at least I would be with her again,
thanks to Vernon Shaw.

Neill came over from Seattle in October 1922 on the Matson steamer
"Lurline." She was in the company of Marguerite Colpitz Miller, whom I
already knew. Commander William Anderson, my ONI boss in Oahu at the
time, had introduced them. He had been on the West Coast of the mainland
recruiting girls–business women, clerks with college education, former G-2
and MID workers. Neill came highly recommended by her mentor, an MID
Captain who later got a Navy commission with promotion to Lieutenant
Commander. At the time I knew him only by the name Shaw.

Neill was as excited about coming to Honolulu as a young coed at a big
prom. Her goal, she said, was to live at Waikiki, and, whenever she wasn't
busy with work, she would go swimming and surfing right at the edge of
her back lawn. You'd think that was just a romantic fantasy, but she
immediately got the cottage by the beach, not far from Diamond Head. And
she swam every morning. The truth is Marguerite Miller already knew
about the cottage and had rented it ahead for the both of them.

Neill also said she intended to hike on the plantations, climb volcanoes,
play golf and tennis, and maybe even learn to play Island polo. I thought
early-on she was merely bewitched by the tropical possibilities, like so
many newcomers from cold climates. But I soon came to know intimately
that she was frantic to do something with all that energy of hers.

The silliest thing is that Neill resolved she would get so tanned she could
pass for a native, and within a week she was telling strangers she was "part-
Hawaiian." She told me the same story when we met. She always wanted to
pass for someone else, not as an act of self-loathing or as a coy game but as
a test of her potentialities. And she excitedly said she intended to take full

advantage of the famous nightlife along Kalakaua Boulevard and would dress up like a film star. I wondered at first what kind of creature I had met up with.

Neill liked and admired Marguerite almost from the moment they met, but they had different attitudes and ambitions, so they settled in as friendly roommates. A decade later, though, there would be other, more significant differences. Marguerite at first made Neill feel uncomfortable; I think it was because of her appearance. Marguerite had a long, thin face and an ashen complexion and a way of holding her head back as she looked down at most people, especially women, from her six foot height. Maybe she reminded Neill of someone else. Neill described her that first day in Oregon as being dressed in a granite-hued business outfit, with a double-breasted jacket cut like a man's. The severity of her suit was offset by a pink and turquoise floral scarf wrapped around her neck and tucked into her shirt like an ascot. Neill surmised she wore it because her neck, like her face and torso, was overly long and narrow. Her hair, like Neill's, was cut in a fashionable bob. But unlike Neill's wildly luxuriant mop, Marguerite's was thin and lay limp on her head so that her ears poked through the wisps. Under the arched nose her lips were a thin colorless line whether pursed or smiling, and there was a hint of moustache.

Neill loved to be seen with glamorous people, and Marguerite certainly couldn't be counted as that. Yet Neill was drawn to her eyes. They were iron-grey like her suit and were compelling in their intelligence, and her face shone a confidence and self-acceptance. It soon became obvious to Neill that Marguerite was worldlier as a traveler and more experienced as an agent, and I'm sure she suspected that Marguerite was her better intellectually and wouldn't be dominated. Marguerite had advanced degrees in paleontology, and that was part of her usual cover. She also had been married and quickly divorced, and that kept Neill wondering about her. At the time they met, both of them were idled by the recent Lieutenant Long affair.

They had hiked together in the Cascades, heading out before dawn and packing lunches and extra clothing against the unpredictable fall weather in the Northwest. Neill was delighted to learn that Marguerite, despite her length of limbs, proved to be strong and durable. They would return to Portland after nightfall and have a late dinner at a hotel dining room, where they talked for hours about Hawaii and the places Marguerite had reported from. It might have been those long talks in the afterglow of strenuously satisfying days in the mountains that transformed Neill's restlessness and need to leave her family into a love for travel.

How could I now feel jealous of a person Neill was adventuring with before we ever met? Why does just the thought of their moments of public intimacy at the end of a day's climbing cause my heart to go faint? I suppose I've been so blended with Neill, and for a time believed she was so completely absorbed into me, that her whole life was mine, too. But of course we had our separate pasts, and her early times with Marguerite were merely athletic and collegial. So there was no romance but a tentative friendship which lasted even after Marguerite left the cottage to resettle with her former lover, who had returned from a posting in China.

Marguerite and Neill reunited in the Thirties when Neill returned to Oahu, but by that time I was out of government work and thousands of miles away. Neill's life seemed to go in circles like that, looping back to places and people she had left, as if she were trying to get something right the next time or she was fated to keep revisiting her past. She did that with me, too, and I had to learn that she would be off to another place and other people no matter how often she returned, and all I could do is hope I would be with her again.

Within a month of her arrival at Honolulu, Neill had gotten a job at Hawaii Ice, training the sales staff and customers and doing their publicity all over the island. I was a stringer for AP and the San Francisco Chronicle at the time, but the urgent work both of us did, though she didn't know about me at the beginning, was for Commander Anderson. It's odd, but after all these decades I still feel reluctant to talk about the work. Maybe our old vows are more durable than we are. That would not be completely true of Neill, but she always was full of surprises and I still might misjudge her.

A copy of a very early letter she wrote to her youngest sister Jane came into my hands and I kept it. She wrote to Jane often from Hawaii, and she showed me many if not all of her letters before she sent them to Jane. It was a practice we all did as a check on security, even Anderson. That early letter displayed her infatuation with Hawaii and her willingness to cover over inconvenient facts.

> *Dearest Janey,*
>
> *Our little cottage by the sea now feels more like home and grows more welcoming by the hour. I have bought a rattan couch and hassock with cushions of brightly printed cotton ticking and ocean blue verge and placed it on our lanai facing the beach. Mornings like today I can lounge*

on my Islands settee, coffee in hand and books and letter paper on the table, and watch the bronze bathers going down to the surf. I am brushed by the onshore breeze and the fragrance of a thousand blossoms, jasmine and orchid and papaya blooms. Oh Janey I wish you could come out here to enjoy this luxury with me! But I think it wise that you are determined to finish with school before moving on to anything else.

My roommate, Marguerite, has found a job in publishing. She has a fiancé and might not be long for the single life. If she leaves our little "hale" (house), I shall have to find another room mate, as I am unwilling to lose this paradise of a spot to somebody else. It's as glorious an Eden as any I've ever seen on the mainland. It's very easy to meet people here, all kinds of people from all around the world. My new position at the ice firm gets me out and around the island in my own company auto several times each week. I make sales presentations and put on training programs for the refrigeration ignorant, which includes almost every businessman in the Territory. But this way I get to meet all the merchants and hoteliers and learn about their social connections, which is very useful for a single woman looking for someone to share the rent. I also get introductions to the higher-ups of the island, for example this weekend I am learning to play Hawaiian polo as guest of the Commander of the Naval Base. Polo came to the Islands from Australia, so it's not played as we do on the Mainland, but they promise me a good ride and a nice party afterwards. I shall need a new wardrobe for such an occasion, don't you think?

Give my love to the family, and please write back to me right away. When my ship comes in I wish that you will be on it. Best love,

Neill

She had an ideal situation—an easy job, a car, a place on the beach and some exciting undercover work to do. When we first met it was accidental, in more senses than one. Anderson hadn't told her about the rest of us, perhaps because as a newcomer to his operation she was on probation until she proved what Shaw had said about her was true. We, on the other hand, had been briefed about her before she left Seattle. But it really was mostly a coincidence that she and I met, and it was sooner than Anderson had planned. It happened because of her road accident.

Neill wrote offhandedly about the incident in her Petticoat Vagabond book, but she entirely omitted meeting me. What actually happened went like this. She was on the coastal road to Kailua, driving to a sales training seminar and hoping to meet a potential new roommate there who would help her cover the cottage rent. On a short stretch approaching Makapu'u Beach, the road narrowed to skirt a lava cliff and the verge dropped off sharply to the sea on the opposite side. With barely two lanes and no shoulders, the pavement would just allow two sedans to pass one another if they were careful.

Motoring along at nearly top speed in her little company Ford, Neill looked ahead and saw a plantation truck weaving toward her. She doubted that it could squeeze past her coupe, even under the control of an expert driver. But the driver coming at her appeared to be asleep or drunk. Neill switched her headlights on and off and tooted her horn as she slowed, but the truck bore down, tacking from side to side. She didn't want to go into the ocean, nearly fifty feet below the road's edge, so she opted for split-second timing. As the oncoming truck neared her front bumper, the driver rhythmically drifted to his left, just as she had anticipated. Neill swung sharply to her left, toward the rock wall. The little Ford's right rear fender was clipped by the passing truck, the momentum spinning the coupe into the cliff and crushing it like a tin toy. They did, after all, call them Tin Lizzies.

The swerving truck continued on around the bend toward Honolulu, and Neill was left pinned in the wheezing wreckage, sitting dazed and feeling cold, as she watched wisps of white smoke rising from what had been the hood of her car. The hulk was upright and facing south, the way she had come, and the passenger side was smashed into the lava wall. Poor Neill was numb and bruised but not bleeding seriously, and she pried herself free from the tangle of steering wheel, shifter and crumpled seat. She climbed out the driver side window, pleased that her bones appeared to be intact, even though she began to feel splotches of pain emerging and spreading everywhere on her body. The first northbound driver stopped and offered her a lift to Kailua.

The driver said he was an Army NCO in the medical corps and this was his day off. He quizzed her as they drove. Neill guessed he was trying to find out how seriously she was injured. She answered his questions politely and reassured him that she wasn't badly hurt. She said she might have been in shock for a few minutes. She also told him about how she had survived because of her skill and her constitutional good luck. He replied that she had just been in a frightful wreck and that didn't sound to him like such fine luck.

The sergeant dropped her off at the territorial marshal's office, where she phoned her local host for the sales seminar and then her boss at the ice company. Her main worry, it seems, was that she would lose her ice job and have to tell Commander Anderson about the accident. If her luck held, he would be forgiving and help her find another job as cover; if not, it could mean the end of her sojourn in Paradise.

Mr. Nakamura, the owner of Hawaii Ice, was stunned by the news, but he was wonderfully kind and his concern was only about whether Neill was safe and unhurt. He told her to have the disabled Ford taken to Honolulu and he would order a new car for her in the morning. Don't think another thing about it, he advised. Neill said she felt a familiar sense of reprieve, rescued safely first out of a potentially fatal crash and then out of potentially dire consequences for her budding career. She decided she wouldn't have to tell Anderson anything about the event.

Two days later, just as a new Model T roadster was delivered to Neill, my AP editor put me on the accident story, and I went out to visit her. My journalistic specialties were transportation and working women's careers. Anderson, of course, knew about the crash and thought it would be a good opportunity for me to verify Neill's report about how she was settling in.

Neill showed me to her lanai, where we sat side by side on the wicker couch. She gazed warmly at me, as if I were an old friend. I showed her my credentials and said, "I'm Geraldine Sartain, but you should call me Gerry."

We had iced drinks and looked out to the beach as we talked about the accident. She continued to look at me appraisingly, up and down, and I happily received the attention.

"You look amazingly well, Miss James," I said, "considering the catastrophic nature of your crash." And she did look well. She was slim and athletic looking, and she had fierce dark eyes that could suddenly grow all soft and yielding.

"I feel as if I had been tumbled in a barrel over Niagara Falls, but I have no broken bones, and I am confident I could scale a mountain today if I had to. But surely an automobile accident is not very interesting news for your papers?" She obviously was puzzled by my visit.

"It interests me," I said. "I have a longstanding desire to tell stories about the place of automobiles in our society, whether it is in my home area of California or in the Territories or in Timbuktu. The auto is both an instrument of emancipation and the destroyer of history. I also have an interest—a political interest, if you will—in writing about independent women who are employed and who overcome challenges, especially the challenges of operating an automobile. Your situation sounds like it brings together two of my favorite and best received writing topics. And what brings you out to Oahu, Miss James?"

"Oh, the lure of the road and the sea, I suppose. I'm a vagabond at heart, and I plan to travel light and far and see everything there is to be seen. But in Waikiki I think I have found a true haven, or maybe that should be heaven. It's the most delightful spot I have ever lived in."

"You found work almost immediately upon your arrival, did you?"

"Yes, apparently my credentials and skills are in great demand in the Islands. I have a background in merchandising and journalism, well, light journalism," Neill smiled sheepishly. "And I worked for the government in Washington D.C. and the Northwest, too. Executive secretary."

"I'm sure your skills are highly valued here, Miss James. Yours is a pattern I have seen quite often since my own arrival in Hawaii last year. To get on well here most of us hold multiple jobs, and I would expect that you do or soon will, too."

I was testing her. She clearly knew nothing about me and she was sticking to her cover story. I suppose I also was trying to give her an opening to recognize we had something else in common, perhaps hoping that later she might not feel so untrustworthy and excluded. Yet there was the probationary status Anderson had imposed, so in a way I was being naughty.

"Well I can't say what the future will bring me, Miss Sartain—sorry, Gerry, and by the way, do call me Neill—but I confess I am just lucky to be alive after that horrible truck driver almost ran me into the ocean. If I hadn't reacted quickly and decisively I would not be here talking with you over mango juice. My employer thinks so highly of my work he never thought of asking for reparation for the car. Did you see my new roadster?"

We walked out to the road, where her new Ford was parked, and she gaily showed me the electric starter button on the floor and the array of transmission pedals and the flipper on the steering wheel that served as a throttle. She commented that her little black convertible could be made to function as a conveyor belt or water pump or mill saw, just by removing a wheel and connecting it to other machinery. I would later write a glowing essay about her love for autos and skill in operating them.

After two hours of leisurely talk on the lanai, I made ready to leave. The official interview had been over almost before it began. "Surely you will have guests coming this evening, since it's Friday, or you'll perhaps need to prepare yourself for a night out somewhere. So I should be off."

"In fact, Gerry, I am still recovering from my bruises and bumps and felt it was too soon to go dancing. So I'm planning a quiet dinner here in my little cottage for this one night. I would just love the company, if y'all have no important engagement for this evening. There's a nice white wine in the ice box, and I was thinking on asking Mama Lao to bring down something Chinese from her kitchen. Would that be suitable? And maybe we can talk about what other jobs you and your friends are employed with."

I stayed for dinner, and by the time Neill and I slowly walked up the white stone path to the road, long after midnight, we were both flush with the first excitement of a potential romance. We didn't discuss work for Anderson, but we had agreed to live together.

I found Neill to be forceful, daring, guileless, even a bit naïve–or so I then thought–my ideal of the new woman who not only was out to explore the world but had the fearless eye and social charisma to conquer it. Neill later told me she envied what she called my "easeful intelligence." She said I was "serene" and that appealed to her. Serenity never came easily to Neill, though she aspired to it. We had sensed in each other a hunger, a vague and searching desire, and there was something else shared and unspoken, perhaps a feeling of being special and different when we were together. I thought it was the first bloom of love, and I wondered what Neill made of it.

Within a few days we had rearranged the contents of the little cottage by the beach to accommodate our wardrobes and furniture and our very different tastes in décor and domestic habits. I have always been an indolent, unworried procrastinator, and if that's serene then I'm it. But Neill immediately put into action her tremendous energy and will to control everything. She organized a daily routine of chores, social activities and sports for both of us. We did stretching exercises and swam in the ocean every morning and played tennis or golf several times a week. I was always exhausted, always sore, and the happiest I had ever been.

During the day Neill was off around the islands on her marketing and training work for Mr. Nakamura's ice company. My work as a journalist allowed me to schedule most of my own assignments and writing times, so I had the freedom to take total responsibility for our meals, which I loved to do. I put my cookery skills to work and prepared the most sumptuous meals I could imagine, spent freely on them, not just occasionally for dinner guests but for the two of us every day. When I couldn't avoid arriving home late we would dine at Mrs. Lao's Island Wok on the beach. I was losing the battle to keep my weight in check, despite our strenuous exercise routine.

Neill was an ardent lover, overheated and always available, but she was not warm in her heart. She was athletic and demanding in bed, willing to do anything and always turning our little games into elaborate dramas. Still,

there were long hours when she would seem to relax and enjoy my brushing
her thick hair or massaging her with oils, or we would lie entwined in a tub
of hot water until almost falling asleep. She had an appreciation for the
voluptuous pleasures.

After a short while, though, each of us for different reasons began to
grow silently uneasy over the other's unexplained absences from home,
which I later would learn was already an established pattern in Neill's
affairs. She would be gone for a few extra hours several times a week,
probably to eavesdrop on the Hawaiian Freethinkers Club or the Asian
Workers Union and to write reports for Anderson in secrecy. She usually
told me she had paperwork to do at Mr. Nakamura's office. I knew
generally what she was up to, but still I began to wonder at this ease with
deception that bordered on delight. I both admired it and feared it, because
it was such a struggle for me to keep anything from her. At times it
infuriated me, but I couldn't say anything.

I sometimes wouldn't be at home during the daytime when Neill
expected to find me there. When she asked me where I'd been—she would
grill me mercilessly—I would say as breezily as I could that I was out
following a story. Or sometimes I'd say I was restless and went into the city.
I never felt entirely convincing. It was awkward for both of us, because Neill
needed more control over information about my affairs and I couldn't know
how devoted she was to her assignments or whether she was just playing
the cat with a mouse. Actually I think I was jealous of everything about her
and it had little to do with our absences.

Just as the tension was turning to mutual resentment and silence,
Marguerite Miller came to the rescue. She had had a talk with Anderson
and persuaded him to let Neill off probation early and for us to tell her
about the network. It was Marguerite who took on the task. She met Neill
at the door of Hawaii Ice one morning and said she thought they ought to
talk privately, before she went on to her work at a dig up the coast. They
went out to Neill's roadster, which was parked under a porte-cochere, and
sat in the front seats and smoked Pall Malls. My diary from that time
dramatized what Marguerite coolly described to the rest of us the next day
in Anderson's office, and I still feel guilty for having listened. But it was
pure Neill.

"I mentioned to Commander Anderson that you have a new roommate,"
Marguerite began.

"You've been checking up on me, have you?" Neill smiled but her dark
eyes were grave.

"He asked after you. He likes to make sure his people are comfortably safe and satisfied. I told him I would look into it. In that sense I guess you might say I was checking up on you."

"So what did you tell him?"

"I told him Geraldine Sartain had found you and had become your companion. He was very much relieved."

"So. And why are we having this little chat?"

"Sartain also works for Commander Anderson, Neill, and he is pleased that someone as disciplined and dedicated as you will be her housemate. Geraldine is a gifted worker, both in her news reporting and in our business. But she has no sense of urgency, and we know she could be much more productive if she had a constant good example."

"We? Why I had no idea." Neill's face showed curiosity but her imagination must have been swirling. Had Marguerite been her boss all along, since Portland? Had I, Gerry, been assigned to keep tabs on her while pretending to be her partner at home? This would have been crushing to Neill. "Does every girl in Oahu work for Anderson?"

"Almost." Marguerite scanned the grounds before continuing. "Both G-2 and ONI have brought in a lot of unofficial personnel, many of them girls like us, contract information gatherers and observers who have other jobs. The sort of work you and I and Geraldine are doing—checking on the labor activists and radical groups, sniffing out Comintern recruits and keeping track of Nipponese agents—all of it has proven very useful to our government, because as you well know they can't use career agents anymore. We're countering two main threats, plots to undo our capitalist way of life and install communism, and the Japanese spying on our military assets and strengths. We're doing the eyes and ears work, the real, tangible, front-line work, Neill, and that requires a lot of diligent eyes and ears."

"Spare me the flag waving lectures. You sound like a propaganda recording. I know all that, and I assumed you and I were not the only girls pretending to be reporters and stenos and scientists. I just want to know where I stand. Who's really my boss?" Neill's eyes were bright with excitement, and her shag of black curls seemed alive in the morning breeze. She was always energized by the drama of secrecy.

"Whoever gives you the contract. Shaw turned you over to Anderson, and for now he's our operator, yours and mine, and as it happens, Geraldine's and more than a dozen other girls'. I'm just one of many, though I'm a little older and have a longer tenure with government than most."

"So, is that why you came to see me today, to tell me about Gerry?"

"That's part of my purpose. Since I'm an old-timer, Anderson wanted me to help you adjust to your arrangement," she puckered her mouth as she said it. "One of the cardinal rules of the work we do, Neill, is to keep the personal things away from our assignment. We don't talk about our work to our lovers and family, even if they're in the same line of work, unless we are on assignment together. That way we don't burden each other with unnecessary secrets. And we don't let emotional attachments confound our judgment at work or interfere with our effectiveness. Take a caution offered by an old hand, Neill, be careful not to let Geraldine come between you and your assigned responsibilities."

Neill was silent for a while. "You and I talked pretty openly in Oregon. How's that fit?"

"That was just between a couple of out-of-work agents, Neill, colleagues reminiscing."

Neill finished her cigarette and ran her hand through her unruly hair. She said she had misjudged me. And now, knowing of what she called my easy-going innocence, she was even fonder of me than before this conversation began. But Neill was confident that her attachments wouldn't interfere with her work. She believed it never had, and it never would—the adventure of work, if not its purpose, always came first. It was my burden to learn this over time. But she made her own decisions about whether to violate the rule or not, just as Marguerite did.

"Yeah, I know all the policy stuff. But don't you think you should be saying this to Gerry, rather than to me?"

"We already have."

Neill said she had to go inside. She thanked Marguerite for the visit and said to tell Anderson there's nothing for him to worry about.

That evening I had a seafood feast ready for the table when Neill came home.

"My, how lovely. Y'all must've been working all afternoon to put up this glorious supper."

"I knew you wouldn't be home until late," I said, "so I had plenty of time for the kitchen. Sit down and let me make you happy."

As she picked up her fork Neill said, "I know you work for Commander Anderson, and I know you know I do, too." So I'm thinking maybe we don't have to talk about this or worry anymore about such things."

I agreed, but the next night she told me what Marguerite had said, confirming what I'd heard in the office. I wasn't up to preventing her from violating the rule, but at least we didn't worry any further about secrecy or fidelity. Still, she couldn't resist telling me about her conversations with her targets, and I was left to wonder who was supposed to be good for whom. Our lives together eased but nonetheless became more fragile because Neill was so aggressive at her work. I had a poor understanding of her passion for it. In her boldness, she cracked an important Japanese espionage ring, and I should have predicted how the result would affect us.

It began when Neill infiltrated a group of Japanese residents of Oahu who had formed an association to promote social and business contacts in the maritime and agriculture industries. She attended their meetings as a public relations advisor and at first was treated politely but distantly. From observing their afterhours socializing for two months, she began to suspect there was another organization operating beneath the public one. She decided to penetrate the small group of bespoke-suited businessmen she had seen surreptitiously swapping portfolios and gathering for private discussions after the late parties.

She chose an elegant but rather homely man who frequently wore the most expensive clothing and seemed to be at the center of the document exchanges and side conversations. She told me she smiled demurely, touched him lightly on the wrist and purred in her baby Japanese, "*Okuro-san, anata-wah konya desuka?*"

Mr. Okuro swung around suddenly to face her, at first looking shocked. The frown on his flat, pitted face almost immediately melted to a broad grin, and he flashed his eyebrows. He answered her in flawless English. "I am very well this evening, Miss James. You surprised me with your excellent command of the Japanese vernacular."

Relieved that he wasn't going to carry on in Japanese, Neill said, "Oh, I'm just trying to learn. And I am pleased that you are well, Mr. Okuro. I see your glass is empty, though, and it would be impolite of me not to offer you a nightcap."

They soon became frequent dinner companions, and despite Mr. Okuro's free spending, Neill's expense account began to show substantial charges for entertaining him. After a time he began encouraging her to pass a few hours more with him, to accompany him to his hotel room for a nightcap—he'd learned the word from her the first time he recalled noticing her. Neill managed to find credible excuses or would look down at the floor and say she had attachments she first must resolve before becoming closer with him. She always called him Mr. Okuro.

He was very patient and circumspect, but after one late dinner with too many glasses of champagne he whispered to her that he had important defense work to do for his government. She could see he expected no necessary *quid pro quo*, just a hint of a promise would do.

Neill edged a filled champagne glass toward him and delicately asked him to tell her more about his important work. He drank it down quickly and grinned at her. His face was blotched red and moist, and his eyelids sagged over glassy eyes. He leaned into her neck and said he and his people have information that is very delicate, yes, very valuable. That was all he would say, until Neill suggested that maybe it was time soon for them to go up to his suite, where they could talk in private.

"Oh, but I can tell you some now," he recanted in an urgent whisper, slurring the sibilants. "Yes, I should tell you. You are so good to me, and you love Japan so much."

Neill put a finger to his lips and shushed him. She took his arm and guided him from their table across the lobby and all the way up to his rooms. He kept telling her how important his group was and what glory they would have once their information reached Taiwan and Tokyo. He gave her the key and she led him to the bedroom. Before she could think of a way out of the situation, she heard him groan and saw him crumple like a felled sapling onto the bed. She lifted his legs and removed his shoes. She loosened his necktie and collar, checked his identification and stepped out of the suite.

Anderson was delighted when he got her report. She had recommended that a Japanese double-agent be installed in the businessmen's circle, and Commander Anderson promptly arranged it. Within weeks the infiltration began producing high quality intelligence about Japanese espionage of U.S. military installations.

Anderson rewarded Neill with an assignment to find evidence about people named on what was called The List. He gave her a sheet of paper on which 157 names had been typed, all Japanese non-citizen residents of Oahu. Some were officers of the four Japanese banks in Honolulu. Others were businessmen and administrators; some were teachers in Japanese language schools. Many of the names on The List had been lined out. Those persons already had been arrested or deported. Soon all 157 would be either imprisoned or sent back to Japan, and all that was needed was evidence that they were in leadership roles among Japanese groups in Hawaii. It was an interesting sinecure.

To meet the bankers Neill used her old connections with the Japanese networking group, where she was remembered as the honorable but mistreated ex-girlfriend of the disgraced Mr. Okuro. She also spent many evenings at Japanese Language schools, gradually learning basic spoken Japanese while she was learning about the schools' leadership. Contrary to Neill's frequent claims in her books that she was quick to learn languages and had fluent French, Spanish and Japanese, I knew she struggled with anything that required long, disciplined study. She nearly failed French in college, her records showed, and her Japanese remained patchy, childish and error-riddled as long as I knew her. It wasn't for want of effort. She practiced for long hours at our cottage, grimly mouthing Japanese conversations to herself. She later would have the same struggle with Russian. Nonetheless, Neill created an impression at the ice company and among ONI officers that she knew Japanese, and she deftly avoided situations that would require her to actually converse in it, despite her dutiful and dull practice at home.

My public career improved, too. My published Chronicle and wire articles were accumulating into a coherent package and so my reputation as a journalist with specialized knowledge of automobiles and women's employment matters grew across Hawaii and extended to editors on the mainland. I was given a byline. As a feature writer I had access to the importers of auto parts, gasoline distributors, auto sales forces and dock workers unloading products for the popular new mode of transport on the islands. That coincidentally helped me in my ONI assignment, though Neill sometimes told me I was too lackadaisical about my contract work. I was probably too lackadaisical about my newspaper work, too.

But those were our salad days in Hawaii. I loved to ride in Neill's little Ford roadster, though I have always been a timid driver myself. Whenever we could find the time, we toured remote roads around Oahu on weekends, lodging at plantation farms or camping in an Army surplus canvas tent. After our first night in the tent, Neill taped insect netting over the entry flaps and sewed extra material on the side to act as a sun awning. We climbed every peak in the Waianae Mountains.

I gradually began to gain some strength for mountain ascents. On a glorious vacation, we booked passage to Hawaii and climbed the storied volcanoes on that island. The best part was reaching the edge of the broad shoulders atop Mauna Kea, hand-in-hand and laughing madly in our exhaustion, dizzy and gasping for breath. I should say, *my* exhaustion–Neill had to pull me up the last hundred meters or I wouldn't have made it.

Back on Oahu we climbed again through the thickets and rocks of the Waianae Range and slept under the chill fog on the rim of Mount Ka'ala.

For a magical six months we were together, and it really was Paradise. Neill wrote triumphant letters to Jane, telling her about the polo lessons and mountain climbing and the glamorous luaus on Diamond Head. She rarely mentioned me and when she did she portrayed me as just a roommate. What did I care? I was more satisfied than I'd ever thought possible.

Jane always wrote back respectfully, showed polite interest but no envy. "I sense our paths converging one day, as I too love the delights of travel and the challenges of adventure," she wrote. They agreed that when Jane finished business school she would come to Hawaii for an open-ended stay with her elder sister. I don't know what Neill had in mind for her roommate.

But it was not to be, at least not in Hawaii. One rainy morning at the beginning of May 1924, Neill was delivered a telegram from Tokyo.

> HAVE IMPORTANT WORK FOR YOU HERE STOP ANDERSON ON BOARD HIGHLY APPROVES STOP POST IN EMBASSY AWAITING REPLY YOUR ACCEPT PRONTO STOP SHAW.

Neill's reputation for success at work was propelling her away from me. She knew she couldn't pass up the chance to work again for Lt. Commander Vernon Shaw, especially now that he was stationed in Japan. She also knew she would have to tell me, but she decided to do that only after she had replied to Shaw. She drove to the Western Union desk at the Moana Hotel and sent her acceptance to Shaw:

> WILL BE ON FIRST STEAMER AVAILABLE HOLD POSITION AT EMBASSY FOR ME STOP MORE SOON STOP NEILL.

I had been on assignment all day and returned too late to make our dinner. We decided to eat at Mrs. Lao's restaurant, a short walk from the cottage. We sat at our favorite beachside table. The flames of two fat candles on the table undulated like hula skirts. Over drinks we told each other about our day's activities, all as usual. I told Neill about an interview I had conducted with a woman who recently switched jobs for better working conditions and was promptly fired.

"Speaking of changing jobs, there's something I need to tell you," Neill said.

"You're not leaving Mr. Nakamura, are you? He's been very kind, and that's easy and steady work, about perfect for our situation."

"I have received an offer of an important position. In Japan."

She spoke calmly, almost emotionless. She showed no sadness, no regret, just looked straight at me, as if she were reporting the weather.

"Oh Neill. Oh my Neill." I sensed what was coming. "Are you going to take it?"

"I've already accepted. I'm sorry. I mean I'm sorry for us, because I am very happy here with you. But I will be in the embassy, and I'll get to work with Shaw again, and you know what a decent man he is. I've booked passage on the Empress for Friday morning."

I nearly fainted with heartache. But I told her I fully understood even though it would be difficult to accept. Neill got up, said she'd eat later and went off to the cottage to begin packing. At the time, I thought it was the beginning of the end for us.

IV

Vernon Shaw

> Let us measure our values together:
> One fine morning we'll go wandering off.
>
> —Tso Ssu, "Summoning the Recluse, No. 2"

Neill had been with us in Tokyo a little more than a year when she told me she was unhappy. It was one of those fresh autumn mornings in the capital when the sun would shine brilliantly and the air would be sparkling clear after a cool night rain. She brushed past Marta, my administrative assistant, and strode into my office without an appointment.

I knew something was wrong whenever she came at me with such force. She placed both hands on my desk, leaned toward me and drawled, "I am not a bit happy."

At first her complaint puzzled and annoyed me. I had given her the best assignment and the most sensitive task then under my command: to monitor the Kokuhonsha Party. And she had been doing exceedingly well. She kept abreast of all the English language press and had worked with one of the embassy translators to comb documents and the native press. She did a massive amount of eavesdropping. Compliments were coming in from both G-2 and State, who were very pleased. Following the Imperial Hotel dustup we put her in a pretty house on a quiet alley with three servants, a place we found for her after we returned from a Karuizawa hiatus. She wanted to get away from the Imperial Hotel—adored the address but couldn't abide the noise and lack of privacy there. So we found her a place to live. She wasn't as yet unhappy with her pay. That would come later.

Somehow I convinced her, without pulling rank, to sit down. And then we talked. What bothered her, she told me, was that she was languishing. That's how she described it, "languishing." She would never say she was bored. She didn't like to think of herself as the sort of person who would find anything in her life boring, and more to the point she didn't like to think anybody else would think that. But languishing, as if she was being neglected, like a pretty girl still waiting to be asked to the party.

I doubted it was that she felt under-noticed—she always seemed to know when someone was aware of her, and she could *make* people notice. It was more that she was feeling undervalued and under-utilized, and the lack of excitement was like a deficiency in her diet. Arousal, attention and action, I had theorized, were her nourishment. If she wasn't aroused, she was like an old loaf of bread on the sideboard, growing stale and eventually decaying. I think that was what she feared, decay from ennui. What aroused her was facing something new and risky and taking *control*, doing something reckless and making it come out well and being noticed for it. In her work, she needed to be as near to a threat and as unleashed as possible, always. It was the source of her sense of self-importance. My job was to make sure the leash was at least attached and to keep her safely at work.

It so happened that I had just been given authority to issue Neill a cryptonym. Only those agents who could be expected to have continuing work in highly sensitive missions were designated by coded name. The others were given numbers or simply remained undesignated occasionals. This bright morning would have been a fitting time for the award, but I decided to postpone telling her for a week or two, to give the impression that it was a consequence of her complaint of languishment. It might look like an advancement that I would have acquired for her for that reason. This was a technique we often used for creating personal loyalties, particularly important in the case of agents who needed inducements to remain faithful, and I then suspected Neill might be one of those.

From all indications, her first Japan tour had deepened her attachment for our work. The history of that tour is the story of her first assignments under her code-name and how she nearly brought the East Asian operation down because of her innate recklessness–but at the same time probably saved it from certain loss. When I wrote my memoir I couldn't tell all the details, but I believe her work ultimately could have influenced America's involvement in the Second World War.

Two weeks following her complaint, I summoned her to my office and told her my superiors in Washington had agreed to issue her a code-name. Now Neill would be an insider. "Kokio" was selected by a panel at M Street from a block of allocated sobriquets kept by the DMI. It was the Hawaiian for a hibiscus, and Neill loved the association.

"Oh my heavens. I am flattered and grateful," she said.

"It's not flattery," I told her. "You well deserve the recognition. Your reports have become required reading, not just for the analysts but the top policy folks as well. We want you to stay on and we're now confident that you will always put your work first. We don't want you to become rusty." I meant, but didn't say, to become indifferent.

Neill had plenty of time available to devote to her work. Having left her companion in Hawaii, she was living a subdued, if not ascetic, life and had been doing so since arriving in Japan. She hadn't found any suitable romance, although she was said to have considered the embassy staff and the international set around Tokyo, Yokohama and the legation retreat of Karuizawa. My assumption, having perceived something a bit unusual about Neill from the beginning, was that she considered all of them, men and women. Yes, women too. I am no prude, but this was *not* something people talked about, certainly not Neill. Yet her attraction to her own sex became obvious to me and I incorporated it into my overal handling of her without ever mentioning it–to her or anyone else.

Despite her telling many people she was one-eighth Japanese, she seemed uninterested in personal relationships with any natives. It appeared my secretary Marta Carlova had become the closest of her colleagues, but Marta had lived for some years with one of the clerks. (She was given the name Ruby in Neill's first book.) Marta was a shy, bookish woman who didn't socialize much outside the office. She was shaped like a pumpkin, decidedly not athletic, was fluent in Japanese and Mandarin and very smart, and thus was someone who would not be of much personal interest to Neill James, though I imagine Neill admired her. Marta and Ruby had been in the Naval Attaché's office a good while before my arrival, and I owe my survival on that tour to their competence and loyalty.

I briefed Neill on her first assignment as Kokio. "I want you to take a vacation from the embassy," I said, "and go to China, locate an important source of ours in the North and see if you can get a look at his operation in Mongolia. We're interested in verifying the field reports that have been coming from that quarter. We also need to learn what the intentions of Chang Tso-Lin are toward the Japanese in Manchuria. We have some indications trouble is brewing in Mukden, either with the Republicans or somehow involving the Japanese interests."

Neill frowned and brushed her fingers through her hair. "Who's this source of ours?"

I told her about Mack Young. "Soldier of fortune, former NCO named John McKenzie Young. He works for Andrews of the Natural History Museum on the Third Asiatic Expedition, but Andrews is away much of the time, usually in North America on lecture tours and fund-raising. Reports used to come from Andrews, who has a cryptonym, but now it's mostly from Young, who doesn't. He's been carried as an occasional, contracted on Andrews's say-so, but he's very tough, very clever and determined. His history is a little sketchy. We think he's Canadian, but he served in the U.S.

Marines. Marta will get you the file. Just a reminder, all reports from Kokio will be for my eyes only."

She looked squarely at me and nodded.

Following three weeks of intensive study on the Chinese Republic and the warlords and familiarizing herself with Young's personnel file, Neill embarked for Tientsin on the small steamer Duchess of Liaoning. I sent Marta and Ruby along with her, the better to mask the real purpose of their sojourn. I reasoned that there would be fewer questions asked if they were to pass as three women junior diplomats out on an adventurous vacation trip to places on the cusp of great change. It would help of course that Marta had Japanese and Chinese, and she was an able field hand.

They encountered some rare November storms, which chilled their spirits from Tokyo to the mainland and beyond. Cold squalls lashed the port of Tientsin when the three vacationers debarked. They took refuge at the garrison's civilian hotel, the converted German-Asian Bank, and did not go out for sightseeing. Neill, however, wandered through the concessions district for half the night, to the northeast and the Japanese neighborhoods, back to the French on the southwest of the U.S. garrison, across the Hai River to the Italian concession and through the remnants of the old Russian neighborhood. She made note of every group in uniform, estimated their numbers, and recorded what they appeared to be doing under the glaring streetlights and in dim courtyards. She reported her suspicion that there might be a Japanese troop buildup in progress.

The next morning she had already finished her first cup of coffee when Marta and Ruby came down to join her for breakfast.

From Tientsin to Peking they traveled by first class rail carriage. Neill would have known from Young's dossier that he frequented the bar and dance pavilion in a certain Peking hotel, popular then but now lost to history. The three travelers lodged at the same hotel, and at the first tea dance following their arrival Neill made contact with Young. She reported that it was easy for her to identify him from his file photos–handsome without being glamorous, the physique of a natural athlete, a face that had the lines and florid color of someone who lives outdoors. It was a symmetrical face with a large, square chin and a broad forehead, topped by wavy chestnut hair. She said his quick eyes constantly and coolly scanned the room, as if searching for an enemy or a lost companion.

Neill's reports always were detailed and dramatic. Marta's were detailed and objective. I used both to piece together the whole story of their mission.

"I understand you're Dr. Andrews's right hand man." Neill had approached him as he stood in line for dance tickets. He examined her up and down and broke into a grin, looking like someone who had found his lost companion.

"Why, hello there. Now please correct me if I'm mistaken, but you must hail from Louisiana or Mississippi." His voice had a hint of Scotland in it.

"I'm a long way from my origins in little ol' Gore Springs Mississippi. And you don't sound like a native-born American, if I'm not mistaken."

"Canadian. McKenzie Young. Call me Mac."

"I'm Neill James, from the American embassy in Tokyo." They shook hands and Neill gazed up at him with appraising eyes. She proposed that they move onto the dance floor. Like Neill, he was a smoothly athletic dancer, and they moved together easily. Her style was flamboyant, his was gracefully controlled. They danced every number until the band packed up their instruments and silently disappeared into the night. When they finished the last dance Mac left his hand on her waist and walked her to the exit. He suggested that she might enjoy riding polo ponies with him the next day. She hesitated, said she would have to rearrange some appointments, probably hemmed and hawed and sucked her teeth, and only then agreed.

They played polo in sheepskin jackets, necessary protection against the bracing early winter weather. For much of the next week, they took in the sights around Peking together–the Forbidden City and the Summer Palace, the Jade Fountain stream in the Western Hills and various pagodas and gates in the old walled city. Neill said Mac seemed to know a lot about the Manchu Dynasty history and relish the opportunity to serve as tour guide for a vibrant young American and her two companions.

One night while dining at the hotel, Neill asked Mac about a camel train they had seen in the Native City, outside the legation district. Mac spun a detailed account of the natural history of the Bactrian camel. "It's two times the camel as the dromedary," he joked, and he told the visitors the double humps do not carry water but are filled with fat, fuel for long periods of work without rest. "All Bactrians can eat anything that grows and can go more than a month without water," he said.

His expression turned melancholy when he talked about the shrinking number of wild camels in the Steppe. "Like horses before them, the wild Bactris have been displaced by their domesticated brethren. They've been tamed, herded into work trains, given jobs, and they've forgotten how to get their own food. They learned to fight each other when there's no question of reproducing, just like domesticated humans," he said.

"When there's no question of reproducing," Neill interjected with a smile, "undomesticated humans seem to prefer romance to fighting."

"Those do appear to be the alternatives, don't they, romance or reproduction. But too bad for our camels—they've all forgotten how to be undomesticated. If we don't keep them busy or separated, they'll fight to the death. So, one of my jobs is the tender care and supervision of two dozen of the beasts."

He ended his lecture by noting that he would be leaving for the Gobi Desert in a few days to check on the Andrews Expedition's equipment and transport. His usual job was to provide for campaign security and to manage the motor pool, and he needed to check his Dodge sand-wagons. He also had the string of camels, which were vulnerable to thieves, he said, most notably the Christian warlord General Feng Yu-hsiang. And he needed to vouchsafe the security of supplies in Kalgan.

"That sounds so very intriguing. I would give anything to be able to tag along, at least to Kalgan." Neill placed her hand on Mac's wrist as she spoke.

"I was thinking of inviting you along. It's a good season to go up there, not too dusty, and the really foul weather hasn't come in yet. Can you be ready by Thursday morning?"

"We'll be at the platform before you," replied Neill.

Her job completed, Ruby kissed Marta goodbye at the central railway platform and returned to Tientsin and Tokyo. At the legation Neill and Marta obtained their border crossing papers, embossed with General Feng's stamp. The packed train to Kalgan had no seating for the Westerners except in the foul-smelling dining car, so Neill, Mac, and Marta drank tea there for the bumpy, noisy sixteen-hour trip to Kalgan. They arrived at midnight and two of Feng Yu-hsiang's militiamen immediately fell in behind them and shadowed them for all the time they were in Mongolia. Mac said it had become routine and to pay them no mind. As long as they didn't photograph military installations or operations and did nothing obviously criminal, they wouldn't be questioned.

He put up the women in a safe house run by female missionaries from the United States. Never one to miss an opportunity for social advancement, even in a remote province, Neill had packed what she called "an evening frock," just in case. Against the expected winter chill she also brought along a fur coat she had bought years ago in Portland, Oregon.

And so, dressed for a formal reception, she accepted an invitation to a dinner party thrown the following night by The British American Tobacco Company and the American Consul, Samuel Sokobin. Sokobin was a long-time China hand in the State Department, having been posted to various Chinese cities since the mid-Teens. Now he ran the stations at both Mukden and Kalgan—or as the Republican Chinese called it, Ch'angchiakou—both considered hot spots for revolutionary conflict. He had come up to Kalgan from Mukden just for this event. It's unclear why the dinner was put on, but Neill claimed in her first book it was to honor her and Marta. Marta surmised it was political, and she was right. We knew State wanted our help in the Northeast, and I had offered Neill's assistance, though I hadn't an opportunity to alert her to it.

That night it was immediately clear to Neill that Sokobin was eager to talk with her. Mac made the introductions, and during drinks before the grand meal the Consul asked Neill to join him on the chilly verandah of the BAT mansion.

"I've been told, Miss James, that you are both on vacation from the embassy and on assignment to do some observation of the Expedition and Manchuria." Samuel Sokobin was a natty, affable looking man with shiny round cheeks and gold wire glasses. He easily could be taken for a senior professor or rabbi. His hands, Neill observed, were soft and thick.

Neill was unsure how much to tell the Consul. "Why Mr. Sokobin, now I wonder who would've told you that?"

"Your naval attaché, a Commander Shaw, sent me a secure cable. He said I could put my trust in you."

"Vernon Shaw is my mentor, Sir. I stand by anything he might have told you."

"*Nemma, hen hao.* Oh, forgive me, that's a bad habit of mine, slipping into *p'u-t'ung hua*. Most days I talk more in Chinese than in English. But that's splendid. Shaw wanted me to ask you to be on the lookout for signs of Japanese industrial activity north and west of Changpenhsien. That's of course in addition to your original brief. We're especially concerned to know what sort of wedge Japan is planning to place between the Soviets and Peking. Policy on Soviet Russia is very fluid just now, particularly since Sun Yat-sen's death. They've been stirring up revolutionaries in the south while mollycoddling Chang Tso-lin, and we sense there's tension within the GMD, which will be trouble for the Soviets and which the Japanese will try to exploit. We need to know as much as possible about both the movement of Russians in Mongolia and what the Japanese are up to."

"Of course. I can do that, and I already have the means. If you reply to Commander Shaw, please tell him I will honor my brief and put my attention on these other concerns as well. Thank you, Sir, for your instruction. And your trust."

Consul Sokobin abruptly shifted to telling Neill about the currently popular dances in Kalgan and Mukden. He took her arm and escorted her into the dining room, all the while discoursing on the musical culture of the international set.

It was a grand evening for the dozen industrialists, scientists and diplomats in black ties and the two women visitors in gay party dresses and shawls. They sat for a six course meal accompanied by French wines, efficiently served by Chinese houseboys. Late into the evening they drank scotch and danced to old recordings of songs on an American Victrola. Mac and Neill again were the last couple on the dance floor when the music ended. The next morning they set out for Changpenhsien in Mac's Dodge, recently equipped with aircraft tires for maneuvering in the Gobi sands.

Neill kept voluminous notes, writing down in steno script every detail of the countryside, every conversation she had with our contacts and the Chinese and Mongolians they met along the way, every road sign and vehicle, every excavation, construction site, antenna and soldier's uniform. For cover, she told Mac she was thinking of writing a book about her travels and these would be her field notes. He certainly would understand the concept and necessity of field notes for a travel author, and it would make sense to him that she would want to keep them private for now. He probably guessed her real purpose. He showed her how to protect her notes by hiding them within the lining of her cabin trunk.

Risking detection, she had brought along a small camera and took tourist photos, but when the shadows looked the other way she quickly shot pictures of intelligence targets. Marta took notes on the sojourn for her reports to my office. We always tried to secure redundancy as a quality check and, as I say, to fill out the story.

A dry storm had risen in the Gobi by the time they arrived. Mac Young led the women through the blinding dust to a sturdy canvas tent, which would serve as their overnight lodging. He invited them to a late meal in the expedition headquarters hut. It was a more elaborate collection of tents connected by canvas tunnels that constantly rumpled in the wind. The whole compound was set in a revetment criss-crossed by slack lines for orientation during storms and surrounded by a crude wire fence.

At dinner Mac introduced Neill and Marta to the five other people in the camp. "These young women are on vacation from the American Embassy in Tokyo," he said. "They have a personal interest in our work and were courageous enough to come out here for a look. We're going out to the Chahar borderland at Dukou tomorrow."

Seated around one end of the low table were three young archeologists from North America, graduate students on one year research grants. An elderly Chinese man called Fan-yi rushed back and forth from the kitchen tent. He served as translator and unofficial house-boy. Sitting across from Neill was an Army officer Mac introduced as "Butler the photographer." Lieutenant Butler said he had requested the Expedition assignment to have an interesting adventure away from garrison duty and his routine public relations work in Peking. The Army officially sent him out to document the fossil discoveries so there would be no question of ownership later. Mac had other ideas about Butler.

When Fan-yi served the soup, Lieutenant Butler asked Neill in a vaguely Southern American accent where she hailed from.

"My home is in Tokyo now. I've been there a year, and before that I lived in Hawai'i."

"Y'all sound like maybe you come from down my way, originally."

"Where would that be?"

"Little town in southern Arkansas." He pronounced it Ar-KANsas, and Neill smiled.

"Well isn't it strange then," she replied, "that they call you people ARKansawyers."

Lieutenant Butler smiled weakly and immediately busied himself with his steaming soup. Mac suggested that the graduate students tell the visitors about the projects they have planned for the 1925 explorations, and the rest of the evening was a lively discussion of dinosaur eggs and bone fragments, accompanied by several jugs of barley beer.

On the way to Dukou in the sandwagon the next morning, Mac pointed out how the landscape changed from dry, rocky hills to nearly flat, dusty desert, from dark grays and cocoa browns to ever softer tans. Then abruptly he said, "I didn't bring Butler along because I wanted to let you know there's more to his being here than he's letting on."

"I'm not sure that would make a difference to us," Neill said.

"I would assume there's more to your visit, too, but he's not a very pleasant addition to the camp and not nearly as easy to look at as you." He glanced quickly at Neill.

"Things never are quite what they seem, are they."

"There's a growing Army intelligence presence around here, and he's the tip of their probe. G-2, I've heard, and I think your folks at the embassy might want to know they're gathering information in the border areas, and Navy might be, too."

"My goodness, they are busy indeed. And I thank you for trusting us enough to share what you think. But it makes little difference to a couple of women on a winter's holiday." Neill gave Mac a genuine and grateful smile. Their shadows struggled behind in an open phaeton with hard tires.

After touring some old sites from earlier years, they retreated to the Expedition camp ahead of a renewal of the storm. Butler was nowhere in sight, and when they prepared to leave for Kalgan the next morning, Fan-yi said the photographer had gone off with the students to a nearby village where some Japanese fossil hunters were gathered. Neill later wrote that it was impossible to know who was watching who or how many layers of watchers there were in the Northwest.

Mac pulled Neill aside before they boarded the sand-wagon. "I was wondering if you might be interested in returning as my guest sometime in the next year. I'm going to be on the project at least that long, and I would very much enjoy your company again."

Neill studied his earnest face and thought for long moments before answering. "I have had a wonderful time on this excursion and it's mostly owing to you. But as I said, things never are quite what they seem, and I'm always looking over the far horizon for a new adventure. I'm afraid I should not give much encouragement about returning. Let's say I'm intrigued but I am not committed."

Mac cocked his head and raised his eyebrows. "Okey-dokey," he said and headed for the Dodge.

Upon their return to Kalgan, Marta and Neill gave Mac their grateful farewells. He was returning immediately to resume preparations for the 1925 campaign of the Expedition, and the women were destined for Mukden and Korea. At the railway station the two shadows vanished for good. Neill watched the dashing J. McKenzie Young stride off alone down the dust-blown street. She turned to Marta and said, "There goes possibly the only man I've ever met who truly excited me."

Once back in Peking, they booked rail passage to Mukden. The ticketing agent tried to talk them out of going. He pointed out that it was dangerous territory now, the warlord Chang Tso-lin was in control of the entire Northeast and was headquartered at Mukden, and even Tientsin, which they would have to transit, was unsafe. Conscious of the urgency of their assignment and what Neill called "the feast of danger" ahead of them, they insisted.

They were locked into their compartment for the overnight trip. A uniformed guard stayed outside their door until they arrived at Tientsin, where they were escorted directly to another train. From there to Mukden it was the same arrangement, but on this leg they were allowed to go to the dining car for meals. Neill watched from the compartment window and made notes of everything she saw. She counted the carriages of passing troop trains and estimated the numbers of soldiers. The grey uniformed boys with hats pulled down over ears were packed standing up in open coal hoppers. She observed day and night, even working in the light of the wintery moon.

It was bitterly cold when they arrived at Mukden, and Neill put on her fur coat. An American woman met them at the depot. "Call me Julia," she said. Samuel Sokobin had a place for them to stay, and Julia told them the Consul would like them to join him for lunch the following day. Julia led them to a taxi and escorted them to a western-style hotel near the consulate. Marta's work began in earnest, estimating the public support for Chang Tso-lin and his military strength. She pored over Chinese newspapers and eavesdropped on conversations, and she closely watched uniformed troops to note what their civil authorities seemed to be. The city was orderly and peaceful, but there was bustling movement of people along roads heading out of the city, and crowds waited at the railway station to board trains south. She also had to keep track of Neill.

At lunch the next day Samuel Sokobin sat between the visitors and calmly described the gathering storm of war. It remained unclear what Japan would do in case the Nationalists were to attack along the Korean border. The White Russian community in Mukden and other Northeastern cities were frantic about rumors of Soviet dominance on the Nationalist front. The remnant White Russians contributed to instability, he explained, not just because they remained poor and underemployed but also because they could become the next wave of refugees. He asked Neill if her observations yielded anything valuable. Marta paid close attention to her response.

At first Neill was reluctant to tell him anything about her intelligence gathering. She said she would report to Commander Shaw and he would decide the worth of her work. Sokobin went pensive. He daintily folded his linen napkin.

"I'm afraid there's not much time left to us, Miss James. You can send a wire under your code-name to him and report your findings. But there's one thing I would find of incalculable worth, especially if there is no delay, and that's to learn what you saw of Japanese developments northwest of here. After all, I am the official on the hot seat." He turned a sad, tired face to Marta and then back to Neill, his smooth cheeks now sagging a bit under the wire glasses.

"I can't send everything to Shaw, Sir. There's too much, and I do not know enough to be able to digest it for him. Besides, there are the photographs."

"You took photos? How enterprising. Most extraordinary. May I ask . . . ?"

Neill was flattered and began to feel overly confident in using her own discretion about sharing her information. "I need to have them developed, but I think they are of fuel extraction and processing sites and a coking plant. Japanese for certain."

Sokobin said he could have the work done in two hours, and he would help her send a summary to Tokyo by secure cable. Neill and Marta resumed the morning's sightseeing around the old quarter of Mukden and returned to the consulate building for tea and the telegram.

When her cable came in I replied almost immediately.

YOURS RECEIVED STOP IF MATERIAL BEARS OUT KOKIO IN FOR MOVE UP STOP BE AWARE BORDER TROUBLES STOP NAVIGATOR.

Neill was unable to send me the photographs and neglected to mention them in her cable.

"What border troubles?" she asked Sokobin.

"Chang's folks aren't getting along these days with the Japanese border guards, and the Japanese in Korea are jumpy because of the Nationalist gains. It seems they don't know who they'd rather fight."

"Can we get through to Seoul?"

"You have your embassy papers. That gives you diplomatic protection. But don't push it too hard. If worse comes to worst, get in touch with me. I have people in that area who might help."

He gave Neill her film negatives and copies of the prints, which she slid into the trunk lining with her notes. The following morning they were on the luxurious Manchurian Express, headed southeast for Andung and the Korean border at the mouth of the Yellow River. In instructive contrast to the dirty, war-torn carriages of the trains in China, the Japanese train was sumptuous, spotlessly clean, a sleek, blue rolling hotel, and Neill enjoyed the reward of luxury every adventurer seeks at the end of a difficult journey. But it wasn't quite the end of Neill's and Marta's journey.

At the border Japanese guards examined each passenger's papers and searched each piece of luggage. Neill's cabin trunk stood in an alcove beside the compartment door. A tall, very thin guard peered through horned-rim glasses at their diplomatic papers and passports. Marta told him in flawless Japanese that they were vacationing.

"In winter?" He gazed down at her incredulously.

"We have less work to do in winter," Marta replied.

"Why were you in Kalgan? What were you doing there?" The guard looked from Marta to Neill, as if he was asking them both. Neill smiled amiably.

"We were invited to inspect the Natural History Museum Expedition." Marta hoped Sokobin would say the same thing if they had to turn to him for help. The guard looked through their suitcases, making little grunting sounds to himself as he searched. When he turned to leave he spotted the cabin trunk. He pulled it out and asked to have it opened. Neill unlocked it and stood back. She had hidden her camera in a boot packed under some hiking clothes and two cloth bags filled with souvenirs. They had bought a few drawings, some small dolls, Russian jewelry and Mongolian hats and gloves at the bazaars in Kalgan and Mukden.

The grunting went on as the Japanese guard carefully examined each item. He pulled up the boots, felt inside them and replaced them in the trunk. He ran his hand over the lining of the trunk. The grunting suddenly stopped. He again ran his hand all around the inside of the trunk, this time more slowly and in silence.

"*Kokoni ite.*" Stay here.

The guard left the compartment, locking it behind him, and got off the train. Neill and Marta could see him join two other guards on the platform. They talked animatedly, then reboarded the train and returned to the compartment.

"Please go outside."

Marta and Neill took their coats and followed one guard out to the platform while the other two hauled out the cabin trunk. They were joined now by two of Chang Tso-lin's soldiers, always on duty at the border crossing. The three guards and two soldiers spoke hurriedly in sketchy Japanese mixed with a few Mandarin words. There seemed to be a disagreement. The border guards opened the trunk and gestured toward its contents. Neill held her breath.

"From what I can make out," Marta whispered, "they're having a jurisdictional dispute. Could be about rank. The Chinese think we've stolen something. The Japanese guards think we've broken some sort of rule about border crossings."

"The souvenirs," Neill said. "They must think that junk is from the Expedition."

The warlord's soldiers brusquely reached into the trunk and pulled out the cloth sacks of souvenirs. They held them up to Neill and Marta. Marta told the Japanese guards she has receipts from shops for the items, if only they will allow her to fetch them from the compartment. A guard escorted her and they quickly returned with the receipts. After examining the papers, the soldiers tossed the bags back into the trunk and walked away.

"You have violated the law, and you will not be permitted to enter Korea," said one of the guards.

"We have diplomatic privileges. You can't detain us." Marta spoke with as much authority as she could muster.

The guard reached into the trunk and removed the boot and shook it. The camera dropped into his hand. "No cameras."

"Any film in it?" Marta whispered to Neill.

"It's empty. Let them have it."

"You can keep the camera. Give it to your eldest son. Just please let us get on our way. We must not be delayed for our arrival at Seoul. We must meet diplomats in Seoul."

Snowflakes began to fall and swirl around the platform. The guards conferred for a few seconds behind their gloved hands, then returned travel documents and the boot, without the camera. They closed up the trunk and hauled it back to the compartment, said thank-you with a little bow and left the train. Neill and Marta slumped into their seats and laughed. Snow was falling on the shiny blue train as it crossed the Yellow River on its way to Seoul.

I met with Neill and Marta the morning after their return to Tokyo.

"Your debriefing will begin this afternoon," I said, "but I wanted to tell you right away how pleased I am with your outing to Kalgan. While you were at play in Seoul, I received the photos from Sokobin by normal diplomatic pouch. High risk but probably uniquely useful. The reports you sent were most appreciated in Washington, and I was asked to convey thanks to you. Both come through it unfazed?"

"I'm exhausted and coming down with a cold," Marta said, "but I'd do it again in a second."

"It was a wonderful vacation, and I'm already chomping at the bit for more of that kind of work," Neill added.

I excused Marta and asked Neill to remain. I felt it was necessary to explain the dicey situation she was in. We sat on the sofa.

"There are a couple of fine points I need to make regarding Consul Sokobin," I said. "He's among the very best of FSOs, unquestionably loyal and capable. And I'm sure he can be persuasive. After all, he is a diplomat. But—and here's a fine point—your assignment was to produce intelligence for my eyes only, and that includes not divulging to anybody else, even a senior officer of our government, any information you have collected. The photos were a bit ahead of your assignment, a bit outside of it I might say, but they could be exceptionally important. Time will tell. I appreciate your initiative and calculation of the risks. For that we will reward you. But I have had to make a notation in your file that you failed this time to stay in chain of command for security."

Neill looked genuinely perplexed. "I made a mistake when I mentioned the photographs to the Consul. He made it sound like the fate of all northern China rested on them."

"As it turned out, he wasn't exaggerating. And you would have been in a bigger mess if you hadn't processed the film but had left it in the camera. So in that way you were very lucky. The lesson in this discussion, though, is about following the rule and being loyal. When given an order, especially about security, even though you might be in the field on your own, follow it to the letter and to the end. You won't always know everything about the operation. This one is risky for you. If the photos turn out to be as valuable as they might be, as good as Sokobin thinks they are, you'll be the winner. If not, things could go the other way. I will keep my ear to the rail and will let you know if anything comes of it. In the meantime, you still have my full confidence and my thanks for a job well done."

Neill looked like she didn't know whether she had been chastised or congratulated. It probably sounded like both and I meant it as such. For the next few weeks she filed her reports and did routine office work, scanning newspapers and evaluating field reports sent in by other agents. She was languishing again, this time in what we at ONI called "casual status," not a form of employment but just keeping busy while awaiting the next assignment, and I didn't want to prolong the languishment.

She wasn't good at marking time. In her restlessness she decided she was being underpaid by the embassy, her official employer in her cover job. She wrote a letter directly to the Secretary of State, complaining that it was impossible for a single woman to live respectably in Tokyo on her clerk's pay of 2,500 yen a month. She also might have thought she was helping protect her clandestine role.

Such an act was unthinkable for anybody in her position but Neill James. Ambassador McVeagh was not pleased when he learned of her letter. He received a copy of it in the next month's diplomatic pouch from Washington, accompanied by a handwritten note from Secretary Kellogg:

> Charles, would you kindly see if less costly lodging can be found for Miss James? Cordially, Frank

The Ambassador instead turned over Neill's letter and a copy of the note to me and said it was now my problem. I filed the Secretary's note and tossed the complaint letter into the burn basket.

The winter turned to spring, and still Neill heard nothing. Then one day in early April 1926, just as the cherry blossoms were coming on, I received the findings and notice to move ahead. I asked Marta to tell Neill Commander Shaw would like to have lunch with her. "Tell her we have news, but do not reveal it—I want to frame its reception."

I took a private dining room at the Royal Akasaka Hotel, across from the embassy. We sat on tatami mats with our feet in the warming pit and chatted while the first course of the meal was spread. When the servers had left the room, I gestured for Neill to come closer.

"There's news about Samuel Sokobin you need to know. He's been removed from China, posted to Kobe. It might be the end of his career."

Neill eyes narrowed, as if this discussion might not be favorable to her at all. "My goodness, I should think Kobe would be a plum," she said.

"Not for Sam," I said. "He's a China hand and always has been. No, he's fallen from grace. His higher-ups in State don't accept his findings. They don't believe the analysis and predictions he based on your work. They've been very displeased and wanted him to retract his forecast, change the analysis. He's refused to budge, so they've sidelined him, parked him in Kobe. I've heard he's headed for England shortly, probably Birmingham, where all good FSOs end their careers."

Neill frowned. "Oh no," she whispered.

The waitresses returned and went on serving our meal. When they were gone, I continued.

"I feel bad for Sam, we all feel bad for him. He's probably the best China person they have in State. This will produce big gaps in understanding what's happening there, just at a time when everything hangs in the balance, when there's such turbulence that anything can happen, and Japan will be the blade of the sword that inflicts the deepest wound on the Chinese people."

The waitresses returned again and busied themselves around the low table for another few minutes, while Neill and I talked about plans for the holidays. Then we were alone again.

"Our people don't agree," I continued. "We think Sokobin's analysis is correct. In fact, we're so sure of it that a special report already has been delivered to the Secretary of War and the Vice President. We think our view will win out, policy-wise. Top people at ONI all know your field work has been important to the analysis, and they are very pleased. They also appreciate your report on G-2 in the theatre." I studied Neill's face, trying to see if she looked happy.

She later wrote in a letter to me that she wondered then if the goal of the game is to please the higher-ups and to not displease anybody who can affect your welfare and future. She smiled weakly. "What does that mean for my work? I mean, will I be allowed to continue? Can I do something worthwhile again?"

"It's better than that." Telling her this part was my reward. "A major assignment is being pieced together for you in headquarters. It might take some months to arrange everything, but you will be very pleased I'm sure."

Neill wrote that she now thought being pleased and being displeased perhaps was merely a way of talking about appreciation rather than formal approval. Maybe it involved more of a personal standard than an official assessment.

"So it's good?"

"Very much so, Neill."

"What will I do in the meantime?"

"Two things. I have some material I want you to study, investigative reports and historical documents related to your next assignment. And I want you to write some analysis of your own, based on your observations of Kokuhonsha. We need to have a strong sense of where they're headed, who is going to dominate inside the party, what effect they will have on the government and in particular on foreign policy and military plans. You'll have plenty of reading to do."

Neill later told me she left that lunch meeting feeling as if her feet weren't touching the polished floors of the hotel lobby. She hadn't realized how worried she had been since the January day when she was placed in casual status. Now she had work to do, and there would be a new assignment, probably with more responsibility and maybe with another rich dose of adventure, as soon as the plan was drawn up.

She dutifully took the train every day from her house in Shinjuku to Akasaka and sat at her desk for long hours, poring over reports, intelligence summaries, and briefing notes. Marta brought her recent books on the history of Comintern and the rise of the American Communist Party. She wondered why there was so much material on a woman named Agnes Smedley, a tall stack of files from G-2 and Hoover's Bureau of Investigation at Justice. Smedley obviously was a radical leftist, probably a communist, but it was entirely unclear to Neill then what Smedley had to do with ONI and Neill's post in Japan.

Our answer came in mid-September. I finally was authorized to tell Neill she was headed to India and then possibly to Europe. Her assignment was to track down and monitor Agnes Smedley, who was thought to be among ultra-leftist radicals in India's anti-government movement. She was told be ready to leave on a moment's notice, but it wasn't until the first of October that she received her tickets for passage to Ceylon.

This is the letter she dashed off to Jane at that time:

Dearest Janey,

Suddenly I am drawn to the south and east, to the endless summer of mysterious La India, so I will be leaving my pretty house on the canal and my little job at the embassy post haste. I've booked passage on the Pacific Queen, a nice 2nd deck outside cabin, leaving on Sat. the 9th. Alas this means we will not be able to live together here in Tokyo, and I so want to see you. I will make you a promise that I will visit you there in New Orleans soon as I return from this adventure. I aim to cross Europe and be back in Dixie before facing another northern winter. My travel last year in Mongolia and Manchuria are to thank for that.

I loved your note about your birthday gift wch (note) arrived last Thurs. I'm made happy to know that the porcelain doll arrived in one piece and the kimono actually fit you. I am taking my dolls with me, not trusting that the collection will make it to my next destination unattended. My hope is to get a temporary appointment in an embassy in Europe to tide me over, and I've sent out inquiries. Maybe by the time I arrive in Bombay I will know where I'm headed from there. Will write again when I alight. I feel like a migrating butterfly, staying ahead of the storm. Please be patient with me and take good care of yourself.

My Best Love, Neill

By October ninth, however, Neill already was in Colombo, Ceylon. She had left Japan a week earlier than she said in her letter.

Ambassador McVeagh sent an urgent cable to Washington:

MISS NEILL JAMES HAS RESIGNED STOP PLEASE APPOINT A MALE CLERK AS HER REPLACEMENT STOP MCV

V

Geraldine Sartain

> Let the people who never find true love
> Keep saying that there's no such thing.
>
> —Wislawa Szymborska, "True Love"

Neill came back to me, at least for a short while. We were together again in Berlin and Paris, one brief reunion for barely half a year, and then she was gone. I learned by then to accept her desolated need: She would always be leaving someone.

She had resigned at the Tokyo embassy, apparently because Shaw had secured a new assignment for her. So her contract with the Office of Naval Intelligence was renewed, and she was provided with a second passport, an obviously fake one. When I saw it I worried that she had been set up to be found out. The new document was issued at Tokyo but she retrieved it from a courier pouch in Ceylon. Her entry permit into Germany already was stamped in the first visa page, showing she entered Germany before she arrived at Bombay. The passport listed her occupation as "Secretary (Member of Staff of American Embassy, Tokyo, Japan)," which State certainly would have denied because it wasn't true, and it had a mistaken birth date for her, January 03, 1899. The wrong date, of course, could have been because of her own finagling.

When we met up in Berlin, Neill violated the basic rule again and told me all about the harrowing trip that took her from Japan through South Asia and Eastern Europe and finally to the Charlottenburg apartment. It put me in an awkward position, but I knew she needed desperately to tell about it and so I listened. She thought she was in pursuit of Agnes Smedley, and she had little idea of what she was up against. I later had occasion to review all the files created during that period, so that I could complete my unit history for the departmental archives, which was the encore aria at the end of my own little ONI career. They always made full use of their journalists, just as they did of their stenographers. Neill's logs were very complete and colorful, and that made my final job both easier and unexpectedly melancholy. It was like hearing her talk to me again, the way she used to do long into the night at our cottage near Diamond Head.

Shaw, by then a Commander, instructed her to stop first in Shanghai, where she could easily pass as a traveling woman of independent means. That role—the vagabonding rich girl—must have felt just right to Neill, and she registered at the Astor House, where she would inevitably rub shoulders with the world's most influential capitalists. After all, Shanghai was already a major crossroads, and the stock exchange had been established at Astor House. She delighted in not having to leave her hotel when she wanted to attend the famous tea dances of Whangpoo Road, and she commented on it, without explicitly bragging, in a letter to Jane.

After Hawaii, I had spent a brief time in Shanghai. And I saw Neill on my way down there through Tokyo, but she was about to leave just then on what she said was a vacation to Mongolia and Korea, so we had only a few hours together in a hotel restaurant before going our separate ways. She seemed to attract interesting and dangerous assignments, especially compared to mine. But my journalism was always more important to me than the government work, and eventually I saw to it that my reporting became my only work. But I do think for a long time Neill adored the secret assignments. I did not know her as Kokio until I began writing my unit history.

Her task in Shanghai was to find out whether the revolutionary forces of the Guomindang could be successfully stopped there. At the same time, Shaw thought she might learn something about a drug trafficking and gun-running American named Paul Crawley. State wanted to get the goods on him for sneaking heroin into San Francisco, and Shaw believed a lead on Crawley might help ONI relations with several ambassadors. But Crawley always worked in the company of traitors, opium dealers and the lowlifes who ran prostitute rings, so Neill was poorly prepared for that sideline. Her cover identity was all wrong, and she was unsuccessful in getting close enough to Crawley to learn anything of use. She was unenthusiastic about that job.

Her report on Chiang Kai-shek's GMD, on the other hand, turned out to be provident. At the time, the GMD still included large contingents of leftist revolutionaries, Communists, Comintern enlistees and Soviet advisors. That was before the break with Mao. Chiang would soon expel the radical leftists, but in the fall of 1926 Washington was afraid of a Soviet-style revolution all across China, and they hoped Shanghai would be the unconquerable holdout against Chiang's army.

Neill made her secure contacts through the YWCA, where there was a convenient message drop. After weeks of observing and interviewing, listening to rumor mills and taking scow trips far upriver, Neill reported that Shanghai was ill-prepared for defense. The Chinese civilian population, already lobbying the foreign powers for a larger say in government and the courts, not only wouldn't oppose Chiang but were downright joyful over his successes on the front. The GMD forces, Neill wrote, would be welcomed as heroes by the Chinese in Shanghai, and she added that stories were circulating about political rifts growing within the GMD leadership. She would be proven right a few months later, when on March 21 GMD bullets cracked the masonry façade outside the very room where she had stayed at the Astor House, and the Shantung Guard promptly negotiated the city's surrender. Both Nanjing and Shanghai fell to Chiang in quick succession. The capital was moved from Peking to Nanjing. Looking back, I was very much afraid for Neill.

Shaw defended Neill's report against doubters in Washington and sent her on her way to Ceylon, where Agnes Smedley was scheduled to attend an economics conference. Based on her earlier file reading, Neill figured that Smedley must be a well-intentioned idealist, a believer in a future world free of exploitation and classes, without poverty, illness or ignorance. To Neill this was ironic, considering that Smedley was described in her dossier as always penniless, often mentally ill, and a self-labeled ignoramus who was totally uninterested in political theory and all too willing to manipulate her wealthy benefactors into supporting her quixotic schemes. She also was said to encourage the use of violence to obtain freedom from whatever she saw as oppression. No passive resistance and civil disobedience for her.

I suspect Smedley's hunger for change and impatience with theory sounded familiar to Neill. Neill knew she herself couldn't muster the political commitment that came naturally to Smedley, but she always favored action and competition over contemplation and compromise, and both she and I would have appreciated Smedley's struggle for sexual freedom and social equality with men.

Or so it seemed from what was in the file. Neill would find out otherwise over the next decade, but when she arrived in Colombo on October 8, 1926, she believed she knew the character and motives of her elusive revolutionary. Her contact at the consulate, however, told her Smedley never arrived at the conference in Ceylon. Instead she was thought to be living in Berlin with her lover and political hero, the Indian revolutionary Virendranath Chattopadhyaya. Everyone in the India nationalist movement called him Chatto, and that's how Neill wrote about him. Disappointed, Neill immediately cabled Shaw for instructions, using the medical metaphor that Smedley had created for contacts with the Indian radicals.

PATIENT FAILED TO SHOW FOR APPOINTMENT STOP CURRENTLY UNDER OBSERVATION BERLIN RESIDING WITH DOCTOR PLEASE ADVISE STOP KOKIO.

She heard nothing for a few days, and she took the opportunity to see the sights and enjoy the night life of Colombo. Shaw's delayed reply was optimistic.

> GO TO BOMBAY THEN AGRA FOR MEDICINES CONTACT EYE SPECIALIST SULLIVAN HOTEL CECIL BOMBAY STOP ASSIST WITH CONSULTATION ON PATIENT NEW PRESCRIPTION FORTHCOMING STOP NAVIGATOR.

The so-called eye specialist was in fact a British double-agent then residing in Agra as a Sikh revolutionary named Bhuma Singh Sharma. In her first book Neill wrote that she traveled from Manila to Agra with a Major Sullivan and his wife. That was meant possibly to mislead and entertain readers. She actually had been traveling alone until she arrived at Bombay. There the station officer, a former Marine Major named Ernest Sullivan, guided her through the throngs milling about on the steamy riverbanks to the two room diplomatic mission on Bandra Road. Major Sullivan briefed her about her contact in Agra.

"The Brits are more interested in Smedley than we are, and we're doing them a big favor, an important favor, and we'll incur their debt. Bhuma Singh Sharma will have information for you and some key introductions that might help you get the goods on Smedley. There might be some other chores we can do for them as well."

"What kind of goods are we talking about?" As usual Neill was being coy. She knew the game was to find a way to extradite Smedley to the United States, and she suspected it might have something to do with her reported marriage to Chatto.

"We think she's traveling without a passport, as she's confined to Berlin. And she might have violated the espionage act, but like the last time, there's no proof of it. The espionage charge might depend on our being able to show a connection to Münzenberg. Either way, it would please our English friends if we had a solid reason to return her home indefinitely."

Neill smiled knowingly, made a note to herself to learn more about this new character Münzenberg, and asked for a ride back to the train station. Sullivan walked her out of the office building and waved over a pedicab.

"Do take care," he said. "We don't know much about Singh Sharma except that he works both for Whitehall and the Indian revolutionaries, possibly even OMS."

Neill doubted that any British agent could survive for very long as a covert double within the cobra pit of Indian politics, let alone within the international arm of the Soviet government. Singh Sharma must be quite a chameleon, she wrote.

It was thirty-three degrees centigrade when Neill boarded the mid-afternoon train at Victoria Terminus in Bombay, and the humidity made her feel as if she were soaking in a warm bath. For the first few hours of the twenty-eight hour trip to Agra she sweated under a tiny ceiling fan in a velvet upholstered compartment she shared with seven members of an Indian family. But by the time she reached Nasik, it was amber dusk and the mercury already had dropped into the low twenties. She arrived in Agra late the following night, her blouse salt stained but dry and her makeup long since rubbed away. It was nine degrees centigrade outside and Neill was trying to recall where she packed her fur coat.

She stood on the bustling platform by the baggage car, waiting by a lamppost for her cabin trunk. The bricked platform had been washed, and travelers trudged through the cold puddles under cones of light and hurried along their way into darkness. Three or four Indian men waited with her, eager to offer assistance for a few copper coins. From behind someone grabbed the handle of her grip, almost snatching it from her hand.

"May I serve as your guide and bearer?" The voice was melodious, and there was an accent that suggested the colonial upper classes. Neill swung around to see a slender youth dressed as a Sikh soldier in winter uniform—loose bloomers tucked into boots, a tightly belted jacket with epaulettes and holster straps, and a gleaming white turban. The soldier's flawless complexion was the color of well-milked coffee. He smiled and bowed slightly.

"And you would be?" Neill was alarmed but tried to look placidly annoyed.

"Bhuma Singh Sharma, at your service, Miss James."

"Oh yes. Thank goodness. There's my trunk. Y'all might get some help for that."

The soldier took the grip, waved one of the waiting men over to fetch the cabin trunk, and the three went off to the man's cart and donkey. They rode without speaking for nearly half an hour through streets still teeming at midnight with chattering people huddled around barrel fires, and with cows, hens, dogs and every sort of conveyance. Turning into a quiet, darkened neighborhood, the driver and Bhuma Singh Sharma exchanged a few words in Hindi, and they stopped in front of a tall brick building. A yellow light flickered by the entrance.

Neill and Bhuma Singh Sharma set chairs at a tiny kitchen table in the only spacious room of his third floor apartment. He pulled a bottle of first-rate claret from a sideboard. Neill noticed his delicate hands, which were narrow and long, with skin smooth as pudding.

"It is late, I know," he said, "and you have been traveling for nearly two days. But we must talk before trying to sleep. Sleep never comes easily in Agra, and we may have little time to talk later." Again, that high, lilting voice from Cambridge and Delhi.

He poured two glasses of wine, sat opposite Neill and began what sounded to Neill like a lecture.

"You are in pursuit of Agnes Smedley, alias Alice Bird, also known as Violet Ali Khan Hussain. You are on the wrong continent. I understand now you already know this. She was last known to be living on the Charlottenburg in Berlin with Chatto and three other nationalists, including Chatto's sister. As we sit here sipping our plonk she is making arrangements to travel to Brussels for the First International. It will be hosted at the Palais Egmont. If you can intercept her there your job will be good as done. There is no plan to bring her to India. Actually, the revolutionary front leaders are carefully preventing her from entering South Asia. They fear it will weaken the Soviet support for the movement. She is an independent outsider, indeed prefers things that way, as it gives her maximum freedom to follow her inclinations, which are subject to changing allegiances and alignments. One thing is always and abundantly clear, however, and that is that she will be firmly on the side of the downtrodden and against the privileged. She is labile, fickle, politically naïve and disinterested in theory but nonetheless ideological. She is fearless, both fragile and iron-willed, both promiscuous and love-starved, often very well connected and . . ."

"First International of what?"

"Oh, the Congress Against Colonial Oppression and Imperialism, something dreamed up by Comintern, don't you know? It will be closely watched by Moscow, both before and when it actually goes off. We rather suspect its main purpose is to sort out the alignment of Münzenberg behind either Chatto's people or Roy's loyal band of Soviets." Bhuma Singh Sharma paused a few seconds to study Neill's puzzled expression. "For Indian independence, you know."

Neill began to sense that she was falling behind in the pursuit, wading in mucky waters and approaching quicksand, and she felt neither useful nor particularly welcome here in Agra but rather something of an annoyance.

"I will have papers for you tomorrow and you can be on your way to Berlin. I will instruct you how. It first will be necessary for you to go to Prague and Dresden, and I hear you have school in Munich. But there will be no swallow assignment, which perhaps is your specialty? All of it will be straightforward mule work and study."

Neill was reminded of affectionately being called a swallow by her Tokyo colleagues, a slang word for agents who use seduction to extract information. She liked hearing it then, but coming from Bhuma Singh Sharma it had a taint of insult, and she was dismayed to think that she was earning a reputation. Or was he accusing her of trying to seduce him?

She replied, "I can manage any sort of assignment along the way, but I must continue with my original brief."

"I fully understand." Bhuma Singh Sharma swept up the glasses and wine bottle and gestured toward a daybed. "You can sleep there. I will be in the vestibule. This is a secure building, but conditions change very rapidly in this neighborhood. Good-night."

An hour later Neill was awakened by a blade of light coming from the vestibule. Through the partly open door she could see Bhuma Singh Sharma undressing. He must have had other business, Neill thought. She watched as he carefully unbuttoned his tunic and folded it before placing it somewhere out of her view. He removed his trousers and Neill saw that he was wearing a sort of corset that extended down the thighs, the kind that was in fashion for women decades earlier. He tossed the pants aside and slowly uncoiled the white turban. Long, black ringlets of hair fell around his head. Then he removed his undershirt and Neill could see his chest was wrapped in gauze. When that came off Neill's confusion dissolved: She was looking at a slender but full-breasted woman.

Her pulse would have quickened, not just from discovering the deception but from the sudden change in her understanding of who or what Bhuma Singh Sharma was. She also would have flushed with anger because she realized Singh Sharma's comment on her being a swallow was meant to insult her.

At dawn Neill was up and dressed before he came into the kitchen. She resolved to remain disciplined and not demand to know who her guide really was. She would find that out later. For now there was urgent work to be done. He made a quick breakfast of honeyed kitchari and yoghurt. There were document packets Neill had to strap to her waist under her dress. While they drank coffee Singh Sharma stamped entry permits into her passport and briefed her about border crossings in Eastern Europe. She was booked on an oiler through Hormuz and Suez and would disembark at Naples. Neill was unhappy with the coach class rail passage from there but didn't tell him she thought she would upgrade her tickets once she arrived in Italy.

An old man met them at the front door and escorted Neill to a closed pedicab. Neill turned to say goodbye to Bhuma Singh Sharma, but he had vanished.

There were stops in Munich, Prague and Dresden on the way to Berlin. Neill delivered the documents at her drops and managed to take in a day of sightseeing at each city. She was several weeks in Munich, where she received an intensive course in spoken German. From rising until bedtime she was totally immersed in *Berlinisch* and forbidden to use English. Much later she would write of the journey in her first travel book as if she were on a leisurely wander through North Africa and Europe, with no firm destination or schedule. In fact, she knew it was important that she get to Berlin quickly, because Smedley was thought to be heading soon for Moscow and China. Smedley had applied for a passport, and the State Department was trying to find legal reasons to deny it to her. To this day, I don't know if she was aware I was living in Berlin then, and I had no idea of where she went after Japan.

For Neill the journey was no vacation. She traveled mostly alone and had a serious flu along the way. She had very poor French, no Italian and the most rudimentary traveler's German. Except for the time she passed with her instructor she mimed or insisted on English, and no foreign speaker of English could understand her dialect. It was a lonely sojourn.

Her elderly language teacher in Munich was a rotund, politely officious man called Fritz. He accompanied her to Prague and then on to Dresden. Her lessons continued for those few extra days, as she practiced conversational *Berlinisch* with Fritz on the train, on walks around the cities and at meals. An hour out of Prague Neill broke with her discipline and blurted out the question she had been longing to ask. "Now just who is this person who calls herself Bhuma Singh Sharma?"

"Ah, you met her in India, huh?"

"I am her mule."

"Very good person, that one. Brave and clever and independent. Do you know how old she is?"

"Haven't a faint idea."

"Nobody does. There are many mysteries about her."

"She's Indian?"

"English, that much is known. Mother was Russian, Jewish, from Petersburg, before it was Petrograd, before it was Leningrad."

"When did she start dressing as a man?"

"Just for effect, a disguise. You say what, a one of a kind? Like special roles in the drama. In London she is Vivienne Cross, society lady, in Budapest she is called Countess Brankaskaya. I do not know her birth name, but she has an appointment at Heidelberg as Vivina Grosz and translates literature. She has a home there. They say she knows at least seven languages."

"Oh my, I am humbled."

That night, Neill had the first of the dreams she told me about involving Bhuma Singh Sharma. She watched him undress again, and she saw him transform into a woman as the clothing came off like a chrysalis. Naked, Vivina slowly turned around in the wedge of light from the passage. She paused and gazed at Neill and continued gazing as she came through the doorway toward her. Neill saw an amber glow around Vivina's body and up between her legs, the tawny light from behind her shifting like a late sun through clouds.

Neill arrived in Berlin the same day in late December that Agnes Smedley received notice her passport application again had been turned down. The letter said she had been writing for Anti-American publications and was associating with members of the KPD, Germany's communist party. Smedley had just dropped out of graduate school at Berlin University, where she had previously taught a course on India's political history and where her articles were used in the curriculum. She was struggling because of her lack of preparation for academic work, or perhaps it was a lack of interest in academic theory. In any case, she had become entirely preoccupied with preparations for the Brussels Comintern congress. But she still was without a passport.

Neill needed to set up housekeeping and obtain a cover. I had not been notified that she was coming, so I couldn't help her. But our Naval Attaché had a fifth floor bed-sit in a boarding house just down Wilhelmstrasse from the embassy, and he made that available to her while she went job hunting. She disliked Berlin from the start and only wanted to finish her work and leave as soon as possible. She also couldn't abide the boarding house, with its noisy communal meals and constant bustle of international transients. Neill was fantastically energetic and loved to meet people and entertain, but she needed a hideout, a quiet place to restore her troubled soul from time to time. And don't we all? Neill used to say, "Pity the refugees and the deranged of the world, who have no hideout."

I don't know how it came about, maybe Commander Shaw had contacted our NA, Captain Bradlee, or maybe it was just because Bradlee knew that most of the Comintern activity and safe houses were on Charlottenburg. But Neill was told she might consider offering to share my apartment. I had been living on Charlottenburg since arriving in Berlin the year before, and everybody knew Smedley now was in that neighborhood, ever since her break with Chatto. Münzenberg's headquarters were less than a block from my apartment, so it would have made sense to send Neill in my direction.

We met at Alterhund, a women's café around the corner on Ubertiergarten. Neill roared back into my life with the force of a hurricane. She didn't seem surprised to learn that I had been moved to Europe, and she kissed me with an intensity that made me sorrowful. She seemed so terribly lonely and alienated, almost traumatized, as if she had been off fighting a horrible war during all the time since she left me in Hawaii. She said she was still feverish from the flu she had been battling on her travels, but clearly she was worked up about the hunt for Agnes Smedley and the flu was long gone.

I told her she looked elegant, a word she loved, and she did look elegant, what with her cape and matching wool pillbox, which she wore over her ears, her broad-shouldered crème suit and silk neck scarf. She looked like a fashion model in a New York salon ad, except that her chin, just as always, was too proud for any fashion model. The fierceness and hunger still flared in those dark eyes, and I felt the same excitement I had felt when we first met at the cottage on Oahu. She had a way of looking at me that felt like the gaze of a wild animal.

After she said how much she had missed me since Hawaii and we finished talking about her move to the apartment, Neill went right to work. "What can you tell me about this guy Münzenberg?"

"Not much," I said. "If you can risk it, you might ask for a briefing by Captain Bradlee's office. But from what I've heard, Willi Münzenberg is openly recognized as a Comintern impresario, sort of a front-line link between the Germans and national independence movements, including the Indians. He was a social-democrat, then he got into the Reichstag and founded the KPD. He's also very close to the Soviets, ever since the Cheka days, and now we don't know if he reports to OGPU or the KPD or the other way around, possibly both. They say he's smooth, unctuous, a nice old man sort, though he's only in his late thirties."

"Is he dangerous?"

"He seems more of a company man, working the inside politics and manipulating people, rather than hurting them or making them disappear."

"I think he's behind Smedley," Neill said pensively.

Her cabin and steamer trunks arrived the next day, and she quit the boarding house and moved in at 51C Charlottenburg. We put the apartment in order and resumed living together much as we had five years earlier. There was a good little kitchen, so I could cook until my heart was content, and now I had my darling to cook for again.

Somebody, most likely Bradlee or Shaw or the both of them, got Neill a billet at the embassy. It was temporary, three months was all State would agree to because she had been such a pest in Tokyo. Shaw later said that that was all the time he wanted to give to the Brits anyway. I was filing features for the *Chronicle*, mostly about the German automobile and health industries, and my time was entirely my own whenever Captain Bradlee had no demands.

Unlike the late days in Hawaii, Neill pushed herself relentlessly in her ONI work. She was mad to get access to Smedley. She seemed obsessed by the possibility of meeting with her, and she said again and again, "I *must* see what she looks like and hear her voice." I kept telling her I didn't want to know anything about her work, and she would say it wasn't about her work, it was more important than that. My surmise is that Neill came to identify with Smedley, and that's why I said nothing about her giving me the details of her assignment. I often was successful in distracting her with a long walk in the Tiergarten, but the next day she would be fuming and plotting about meeting this person or that person who could connect her with her quarry.

Neill decided to pose as a writer, and I believe it is the first time she imagined herself as an author, rather than an advertising or publicity hack. She learned that the Berlin office of the Chinese Information Bureau was being set up near Münzenberg's office. It was a British operation, started up in London by a group of renegade Labor MPs and diplomats who by this time had sympathies with the League Against Imperialism, and our branch was to be run by an old Cambridge don and socialist diplomat named Reginald Bridgeman. Our Münzenberg files told her Bridgeman knew Smedley and that he had protected her from the State Department's investigations, and recently he appeared to have employed her as a propagandist at the Chinese Information Bureau. So Neill decided to persuade Bridgeman to hire her, too.

She easily got an appointment with Bridgeman, just sent over a note with her card that said Miss Neill James, Authoress, Shanghai and Peking, China. His boy brought back an invitation for Neill to join him the following morning for a coffee at his new offices. It didn't take Bridgeman long to start probing into Neill's motives.

"You say you've written on Kalgan and Mukden, Miss James. That's an area of great interest to our followers."

"Yes, Sir, I spent some considerable time in the North and Northeast."

"I sadly confess I'm unfamiliar with your work. Do you have a résumé and bibliography?"

"I do." She handed him the papers she had created the previous night.

Bridgeman scanned the list of writings. "And your portfolio? Letters of support?"

"This is happening all so quickly, I have just arrived from Bombay, and my personal effects trail behind me somewhat. Should have those things in a few days."

Bridgeman smiled indulgently and sipped his coffee. "Well, lovely indeed. Perhaps we should talk again when you have your complete packet. Meantime, you are staying . . . ?"

"With a colleague, an old friend, just up the road a piece."

"Wonderful. It's such a pleasure to meet you, Miss James. Perhaps you'll call again." He rose from his desk chair and started toward the door.

"My friend tells me another American writer is currently in your employ. I dearly would love to talk with a fellow author and girl from my part of the world. I am sure we have similar views on many things, including India and China."

"Oh? And that would be . . . ?"

"Miss Smedley. Agnes Smedley? Her wonderful articles in *Modern Review* have truly inspired me. I am especially fond of her writings on Danish artists and politics in India. Do you know how I might meet her?"

Bridgeman studied Neill's face for a long moment. "I shall see if I can arrange that."

A week passed without a word from Bridgeman. One morning she told me she was fed up with waiting and would demand to see Smedley. I kept telling her I didn't want to hear anything about her pursuit of her targets, but she repeated that she considered this to be both an official and personal matter, improbable as it might sound. She headed off to the CIB address with a renewed head of steam.

She strode into Reginald Bridgeman's office with her hand extended and a broad smile on her face. "Good day, Mr. Bridgeman. I wished to tell you that my belongings still have not arrived from India or wherever they might have been delayed en route. But I also wish to renew my request to visit with Miss Smedley."

"Ah, Miss James. Thank you for your diligence. It demonstrates that you have a strong and genuine interest in us. When your portfolio arrives, do please bring it in. In the meantime," Bridgeman was gesturing toward the entrance, "if you have any questions, please do not hesitate . . . ." He extended his hand.

"Smedley. Can I see her?"

"Well, I'm afraid Miss Smedley is indisposed at the time. She is terribly busy, as you can imagine, what with her work on the clinic and her writing. And you might know that she is preparing for an extended journey, as we are shortly posting her to China. So, no, I doubt that a meeting will be forthcoming. Sorry."

Neill thanked him and left, furious at having been turned away. Smedley, she thought, must have dismissed her. Or perhaps Bridgeman suspected Neill wasn't being truthful and once again was protecting Smedley.

She would try one more time before her chase would be abruptly ended. In Prague Neill's teacher Fritz had introduced her to a translator who knew Vivina Grosz. He wanted the translator to hear Neill's pronunciation of American English, because they had never heard authentic Mississippi speech. The translator also was a friend of the antiwar artist Käthe Kollwitz who, in turn, was close to Margaret Sanger and, the translator said, another American named Agnes Smedley. Neill also learned that all three were currently in Berlin, working together to establish women's health and birth control clinics across the city.

At the time, late spring 1927, Kollwitz was showing her new woodcuts at the Galerie Ferdinand Möller. Immediately after leaving the CIB offices, Neill made her way to the gallery and arranged to see Käthe Kollwitz. When they met that evening, Neill convinced Kollwitz that she was interested in writing about birth control in colonial countries including India and China, and it was important for her to talk with Sanger and Smedley. Kollwitz agreed to set up the meeting.

The following morning Neill told me she had dreamed about Bhuma Singh Sharma again, the same dream except that this time Singh Sharma looked slightly Chinese and there was a baby in her arms when she entered Neill's room. Neill rarely remembered dreams, but she said this was a very clear and powerful one, and it appeared to disturb her.

A note dropped through the mail slot. It was from Kollwitz, inviting Neill to tea at her apartment two days later. "Agnes Smedley will join us and is eager to meet you, and we shall discuss the clinics," the note said. Neill sent back a quick thank-you and said she will be pleased to attend the tea. She devoted the next day to shopping for a pair of workman's trousers and safari shirt that would fit her, and when she left 51C Charlottenburg for Kollwitz's apartment she wore them and her hiking boots, as if she were already on the front lines in China.

She hadn't been gone five minutes when Shaw telephoned and asked, "Has she left to see the artist?" He had correctly assumed I knew what was up.

I said she was on her way.

"Get her back. Our friends now wish not to disturb the subject but to allow the work to proceed. Just keep her from disturbing the subject of the work."

I told him I understood, which was frighteningly true. The British now had a different plan for Smedley, and it involved not repatriating her after all but allowing her to go deeper into the networks of Comintern and Soviet agents in British colonial areas, probably in East Asia. They would use her to lead them to Comintern and Russian espionage and propaganda work in China and Hong Kong and eventually, they hoped, in Japan and the United States mainland. If Neill cozened up to Smedley and was found out to be under cover, the U.S. intelligence relationship with Britain might be badly damaged and any potential future intelligence from trailing Smedley would be lost.

I rushed out to the street and ran toward the Klopstok and Händelstrasse, where Kollwitz's apartment overlooked the park. I was never the athlete Neill was, and I was panting pathetically and slowing down as I turned the corner onto Händelstrasse. I thought I might have to stop to catch my breath, maybe sit for a few seconds on a sidewalk bench. But I spied Neill just entering the apartment building, so I desperately pushed myself forward, struggled up the stoop and into the foyer and, all but dead with exhaustion, used my last breath to shout her name. Over my panting I could hear footsteps on the stairway, then nothing, and then footsteps again, as Neill came back down to the entrance. I was doubled over with my hands on my knees, trying to breathe.

"What on earth are you doing here, Gerry?"

"Don't go in. Come outside with me," I wheezed.

"I thought you weren't supposed to mess with my work. And here you are interfering, just at the moment I have been waiting for. Well, I'll just see you at home." And she turned and headed for the stairs and her tea with Smedley.

"Shaw called. It's his instruction," I said.

"Well why in hell didn't you say so."

We walked down to Brükenstrasse and returned to 51C by a long, slow circuit through the park. We sat on a bench in a quiet cul-de-sac, Neill looking rather silly and sad in her peasant clothes and boots. I told her what I suspected about the change in policy on Smedley, and she listened thoughtfully. I saw regret on her face, as if this were the end of a stage play she wished would go on and on. We talked about the necessity to take up whatever assignment our agency had for us and the equal necessity to discontinue, to disappear, to become as nothing, when the work called for it.

Her mien changed abruptly when I told her Shaw said there might be other opportunities for her to befriend Smedley. She said she knew they would someday meet up because she felt a unique bond with her, both of them so disconnected to their families, so passionate about the world, so committed to being strong women. Had I known more about Smedley I might have thought Neill was inflating her own passion and commitment, but at the time I agreed that there were similarities and accepted Neill's obsession with the chase.

Shaw almost immediately reassigned us. He made clear that we weren't being sent on as a pair and it was not for punishment. But, he said, there was equally important work that called each of us to Paris and we might as well continue to live together. I'm sure he meant important work for Neill. He believed we were a good influence on one another, and I for one agreed with him. I think his opinion on that mattered little to Neill.

Within a week of arriving in Paris we found a bright little apartment in the Val de Grâce section of the Panthéon District. Neill had a talent for finding posh digs that were affordable, and in those days rue Val de Grâce was one of the best left bank addresses. Luckily for me, my editors at the Chronicle and the World Telegram had story ideas for Paris, and so I was kept busy with my work as a journalist. It was lucky also because ONI had precious little for me to do except keep an eye on Neill, while Neill had a peach of a contract that paid her handsomely and put her back with the American Legion.

It was a pleasant interval for us, those few months in Paris. Weekends we often slept late, and we had countless lovely dinners at the small cafés in our neighborhood. We took walks along the Seine and wandered through the bookstalls on the east bank, and sometimes we would take a picnic basket and a bottle of wine and go by train to the countryside for an afternoon, Nanterre, Versailles, and one time all the way to Chantilly. I was never so in love.

Neill was disturbed, though. She continued to have dreams about Bhuma Singh Sharma, always the same events but sometimes with a crying baby Singh Sharma would put on the floor, sometimes with a baby that seemed to be dead, and the dream would end just as she was about to embrace Singh Sharma transformed into Vivina. She would wake me and turn on the light and ask me to hold her. I wondered if it was her work or if something happened when they had met in India.

At the time I only knew she worked for the Legion and went to the Trocadero every day. There was to be a national convention in Paris, and to get in she used her connections from one of her earliest jobs, something for the War Department in Spokane, Washington. The files showed that she once had organized civilian intelligence groups among the Northwest's American Legion posts. Now she worked for the Legion's organizing committees making preparations for the great Champs-Élysées parade and the general sessions of the Auxiliary. She was supposed to be personal secretary to the National Adjutant, a man named Barton. I later learned that she was monitoring tensions between ultra-right factions in the Legion and radical opponents they attracted from Europe's socialists and communists, who came to the convention site like ants to a picnic. It was a way for the Allies to take stock of left-wing internationalists and Comintern networks, a quality check on their intelligence. It was valuable work and easy for Neill, and it posed few risks.

Shaw apparently was like that with Neill, giving her a sinecure with high pay after she had taken on some risky or exhausting assignment. But his control and authority only went so far. Before the Legion's parade took place, Neill suddenly was let go.

She came home a few days before the convention began and said, "I just received my pink slip. I've been discarded like a dead weasel."

"Shaw did it?" I asked.

"No, no. Some faceless bureaucrat back in Washington, I suppose. The letter was waiting for me at my drop. Just go away, it told me. Now what am I going to do?"

I suggested that she could find work around Paris, surely something would be available. She told me all the silly arguments that much later appeared in her first book, where she pretended that we were just visiting Paris. I wondered if she really didn't want to stay in Europe, if maybe something so distressed her that she just wanted to move on.

"I admit they've offered me something close to my sister, in New Orleans. But I will be tightly strapped to get from here to there. I managed a letter of recommendation from Barton, just in case."

I asked her not to leave, but I knew she would go. That night she read to me a letter she had composed to her sister Jane.

Dearest Janey,

I am soon to be on the road again, this time heading back to Dixie and to what I hope will be a milder winter than any I've had since Hawai'i. My work at the American Legion National Convention is now done, the grand events to start up day after tomorrow, and they have no need for my services anymore. The State Dept owes me the costs of my travel home, and I intend to collect that plus my salary en route when I pass through D.C. They do not seem pleased to communicate with me about the matter, though, and I suppose that's why diplomats are called masters of silence.

My boat leaves Cherbourg on the 20th and arrives in NYC the following Monday, the 26th. I will do some good old American style shopping in New York before traveling to Washington—is there anything special you would like? Of course I will come as quickly as I can to

Memphis, I so want to see you. My destination then is New Orleans, where I already have arranged a job with the Louisiana Ice Company. Why not take advantage of all my ice experience from Hawai'i? Can you come to N.O. with me? Surely your training and job record will make it a cinch to gain employment there. And it is such a siren among cities, I always believed we would be together in New Orleans. Please think on that, will you?

My Best Love, Neill

The State Department paid her nothing, and there never was proof of a telegram promising her return fare and salary for her trip to the United States. Neill failed to see how inconvenient she had been to State, and I heard that for the following decade she continued to appeal to her contacts for jobs at embassies, always without success.

I went up to Cherbourg with her that Tuesday in September 1927. It was a cold, grey day on the coast, and the wind was blowing sharply as we kissed goodbye near the queue rope at the dockside. Almost in spite of the bleak weather and my sadness, she was gaily dressed in a flowered silk dress and her fur coat, and she had a broad smile of happy anticipation on her face. The wearied look of distress I had seen for the past month was gone, and she glowed as she waved from the canopied gangplank, then turned around and headed up to the deck and out of my life once more.

I have often wondered if I ever appear in Neill's dreams. Ten years after she left France her first book was published. When I read it I was pleased to see that she mentioned me and our months together in Paris, although she omitted all but the slightest reference to our home near Honolulu and left out completely the times we were together in Denmark and Florida. Even now I occasionally have dreams about her, but they occur ever less often as the years go by.

VI

Documents

> Access to public records gives citizens the opportunity to participate in public life, help set priorities, and hold their governments accountable.

—The Carter Center, Americas Program

U.S. Department of Justice

BUREAU OF INVESTIGATION

Washington, D.C.

```
BOI/ DOJ: 080-2241
CONFIDENTIAL / RESTRICTED ACCESS CATEGORY K
```

Case File Origination
Case Officer █████████

Date: November 07, 1927

Subject: JAMES, Nell Neill
DOB: January 03, 1899
POB: Grenada, Mississippi

PREAMBLE:

The Subject, having been intermittently employed in U.S. embassies at Tokyo, Japan (August 01, 1924-November 01,1926) and Berlin, Germany (April 01, 1927- June 15, 1927; cf. employment records as addendum A), and having been known to be in contact with possible foreign espionage elements and other United States citizens believed to be working for the Communist International, was made the Subject of directed surveillance beginning January 01, 1927, all watch reports and recording being conducted under jurisdiction of the U.S. Department of State.

As of June 30, 1927 the U.S. Department of State ceased all mission responsibility for non-domestic espionage and counter-espionage and for negative intelligence as it applies to United States citizens operating beyond the borders of the United States. As a consequence of this policy and mission change, ██████████ directed that the Bureau of Investigation take up surveillance and reporting on Subject for purposes of strategic coordination of counter-espionage and negative intelligence analysis and action.

SUMMARY ASSESSMENT:

Subject worked as contract agent ██████ Office of Naval Intelligence beginning June 1922 or earlier. ██████ reported Subject previously had undercover assignments for G-2 and its predecessor Department of War units as early as 1918, while employed in stenography positions for Quartermaster General; however, G-2 and ONI have not released any records pertaining to this reported employment in negative intelligence.

█████ has placed Subject in Agra, India, with known British-Soviet Russian double- and suspected triple-agent, █████, as above. Thereupon Subject was observed to frequent the Berlin offices of League Against Imperialism (LAI), the Comintern-inspired successor organization to League Against Colonial Cruelties and Oppression (LACCO), both created under direction of international Comintern figure W. Muentzenberg. There Subject discussed her application to do propaganda work for LAI with Berlin LAI Chief █████, who was an active British Foreign Office agent and ex-Member of the British House of Commons. Although █████ never reported his contacts with Subject, he was thought to be protecting the American radical activist and writer Agnes Smedley and wanted to divert attention away from his Berlin offices.

Subject lived in Berlin, Germany, and later in Paris, France, with an American journalist named Miss Geraldine Sartain. It is not known whether Sartain knew of Subject's contacts with █████. Sartain remains in Europe as of this assessment.

In Paris Subject had frequent contacts with █████ under cover of employment at the National Convention of the American Legion. Upon termination of her ONI contract she returned to the United States, arriving New York City September 26, 1927 and subsequently traveling by rail to Memphis, Tennessee via Washington, D.C. She currently resides at 2308 Napoleon Avenue, Apartment J, New Orleans, Louisiana. Subject has accepted employment in sales with the Louisiana Ice Company.

RECOMMENDATIONS:

(1) That the Bureau continue routine surveillance of Subject's activities and reporting thereof, with main responsibility assigned to the New Orleans Field Office until further notice;

(2) that Subject's financial records be reviewed and current financial transactions and holdings be audited without disclosure and made part of the confidential record; and

(3) that the file be flagged for status revision when any indications of contacts with suspicious persons or organizations listed as potentially subversive are observed.

FOR THE ASSOCIATE DIRECTOR, by ████████████
APPROVED ████████████
BOI/ DOJ: 080-2241 CONFIDENTIAL / RESTRICTED ACCESS
CATEGORY K

———

// CLASSIFIED SECRET – ROUTINE //

Field Record ONI: 017-1887 Date: 17 NOV 27

Created by: Navigator

File at: Contractor Kokio

Directed the intelligence officer of Eighth Naval District, New Orleans, Lt. B.R. Price, to establish dead drop and secure comms for Agent Kokio. He was informed that Kokio is now on contract for counter-espionage throughout the District and has clearance to debrief foreign vessel boarding inspectors. Kokio will liaise with DIO and Commandant 8th ND and report to me at ONI HQ. Cover established through Louisiana Ice Distribution and Sales Corp., New Orleans and Biloxi, Mississippi. Agent Kokio resides alone at 2308 Napoleon Avenue, Apartment J, New Orleans, ▆▆▆▆▆▆ remains in Memphis, Tennessee.

–RESTRICTED ACCESS–

———

WESTERN UNION TELEGRAM

1928 MAY 05 AM 10 45

NO ACTIVITY FIVE MONTHS NEED WORK STOP WILL TAKE ANY NEW LOCATION IF RATE RIGHT STOP TRANSPORTATION EXPENSES REQUIRED PLEASE WIRE IMMEDIATELY NEILL JAMES CARE OF BAYOU GRAND HOTEL NEW ORLEANS STOP NEILL.

———

WESTERN UNION TELEGRAM

1928 MAY 23 PM 9 11

ASSIGNED TAMPA FLORIDA WILLIAM BEERS COMPANY SEE MR JOHN MARSHALL STOP PASSAGE PAID ON STEAMER SUN CITY DEPARTING MONDAY 29 MAY STOP FIND LODGING FOR REIMBURSE STOP SHAW.

———

FLORIDAN PALACE HOTEL

A Francis J. Kinnard, Jr. Landmark Property
Home of the Sapphire Room

905 North Florida Avenue, Tampa, Florida
Tel: Neptune 8-1001

June 4, 1928

Dear Shaw,

The only habitable spot in this entire overcrowded town is the Floridan, so this is where I have landed. It is a marvelous new structure, the tallest in all of Florida, and not at all unreasonable. I still await the arrival of my steamer trunk. I have my breakfasts in the garden court, and the maid service is world-class. I walk on the beach every evening. May I stay here forever?

I am lucky to have survived the crossing. That leaking tin can the "Sun City" barely avoided capsizing. Dread to think what might have happened if there had been a Gulf blow—the damned tub would now be at the bottom of Tampa Bay.

Mr. Marshall was ever so accommodating, and William-Beers seems a well positioned firm, just what fills the prescription. I will have my own car to travel about in and no set schedule of hours.

I don't suppose you could see your way clear to have G.S. come over here could you, even for a brief while? In spite of the hoards of seasonal visitors from Nu Yawk, one feels a bit isolated on this peninsula. In any case, I shall begin work next week.

Yours sincerely, Neill

———

John Edgar Hoover
Director

U.S. Department of Justice

BUREAU OF INVESTIGATION

Washington, D.C.

July 12, 1928

Memorandum for the Director

In regard to the file on Nell Neill James, ref. BOI/DOJ: 080-2241, it now is known that James is living at a garage apartment attached to the Tampa address 4097 Windward Drive. She is employed as a sales development agent at the ice wholesale and supply firm William-Beers Company of St. Petersburg. She lives with Geraldine A. Sartain, an international journalist with whom she shared lodging in Berlin, Germany and Paris, France per earlier reports.

In view of the aforementioned change of location by Miss James, I made personal contact with the Office of Naval Intelligence and requested Capt. Vernon Shaw to share records on her and to direct her to liaise with the Bureau. Captain Shaw referred me to M.O.U. dated November 15, 1927, and December 06, 1927, delineating agency areas of responsibility in the Gulf Region. He would provide no further information and suggested that I have my superiors contact DNI, Capt. Alfred Johnson.

The Orlando Field Office will maintain current surveillance and reporting activities until further instructions are forthcoming.

Respectfully submitted, T.F. Baughman
Interim Agent in Charge, Florida Field Office, Orlando

––––––

John Edgar Hoover
Director

U.S. Department of Justice

BUREAU OF INVESTIGATION

Washington, D.C.

October 25, 1929

Memorandum for the Director

Pursuant to telephonic instructions, a review of the status of Nell Neill James, Case file BOI/DOJ: 080-2241, was conducted by the undersigned and Agent Francisco Tremonte during the week of October 13-19, 1929. It was found that James has been resident at Orlando, Florida, since at least June 1929. Previous to that relocation, James continued to live at the aforementioned 4097 Windward Drive, Tampa, Florida. (See Memorandum for the Director dated July 12, 1928.) In the interval James attended a sales training school at Chicago, Illinois, under the sponsorship of the Florida Ice Manufacturers' Association. The exact address where the training facility was located is not known.

James currently lives alone in apartment 7B at 1201 Coral Road; however, James travels extensively throughout southern and central Florida and rarely is at her Orlando residence. An interview was conducted by the writer on October 15, 1929, with Mr. Fredrick Shavitsky, Assistant Director of the Florida Ice Manufacturing Association. Shavitsky told the writer that James has performed excellent work and is expected to remain in FIMA employ for the indefinite future.

T. F. Baughman, Field Agent in Charge, Orlando Office

––––––

ONI/NAVIG SECURE TWX O1201930: 1140AMEST//SECRET CW//

YOU ARE DIRECTED TRAVEL TO BOSTON MASS FOR FINAL TRAINING CNSY LOCATION NLT 01271930:0800AMCST STOP ALL TRAVEL MOST CONVENIENT MODE AUTHORIZED STOP ASSIGNED

TO SAN JOSE COSTA RICA FOLLOWING TACTNG CONTACT CMDR J G RICE GRAN HOTEL STOP TWX WHEN ARRIVE COSTA RICA STOP NAVIGATOR

———

ONI/KKO SECURE TWX 02031930:0935AMCST//SECRET CW//

ARRIVED SAN JOSE YEST MET RICE WHO GAVE DEAD DROP AND MADE WORK SCHED STOP WILL BE IN REMOTE ONE WEEK THEN COASTAL ONE WEEK THEN RETURN SAN JOSE BEFORE WORK IN PANAMA STOP INVOICE FOLLOWS BY ROUTINE POST STOP KOKIO

———

ONI/NAVIG SECURE TWX 04021930:0330PMEST//SECRET CW//

RETURN PASSAGE TO FLORIDA AUTHORIZED STOP GOOD WORK ALL PLEASED STOP NO FURTHER CONTRACT NOW BUT SOON NEW SOUTH PACIFIC WORK NEW ZEALAND POSSIBLE STOP MORE INFO ASAP BUT POSSIBLY 3 MONTHS WAIT STOP NAVIGATOR

———

John Edgar Hoover
Director

U.S. Department of Justice

BUREAU OF INVESTIGATION

Washington, D.C.

May 02, 1931

Memorandum for the Director

In reference to file BOI/DOJ: 080-2241, Subject Nell Neill James, your request for a final report and recommendation for disposition of the file was received. A review was conducted of the case file and all reports appertaining thereto, and requests for further information were issued to relevant agencies of national governments where James had been active since origination of the file and to both domestic and international civilian informants. The following summarizes all information received pursuant to those investigative activities and the subsequent review by this office.

After a two week period of training in Boston, Massachusetts, paid by the Florida Ice Manufacturers Association, which coincided with participation in the Annual National Convention of the Ice Industries of America in Boston, James returned to Orlando, Florida, and worked again in ice sales promotion throughout the State until approximately mid-

December 1929. She resigned her position at the Florida Ice Manufacturers Association and traveled by steamship "Caribe" on December 20, 1929, from Miami, Florida, to Havana, Cuba. Three days later she departed from Havana by steamship "Queen of the Pacific" for Panama and Costa Rica, arriving at Puntarenas, Costa Rica, and by rail to San Jose, Costa Rica, where she began work for the publisher Otilio Ulate Blanco, promoting newspaper sales for "El Diario de Costa Rica" throughout the country. On Saturday, March 22, 1930, James departed Puntarenas, Costa Rica, by steamship for Colón, Panama.

After two weeks in Panama, James's sister, Jane Elizabeth James, joined her at Colón. On April 04, 1930, Jane Elizabeth James departed Colón, Panama, for New Zealand on the steamship "R.M.S. Rangitata", and Nell Neill James (hereinafter referred to as James) departed by steamship "Stuttgart" for Havana, Cuba. By April 10, 1930, James was in Miami, where she remained, apparently without employment, until July 24, 1930, when she embarked at Miami on the Munson steamship "Munargo" for Havana, Cuba. On July 26, 1930, James departed Havana, Cuba, on the White Line steamship "RMS Majestic" bound for Panama. She departed Panama at Balboa via sea embarkation on August 08, 1930, bound for Auckland, New Zealand on the New Zealand Line "Remuera".

In Auckland, New Zealand, James was known to have worked for the agent (name unknown) through whom she obtained her work in Costa Rica. She and her sister, Jane Elizabeth James, conducted a publicity campaign for "The Manawatu Daily Times" newspaper in Palmerston North, beginning on approximately September 02, 1930. The sisters completed their work on that campaign on or about January 30, 1931. James and Jane Elizabeth James appear to have been stranded in Wellington upon termination of the newspaper publicity campaign. City records show they purchased a penthouse and roof garden of the Empire Commercial Building, where they installed a fee-based miniaturized golf course on the roof. The enterprise was unsuccessful, as the sisters paid no business or real estate taxes and within three months turned over the business to creditors.

Upon termination of their business activities in Wellington, Jane Elizabeth James departed by air transport to Honolulu, Hawaii. James remained for some days in Wellington, until she departed by sea for Suva, Fiji Island, apparently for an extended vacation. James left for Honolulu aboard the "S. S. Niagara" on March 13, 1931 and disembarked at Honolulu March 15, 1931. James and Jane Elizabeth James took up residence first at the Fernhurst YWCA facility and later at a double beach bungalow on Waikiki. Jane Elizabeth James gained employment at the tourism magazine "Paradise of the Pacific", but one month later departed by sea for Shanghai, China. The reason for her departure currently is unknown. James took up a position at the Institute of Pacific Relations and was still employed there at the time of this report.

As there have been no critical contacts during the period under review with known or suspected Comintern members, radical revolutionaries, seditionists, or espionage or counter-espionage agents by either Jane Elizabeth James or Nell Neill James, it is this office's recommendation that surveillance be suspended and file BOI/DOJ: 080-2241be placed in the Pending category according to the Bureau Records Disposal Schedule.

Respectfully submitted,

F. T. Baughman, Supervisory Agent, Southern District

——

GRAND PACIFIC HOTEL

Located on the Victoria Parade
the Pride of the Islands

Suva, Fiji

7 Feb 1931

Dearest Janey,

I have been encamped at the Grand Pacific, a most unique and unexpectedly luxurious place, just like living in a stateroom of a great ocean liner. There even is salt water in my bath tap and a ship's prow above the gardens. I have no work and no money, but fate and my good luck will see me through. This is a magical place, and when it rains in the evening you can sense the presence of Mr. Somerset Maugham, or so the natives say. I have never read his stories, but he is talked about like a god in the hotel salon here all the time.

Can you wire me a bit of cash, a few hundred to tide me over? I'm sure by now you must be settled on Oahu, and I'm ever so glad to hear about your position at the magazine, writing and editing cover to cover. As you might guess, I have itchy feet again but my pockets are empty. And that Maori girl I befriended kept my jewelry and stole most of my lingerie, which I had to replace and which has me without enough for a first class to Honolulu. So woe is me, but the sun is shining and there's always a fine ship awaiting at the dock, and while I'm here I'm having a grand time.

Please let me know where you are staying, so I can mail direct to you. In the meantime I shall continue to send to you at the WU express office.

Best love, Neill

——

Honolulu, Oahu, Hawaii

February 12, 1931

Dear Neill,

How wonderful to hear from you, but how horrible that you were robbed! You put such trust in girls who attach themselves to you that you are an easy target. I hope you have been able to eat decently and are not piling up too much debt at the hotel. Have wired some money and hope it is enough for now.

You must leave Suva and come here. There is work to be done, and we can live together, just like 20 years ago at home, not in hotels or train compartments or ship cabins but in an apartment or a cottage near a beach. We both need that sort of life at least for a short while, something resembling settled-down and restful.

You are needed here. More than one opportunity have been put in place for you, just waiting for your arrival. I am receiving mail at the YWCA Fernhurst House, Honolulu, and you can write direct to me there, but it would be better if you can catch the Niagara right away and come up to Hawaii.

Your loving sister, Jane

———

WESTERN UNION TELEGRAM

1931 MARCH 12 PM 11 45

CASH RECEIVED JUST IN TIME STOP LEAVE TOMORROW ARRIVE 15TH HONOLULU ABOARD SS NIAGARA STOP MEET ME AT PORT STOP NEILL

VII

Vernon Shaw

> We are never deceived; we deceive ourselves.
>
> —Johann Wolfgang von Goethe

ONI needed a replacement for Marguerite Miller at IPR. She had been chosen for a new assignment in Shanghai and within six months would be leaving the Central Secretariat at Honolulu. We wished to have continuity at IPR as it had become a valuable source of information on both the Chinese situation and Japanese capabilities and intentions. Neill James and her sister had completed their work in New Zealand and Melanesia, so she was available for the job as Marguerite's replacement. Neill's skills were a good fit, and she was eager to work. We found the IPR job also to be a very productive cover.

The sister, Jane, had established cover already at a territorial tourist magazine and was reporting to us on travelers and the transport industry. It was only her third contract, and she had no code name, although if she had stayed with us I have no doubt that in time she would have been given one, as she was very able and dedicated. After Palmerston North, Neill had taken on some extra observational work at a number of islands—she was always short of cash, so I scraped together some experimental jobs—establishing a prototype for later intelligence gathering efforts in the South Pacific. At the end she lagged behind in Suva, for some reason still unclear to me. She later said it had been a vacation, but she seemed always to be on vacation, even when hard at work. I had guessed there was a romantic affair, for she seemed always to be involved in one of those, too.

The surveillance was important because we suspected the Japanese continued to violate the Washington Naval Treaty, and we needed to know more about the South Seas Trading Company. Neill James delivered the goods. She reported that the Company was active on most of the Japanese-held islands, was stockpiling munitions, and was staffed with Japanese naval officers, all of which much later was confirmed.

We put the two sisters up at the YWCA until we could lodge them in a residence at Waikiki, and that arrangement pleased Neill very much. By this time, the early spring of 1931, I was back in D. C., and for the Asia work I had to rely entirely on field reports plus Neill's eccentric and erratic disclosures of events in her personal life. I knew I could trust the quality of her official reports, but outside the job her stories always had a ring of exaggeration or strategic omission, which is why she had become so valuable to us in time, as long as we could trust that she was using her facility for deception for the right purposes. For longer than usual I had to keep watch over her.

Neill launched herself into the IPR staff job and found everything they did to be of interest. She quickly learned their pecking order and procedures, and she cooperated fully with Marguerite's training, although she bristled a bit under her supervision, perhaps because of their earlier encounters in Oregon and Honolulu, when Marguerite was more of a colleague, chaperone and advisor than supervisor. But quite unexpectedly to me, at IPR Neill became fascinated by the scholarly work that flowed through the office. She was not much of a scholar herself, but the academic studies of political economy and geography appeared to absorb her attention. Within a year she was pressing Elizabeth Green to let her write book reviews for *Pacific Affairs*. We thought that might be a little too risky to her cover, but eventually Neill prevailed, and by mutual agreement she published some brief reviews and, following Mrs. Green's policy, signed them only with her initials. I believe it was the first writing of hers of an intellectual sort she had seen in print. At the Shanghai conference Miss Green was re-elected to the editorship and happily Neill's name never made it to the masthead.

Planning for the Shanghai conference had been completed by the time Neill arrived at the Institute. I directed her to learn by shadowing Marguerite when the Central Secretariat staff traveled to China for the fortnight of the meeting. All the speeches and colloquia and roundtables, and all the academic papers—even some of the casual remarks in general sessions—all of the proceedings were recorded, either steno-graphically or mechanically on electric Columbia Dictaphones, which IPR had shipped in from California. Furthermore, all the recorded proceedings were managed by Marguerite's office, translated when necessary, copied and filed. We saw everything. But more importantly, my people in the field had a legitimate framework within which to meet the more highly connected leftist thinkers of the Pacific region and especially those who wrote about China. Charming highly connected people was Neill's forte.

That was the event when she first met Katsushi Uchida of the East Asia Industrial Company, Dr. Hu Shih, and Professor Chen Han-seng, the Chinese scholar we already knew to be in the Far East Comintern. Those contacts would prove useful later on to Neill and, through her, to our efforts to learn about Smedley and others in the Sorge espionage ring. For the time, Smedley was unwittingly being helpful to our British opposites, so we needed to know about her but not alert or intercept her. We considered her as a link to Sorge and Hotsumi Ozaki and hoped we might intercept their intelligence. We were less concerned about Muenzenberg. If the information suggested Smedley was a Comintern agent or otherwise was actively disloyal to the United States, Neill would track her down later. It was delicate. Our main purpose at the time was to apply what we would learn to improving War Plan Orange.

At first, it didn't go very well. In October and November 1931 when the conference took place, we believed Smedley to be living in Shanghai. But even though many international writers dropped in as occasional guests at the general sessions, she remained away from the proceedings. Neill transcribed a conversation she had had with Prof. Chen Han-seng that touched on Smedley, shortly before the plenary session:

Miss James: Professor Chen, I thought your paper on farmers' problems in the South of China was an awfully creative work. I learned so much that I am now most eager to read your next book.

Prof. Chen: Thank you, that is very kind. I do not however think of my writing as creative but only as a kind of reporting out. I merely say what few facts I have learned by diligent study.

Miss James:: You are too humble, Professor Chen. I dearly would love to talk more with you about interest rates and the lack of cash in the countryside and how they might be connected to development. As a world traveler I want to learn as much as I can about the people who work the land.

Prof. Chen: We cannot talk about interest rates anymore, Miss . . . , ah?

Miss James: James, Neill James.

Prof. Chen: Yes, Miss James, because the right word is usury, and it grows worse as currency grows weaker and weaker. Soon currency will be worthless and usury rates will be impossible. That is what has happened before every revolution in China's history, even in ancient times.

Miss James: Oh yes, "the Mandate of Heaven is carried upon the backs of the peasants." I understand one of my countrywomen has written extensively about peasants and land reform in Southern China, Miss Agnes Smedley?

Prof. Chen: I have heard of her name. I do not know her. I think maybe she is a sort of popular writer, maybe journalist.

Miss James: I heard that she is living here in Shanghai. I was hoping you might introduce me to her.

Prof. Chen: I regret that I cannot, Miss James, as I do not know her.

Chen was then surrounded by admirers, and Neill was left to make her notes. She had underestimated the need for *kuan-hsi*, what the Chinese call connections, before making a request. Her approach to Dr. Hu Shih, the grandest intellectual of all China, was somewhat more cautious and consequently more productive. She visited with him at breakfasts and brought mail to him whenever it arrived at the lodge. He was taken by her compliments, and when eventually she asked him about Smedley he immediately acknowledged that he knew her and had worked with her.

"Alas," he said, "I would like to help you to meet with your countrywoman and have conversations, but unfortunately she is too busy assisting her friends, the publishers Mr. and Mrs. Noulens, on a very important legal case."

He was being a bit evasive, but it was corroborative information. Smedley was busy maneuvering to defend herself from accusations in the press that she was a Comintern leader in Shanghai, while she also was rounding up support for Mr. and Mrs. Hilaire Noulens. The Noulenses had been arrested by the Nationalists as suspected Comintern agents and had been convicted and sentenced, in the case of the husband to be executed, and in the case of the wife to life imprisonment. They were in fact the Swiss couple Paul and Gertrude Ruegg, and they were important Comintern agents in the Far Eastern Section. Smedley had written propaganda for the Noulens group, and she was helping the defense to keep her out of the story. Hu Shih had known of the arrests and sentencing but said nothing to Neill about all that. The Rueggs later were released when the Soviet Union intervened, and the couple disappeared from history, probably back to Moscow. Muenzenberg, we later learned, helped get them off by writing directly to Chiang Kai-chek. But at least Neill had met Hu Shih.

Back in Hawaii, Neill replaced Marguerite Miller. Now there would be no buffer between herself and the rest of the Central Secretariat. Now nobody would know the details of her double roles at IPR, and she alone was in charge of maintaining the integrity of her cover. This is the reason we worked so hard to stage the next conference at Banff. It gave Neill a plausible reason to travel a circuitous route from Hawaii across the Aleutians and down the Alaskan and British Columbia coasts before taking up her duties as Secretariat hostess. In fact that was how she arranged it, by going on one of her annual vacations. Coincidentally, she wrote valuable reports on her coastal observations. Banff also was most convenient for us because all foreign participants would need Canadian entry documentation and they would be sequestered for a week, held captive within a luxurious resort in the wilderness by their own obsessions and ambitions. It greatly enhanced our opportunities for access.

Both Hu Shih and Chen Han-seng were in attendance again and gave papers. Owen Lattimore and Ada Comstock and Mr. and Mrs. Luce also attended. I of course did not, but Newton Baker, who had been the Secretary of War when both Neill and I began our careers, participated vigorously in the roundtable discussions.

Neill was so busy during her twelve days in Banff she scarcely slept. Her reports disclosed that she supervised the clerical staff, gathered all the transcriptions, took stenographic notes of panel presentations, copied studies and other documents that would provide vital information, and tirelessly labored to establish personal contacts with conferees who might be useful to our work. Her personal notes and telegrams expressed regret that official duties prevented her from enjoying the recreational activities as much as she wished.

One leisure event she participated in, however, was a near-catastrophe but eventually would pay good dividends to Neill and ONI. The Canadian entertainment committee provided conferees with many diversions, some of which were among Neill's favorites. Banff Springs Hotel has first-class golf links and tennis courts, and there were forest paths and streams for exploration and contemplation. The Committee hired wranglers to guide the more hardy guests on horseback rides into the surrounding mountain forests and glens. Following a raucous afternoon of cocktails on the vast stone patio, a group of historians and publishers persuaded Dr. Hu Shih to go on a trail ride. Prof. Chen Han-seng could not be moved to join them.

Neill had just come out to the patio from her office work when she overheard the laughter and teasing. Somebody had placed a large western cowboy hat on Hu Shih's head, and he grinned but looked helpless as the group headed off to the stables. Neill saw an opportunity and quickly went to her room to change into riding clothes.

The wrangler helped Hu Shih get aboard a huge grey gelding with dark spots on its rear. Neill's mount was an Arabian mare, tall for her breed, with shiny copper coat. She caught up to the line of horses and riders just after they entered the forest beyond the resort's broad lawns. Hu Shih bobbed along atop his horse, pulling the reins with both hands and looking like he was swept away by events beyond his control. The string headed up a rocky, shadowy trail through fir and spruce groves until reaching a mountain meadow and a small glacial lake.

Neill's horse was immediately behind the big grey gelding when something huge and dark crashed out of the woods and entered the meadow off to the right. One of the horses spun around and galloped away, its rider flopping in the saddle like a rag doll before falling off. The intruder, either a grizzly bear or black moose, veered at high speed toward the line of frenzied riders, whose horses by this time were spinning and rearing in a maelstrom of dust.

The guide shouted for people to turn their frightened horses around and gather together in a half-circle. Dr. Hu's horse began to hop nervously in place, first the front end and then the rear. Neill could see it was the prelude to bucking and breaking away. The harder Dr. Hu pulled on his reins, the more agitated the horse became and the wilder it hopped about with its head reared back. He began to lose all control and quickly was at the mercy of his bucking horse. Neill moved her mount up next to his, took his reins and used her horse to steer the grey gelding into the middle of the gathered riders and horses. She steadied both horse and rider as the group now faced as one the danger coming toward them. Just as suddenly as it had entered the meadow the intruder, now clearly an adult grizzly, turned aside and vanished into the forest.

Dr. Hu had lost his hat and he was wiping his face with a handkerchief. Neill's letter about the incident said he was drying his tears, but it could have been sweat or dirt, for Neill had remarked on the cloud of trail dust from the panicked horses. Dr. Hu recognized that Neill very likely saved his life by her quick and decisive actions, and he couldn't have been more grateful. At that night's after dinner gathering on the patio he proposed a toast to his "rescuer and grand friend from Shanghai, Miss Neill James." She had secured her future letter of introduction to Smedley.

By the time Neill arrived again in Shanghai, Smedley already had departed for Peking and Moscow. Neill had resigned her IPR post in December of 1933, and the Central Secretariat immediately abolished the job, leaving office management to the Acting General Secretary, Charles Loomis. Mrs. Green also left IPR that December, after seven years as editor of *Pacific Affairs*, and the journal was revised, both editorially and administratively, changing from a specialist's monthly to a less technical and more generally accessible quarterly. It was apparent that the Pacific Council executives of IPR sought a lower profile, as suspicions about their leftist agenda were on the rise, especially in the United States and Europe. We closed shop there.

Although Dr. Hu Shih and Agnes Smedley were temporarily estranged over his criticism of a story she had circulated about Chinese prison conditions, he nonetheless wrote a strong letter for Neill. She carried the letter and another from Owen Lattimore with her on the S.S. Coolidge when she left Honolulu for Shanghai. Chen Han-seng remained aloof but promised to help her get around in China should they meet again. We still had no hard evidence on Smedley but wanted to know more about who her contacts were.

It was the end of February 1934, and we had been trying for the previous two months to teach Neill Russian, in anticipation of her future work in the Soviet Union, we hoped alongside Smedley. Neill worked diligently at her studies, but she had no natural ability for languages, and all the training in German, Japanese, and Russian we provided over the years mostly went for naught.

Her sister Jane, on the other hand, was ably learning Chinese in Shanghai. She had fallen in love with a suave young American Marine, Lieutenant Francis B. Loomis, Jr., who was the only son of a top American diplomat, no relative to Charles Loomis. Lt. Francis Loomis's father had been an American newspaperman and business executive and, besides serving as Ambassador to Venezuela and Portugal, had once been Acting Secretary of State. Some records show that he also had been involved in intelligence operations in Brazil and Japan. By the time of Neill's arrival in Shanghai Jane and Loomis were engaged to be married. It was an influential, wealthy family, and Jane had done well to become part of it. From that point forward, though, she rarely took contracts for work with us.

Young Loomis escorted Neill and Jane to sights around the international settlement, while Marguerite Miller saw to the details of Neill's travel papers for the Soviet Union. In her first book, Neill told a story about coercing a Soviet Consular official into issuing her the visas she needed. That was a sham. In actuality we prepared three visas and two passports for her, which if undetected would allow her safe passage through multiple border crossings, in diverse situations, that is, if she protected the documents properly.

She would put her documents to the test within a week. After a brief vacation of sleepless nights carousing the international clubs along the Bundt and frantic afternoons at the horse races, where she lost most of her savings—only Neill James would have called this a vacation—she bid farewell to Jane and the fiancé and friends and sailed for Dairen. We had an agent in place there, a Honolulu Japanese who had attended journalism school at Manoa and went to graduate school at Columbia University. George Sakamaki was stationed as night editor of the *Manchuria Daily News* and had an inside source in the Manchukuo Railway. It was George's suggestion that it might profit us to have our agent travel by rail from Dairen to Vladivostok, where observations could be made of Japanese military movements and Russian responses on the Far Eastern borderlands. It was rumored that Vladivostok was being converted from a commercial to a military port, and ONI wanted confirmation.

At Dairen, Neill's papers were accepted by Japanese guards without question, and she went directly to the train terminal in the company of the flamboyant American businessman Harry Yang, George Sakamaki's inside man. Yang represented several railroad equipment manufacturers and enjoyed security with the Japanese, Chinese, and Russians because the entire South Manchurian Railroad ran on American-made parts based on American measurement standards. If anything untoward happened to Harry Yang, the rail lines would soon shut down.

Yang saw to it that Neill had passage to Harbin, where she would deposit her cabin trunks and other luggage, and then on to the Russian border crossing at Mudanjiang. She was to spend three days in Vladivostok and return through Harbin on her way to the northern border at Manchouli. He arranged for her to share a compartment with two Russians and one Japanese, all government officials.

On the overnight trip to Harbin, Neill struggled to stay awake so she could eavesdrop on the conversations, which the others conducted in childish Mandarin, the lingua franca of the region. She didn't understand much of what was said, but she could transcribe steno-graphically the sounds she heard, pretending she was writing letters and her diary. That was the sort of detailed effort she typically devoted to her assignments and remained to the end why I kept turning to her. I have often wondered why she was so exceptionally good at transcribing foreign sounds but so limited in producing them.

Spring already was coming on in Dairen but in Harbin it was still mid-winter, and Neill pulled out her fur coat before locking her travel trunks in storage. The porters and conductors on the train to Mudanjiang now were all Russians, and the only Japanese she saw were a few soldiers on board and the many troops positioned alongside the railroad tracks at every town and coaling station. Through the long, grey day she peered out the window at new Japanese food distribution warehouses, machinery factories, lumber mills and munitions centers. She kept scribbling steno notes in her diary. When the train arrived at Mudanjiang she learned that it was now called Botankou, and the sprawling military post she saw under construction as she approached the city was the Japanese Botankou Command depot.

It was late afternoon and Neill was no doubt glad she had her coat. George Sakamaki had told her to show her Moscow visa at the Russian customs office in Botankou and to tell them she was a friend of Harry Yang and an international journalist on her way eventually to Moscow. Her report described an unpleasant conversation.

"Why going to Vladivostok?" the uniformed customs officer growled.

"I know it is the most southeastern point in all of Russia, and I want to stand at the edge of the continent."

"Are you being poet?"

"I am a journalist."

"So you are planning to write about edge of such a continent?"

"I plan to report on the new era of recognition between your country and mine. When I arrive in Moscow."

"And you are finding era of recognition in Vladivostok?"

"I would wish to just tour your lovely city, to practice my baby-talk Russian."

The officer asked her in Russian what sites she wanted to see in his lovely city. Neill stared at him for a long moment.

"It's awfully cold in here. Might we continue this in the lounge?" She smiled at him.

"Only few more questions. How long are you thinking to stay?"

"Oh three days will be nice. I think three days."

"Have letters?"

Neill handed him her notes of endorsement from Harry Yang and Owen Lattimore. He glanced at them, rose from his chair and told her to stay put. In a few minutes he returned to the interrogation room.

"You must be coming back here three days at this time." He returned her letters and gestured for her to pass through the station. Neill pictured the officer gazing after her as she left the room and reaching for his telephone.

She knew she would be followed in Vladivostok, just as she had been on all her earlier travel in China and Manchukuo. The Chinese and Japanese agents then had practically kept stride with her and didn't try to hide their surveillance. The Russians, however, remained out of sight, and she could never tell to what degree she was under observation. The consequence was that she could take no photos and remained emotionally tense, not a customary feeling for Neill. She said she got used to the feeling, though, and it would serve her well for a time in Moscow.

She went directly to the waterfront, where she caught a glimpse of the new fishing port, still under construction. She speculated that it readily could double as a naval station for heavy cruisers and battleships. It's unclear how she learned it, but she also reported there were cadres of prisoners constructing a major fortification on Russkiy Island, just off shore, and she noted it was armed with extremely large caliber cannons. "The Japanese Imperial Navy will not invade Vladivostok," she wrote in her report.

As she neared the fences enclosing the fishing port construction, she was grabbed by each arm from behind. Two Russian men in business suits turned her around and escorted her forcefully across the paved wharf to an alley between warehouses. It was already dusk.

"You will please be walking calmly with us to exit and car. Thank you."

They drove her back to the processing station at the border, where the customs man took her entry permit, returned her passport and told her she must leave.

"I had permission to tour your city for three days. You said three days."

"Some people are thinking maybe you are too curious. There is nothing more to see. Good-bye, Miss Neill James."

"But I haven't seen most of your sights in Vladivostok."

"You have already being on southeast end of continent, Miss Neill James. Now you can leave and write articles. Remember to obey official signs in Moscow, or you will be having big trouble, maybe just because of curiousness."

Neill hired a driver and made her way to the depot, arranged her ticket exchange and set off for Harbin. She hadn't spent five hours in Russia, but she made it worth the effort.

At the Manchouli border crossing on the Gobi Desert an elderly Russian customs agent took a long time to examine her papers. He told her they knew she was asked to leave Vladivostok and cautioned her to stick close to her Intourist guide. The Intourist official examined the contents of all her luggage, leafed through her books and letters, and wrote in his ledger a list of each of her belongings. It was a lengthy procedure and a long list, as Neill traveled with two cabin trunks and six suitcases of various sizes. She had left her golf clubs, tennis racquet, and climbing gear in Shanghai.

After half a day of processing at the border, she departed for Leningrad and Moscow on the Trans-Siberian Express, an eleven day journey. Our papers were good enough to get her into Russia. Because diplomatic relations had only recently been established, we had not had enough time to set up a network at the new mission in Moscow. Neill would have to fend for herself, find work, try to set up a dead drop outside the embassy—all this because Ambassador Bullitt was at first unsympathetic to our work.

Nonetheless, immediately upon her arrival in Moscow, Neill attempted to land a job at the Consulate General's offices in the Savoy Hotel, which was the temporary home for our diplomatic corps while the new embassy was being readied. They put her off for a few days and then told her only men need apply. Apparently word had gotten around in State. She lodged, as long as she could afford to, at the Metropol, then moved to a boarding house near the Savoy, farther north on Rozhdestvenka.

She was struggling, had no connections, and sent forward only the most euphemistic cables, although she was collecting enormous amounts of observational intelligence, including information about the New York Times columnist Walter Duranty. Duranty was a known Stalinist, and Neill had been alerted to his likely presence in Moscow. Outbound cables were dirt-cheap, but the security was poor and she couldn't find a good location for her dead drop, so she had to be cagey. I realized with alarm that our leash was by now altogether unhooked. We felt it was time to intervene, and I clear cabled her at Moscow's Intourist office:

INTERNATIONAL CABLEGRAM INTOURIST 20APRIL1934:0230PM.

SORRY JOBS FELL THRU WILL WIRE FUNDS STOP FOR ADVICE SEE ALEXANDER WICKSTEED SAVOY LOBBY MON EVE STOP CARE LUCK & CAUTION STOP SHAW

I had asked our friends to help out because we had no contacts on our side, and they were in our debt. The Moscow site was so recently established that we knew of no other American civilians in Moscow aside from Smedley and Duranty, both of whom were subject to our investigations, and at the time we weren't sure where Smedley was. The Brits suggested Professor Wicksteed, who might be able to put Neill in touch with Vivina Grosz.

Just then, Grosz was visiting Moscow as the Baroness Brankaskaya, for whatever reasons we weren't privy to. We knew the Soviets had abandoned the days of the week, and the meeting would only seem more innocuous by openly specifying the day. We also were aware that she would be watched anyway.

Wicksteed, an elderly English teacher in laborer's attire who was on the faculty of Moscow's Institute for Foreign Languages, told Neill to return to the Savoy the following afternoon. He would introduce her to Baroness Brankaskaya and the two women could talk privately in the lounge.

Neill was prompt and recorded the conversation verbatim. The transcriptions she eventually got to us included the only exchange she had with Grosz, labeled here as B.B. They met at the lounge of the Savoy as Wicksteed suggested and sat by a heavily draped window overlooking the intersection with Pushechnaya Street and the old Sophia church. We knew the NKVD had taken over the church for a warehouse. The Baroness laid her silvered purse on the table and silently studied Neill's face.

N.J. Well well, we meet again. Although I must say I would never have recognized you.

B.B. You would not have recognized me, Miss James, because we have just received a first introduction, luckily by the estimable Mr. Wicksteed. He well knows how to bring together people with convergent interests.

N.J. I see. Well, Baroness, *my* interests are being thwarted. I don't seem to be able to land a temporary position without an extended visa and I can't get a longer stay visa without a job.

B.B. Yes, it is a common problem here. The usual solution is to arrive with sponsorship and a clear agreement for work. You apparently had insufficient assurance of a position?

N.J. Oh I've been put off by the embassy and our Mr. Bullitt. They say only men need apply. It appears that would be against the law here. I'm still pestering them, though.

B.B. Your recognition of the Soviet Union last November meant that the diplomatic mission here is U.S. territory, and only U.S. law applies, not Soviet law. The ambassador's staff might be wrong but they are legal.

N.J. I would feel terrible if I had to leave before I got a good chance to do my work. I believe there must be work here to do, even for a stenographer with but little Russian.

[long pause; BB studying the Sophia Church]

B.B. Indeed there is much to be done, and we can help one another in that regard. But you will either run out of money or run out of time, unless you find gainful employment. I can give you introductions, but you must make your own case, and you must remember that Intourist will not and cannot help. I will give you an introduction letter for Mr. Wicksteed's Director. Maybe you can teach Japanese?

N.J. That would be most helpful and very kind of you. I will be sure to follow up that lead. I also am annoyed that I can find nobody who knows the whereabouts of my countrywoman, whom I came here hoping to meet.

B.B. That woman has departed for the United States. I do not know when she will return, but because of pending editorial matters it's nearly certain that she will do so. Perhaps by then someone in your legation will be able to make contact with her. Or your paths might cross elsewhere–you both travel about so much. In the meantime, you might enjoy an evening at the Visiting Writers' center. My acquaintance Sonja Kuczinski will be an important person for you to meet, both in your search for a position, as she knows many people here, and in making a future contact with the American woman you have missed. I will leave an invitation and door ticket for you. But be mindful that Sonja has deepest ties to this government and loyalties so exclusive that caution is the watchword in all dealings with her, public and private.

She got paper from a waiter and wrote a brief letter to the Institute for Foreign Languages, recommending Neill to teach Japanese. Then she gave Neill an envelope containing a stub ticket and an invitation inscribed Writers' Solidarity Center Reception for Visiting Dignitaries. Without another word Baroness Brankaskaya picked up her purse and walked into the lobby to join Wicksteed, as if she had taken a short visit to the powder room.

Neill knew she was incapable of teaching Japanese, but she valued the gesture. She went to the writers' gathering at the Solidarity Center a few nights later. It was an unusually warm spring evening in Moscow. She left her fur coat in her room and dressed as a Komsomolka, a revolutionary peasant girl from the Youth League. Resembling a flamenco dancer without earrings, she wore a blue work shirt over an ankle-length, colorful skirt, and she tied a red scarf around her throat. Her bobbed hair was tucked under an engineer's cap. She wrote proudly to Jane about her costume, but the double irony of it escaped her, as the Komsomolka were famously frustrated in their quest for equality with men, and in the mid-Thirties they still had little official or social power in Soviet society, despite their political radicalism.

Her long cable to Jane describing the party suggested to me that the visiting writers took her get-up to be a satirical statement and complimented her on her cleverness. Back on M Street, we breathed a sigh of relief.

Neill and Sonja Kuczinski had a private conversation in the lounge. They shared gossip about Käthe Kollwitz. Kuczinski said a journalist named Johnson had been visiting from Shanghai and he seemed to know Agnes Smedley. The Baroness had suggested that a note of introduction from Sonja Kuczinski to Mr. Johnson might help Neill gain access to Smedley, if ever they both returned to China. Kuczinski pressed a small envelope into Neill's hand as they were saying farewells.

It would be some years later when we discovered that Mr. Johnson actually was Richard Sorge, the mastermind of the most important espionage ring in the German-Soviet-Japan-U.S. theatre. Neill returned to her room and sealed the envelope inside the lining of her cabin trunk, just as Mackenzie Young had taught her to do, and that might have saved her life.

I knew she was at loose ends when I saw the cables to her sister, Jane. She had stopped writing letters and relied exclusively on telegrams, because from Moscow it cost mere pennies to wire a message of some length to the U.S. We intercepted many cables, the majority from Neill to Jane, who had married Lieutenant Loomis and was then living as a housewife in the military residential compound at Shanghai, just north of the French Concession. Neill bragged about her rich social life in Moscow, although apparently there were no lovers, or she chose not to disclose any liaisons, and bitterly complained about her unemployment.

The exchange of cables that foretold of Neill's downfall was sent just days before her arrest:

INTERNATIONAL CABLEGRAM INTOURIST 11JUNE1934:0930AM.

DEAREST JANEY IM FEDUP WITH HUMID SMELLY AIR POVERTY & NVRENDING SEARCH FOR WORK STOP HAVE TRIED AT SOCIETY FOR CULTURAL RELATIONS AMERICAN DEPT BUT NO LS VISA KILLED JOB OFFER STOP AM AT WITS END STOP WENT TO BALLET LAST NITE SAW IRINA BARANOVA 15 YEARS OLD & GORGEOUS STOP SHOPPING REMAINS DISMAL NO LUX GOODS STOCKINGS COSMETICS BUT GOOD SOUVENIRS STOP HAVE SENT YOU DOLLS STOP MORE NEWS SOON ALL LOVE NEILL

Jane replied later the same day:

USE TOURISM BACKGROUND TRAVEL WORK EVERYWHERE MEANS JOBS STOP TRY AGENCIES BUREAUS COMPANIES STOP FRANK PROMOTED WE ARE OFF TO SINGAPORE TO CELEBRATE STOP LOVE JANE.

Neill either forgot Baroness Brankaskaya's warning about Intourist or she might have had in mind becoming a mole. In either case, and possibly because of her sister's suggestion, she ignored what we had told her about NKVD's penetration of Intourist and promptly applied for the position of English language liaison at the Intourist Moscow Bureau. Her application was politely received, and the desk officer told her she would be contacted within a week.

The best we can surmise is that she was taken into custody on or about Wednesday, July 4th. The irony of arresting her on Independence Day apparently was not lost on the NKVD. At her first interrogation she was congratulated for representing a nation that was born in revolution. She was accused, but not charged, of overstaying her visa and committing economic crimes against the State, both punishable by up to twenty years in prison. She was interrogated only one more time, and she stuck to her story of being a business woman wandering around the globe for fun and adventure.

We of course immediately got the embassy on her situation. I knew there was something amiss as soon as word came from the Brits that Vivina Grosz notified them Neill had either left Moscow or disappeared. The cables had ceased, and shortly Jane Loomis wired me with concerns about her sister's safety, saying she had not heard from Neill in a suspiciously long time. I assured her the Ambassador personally was making inquiries.

But there were Soviet denials and delays. Neill it seems initially had given a false name, telling them she was Mae Foster, and they had one of her passports, the Foster one, and luckily it was not very well made. Neill eventually told the interrogators she knew she had overstayed her visa and therefore feared for her safety, and she believed someone had planted the false passport on her out of spite but she had to use it because it had favorable dates. She suggested it could have been a Chinese or Japanese guard at one of the difficult border crossings she had made. They kept her waiting, and nobody came to see her.

She had been taken to Lubyanka, just a short walk from her room at the boarding house but another world in living conditions. That gloomy monolith, a city block in size, contained thousands of cells, none with windows and all dimly lit day and night, stone-cold and furnished only with metal cot, washbasin, bedpan, and low table. The floors were a thick parquet of oak and chestnut, as the structure originally had been the headquarters of Russia's largest insurance firm. Now it was a warren of suffering and total isolation. There was no way we could penetrate it.

The more recently installed walls were reinforced and sound-proofed, so prisoners had to contend with the crushing absence of voices, traffic noises and bird calls. All that could be heard was fading sounds of heels clicking on the parquet. Like thousands before her, Neill soon began to sing songs to herself, and she recited aloud every poem she could remember, every prayer, joke, vaudeville skit and radio advertisement. The food was bad and scant. She had two feedings each day, always the same soup of root vegetables and kale with a chunk of black bread. She exercised daily in her cell, but she later would say her greatest agonies were that she had no news from outside and she could not see the daylight and the stars at night.

Official forms slowly moved back and forth, meetings were held, and diplomats hinted at possible exchanges and compensations, but nothing happened until the middle of September, when the League of Nations invited the Soviet Union into membership. We now know the Moscow government accepted the invitation the same day it was offered, the 15th. And with considerable pressure from Washington, a strong majority of the League voted on September 18 in favor of adding the Soviet Union. Senate Republicans, praising old Henry Cabot Lodge, crowed that the event confirmed the wisdom of the U.S. boycott of the League a decade and a half earlier, but the President's people saw it as a move toward greater international stability and American security.

Whether it influenced decisions about political prisoners and detainees—of which Neill was one, since she hadn't been tried or convicted of anything—remains a matter for historians to answer. It is evident, though, that before the end of September Neill was moved out of Lubyanka and set up in a minimum security farm near Leningrad.

With a much improved diet and access to the outdoors and magazines to read, Neill's health and attitude almost immediately returned to their usual robustness, and she began to gain hope for her repatriation. It didn't take long. In her debriefing, she described her exit from Leningrad as "a lark." She was told one early winter morning to report to an office near the entrance gate of the compound. She was to take with her any personal items she had in her room. She gathered up her toiletries and a few changes of clothing, stuffed them into the barrack bag she had been given when she left Moscow, donned a heavy wool sweater and prisoner jacket, and headed for what she expected would be a hearing or another relocation.

The guard, a high-ranking officer Neill described as "a bald, worn out Colonel or Brigadier on his way down the ladder," told her she was being released. Her belongings from the Moscow rooming house had been shipped out of the country. She might pick them up in Helsinki's central police station. She could take her barrack bag and the winter sweater and jacket she had been issued by the prison, but that was all. He handed her an envelope and told her she would have one opportunity to leave with no further repercussions, and this was it.

Neill walked through the gate and didn't stop until she reached a settlement of Ingrian Finns at a crossroads half a kilometer from the prison. There she examined the contents of the envelope. It contained her two remaining passports in her name, implying that she might use whichever one suited her purposes, her letter of recommendation from Baroness Brankaskaya, two cables from her sister Jane which had been intercepted after Neill's arrest, and $32.00 U.S. The money was all she had on hand when she was arrested, most of it from our paymaster.

She reckoned with her situation. She had enough money for transport out of the Soviet Union but it was useless, as it was forbidden to exchange dollars for rubles. It was October in northwestern Russia and she was 4,500 miles from the nearest shore of her home country. She had no food, no maps, little knowledge of the Russian language, and for the coming cold she had only a wool sweater and prisoner's coat.

As was her intrepid habit, she decided to trust in her luck. She would walk until she came to a train station and see what happened once she arrived. She headed southwest, toward the sea, and she hadn't traveled more than two kilometers when she encountered a main rail line. She decided to follow the track southward on a parallel road, and two or three kilometers further on she found a small station and platform. There was no ticket office in the waiting room, but half a dozen people milled around, apparently waiting for a train. Neill turned her eye on a young man wearing boots that might have been English. He grinned broadly when he saw her looking at him, and she turned her eyes aside, looked his way again and then smiled demurely. Neill removed her grey prisoner's tunic and placed it across her lap.

When the youth approached her, she greeted him in her primitive French. He raised both his shoulders in a shrug and she made an expression as if to say "too bad" and gestured for him to sit beside her. He said something in Russian, and Neill made the same shoulder shrug. He pulled out his train ticket and pointed to Viipuri, his destination. Neill began rifling through her bag, as if to hunt for her ticket. Then she pantomimed a moment of panic, then anger, then dejection, as she came up empty-handed. She opened her coin purse and showed him it was empty. She had lost her ticket and couldn't buy another.

Her pantomime of near hysteria went on until she gestured she would like to exchange her tunic for his ticket. He shook his head No, but he opened his wallet and pulled out some rubles. Neill couldn't tell how much he was offering, but she knew she would have to look ashamed, grateful, and aroused at the same time.

When the Viipuri train from Leningrad arrived, Neill had three hundred rubles and she had gotten rid of her prisoner's coat. The youth was very pleased with himself for having saved a pretty French woman from destitution and having acquired a symbol of counterrevolutionary resistance, which was very fashionable among young White Russians. He had chosen to avoid Neill on the trip to the border port. Her luck had held.

At Viipuri, she had to confront two problems. She would be examined by exit customs officers at the border, which was early in the next leg of her travel. More immediately, she was desperately hungry and had no idea where to find food. The conductor on the Viipuri train had failed to ask Neill for her ticket, so she arrived with her rubles intact. To maximize the purchase value of her cash she needed to avoid any official store or restaurant. Perhaps, she reasoned, the Helsinki train would have a dining car that was Finnish. Perhaps she wouldn't be asked for a ticket on board. Would they insist that she convert her rubles at the border? In that case, she would have almost nothing.

As long as the train was in Karelia, the dining car would accept rubles. Neill ordered a full meal but spent cautiously. The train stopped in the middle of a vast wetland where a few shacks had been set up near the tracks.

After half an hour, a Russian uniformed officer entered her compartment and asked every passenger for papers. Neill handed over the passport with the Moscow visa stamp. The officer asked her what was her business in the Soviet Union, and she said tourist. He scowled as he studied her passport and then asked if she had any letters. She wondered if she had made a mistake to hide Sonja Kuczinski's referral note in her trunk, for it might help her now. All she had were cables from Jane and Baroness Brankaskaya's letter of introduction to Sonja. She didn't want to implicate Jane if things went badly again, so she handed the Baroness's letter to the officer. He examined it and, still scowling, returned her papers and left the compartment. Neill watched out the window as the train soon moved away from the shacks and picked up speed on its way to Helsinki.

Neill got off at Pasila Station, mistaking it for the Central Railway hub. That was a lucky error because across the square from the depot was a squat, wooden building with a Western Union sign. Neill spent three dollars of her American money to cable me that she had arrived in Helsinki. I wired her back immediately and sent three months pay. I told her how to get to the American consular legation at the Stockmann Building in the central Kluuvi District. It was a couple of kilometers by taxi, and she now could well afford the transportation. I also told her she had executed her contractual duties in fine fashion and her obligation was entirely satisfied.

An aide to Minister Albright took care of her immediate needs. Lodging was in very short supply, but there was a renovated mansion in the diplomatic section that was being used to house visiting dignitaries, so they put her up there for a few weeks while she decided where to go next.

I was frankly of mixed feelings about undertaking another contract with Neill. While the quality of her intelligence work was valuable and strikingly thorough and marked by courage, there always were problems involving finances and personal relationships, and she grandly overestimated her ability to learn languages and took too many unnecessary risks. After conferring with my superior, Captain Puleston, I decided to give Neill some time to recover her balance and show us what she saw for her future.

I made the long journey to Helsinki for Neill's debriefing. She looked vibrant, if a bit gaunt for all the adversity she had endured in the previous several months. We met daily at the legation. There was a pleasant patio overlooking a park, and we often sat in the morning sunshine over coffee and sweet rolls and talked about her experiences and observations in Russia. She had a sharp memory and an eye and ear for the telling detail.

She said Sonja Kuczinski had looked pregnant, despite her elegant evening gown. And Vivina Grosz was unrecognizable as Baroness Brankaskaya because she had changed the color of her eyes from blue to brown, the brown eyes of Bhuma Singh Sharma, and she wore a hat that covered her hair. She did not remove her gloves when they met. There were other Americans being held at Lubyanka, but Neill could not discover who they were. We concluded they were Ford Motor workers caught in the NKVD dragnet of foreigners, many of whom never came out. Neill was one of the fortunate few to be liberated by a brief crack in the international tensions, or a change of Stalin's mood.

Before returning to Washington, I asked Neill to write in the greatest detail as much as she could recall of her sojourn, starting from Honolulu. I suggested that, cleaned up for security review, she might have a spellbinding memoir or autobiography. I was thinking of future cover for her. She rather liked the idea of writing something more public than intelligence reports and more substantive than IPR book reviews or advertising copy. She said an artist friend had invited her to stay at her home in Denmark, which would be an ideal opportunity to write her memoir, and she thought she might travel around Scandinavia for awhile and then rest indefinitely in Denmark.

We were focused on several new initiatives, and I lost track of Neill for a few months. She came to my attention later in the spring when I saw a report from our man in China, Major Bill Wooten. The progress report said Wooten was being assisted by Jane Loomis. He was setting up a ring, posing as an ex-Marine officer turned businessman, and Loomis and her husband helped Wooten make contacts in the Chinese sector. I was beginning to rethink and regret my decision to allow Neill to drift, when just then a letter came in from her, a long personal history of the intervening four months.

She had wandered around the Baltics, she said, traveling as far south as Danzig, where she visited with Sonja and her husband. Sonja was known there as Ruth Werner and was about to give birth, to a son it later turned out. Some of us wondered if the child's father could have been Sorge, as he was known to seduce every attractive woman he came across. Neill said they quarreled, she and Sonja, after Neill turned down an offer to gather information for her. She then had asked for Neill to return her letter of introduction to Sorge, and Neill was thankful that she had hidden it away and could safely say she no longer had it.

They had talked amicably afterward, however, about Smedley's health, Neill recalling what she had read about the neurasthenia and depression episodes. Sonja seemed deeply committed to Smedley's well-being and success, and Neill reminded her that she longed to meet the radical writer, now more than ever. In the end, they embraced at the wharf in Gdynia seaport at Neill's departure.

With improved weather, Neill headed up to Rovaniemi on the border of Finnish Lapland. She toured the city for a few days and explored the north as far as Inari, well above the Arctic Circle, before returning south through Stockholm, Gothenburg, and Copenhagen. She breezily commented that along the way she had met up with Geraldine Sartain again, and the two of them had later settled in at the home of the Danish friend, from where she was writing her letter.

At this point, Neill was hard at work assembling her notes into what she hoped would be an autobiography. She observed that, at not yet 35 years of age, she might be thought too young to publish an autobiography. Her statement reflected a recent habit of telling people she was born in 1901. We knew her official birth date then as 03 January 1899, but I later concluded she actually was born in 1895. In any case, she eventually gave up on the idea of an autobiography and the following year strenuously blamed the aborted work on us for restricting what she could say.

Her letter hinted that she was in financial trouble again and soon might be seeking work. I wrote back immediately and encouraged her to contact me if she were interested in resuming our professional relationship. I heard nothing from Neill for the next six months. Then I received the following night letter.

NEXTDAYTELEX NEW YORK NEW YORK 18MAR1936:215PM

SEEKING WORK BUT HAVE CONDITIONS STOP LIVING IN NYC FUNDS ALL GONE REPLY TO HOTEL PIERRE STOP NEILL

I cabled her to meet me at our New York Section for a conference. She swept into the room and made a theatrical pirouette, her fur coat oddly out of place in those depression times. But she looked fit and sleek, and her hair had grown and now surrounded her face in swooping waves. I had not seen her since Helsinki, and in that year she seemed to have become more flamboyant and glamorous and yet oddly unsure of herself. She was no longer ready to take on anything but had contingencies to present. She wanted to negotiate any assignment she might be offered.

"I can't take on just any old thing in any location on the damned planet," she said.

"I receive my marching orders and have to find ways to get the work done," I replied. "I don't have any choice in what comes to my desk."

"Now I'll just bet you and your bosses decide together what programs and plans y'all put into action, and you're the same rank as the Director, so you should have considerable say."

"My captaincy was a temporary promotion, Neill. But your point is well taken. On the other hand, once a plan has been approved, we are obligated to do the work. My options are limited to the who, when, and details of the how of getting the work done. Within those confines I can offer you prior discussion of any future assignment. You also could suggest work, since you've been in this business long enough to know what might be worthwhile."

"Okay. That is satisfactory. And what do I call you now, Commander?"

"Shaw will do."

"I have another condition. I need better cover if I am to do covert work. This business of phony passports and fake occupations is just too stressful to continue. I need something reasonable and stable, something that fits me, like the journalists I've known. Gerry has never been troubled by the sorts of interrogations and doubts that come my way when we're on assignment. She's never been imprisoned. I want better cover. Surely we can think of something."

"Obviously, Neill, you've been thinking about this for some time. Any ideas?"

"I very much enjoyed writing my book, my memoir, last year. I don't think it's good enough yet to sell, because by omitting all the secrets it can't be terribly interesting to an average reader. But I've been everywhere, and I'm thinking, what if I was to write a travel book and then take the cover of travel book author? I think I could write travel adventures for women. Most travel books are written for men, for businessmen who actually are going to the places in the books, so they're long on sightseeing and hotels and short on excitement and adventure. I think travel adventures written by a woman for women readers who do not intend to travel or cannot travel would be very marketable."

I wish I could claim that the idea was entirely mine, but it was mostly hers and it became her ambition. "I can see some advantages," I replied. "You collect large amounts of information for us on assignment, and some of the same sorts of information can be perfectly useful in a travel book, if the classified aspects are removed. A travel writer under contract with a major American publisher would get nearly *carte blanche* crossing almost any border in the world. It's actually done often, but usually it's an established author who gets recruited for intelligence work, not the other way around. But we'll see what we can do."

"I've even thought of a title, *The Petticoat Vagabond.* What do you think of that?"

"I suppose it would be up to an editor and publisher. But I wonder if you know how intense the work of a book writer is."

"I can do anything I put my mind to, Shaw. I'm not the least afraid of the demand for hard labor."

"And how would you feel about a requirement that anything you write for publication be screened by the agency first?"

"I would have to think on that for a spell. I just don't know, and right now I don't know who to ask for advice."

A week later I received a note under The Pierre Hotel letterhead. It simply said, "Shaw, thank you for meeting with me. I like the travel writer idea and am ready to go to work. Cordially, Neill."

VIII

Maxwell Perkins

> The great interest in publishing is to take on an author at the start, or reasonably near it, and then to publish not this book and that, but the whole author.
>
> —Maxwell Perkins, letter to Ernest Hemingway, Oct 14, 1930

Miss James's literary career was not long by Scribner's standards, nor of high achievement by any measure, although she did a dashed lot of work in the nine years during which we published her. She wrote five books, most of them full length and none of which took her much more than a year to write. It appears that there was no rewriting before submitting her mss, and there was very little editing, because under the circumstances, I kerbed my instincts to counter her demands, while keeping my editorial advice to a minimum. Nine years, from her first in 1937 until *Dust* came out in 1946, and none of the five did more than 3,200 copies. Still, we made back our investments on each and enough more to keep her on the list through the War.

Our relationship with Miss James started at an inconvenient time. Most grievous to me was that we were losing Tom Wolfe, and he would be gone from Scribner's and me by the end of the year to Edward Aswell at Harpers. If he had been surer of his own talent and did not worry about the need for our editorial practicalities and the needs of the marketplace and just accepted those as necessary accessories, like barnacles on a whale's hide, well, there would not have been such a falling out with us.

I also just had learned Ernest's new novel was done, or all but done, and in need only of his usual rewrite, and I had seen him off on a liner from the New York wharves to his first view of the Spanish Civil War, where he was going to be together with Martha Gellhorn and getting himself in God knows what sort of dangerous situations, both in the fighting and with Gellhorn. Then he came back to New York and expressed doubts about his novel, because it was small and wanted expansion. And so we had to go to work to make a new one and ended selling the short one, and it turned out to be very popular. But, as I had thought, it was not a critical success.

Then after Ernest's wrestling bout with Eastman in my office, he was off again to Spain. Just at that time he was going around punching almost everybody he imagined had insulted him, and he and Scott were at each other's throats, emotionally at least, occasioned I think mostly by their mutual admiration and jealousies.

All the while, Scott was bogged down and deeply in debt, both to the company and to me personally, for I had lent him considerable sums just to keep him in food and shelter and in hopes that it might keep him writing. We needed him to stay at work.

Besides, or seemingly beneath, but of equal weight to these personal and editorial concerns—the Tom Wolfe letter being foremost among my burdens—I had become a Director of the firm, which meant Charles relied on me more and more for business operations. It was a devastating economic time in which to be running a complex company like a publishing house, which in fact is a factory engaged in producing that ultimately intangible product, good literature. We were staying alive, but barely.

Into this milieu in early January 1937 came a note from an agent I hadn't previously known, a Mr. Stein, saying he had an extraordinary writer of women's adventure-travel books and asking if we might consider taking her on for a volume about her recent trekking around the globe. The concept and framework for his writer's book were completed, he said, and all the research had been done, and it only lacked the narrative, which he assured me could be done within a few months, as his writer was prodigiously productive. I told him we always wish first to see a rather substantial sample of the work and previous writings and to get to know the author before accepting a contract. It was my belief that we could as well judge the talent behind a future work by meeting the author as by reading his work. That statement, of course, was poorly conceived, as Mr. Stein immediately said he would have Miss James come to see me in short order to finalize the arrangement.

At the time, women's literature was enjoying unprecedented popularity, and we had nothing in nonfiction of a practical bent about adventure travel; consequently, this contact seemed providential and, contrary to my usual caution, I agreed to take the writer on if—and only if—she would pass muster in a personal interview with me. We settled contingently on an advance of five hundred and a completion date of June 30, 1937. The advance was more than I had wished to give, but the deadline was quite unexpectedly short of what I had thought reasonable—any new writer's agent would have asked at the beginning of negotiations for two years or more. Stein said he would ask Miss James to contact me directly to arrange a conference regarding her outline for the book.

She wrote me from the Hotel Madison Square, barely half a mile from my office. Her first letter conveyed the gist of what she and Stein had in mind: " . . . to put in book form the story of my adventures twice around the world and up and down the longitudes–a petticoat vagabond who not only saw the world alone, but made the world pay for the seeing." The idea of a single woman traveling alone and making her way by whatever work she might be able to pick up as she went had fresh appeal, especially in those times. I wrote back to say the following Monday, January 25, would be convenient.

She pranced into my office dressed like a bluestocking heiress. I immediately had the feeling that she had no idea what we were about but wanted to be in control of the situation. After the usual pleasantries when one first meets someone, she took me aback with her questions, as she seemed offended by my appearance.

"Why Mr. Perkins, you somewhat favor Mr. Dorsey, but for your hat. Why are you wearing that hat?" We were still standing, she four inches shorter than I and looking up at me with her chin thrust out and her intense, dark eyes staring at my hat. She had on a brimmed cloche.

"I am very fond of this hat, Miss James," I replied, "and I think it rather old fashioned for a person to hold to the rule that a man's hat can be worn only out of doors or on stage, except of course in case of the demands of religious proprieties." I liked the way I looked in a hat, and I had read my Edward Bernays, who said a hat is symbolic of authority and independence, and as I was constantly in company of authors, I needed a symbolic prop that conveyed the authority of my office and my independence from the business demands of publishing. But she persisted, as if I had been called to account for something she was taking as an insult.

"But a person gets the strong impression you are about to leave out the door," she said. I also found her deep-Southern accent more than a little charming, and I confess that that annoyed me, too.

"Precisely so," I replied. "It often comes in handy to be thought on your way to another appointment, if one wished to limit the time spent with someone in one's office. Not that this is the case now, as indeed it is not. I am at your disposal for as long as we need for getting to know one another and possibly setting up an agenda for the full production of your book. However, observe that it is not considered ill-mannered for you to keep your hat on your head indoors." I hoped that would be the last of the hat discussion.

"Perhaps, then, Mr. Perkins, your hat is a way for you to learn what it feels like to be a woman."

It was mighty difficult to tell whether she was mocking me for being womanish in my masculine attire or she was crediting me with favoring a woman's viewpoint. I replied to her, "I have often said that what all men lack, and need, is to know what it is to be a woman for a while, so that we can more sympathetically understand the world from a woman's viewpoint." I wished not to discuss the deeper reason for my hat–the plain fact that I disliked the shape of my head, wide and flat at the back, and the look of my hair, with its widow's point and unruliness, but I liked very much my appearance in a fedora, which covered over both those flaws.

"I daresay it always has been that only women understand women," she rejoined, and with that she pulled off her velour cloche and shook her head theatrically, letting fly a cloud of wavy black hair.

She thanked me for the offer of an advance and said she thought it sufficient for her to sign a contract with us without further delay.

"Before talking about a contract, perhaps we should first discuss your intended project. Tell me about your recent travels, Miss James, if you will. I should like to have a sense of the sort of adventures that will form the backbone of the book you plan."

"When I began my vagabond life, at age nineteen," she began, "I had never been farther from my roots on a Mississippi plantation than New Orleans. That was when I took a position, following college, for the War Department. They sent me out West, where I was second in command to the base commanders at two military forts until the War was won. I climbed the highest peaks in the Cascade Mountains, ran a women's fashion emporium and organized veterans groups throughout that region. I moved on to Hawaii, where I was the first to sell ice all across the islands, and while there I scaled their fearsome volcanic peaks. I picked up an executive job at the American embassy in Tokyo and traveled across all of Asia, from China to the steppe of Mongolia."

She looked past me, perhaps at some remembered distant vista in one of those places, and continued. "By taking work here and there as a translator or salesgirl, or sometimes as public affairs writer or embassy staff, I made my way twice 'round the world. I traveled on steamships and pedicabs and primitive trains, or I hoofed it in hiking gear, and everywhere I went I mixed with the natives–the poor and the aristocrats and the outcasts. I got booted out of Russia and was practically shipwrecked in the Caribbean, and I sold newspapers across Costa Rica and later in New Zealand. For a while I was a writer and office manager for the Institute for Pacific Relations and ran their convention in Banff, Canada."

I interrupted her monologue to ask if she had a portfolio she could show me. She said of course she did and would bring it by forthwith. It was, however, when she said that her pace of adventuring had taken its toll on her and she wished to concentrate on taking up a more settled writer's life— well, she appealed to the more compassionate impulse that can overrule good editorial judgment, and I began to hear her story with growing sympathy.

She concluded her self-revelation by saying she had more ideas for future projects. "Mr. Perkins, I must admit that the siren song of further unknown adventures beyond the horizon will always lure me to travels. I wish to become more settled, but there will be plenty more books in the future, too."

In truth, she looked much too fashionable for a rough country adventurer, but she clearly was vigorous and had the bearing of a predator animal about to pounce. I called my secretary to bring up our standard contract, and I told Miss James I had been persuaded by the merits of her concept.

We got down to work and in half an hour had a schedule of milestones laid out for her first book, which she insisted be titled "Petticoat Vagabond: Up and Down the World." It was her invention she said, and she was determined to keep it. I thought the petticoat part a bit too feminine, considering that her obvious aim was to tell the world about her exploits as an adventurer on mountain peaks and remote jungles and wildernesses. And I objected to vagabond as being too close to tramp and all that would entail. To soften the disjuncture, I recommended that she consider angling her story toward giving readers—most of whom would be women in search of a diversion which also would offer solutions to the financial demands of travel, and, like her, mature or approaching such an age—the benefit of her personal example.

She bristled when I mentioned age, but she said she would try to make the case for world travel with no other means for support than one's wits and industry. But she was adamant about both petticoat and vagabond.

She was to give me an outline in two weeks. After that time, I received a note of apology from Miss James, explaining that she had suffered a "severe grip" and promising to bring me the blocked schedule within a few days. It would commence a pattern for the rest of our association—her overly ambitious commitments followed by delays and excuses based usually on illness, which always ended with the heroic production of a manuscript in record time under sometimes the most arduous conditions.

I sent her a book, Winifred Hawkridge Dixon's auto travel "Westward Hoboes," and asked her opinion, to give inspiration and to see if she was a sound critic. Alas, Miss James was not a perceptive reader.

By early April, she wrote to tell me she was making good progress, had been married in the interim and living in New Haven, and was planning new travels, this time a return through Lapland. Within a month she had sent 25,000 words and by the end of May another 20,000. She sent along a clipping from the Honolulu newspaper in one of her June communications to me. The item suggested to me that perhaps the term "petticoat vagabond" might not have originated within Miss James but somewhere else.

When asked about it, she insisted the item was written by a friend who was referring to her forthcoming book. We decided not to pursue it with Stein, but I have since wondered if she actually had borrowed the petticoat vagabond idea. She would later attack another celebrity traveler who used the same moniker, asking us to pursue charges—I think she rattled off plagiarism and copyright infringement among other perceived aggrievements. With Miss James, it seemed, things were always a bit uncertain, and her accountings sometimes looked quite contrived.

Consider the marriage, for example. She said the wedding had taken place March 13 at Riverside Church, but I knew that this was not possible, as on the Saturday in question the Riverside Church was entirely given over to a massive celebration of the Federal Theater Project work done by Hallie Flanagan under the WPA. I know this because Scribner's helped sponsor the event. The new husband, moreover, was supposed to have been some sort of Scottish lord with a peerage history, yet they were living, apparently, in a modest apartment on Chapel Street in New Haven, although she did not change her address from Northeast 83rd in Manhattan to Chapel Street until November. I had not taken her for the marrying sort anyway, as there was something in her manner that told me she preferred the company of women to that of men, although she enjoyed flirting with anybody.

Her manuscript for the first book was drafted by the end of July, and her departure for Lapland, originally slated for August 13, was delayed for some weeks, presumably because of something involving her husband's work, whatever that could have been, or perhaps it was something else she hadn't told me about. She had managed, however, to get herself onto the radio, WOR, as the Petticoat Vagabond, marketing her book even before we had finished making up the proofs. I had rushed her to complete it but now was having a devil of a time getting her book into the fall list, rushed up myself by her vigorous personal and unauthorized advertising campaign.

Before she left for her Lapland sojourn, Miss James wrote to say she would like to see me and would be down at nine-thirty Monday, August 23. She would be arriving early on the Banker's Express, as had become her usual practice. Over coffee at my desk, we exchanged pleasantries, and I asked her how I could help.

"It would greatly ease my mind if I had a letter from you saying I will be on assignment with my sister for my next book. Sometimes I come across a lowdown stinker at a border crossing, and even my U.S. passport and my record of embassy work aren't enough to cut through a bad temper."

"It was my understanding, Miss James, that you will be traveling alone on your adventures." I was taken aback.

"Oh, she'll be just assisting me with logistical things, probably only as far as Helsinki. She's not a rough and ready sort, but she loves the ocean crossings. This time she'll be heading on from Finland to join her husband in China, while I'll be sledding through blizzards and sleeping on the hard floor of camp shacks in the far north."

"We don't give attestations unless the author actually is under contract to produce a piece of work. I don't think we are in a position to skirt that policy, which, after all, is only truthful and logical."

"Well, how about just saying something like I'm one of your authors? That should buy me something."

I resisted the urge to feel damned by faint praise and told her we would provide her a supportable letter, and we did.

I cannot recall who used the term "connected with Neill's work," when describing Mrs. Loomis's involvement, but it probably was Mr. Stein. As it was important for us to be clear and certain about authorship of all books we published and all stories that ran in Scribner's magazine, I contacted Mr. Stein to discuss the role of Mrs. Loomis and the new husband, who was called Harold C.K. Campbell. We met at my table in Cherio's.

Mr. Stein was a compact man of over middle age, with a large brush mustache whose color indicated that he might once have had reddish hair, although now it all was mostly a granitic grey. He asked how it troubled us about Mrs. Loomis and Mr. Campbell. I explained our concern by describing a situation where there had been a problem. "It turned out," I said, when concluding my story, "that the putative author, Doctor B., was discovered not only to be not the author of previous works he had claimed but also was not the person who actually put pen to paper in this instance. It was his amanuensis and lover, Cheryl Pennington, who did the composing, and she was perfectly happy to write his books and stay out of the limelight, considering the nature of their romantic relationship. We had a devil of a time extricating them and ourselves from that dustup."

"I assure you, Mr. Perkins," he replied, "the book you are publishing is Neill James's story, and every word in the manuscript came from her hand, and she in fact traveled where she says she did. Her forthcoming work also will be hers and hers alone. As her agent, I strive to be sure all is on the up and up. I personally guarantee you that nobody else, not even her sister, does any of the composing."

"And Mr. Campbell? Mind you we are not interested in knowing about him outside of our contractual relationship with Miss James, but it would be useful for us to understand what the nature of his involvement in producing a manuscript might be." I wished to protect Scribner's from becoming obligated to redundant editorship—beyond our own professional needs—which might greatly dilute the effectiveness of the work. Mr. Stein suddenly called to mind a freshman boy at Harvard who interned with us at *The Advocate* when I was on the Board my senior year.

He gazed for a few moments at his martini glass. "Mr. Perkins, all I can tell you about Mr. Campbell is what you might already have read in the newspapers. He seems interested in and supportive of his wife's work, but I do the guiding and representing of my authors. When you receive a piece of Miss James's—Mrs. Campbell's—writing, you can be confident it is genuinely her work."

It never became a problem for us, although there were times when I wondered how she could produce such vast quantities of adequate narrative in such short periods. I also wondered how a writer as ordinary as Neill James had learned what became a mature style and confident ease with her subject by the time of her third book, the Ainu one.

The second book was a vividly described tale of adventure above the Arctic Circle in which Miss James lassoed reindeer at a Lapp rodeo and slept in primitive lodges and drove a hide sled pulled by a reindeer all night and day across icy wastelands. She left before the launch of "Up and Down the World," her first, and a month after it came out she sent a postcard to our advertising department giving ideas for marketing the second book, yet to be proposed. She also wrote to us, excitedly describing a fishing expedition on the Arctic Ocean and marveling at the Scandinavian landscapes. She further wanted to know how "Up and Down the World" was selling.

Shortly after the postcards from Lapland, a request from Mr. Stein came in, seeking another $500 advance, this to be toward Miss James's second book. Apparently she had completed her Lapland travels much more quickly than I was led to believe. I informed him by letter that our practice was to not make an advance to an author before a previous advance had been paid for by sales of the previous book, which in the case of *Petticoat Vagabond: Up and Down the World* had not yet occurred. I also told him our policy is to examine the materials and ideas, or a completed prospectus, for a book before we would consider an advance, and we have heard no good reason why the policy should be changed for Miss James.

We sent the advance to Stein after Miss James gave us a chapter outline for "Petticoat Vagabond Among the Nomads," the title we finally settled on. She submitted her mss the middle of February 1939, after several delays because of her anemia and colds. The other celebrity lecturer, who had tried to use the Petticoat Vagabond title, agreed at my insistence to drop the Petticoat and changed hers to Lady Vagabond. Miss James was unhappy but resigned herself to a long campaign to best her competitor in the public estimation and on the lecture circuits.

We budgeted for a modest advertising campaign, and Miss James spoke on the radio about her travels, mostly broadcast on a New Haven station, and lectured around the region. We got good reviews in the Times and Post and New Haven Register, and an article or two came out in Oregon and Honolulu. But after a few months there were no further sales of *Among the Nomads*. The initial run of 2,500 never sold out, and orders stopped within two years of its July 1939 publication. This, in spite of Miss James's diligent and, may I say, somewhat eccentric efforts to market the book. She became deadly serious about sales, for by the time she had completed the draft manuscript of *Petticoat Vagabond Among the Nomads*, she had begun to think of herself as quite a successful author, although she insisted on the title of authoress.

Her idea was to stimulate sales by traveling in a reindeer-powered sled from northern Maine across the upper United States to Portland, Oregon. She had brought home from her sojourn a *pulkka*, which is the Lapp reindeer sleigh, and she searched high and low for a compliant and available reindeer in North America, even trying to persuade the Canadian government to lend her one. None was to be found, except for the one at the Sportsman Show then about to open in Manhattan, and the organizer would not part with it. Miss James cabled me pleading for us to acquire the reindeer and said if we could not she would settle for anything with four legs and antlers.

I tried like thunder to dissuade her, but she had seen a newspaper item about the Show which said there also would be a moose trained to halter. That report put her after any captive moose in the region and she eventually found one at a Maine wildlife farm whose owner agreed to lease the beast to her for a week, which was not one tenth of the time she would need to travel by sleigh across the country, if ever a moose could make it. Miss James decided an event for the press at the Rockefeller Center, starring herself and the moose and pulkka, might be enough of a draw, and that is what she did, after persuading the moose trainer to allow it to be photographed with her in exchange for a small fee.

Late that summer and just after we had had a favorable Times review of the Nomads book, I received word from her that she was vacationing near Saratoga at Indian Lake's Camp Driftwood, which I had thought was being converted to a military training post of some sort. But she said she had been swimming and climbing in the Adirondacks—in training, she called it—and hatching plans for her next book.

She was at work on a novel for juveniles about a Lapp family, and as the youth market was very dependable and profitable, even in those hard times, we encouraged her to go ahead with it. She also announced that her next travels would be around the various islands of Britain and to Spitsbergen and Iceland, which did not seem good choices to write about, in view of the concept we were using and our long-standing principle of thematic unity, and we advised her to drop at least the latter two. We never heard another word about the Atlantic islands travel.

I received nothing further from or about her until the following February, when her mss for the juvenile novel *White Reindeer* came in. It was a lovely little story, and we immediately went about putting it into production for the fall list of 1940. It might have been the only piece she wrote that was the real thing for her, until the latter section of *Dust*.

She telephoned me around the first of May to say she was headed to China and Mongolia and asked if we could provide a document attesting to her being there on assignment for a new book. I said we could if we had an outline or prospectus, and within two days she had submitted a prospectus for a book on her next travels, which omitted China and Mongolia entirely but would center on explorations among the Ainu people of far northern Japan. It sounded a wonderfully attractive sojourn, and we willingly drafted the testamentary for her to take to the State Department for her papers.

She wrote me in a panic on May 6, because she needed the document immediately for her visa application and entry permits, and the letter needed to specify her travel was for a book "on the Orient" and, to be timely, had to be delivered the same day to the passport office in New York. As the State Department's offices were just across Fifth Avenue from us, I ran it over to them myself before going off to Cherio's that afternoon, and then I wondered what sort of fool I might look to be.

The errand must have been important and not falsely urgent, because she spent precious little time among the Ainu, and there was a dashed lot more time spent and risk to herself in her travels among the combatants in Korea, Manchukuo, Mongolia, and China. I wondered then if she was back in the employ of the Department of State. Hemingway later mentioned her to me, when he was relating his astonishment at hearing about the American left-wing propagandist Agnes Smedley and Miss James together behind Japanese lines with the Long March fighters in northern China.

He said, "Who lets these women into these places? They aren't much as fighters or reporters, and they aren't much as women. They don't make very good men, either."

I surmised that he was irritated by their presence, but things were not going well for Ernest and Martha at the time, as she was getting the better reports and reviews and he was not finding the adventures he had hoped to find. I asked Miss James upon her return if she had run across Ernest, and she said they had spent a pleasant afternoon at a lobby bar in Hong Kong.

She wrote about those travels, oddly never mentioning Ernest or Smedley, and her book had a very workmanlike quality, full of good facts and exotic locations, and she had a suitcase full of good photographs for us to use. I suspected something was not quite right, however, because she told us she was no longer represented by Mr. Stein. At first she was to represent herself and trust us to do right by her with the contract, as many of my actual first-rate authors did. We gave her the same advance as before, five hundred, but without Mr. Stein I was unsure just what to expect now, as she was still naïve about the publishing world. As a test of my theory, I recommended an agent to her, but shortly she wrote to say she would be represented instead by Matson and Duggin, by Harold Matson personally. They never contacted us, however, and she ably did the contracts herself.

I also was troubled because she began to question charges against sales for her corrections in proofs, challenging amounts as small as a few dollars. I was not much concerned about the money and quickly forgave her the charges, but my concern was for the fact that there was any questioning at all. We had been exceedingly fair with her, and there were no outward indications that she was in need of additional money. Her chagrin about the business functions of our relationship continued to the end.

We had the Ainu book wrapped up by the end of the year, scheduled for the spring launch. I had barely finished the proofs when she asked for another letter from Scribner's, this time attesting to her plan to write a book on new travels, which would be around South America. She said the note was "just window dressing" for the State Department, and she said her intention was not to tour the South American continental coast as she was telling the passport people but to explore Patagonia. She gave a writer's wink and nod, but I felt terribly awkward being asked to write a possibly misleading document to the Department of State. On the other hand, I never was quite certain where she was going when off on one of her adventures. I chose not to be captious with her about it and did the letter.

Then, three months later I was pressured again to write for her because of a delay in her departure. She finally sent a thank-you note to me in August from Mexico City, where she was on some sort of travel around Mexico. She said it was to study the Otomí Indians, but she already had been among them and had finished by the time she reconnected with us, although she was scheduled to be away for another five months.

In fact she never returned, and I never saw her again. She was horribly injured in a mountain climbing accident and then re-injured in another accident involving a second Mexican volcano, and afterward decided to recuperate in a remote native village, to which she devoted a lengthy section of her last book, that section being perhaps her best writing of all.

It was wartime, of course, and her books did not sell well. She was unhappy with our advertising, the reviews (or lack of them), and the sales numbers. But she was determined to continue writing, at least for the nonce. I sent her books to read while she was in the American hospital in Mexico City, and we corresponded occasionally through 1943. She cancelled speaking tours and, once arrived in her village, settled down to finishing *Dust on My Heart*, hoping to deliver it by mid-year 1944.

Because of her various injuries and longer than expected recovery, the mss did not come in completely until spring the next year, and the contract was signed July 28, 1945. She had asked Mr. Stein to represent her for it, and it was he who sent it, but I never did see him and it was dashed difficult to get through to him except by post.

It was her best travel book, and I concluded from the affectionate tone of it she might have been more attracted to Mexico than to all the other places she had traveled to. Over time, it began to appear that she had decided to settle there for good. I do not know what happened to Mr. Campbell, and Mr. Stein seemed to have pulled up stakes, too, as there was no response from his office or home when we tried to contact him, after the advance was sent out and the book was launched. I surmised he went into another line of work or retired altogether and was no longer interested in Miss James's book publicity.

She had plans for other books, both juvenilia and travel, but we had no further editorial contact from her after *Dust on My Heart* was published. I occasionally wondered what really had happened to her in Mexico. A note or two from her came in to Distribution, each time asking for copies of her books. From time to time I would receive a letter from a fan requesting one or another of her books, but by 1946 all news of her personal situation had come to a full stop.

IX

Vernon Shaw

> I galloped in the high wind's face, this way then that,
> And wandered gazing all over the North.
>
> —Liu Hsiang, "Yüan Yu" [the distant journey]

It was a blunder on my part, compounded by Neill's excesses of self-promotion. Somehow, DNI Anderson and quite possibly Admiral Leahy learned about my author, whose marketing escapades could hardly have evaded detection by their staff. And Admiral Anderson already was not happy about her flirtations with the line between the overt and the covert. I was told they thought her mission to battle zones in northern China and Mongolia both risked too much, as it was redundant with other intelligence gathering activities there, and overstepped her capabilities, especially in light of her earlier arrest in Moscow. It also could have been that Ernest Hemingway or someone close to him complained to people very high in government. I suspect it was partly due to this reason, because I learned from the materials she asked me to safeguard that she did not get along particularly well with him when they met, although Neill and Smedley apparently hit it off.

In any case, in the middle of her anthropology study of the Ainu people, I was reassigned to a short tour of sea duty and afterward to what was then called Analysis and Integration, basically sitting alone in a small office writing policy recommendations based on our field work. I was replaced by the agent who had helped me edit her first two books, Harold Campbell. He initially had a crush on Neill but the feeling was apparently unreciprocated, although they claimed to have gotten married. If they did, it was a marriage of convenience only, for the sake of the work, and I wasn't invited to the ceremony.

Campbell also had been known as Hugh Putterman and before that as Vasily Minkoff, and at one time he had been an engineer of some sort. Neill invented all the other names for him that were posted in their wedding announcement, and forever afterward among outsiders he was known as Harold Child—or sometimes Charles—Kineal Scott McGregor Campbell. He seemed to be between jobs, as I later heard he became an important figure in the OSS. But for over three years we three worked out of the Chapel Street apartment in New Haven, sometimes four and even five days a week, while Neill wrote her books. The two of them kept separate apartments in New York, and Neill maintained a busy speaking schedule.

I of course had other duties. But, little by little over the years, Neill had become central to my own career advancement. I admit to having succumbed to a fascination with her drive and energy and a boldness that bordered on recklessness, as well as her unrepentant ambition, but those would be ordinary without her detachment, which worked against her ambitions. I never had a romantic attraction to her, despite her vigor and stylish glamour, and of course I knew what a one-way street it always was between her and men. I was a dedicated bachelor in any case, and my commitment always had been to my work.

Likewise, Neill was entirely dedicated to doing the best job possible of her work, technically, but she seemed also to be devoted to nothing greater than herself. Sometimes it was as if she was acting alone on a stage, and all that existed was the artifice of the audience and techniques of the drama. I saw her as a lonely person, despite her affectionate letters to her sister and her eagerness to meet new people. There was no denying that she was effective at gathering a certain kind of strategic information, and between us we contributed far more to intelligence findings than her part-time employment would normally produce. She irritated everyone up the line, but usually I had little difficulty getting approval to keep her on the payroll and send her on chancy missions. I probably pushed her too hard.

This, of course, was before Campbell came into the picture. It remains unclear to me where the marriage idea came from, but it could have been the event that was intended to ease him into the role as her eventual director. Somebody else might have been reading her cables and field reports before I sent them forward, but my superiors knew she had become something of a public figure, with her lecturing and radio broadcasts as the Petticoat Vagabond. And yet she didn't have the sophistication to carry it off gracefully and thereby warrant their trust, in view of that exposure. They cautioned me on two occasions about her cover, and she and I had conferences about ways we might minimize any publicity not necessary for her writing work and ways to reassure my superiors of her value to our mission. She agreed to keep a low profile but continued to prove she could not resist becoming chummy with one controversial figure after another and with the press.

She might have known something was up, or she had been so chastened by her imprisonment in Russia that she was being uncharacteristically cautious. Whatever it was, before she left for Japan in 1940 she asked me for a particular favor. The conversation began when I reminded her to communicate from Asia only as Kokio.

"I expect that," she said, "but I want to be certain that my reports go to you and only you."

"Why would that be of concern to you, Neill?"

"My granny didn't raise any fools. Somebody let me or helped me get trapped by the NKVD when I went to the Intourist people in Moscow. The State Department folks should have been keeping an eye out to help steer me away from traps, and y'all must have seen my cables to my sister. I can't believe it was our own people, but I didn't get into that trouble all by myself."

"I'm afraid," I said, "I wasn't watchful enough. I entrusted too much to our friends across the pond, and, yes, your traffic was copied and shared around. That was mainly because at the time you were the whole game in Moscow. As you know, State hadn't even set up their attachés in the legation."

"Well." She paused and frowned. "Now that that's out in the open, what are we going to do? I'm about to leave for a goddamned war zone."

"The best I can guarantee, Neill, is that your communications always will come to me first, and there will be no intercepts or interference by our people before I get a look. Beyond that I can make no guarantees. This is an inherently risky business, risky not only because the other side might uncover you but also risky because our own politics always are in flux. If we were in a chess game, Neill, I might be a pawn and you wouldn't even be on the board. But because you can reveal what this pawn is up to, you have value and will be under constant surveillance by any player in control of any piece. That's the way it's played."

"Couldn't you be a rook or bishop? Really, Shaw, you know I welcome any sort of challenge and I am not afraid of treachery. I will happily climb the tallest mountains, ride the wildest horses, swim raging rivers and eat almost anything on the planet consumed by man. I have passed ten days and nights on a filthy rail coach crossing all of Asia with a bunch of coughing peasants and not complained about it. I have slept on the dirt floor of stinking huts above the Arctic Circle and confronted Japanese border guards behind the lines and ridden a sand-wagon through dust storms in Mongolia, because that has been my job. But I feel undercut and insecure if I think my own organization does not trust me and cannot be trusted to be straight with me."

In this deep way, she still was an ingénue. I told her that as long as I was between her and the rest of the agency she had no cause for worry. I trusted her, because by then, for me, she was predictable. And I hoped she still could trust me. She admitted I had never let her down, even though in Lubyanka more often than once she thought I had abandoned her. But when we met up in Helsinki she felt relieved to learn of my efforts to arrange her release. She seemed satisfied with that, yet my sense persisted that she believed something was up.

In May 1940 Neill left for Japan. We provisioned her with two passports—one for her entry into Harbin as Mae Foster—before starting her research among the Ainu. As the exact conditions were not known at the time, State helped us with some diplomatic papers for her. We had heard a rumor of Soviet troops in the Harbin area, presumably to augment the Red Army in their part of the counter-offensive against the Japanese. It was part of the Soviet Operation *Zet*, all very secret but penetrated accidentally by naive journalists and shared with State. They asked us to find out if it was true and to assess how the Red Army was situated, one of those happy convergent interests for them and us.

Neill eagerly agreed to a week of looking around, and it went without incident. She confirmed the rumor, which led to our finding that the Japanese would be stalled in the northern provinces and to our prediction that they would open an offensive elsewhere in the south. Nearly a year afterward, Hemingway belatedly would make the same observation, although his Gellhorn knew earlier.

The other passport was for her author travel under her own name, perfectly legitimate and with visas for her work on Hokkaido and her travels through Manchukuo, Mongolia, and all of northern China. We hoped to get her as far south as Shanxi so she could link up with the Reds at Yanan.

To facilitate her travels and research among the Ainu, we put her in touch with Dr. Neil Gordon Munro, the Scot who was the foremost scientific expert on them and who lived in their territory for most of his life. He was elderly when she met him, nearing 80, but she charmed him and got him to help her considerably with introductions, documentary sources, and tips about what to expect in her research. She later took credit for much that he told her, but her work as an amateur anthropologist helped popularize the Ainu culture and her book included excellent candid photographs of the people and their ways of living.

She was on the assignment from May of 1940 until the end of April the following year. Her work among the Ainu lasted scarcely more than a month, and I was relieved of my responsibilities for her while she was still in Hokkaido. Campbell sent her a cable at Sapporo to inform her that she would be reporting to him thereafter. She wired him back immediately, acknowledging the change and asking where she could contact me. It would be some time before she was told of my location on board ship, and eventually she managed to get a letter through to me that escaped Campbell's scrutiny.

> *Dear Shaw, apparently you were correct about being a pawn. I am devastated, but will continue to do my duty, and I will do my damnedest to see that our paths cross again.*
>
> *Finished up the Hairy Ainu research and have gone on to some highly interesting treks through Korea, Manchukuo and elsewhere, but I still don't know if it all is deemed successful.*
>
> *When I return to 1175 Chapel, I shall write a brilliant book about these travels, and I only wish that you could be there to take over as my literary agent. You actually are a knight, only they don't know it.*
>
> *Neill*

Her signature had a little circle for the dot over the *i*, a touch that gave me a melancholy feeling. Several years later, I restored myself to the role of Neill's literary agent as A. Monte Stein. But that was after we had both ended our work for ONI and after her terrible injuries in Mexico. At that time, just after she left the American Hospital in Mexico City, she asked me to take several cartons of papers from her apartment in New York for safekeeping. As she hadn't embargoed them from my viewing, I spent a month of humid summer nights in my study reading the files she had collected.

There were detailed, unclassified notes from her travels, work papers we had accumulated for her books, and some letters, mainly between Neill and her sister Jane but also correspondence with Mr. Perkins at Scribner's and with various lovers and acquaintances she'd met on her travels. It was fascinating reading, none of it very surprising, but through it I learned what had happened to her after she went to Hokkaido. I say the contents of her files weren't surprising, but that is only because stories had circulated around the agency about her radio broadcasts and the official consternation over them.

After Hokkaido, Neill had returned to Tokyo to arrange her travel to Korea and Manchukuo. It was late summer and Tokyo was baking hot and tense with the run-up to an expansion of the war. The second Sino-Japanese war had been on for three years. The Japanese were stalled in the north and concentrating their efforts on a new front south of Chungking.

People in Tokyo tried to ignore the war, but it intruded into daily lives because rationing was widespread and the city was a Petri dish for propaganda programs. Patriotism, frugality, national values, and even family discipline were manipulated by information campaigns carried out in newspapers, street demonstrations, and radio broadcasts. In this cauldron of nationalistic fervor, Neill waited for her papers to be delivered to the legation.

As usual, when her movement is restricted she becomes restless and agitated. Her notes tell of her scheme to sell her books in Asia. She reasoned that the Japanese were highly literate and avid readers, and she harbored hopes that her books would be translated into Japanese and Chinese, the way Smedley's books had been translated into Chinese and Russian and German.

Through acquaintances she'd made in the streets of Tsukiji and Ginza, Neill arranged to meet the station manager of radio station JOAK, which she mistakenly thought was Japan's equivalent to WOR in New York. I am reluctant to consider what she would have done if she had known JOAK was in fact the center of Japan's international propaganda war. It had become the main instrument for changing hearts and minds to favor Japan and dampen opposition to Japan's aggression throughout Asia. She enthusiastically made a forty-five minute broadcast based on her Petticoat Vagabond lectures, with praise for the Ainu people and appreciation for the arts, architecture, and industry of Japan. She thought the broadcast would go out to the population of eastern Honshu and perhaps be sent to Osaka and Kyoto to the southwest. But in reality, it went to affiliate stations in China for rebroadcast and was reprinted in international newspapers. Within a few days reports of her broadcast were on the desk of the DNI in Washington.

Before word of caution could reach her from Campbell, she was off to Korea, where she made another broadcast on Seoul radio station JODK. The station manager had sought her out and invited her to address the population of occupied Korea with tales of her travels, which she eagerly did. When Campbell caught up with her by secure cable, she was in Harbin filing Kokio's reports. He told her politely that she was to cease making statements on Japanese radio. She replied by saying she saw no reason why, as the U.S. recently had renewed its full trade agreement with Japan, and she was merely strengthening the public perception of her as a famed travel writer.

His next cable was a direct order.

ONITELEXDC 12AUG40 1100GMT SECRETRESTRICTED

PER DNI ABSOLUTELY NO BROADCASTS PERMITTED STOP STAY ON
ASSGT SEND NEXT REPORTS FROM HSINKING STOP TARTAN

Neill had to reply by unsecured wire, because she was in Seoul.

MOCNEC TELEX 12AUG40 1420GMT KEIJO CHOSEN

REFUSE TO GIVE UP FREE SPEECH RIGHTS STOP MATTER
PERSONAL NOT OFFICIAL STOP NO MALE WOULD BE SO TREATED
STOP NEILL

With that she proceeded by train south to Hsinking, where the same offer
of air time was made by the colonial radio station, MTYC, and again she
gave her Petticoat Vagabond speech. It is unclear how Campbell reacted to
her cable and to her MTYC broadcast, but Neill noted upon her return to
New Haven that there had been a "powwow" in Washington about her
conduct on her last mission. She said her innate good luck rescued her
once again, as Campbell congratulated her for taking aggressive steps to
strengthen her cover as travel writer, and nobody mentioned the
broadcasts again. She wrote, "Still, I expect that somebody's
unmentionables are in a knot over all this, and I might hear about it in
disguised form in the future."

Her path home was intended to take her to Yanan, where the Red Army
was supposed to have been headquartered. But by the time she made
Hsinking, the New Fourth Army massacre had occurred, and the
Communist troops and leaders had repaired to Anhui, near the Yangtze
River. She had already gathered an enormous amount of good intelligence
across Hokkaido, Korea, Manchukuo, and the Mongolian northeastern
border region. Hemingway had arrived behind the lines around that time,
and somebody had told him Agnes Smedley and Neill James had been
through earlier. He had dismissed the report as somebody's fantasy, and he
was right.

Neill's travel had taken nearly eight months, and she was tiring of the
endless hours on trains and buses and the constant surveillance by
Japanese soldiers and police. Besides, Campbell now had her headed in the
wrong direction.

Her patience ran out at the front at Wubao crossing, where
international non-belligerents with good papers were supposed to be
allowed to move freely between the Japanese-held territory and what was
left of China. Nationalist troops blocked her passage, claiming that the
route ahead was too dangerous for civilian travel. She protested and

demanded to see the commandant. Newswire accounts in Asia reported that an American travel writer had been detained at the front and after a physical confrontation was accused by Chiang's commandant of violating security rules and infringing on national sovereignty.

Under the headline "Petticoat Hijacking: American Author Bests KMT Troops," an article in the *Hong Kong Daily Press*, reprinted in the *Shanghai Mercury*, described how Neill had snatched a rifle from a Chinese guard and thrown it on the ground in front of the ranking officer, whereupon she was restrained and dragged into an interrogation facility. She refused to cooperate and demanded that the U.S. Head of Mission be put on the telephone, screaming that this was "a lowdown kidnapping" and a "crime that will become headline news across the globe."

So vigorous was her objection to being held that the troops quickly realized they were inviting trouble they didn't need by keeping her at Wubao. In short order, they forcibly put her on a train to the coast, rounded up the few stringers who plied the border crossing area, and threatened them or attempted to bribe them not to report the story. Upon arrival in Shanghai, Neill looked up the Naval Attaché, who gave her safe passage down the coast. She ended up in Hong Kong, feeling dejected, frustrated, and in need of a few weeks of relaxation.

She stayed at the Gloucester Hotel on Pedder Street near the waterfront. Smedley was then recuperating at a home in the hills out of the city, but she often came to the tea pavilion at the Gloucester with friends in the afternoon. Smedley was hard to miss. She talked so loudly in public that people often thought she was in a fight or drunk, both of which would occasionally be true. The teas when Smedley was present were more like raucous parties at an enlisted men's club than polite tete-a-tetes. The pavilion was on the fifth floor, and Neill often walked down the two flights of white marble stairs from her room on the seventh to see who was at tea, with an eye to joining or eavesdropping on one celebrity or another. If nobody of importance was there, she would take the brass elevator to the ground floor and go out in search of an interesting bar.

In a letter to her sister Jane, Neill described her first and only encounter with Smedley. Neill's field notes also were essential to piecing together the encounter. By that time, we thought Smedley was a legitimate target for us because of her rumored connection with Sorge. He seemed to control all the intelligence flowing among Germany, Japan, and Russia, and it began to seem inevitable that the U.S. would be drawn into the war.

When she heard Smedley's tea party in progress, Neill went back to her room and changed into a silk cheongsam, then returned and presented herself as an admirer of Smedley's writing. She told Smedley she particularly was fascinated by *Daughter of Earth*, and she complimented her on her article about Chu Teh, which had been published in *New Frontiers*. Neill had studied both in preparation for her most recent assignment. That, however, was all she had ever read of Smedley's abundant writing, and she hoped there would be no references to any of her other work.

Smedley turned to her five companions—two Chinese women, another woman who sounded English, a tall silent man, and a rotund American woman smoking a cigar and holding the leash of a gibbon that squatted next to her, eating fruit—and said, "Who is this?"

"I'm Mrs. Neill James Campbell. I write travel books, maybe you've heard of the Petticoat Vagabond series? I write as Neill James."

The tall man rose from his chair, as did the English-sounding woman, but Smedley, the large American with the gibbon and the two Chinese women remained seated. "Never heard of you," Smedley said, looking away and blowing blue smoke out her nostrils.

"Mr. Maxwell Perkins is my editor at Scribner's. I'm sure you've heard of him. He also edits Mr. Fitzgerald and Mr. Hemingway."

"Oh, Hemingway. Jesus, that one. I saw him last night at Tumbler's and thought I might vomit." Her voice had a smoker's growl, and she had the ashen skin and lank hair of somebody who has been ill. But her energy seemed to crackle, there was strength and resoluteness in the symmetrical face, and her slate-blue eyes were both sad and penetrating.

"His new book, *Whom the Bells Toll For*, is a best-seller," Neill said. "It's hard to ignore his notoriety, and having never met him, I am most interested in your opinion of him."

"Get the title right first, dear, even if you've never seen the book. Otherwise, you might suffer a broken nose. If you don't offend him immediately, you can prepare yourself for some bullying, a slagheap of lies and a pinch on the ass. He's the biggest goddamned boor I've met in all of Asia, and I've probably seen every last one of them, from every nation."

"I hear he doesn't handle his drink very well."

"He was roaring drunk before sundown when I last saw him. People were hanging on his every word or else scattering like scared cats. They were the smart ones, the ones who just avoided him. He tried to seduce me, unsuccessfully I hasten to add. Look, dear, there are lots of interesting people in Hong Kong for you to meet. You don't have to waste your time chasing down a money-grubbing bourgeois opportunist who pretends to be just another suffering proletarian."

Smedley was getting aroused by her own rhetoric. "As a writer, everything he creates sounds like the script of a bad movie. His people behave like children, his men are clichés, his women are all two-dimensional pinups. He knows nothing about women and treats them like shit. See how many he kills in his stories, or leaves abandoned and crying. He knows nothing about politics. Mostly it's ignoramuses who buy his books, and unfortunately the world has no lack of ignoramuses. Everyone fawns over him because he's famous and rich. And glib. No. You want to talk to other writers, I'll introduce you, but you'll have to find that guy on your own."

"I would be most grateful to meet your writer friends, Miss Smedley." By now all were seated and smiling politely. New introductions were made and fresh drinks and cakes were ordered. The two Chinese women were Rosie Tan and Eva Hotung, comrades of Smedley in propaganda work for the Chinese Red Cross. The fat American woman with the small ape was introduced as Mickey Hahn from Chicago. The other woman was Hilda Selwyn-Clark, whose home Smedley was using as a sanatorium. The tall silent man was introduced as Mr. Boxer. We took his presence as a sign that the Brits had become aggressively interested in Smedley again, though he could have been there because of Miss Hahn.

"Erskine Caldwell is here," Smedley replied. "He might come by for tea one of these days. You should meet my girl, Hsiao Hung, a brilliant novelist. She's terribly ill, and I don't know how long she's good for this world, but her mentor, Lu Hsun, calls her the finest writer of imagination in China."

"What a coincidence! I have met Lu Hsun, at the Institute of Pacific Relations, where I worked for three years." That was all Neill had to say, and Smedley instantly warmed up. She asked Neill to come sit next to her, and using their first names they began swapping tales of world travel and the Chinese intelligencia and literati. Neill made up much of her stories but created them around the basic facts of her travels and the intellectuals she actually had met at the IPR conferences.

When the gathering ended, Smedley told Neill they would get in touch with her about a meeting or possible dinner with some of the writers then in Hong Kong. A week later Neill received a note from Hilda Selwyn-Clark. It said that, with regrets, Agnes Smedley had left on the sixth of May for the United States and it was not known when she would be returning. In the meantime, following the Smedley meeting Neill went out every day to prowl along Queen's Road and Des Voeux Road in search of Ernest Hemingway. She carried with her a letter she had received from Mr. Perkins, telling her to give his best regards to any Scribner's writers she might encounter in her travels.

The *Hong Kong Telegraph* had reported that Hemingway also would soon be returning to the United States, so Neill devoted most of her free time to finding him, perhaps hoping some of his glamour might rub off and his fame might help her writing career. She knew he was supposed to be out gathering intelligence, whether for the Soviets or America it was unclear, but news reports described him as enjoying a fast social life in Hong Kong while his wife was off in the jungles reporting from the southern front. Neill hoped to run into him before dusk, because she wanted him to be sober enough to remember her afterward.

Neill's field notes said she found him at the street level bar of the Hotel Hong Kong. It was only just after lunch but he already was causing a stir. She saw a broad-shouldered man with a black mustache surrounded by a small crowd. At their feet a man was lying on his back, his face streaming blood. She knew from photographs the man with the mustache must be the famous novelist.

Hemingway growled something and the bloody man turned onto all fours, moaned, and crawled away from the group. He got up and skulked out of the bar. Hemingway rubbed his left fist. All the onlookers backed away except for two men, who guided him back to their table by the street windows. Some newspapers, a nearly empty gin bottle, several plates with scraps of food, and many glasses littered the table. Neill sat at a table nearby and watched and listened.

Hemingway said the guy had it coming, and one of the others, a short, burly man, agreed. "What do you think, Rewi?" Hemingway asked.

The man called Rewi sat taller than the other two. His hair was shaved on the sides so his head appeared to taper to a peak like a mountain, and he had a long, arched nose. He spoke with a Scottish or New Zealander accent. "Just another British busybody. But the easiest way to beat them, Ernest, is to tell them lies. We always lie to them, and they go away."

Hemingway grunted, and Neill saw her opening. She guessed that the man called Rewi was Rewi Alley, an immigrant from Christchurch and the Chinese Communist Party member who recently created thousands of tiny cooperative factories throughout China's rural areas. She had seen some of the industrial cooperatives on her recent travels and had learned about Rewi Alley from Agnes Smedley. She approached the men's table.

"Excuse me, Mr. Alley, but I couldn't resist telling you how I admire your small factory system. I saw countless manufacturing cooperatives in the countryside when I passed through Shanxi and Anhui last month. I was told that you were the man behind the idea."

Alley rose from his chair and took her hand. "You have me correct, Madame, but I believe I do not know you."

"Neill James, Sir, travel writer. The Petticoat Vagabond? Maybe you've heard my radio broadcasts."

"How clever, Miss James. This is Mr. Ernest Hemingway and Mr. Morris Cohen."

Cohen grinned with eager interest. Hemingway looked aside and smirked.

"I'm so very pleased to meet you, gentlemen. Mr. Hemingway, I believe you and I share an editor, Mr. Perkins, at Scribner's?"

"You're one of Perkins's girls?" Hemingway suddenly showed interest. He looked Neill up and down approvingly. "Old Max never told me about you. Are you sure Maxwell Perkins is your editor? Not one of his kids in the office?"

"Well, Mr. Hemingway, I just happen to have one of his letters with me, in case you doubt my word." Neill smiled and waited for him to decide whether to look a fool or call her bluff.

He split the difference. "No need. I'm sure he has a henhouse full of beautiful woman writers he keeps from the likes of me. What's the latest news from Max?" He asked Rewi Alley to order a bottle of gin and some fresh glasses and tonic for the gin, and Alley spoke to the waiter in fluent Cantonese.

"He said Mr. Charles Scribner had been away but now has returned to New York. He has sent the advance for my next book to my account, and he doubts that we can finish it before the fall list. Things like that. I'm sorry it doesn't seem like very exciting news, although I am mightily pleased with the encouragement he gives me and with the advance."

Hemingway poured drinks. He asked her what she was writing, and she described her research on the Ainu people. When she told him about her travels through the Northeast China region, he made a boast about his world travels. "I've traveled to more countries and seen more action than all you travelogue writers put together."

"My travels, Mr. Hemingway, are more like expeditions. I'm not a travelogue writer—no hotel ratings, no recommendations for best restaurants. I'm mostly a dirt floor and hiking boots sort. And I daresay I have seen my share of the world's countries."

"That so? Tell you what, Miss James. I'll match you country for country, and for every country you've been to that I haven't, I'll take a drink. And every country I've been to that you haven't actually been in, you'll have the pleasure of taking a swig. Let's say to be in a country means you have to have passed at least one day and night there. That way we'll see who the worldlier traveler is. Scout's honor."

Cohen raised his eyebrows and downed a slug of his gin and tonic. Rewi Alley looked bemused but said nothing.

Neill focused her gaze on Hemingway. "France."

"France, easy. Paris, for years. Biarritz, Marseilles. How about Spain?"

"Spain. Barcelona, September 1927. Germany."

"Germany. Berlin, 1922, 1923. Austria."

Neill lit a cigarette. "Austria. April 1 to 4, 1927." She eyed Hemingway steadily. "Mexico." Neill was fairly certain Hemingway had never been south of the border, except for the Caribbean islands.

Hemingway paused, looked at Cohen and took a swallow of gin. "Burma."

"Burma. Rangoon, Mandalay, December 1926. Ceylon."

"Ceylon. Colombo, 1932," Hemingway lied. "Russia," he lied again.

"Russia, 1934 to 1935. I was held two months at Lubyanka Prison. Finland."

Hemingway took another drink. "Cuba."

Neill took a slow drink from her gin glass. "Egypt."

And so it went for over an hour, Neill taking a drink for every Central African nation Hemingway named, and he taking the penalty when she named Korea and any nation in Scandinavia or in the South Pacific. Alley was keeping score and quietly not counting countries Hemingway claimed, if he was sure it was a lie. When the gin bottle was empty he announced that Neill had been to 64 countries and Hemingway could name 56. They had lied to each other here and there, but she knew she actually was far more traveled than the famous novelist, and she had a sense that he knew it, too.

Hemingway threw some money on the table and stood and stretched. "Give my regards to our friend Max. Boys, let's get to the betting window at the Peninsula."

With that, the three men walked out of the Hotel Hong Kong lobby, and within a few days Hemingway was on a Constellation flying to Manila. Neill wrote that she didn't know whether she liked him or was offended by him. He had great personal magnetism but he also seemed to be dismissive toward her. He appeared both potentially explosive and childishly vulnerable, and Neill found that ambivalence oddly familiar and comforting. She thought he must be a very confused and driven man, but she felt no inspiration and decided not to mention him to Campbell.

In a postcard to Perkins she said she had met Hemingway "behind the lines," but that was all. She later told Perkins they'd had a pleasant afternoon at a Hong Kong bar. She described the incident in detailed travel notes, however, and in a letter to Jane she alluded to it.

1175 Chapel Street
New Haven Connecticut
May 28, 1941

Dearest Jane,

As you can see I am back home and working hard on my "Grass Mansions" book. I tarried too long in Hong Kong but managed to get some early work done while I was recovering from my dreadful travels across the mainland. Hong Kong is a lovely place to recuperate, and I took full advantage of the polo and tennis clubs, the concession golf course and naturally the tea pavilion at my hotel. I drank a bottle of gin with Ernest Hemingway at the lobby bar of Hotel Hong Kong but waited without success for Erskine Caldwell to come by. Climbed some mts across from the island with Baroness Felicitas von Reznicek, the writer I met going into Tokyo last time. She plans to start some sort of international hiking club.

When are you leaving Hawaii? Do come up when you can, and bring Frank if he's free. We'll stay in NYC and there will be plenty of room. It better be soon, because I'm planning a new travel around South America, and I don't know when it will be approved and my papers will be ready. I hope to go out to the Galapagos and all the way down to Patagonia.

The patterns you sent will be perfect. I can make the singlet and blouse right here. Please hold onto the rest of the dolls, as I don't want to have to move them twice. Thanks for being such a big help. Write back soon.

Best Love, Neill

In fact she had tarried too long in Hong Kong, and Campbell tried to mask her absence by relaying her correspondence to Scribner's as if it had originated in New Haven. When she returned to the U.S. she was debriefed and given some time off, which she used for writing her Ainu book, the one she originally had called "Grass Mansions." She vacationed with her sister and brother-in-law on Long Island and continued to work with Campbell in New Haven until her book was ready and she had her new assignment.

She started the process of readying for departure, had a letter from Scribner's and an itinerary, but there was a standoff with the FBI's Special Intelligence Service. They wanted her to report through them to us, and our people saw that as setting a precedent and so resisted the arrangement. SIS had a package from British Intelligence describing her visit with Smedley in Hong Kong. It contained a report from Charles Boxer, who, as their only agent left in the Colony, had moved closer to Smedley than we'd been led to know. Boxer's report said Neill was overly ingratiating and too unguarded with their target. We argued the opposite, noting that we'd been hoodwinked by our cousins and Boxer but had gained Smedley's confidence.

It took nearly three months to sort it out and in the end Neill went off to a new itinerary in Mexico with a reporting line that went through State to us and a side line to the legal attaché. That might have been her undoing, because SIS kept closer watch on our people than we did, and they gave Campbell information that I wouldn't have had and wouldn't have wanted in the old days.

She was dropped in a Mexican village while still recovering from her injuries from her volcano misadventures. She had a little savings, but they gave her no severance, no return travel and not even a letter of appreciation. There was an inquiry, and I was questioned about the years she worked for me, but in the end they supported Campbell's action and closed Neill's personnel file.

I retired from the military as a naval Captain shortly after the inquiry and went to work on my own writings, beginning with the memoir. I also contacted Neill and volunteered to stand as the hidden man-in-the-middle between her and Scribner's for the Mexico book she had planned. She would need somebody to help clean up her affairs in New York and New Haven, and it would minimize suspicions—by Perkins or anyone else—if we finished off her last book as we had done the others. The agency allowed me to return to duty so I might screen the manuscript, because by then Campbell had left for another employer, probably OSS. I did the work by having Neill send me her drafts and moving them along to Scribner's.

It's possible Perkins knew I was the one who really authored the little children's primer. I always wondered if he had it published it as a farewell gift to Neill and me. But he never mentioned any suspicions.

I went down to Jalisco many years later to visit Neill. It was a sentimental journey for certain, but it also was my intention to verify some of the details for my memoir, which I was about to publish. Neill insisted she had never met me and refused to discuss our collaboration. In fact, I hardly recognized her, as she seemed to have gone native. It was as if she had erased an entire layer of her earlier life and had no regret for it or sympathy for anybody who might have been associated with it. All except for her fantasy life as an ex-author.

Something must have happened on her Mexico assignment that tipped the balance and led to her dismissal. It would have been a terrible disappointment for her, but I sensed that she knew her clandestine career was over and at the same time, maybe because of that, her life as a writer also was put in jeopardy.

X

Marguerite Miller

> *Debo cuidar yo mismo aquellas calles*
> *Y de alguna manera decider*
> *Dónde plantar los árboles, de nuevo.*
>
> —Pablo Neruda,
> "Regresó el Caminante" ("The Wanderer Returned")

Neill James came to ground in Ajijic. I'm the one who in the end was ordered to deliver the drop notice, and as far as I know I was her last official contact with the agency. All that, though, happened at the end of her mostly useless assignment to Mexico. I should say stupid, because it could have been more successful if somebody had just done the right advance work.

When she received the job, neither of us knew I would be going along. But before she boarded at Grand Central, I was told to stay right by her side and make sure all went according to plan—the plan that wasn't. In other words, I was sort of a babysitter, and they had no idea what would happen. They flattered me into doing it by saying I was the only one who could keep up with her. Good grief, I was close to retirement age by then, but even though Neill was nearing fifty, she was as energetic and strong as always. They also said it was the right arrangement because we had worked together for Shaw in Spokane and again for a brief stint under Anderson in Hawaii. In any case, she didn't like the sidekick idea, and neither did I, and neither of us knew at the time about the SIS connection. It was a challenge, because we didn't want to offend each other, so we chose to blame the agency. They had their reasons of course, and I felt I had few choices.

We headed to Mexico in the summer of 1942. Her cover was set up as a trip to collect material for a book about the Otomís, a people who everyone failed to consider aren't very widespread around Mexico. I would be her technical advisor, taking advantage I suppose of my early training in paleontology. The Otomí angle was Neill's idea, and she genuinely had a passion to know why their poverty was so persistent. But the ONI assignment called for her to collect any information she could find on maritime movements in Veracruz and on American companies with German connections operating anywhere, particularly along the southern border. No Otomíes there. Not only that: She was expected to get the goods, any goods, on fellow-travelers and suspected Abwehr agents moving through or living in Mexico. She carried a broad portfolio. But she had to steer clear of SIS agents, who always were suspicious of us. I believe that was my intended role, to help her steer clear of them, though at first neither of us knew it. I was just told to keep her out of trouble and out of Mexican jails, and to assist in her work. To this day I'm not sure Campbell ever told her of the side channel arrangement.

For a short while we had a guide and interpreter named Reynaldo. Neill wrote about him in *Dust on My Heart*, though she fudged the story of how she came by him and called him Maurilio. She also made it seem like she was doing Otomí research for much longer than she actually did. That's okay. And she left me out, which also is okay, especially since I had asked her to. She wrote that her Maurilio had been a protégé of Professor Gamio, the most famous of Franz Boaz's Mexican mentees. She said when she and Gamio talked shop about the Otomí he connected her with the kid. That was inaccurate, and in truth the Naval Attaché at the embassy set it up.

Reynaldo wasn't Otomí. He had come up all the way from Mexico City, where he worked in the offices of Ambassador Messersmith. Messersmith knew Manuel Gamio, and Gamio some years earlier had recommended his nephew as a translator for the embassy. It was hard to tell if her book said what it did because of the agency's editing or because of her wish to be taken for an influential researcher. But I favor the second theory, and in that she was partly successful. In fact, she showed a lot of moxie in the field, and her writings about natives, especially on home industries and the cultures of food, were good enough to be quoted by professionals. Her Ainu work eventually was.

Neill and I worked for three weeks collecting data in Otomí camps and villages around Queretaro and Hidalgo. Most of it happened near Ixmiquilpan. Neill would stay in the camps, sleeping on the ground in her Laplander bag and eating the local Indian diet, mostly corn, nopal, chickpeas and pulque. But only when Reynaldo could wangle her an invitation. I chose to stay in good village hotels whenever I could. Otherwise for both of us it was ordinary Mexican fare in a string of ordinary posadas. We moved about mainly by train, hired car and bus. But while I usually hovered in a local bar and observed, she would hike for hours along the rough trails in the high, dry plains to visit a remote village or fiesta site. I'm sure she liked that part. Many of the adventures described in her "Dust" book came from those few times in actual Otomí camps.

I did keep her out of jail once in those early days. She and Reynaldo were hiking to an encampment along a dusty track a dozen kilometers outside of Ixmiquilpan. They rounded a bend and walked right into a band of heavily armed men in shabby uniforms blocking the road. A big man with bandoliers draped across his chest dismounted from his horse and put his face inches from Neill's. She didn't move her feet and later said his breath stank of tobacco and rum. Her Spanish was so poor she couldn't understand his questions. Reynaldo said something, and the man sent him on his way, back to the Barrio. He found me in the cantina where they'd left me hours earlier, and told me the alarming tale.

I went directly to the *alcalde* and complained that one of my scientific colleagues was being detained on her way to see some Otomí friends. We suspected the *federales* had grabbed her and there would be a jurisdictional tug-of-war if the mayor's office tried to help. I suggested that he might need to say Neill is wanted by the municipality for theft of antiquities, and I wrote a note accusing her of pilfering my artifacts. He immediately dispatched an armed police squad to the rescue. When they arrived where Neill had been intercepted, they found her tied up, the government troops making ready to take her to their garrison. They said her papers weren't in order and they believed she was in the country illegally, an old story for Neill. There was a conference, the note was shown, though it's unclear whether any of them could read it. Neill got the idea, though, and she shook free of a soldier's grasp and ran behind the police line. The big man could see it would be more aggravation than it might be worth, so he remounted and led his troops away. Neill arrived in town triumphantly astride the police commander's horse and the next day gave an interview about her adventure to a reporter from the Guanajuato paper.

We couldn't work among the Otomies for long, not just because of Neill's interview but also because things had begun changing fast across Mexico. The George Nicolaus ring had been cracked, but it was like breaking a Fukuruma doll with half a dozen other dolls inside. There were leftover Abwehr agents spreading around the country, particularly in the coastal cities. Several Mexican oil tankers had been torpedoed, and Mexico had just declared war on the Axis. Things were changing fast for the agency, too. The Coordinator of Information had been disbanded, and the President and Mr. Donovan had created the OSS to replace the COI. Nobody seemed to know how intrusive the civilians at the top would be, or what would happen to the military intelligence units, so our people were desperate to have something important from our field work.

We got a secure cable in Queretaro City that put us on the move. We had to go into the coastal areas so Neill could mix with the international set and gather what information she could find. She took to Mexico with a passion she hadn't shown since Hawaii, and we were busy day and night. In Mazatlan she befriended a newspaper editor who introduced her to a German painter. Her new artist friend told her about a group of leftist émigrés recently arrived and bent on thwarting a Nazi plot in Acapulco. We went there but on the way down passed a few days in Guzman and Uruápan and in each of those cities heard stories about the Germans in Acapulco.

But Mexico already had relocated all Germans, phony businessmen and the leftist émigrés alike, from coastal areas to impoundments in the capital, so by the time we arrived at Acapulco all we could get were stories of disrupted plots and intrigues within the German enclave. Some remnants of the Nicolaus ring were said to be sending information to Germany by microdot letters, transmitted through New York. Those stories had value, of course, and Neill recorded them in detail and sent off summaries when we could get to a cipher telex. That wasn't very often, as Mérida and Veracruz had the only secure communications south of Mexico City, and we never made it to Mérida.

From Acapulco we set off for Oaxaca and across the Isthmus to the southeastern border, which was a wild frontier in those days. In Oaxaca, while I was fulfilling our cover at archaeology sites, Neill rubbed shoulders with international visitors. There she identified someone named Rűge, who was said to have agents in Mexico City. She sent that along. She also encountered numerous young ladies who caught her fancy, and more than once I had to interrupt a seduction. I could keep her out of jails but I couldn't keep her away from the fanciest hotels and restaurants and interesting women. Along the way, she dined with Oaxaca City's mayor and chief of police, who toured us around the municipality, and she befriended a Hollywood film crew. She loved the high life when it was available, and when there was none she romanticized her lack of luxuries.

On the way to the southeast there were steamy, insect-ridden days and nights without sleep on an ancient troop train, as we stopped every few hours at remote villages and then creaked along over high passes and through dense jungle and rain forest. Neill relished the adventure and seemed to search for hardships to overcome. She looked theatrical in her explorer's shirt and flight pants, and she seemed constantly aroused. When the train was stalled by a rock slide, she was the first out and up the tracks to survey the damage and help remove the debris. She wandered around every roadside stop, joined the peasants riding atop the train and got the engineer to let her ride in the engine. Her activity finally wore her down, and she had to curb her impulses and get some rest.

We got as far as Minatitlán, at the southern end of Veracruz, before being turned back. The way south was sealed, so we went up through Olmec country. Neill grew impatient with watching boats and listing their numbers. In one of the Tuxlas she argued for us staying on and really becoming archaeologists.

"There's no more to be added, Margie, we might's well just settle in for a time and collect some artifacts for ourselves. There's a growing market for these things in New York." She gave people nicknames, I think to position them socially.

"Veracruz is a target port, Neill. We have work to do there," I said. "They won't be sending us any paychecks here anyway."

"Then let's just stay on for a little bit, enjoy some diversions. We have enough for at least a week."

We stayed on for the week, and Neill filled a crate with sculptures and weavings and sent it ahead to Mexico City. In Veracruz she immersed herself in work, and some pay came in. She learned about sightings of U-boats, listed all the traffic arriving and leaving port, met every European businessman in the city and filled a fat portfolio with notes. But she insisted we put up at the Gran Diligencias and dine where she could be seen.

Then suddenly she got a fancy to climb a volcano.

————

Pico de Orizaba was visible from outside Xalapa. When we went for a weekend in that ambrosial city, the local officer from the Explorers Club of Mexico told us the season was just coming on. It was still too early to attempt the ascent, but soon, soon it would be good, he said.

"Don't expect me to follow you to the top of Mexico," I told Neill.

"You're no fun anymore, Margie. We used to have fun climbing together, didn't we?"

"We never got the same degree of pleasure from scaling volcanoes, and now I'm in decline and get no pleasure at all from it."

"They say it happens to each of us, but I'm going to put it off for as long as I can," she mused. "Anyway, first we have to get our burden to the NA."

We circled back to Mexico City, where we made our reports and deposited the documents and files we had created. The Naval Attaché suggested we take some time off.

The next afternoon we visited with Maurice L. Stafford, the embassy's Consul General and a man we had worked with before.

"If there had been no work to do in Veracruz, we would've been here sooner," Neill told Stafford. "I need some rest and a massage before I meet the Explorers Club." We were chatting at the terrace bar of the San Ángel Inn. She had wanted to stay at the Hotel Genève, but she knew we couldn't afford it, so instead she walked into the marble lobby of the Genève as if she owned it, made directly for the concierge desk and picked up a wad of hotel stationery and some envelopes. Our first night at the San Ángel she wrote a friendly letter to her editor on Genève stationery, and that would be followed shortly by another to him, both intercepted of course, and when Campbell saw her letters he advised her to move to a less luxurious hotel before someone wondered about the source of her wealth. Neill always believed she could easily hoodwink him, and maybe she had been right until then, but her confidence in her own cleverness, if not in his gullibility, would cost her later.

The embassy folks loved to relax at the San Ángel terrace. It had an inspiring view and was shaded from the relentless afternoon sun by a screen of flowering wisteria and a tangle of flame vine that covered the bar's pergola. Laid out on a ridge, the yard opened to the north and west overlooking the sprawling city.

"They were very excited about your request to climb with them," Stafford was saying. "Apologized for not going to Orizaba."

The Consul was a pleasant looking man who wouldn't stand out in a meeting of American business executives, neither young nor old, his freshly cut blond hair going to grey at the temples, and blue eyes that matched his linen suit. He had cultivated the appearance and speech of the proper career bureaucrat. Neill thought of him as fussy and derivative.

"Well, I couldn't not go, even if it has to be Popo instead of the big one" she said. "I'd die if I knew they were going down into that crater and I hadn't at least asked."

She looked toward the bar and a waiter came over. *"Una ginebra, por favor,"* she said. Maurice Stafford was taken with her Mississippi accent. Unfortunately it carried over to her baby Spanish: *"Powah favowah,"* she'd say.

I ordered a paloma. Stafford made a little brushing motion with his hand while almost imperceptibly shaking his head no, and the *mesero* silently retreated to the bar to fetch our drinks.

"Could be risky, you know," Stafford said. "Plan to camp two nights inside the hole, and it's still fuming from the last blow. Not Mount Hood, this one. Nearly 18,000 feet at the rim, active volcano. Rumbles here all the time, felt one just two days ago. And it's scarcely twenty years since the last eruption. Monstrous, lava flowing out and rushing down the slopes into all those pueblos, ash covering the whole country, lots of casualties, massive losses. Don't know why you'd want to go. Wouldn't want you put out of action." He tended toward the agentless speech of the old guard.

Stafford was idly looking away, gazing across the Inn's reflecting pools and palms and over the riot of buildings, traffic, monuments, church spires, cascades of garbage and grey-green hills that stretched beyond to the hazy western rim of the Valley of Mexico. It was as if Neill had handed over her torpor, like an unwanted visitor, to the Consul. She knew I was immune.

"That's what makes it so interesting, Maury. It would hardly be worth the effort if it were just for the view. Margie and I did our homework on it last night. Besides, we're all experienced mountaineers." She meant the Explorers and herself.

Stafford would have detected a familiar self-regard and firmness in Neill's reply. She couldn't resist a challenge like Popo, and he knew she wouldn't be turned aside. Neill looked up to the challenge—still slender and fit at forty-eight, she had an easy, athletic grace of movement and a ruggedness that seemed incongruous with her mascara'd eyes and polished nails. The embassy people were led to think she was forty-two.

"Indeed. Yes, well, we'll get you out to their center tomorrow morning," he said.

He later regretted his promise. The expedition was set to leave Coyoacán long before dawn. His driver had gone missing and he had to drive us there himself. After introducing Neill and me to the Explorers Club team captain, Stafford said goodbye and sped off in the darkness toward the center of the city.

Neill shouldered her pack, picked up a bundle of crampons, rope and ice axe and followed the lead Explorer, Moisés Abrigo, toward a line of waiting sedans and a panel truck. I took no gear, because I wouldn't be staying on the volcano.

Moisés Abrigo looked too young to be the head of scientific expeditions, maybe in his mid-twenties. He spoke fluent English and had the clear, earnest face of a monk. Twenty-eight climbers stowed their gear in the truck, packed themselves by fives and sixes into the half dozen late-model

Fords and Dodges and headed out for Amecameca, a town settled over half a millennium ago and a victim of many eruptions of Popocatépetl and Iztaccíhuatl.

Our caravan traveled sixty kilometers in three hours, and by the time we drove under the arch that marked the entrance to Amecameca's old center, Neill and I were ready for coffee and some breakfast. The town was still mostly asleep, though, and the cars moved on eastward in the chilly semidarkness. The two snow-draped volcanoes loomed ahead of us like white towers of a colossal suspension bridge.

The four climbers in our car tried to speak English so that we would understand them and be interested in talking with them. It was one way they could get the measure of Neill before the ascent. Sitting next to her on the front seat was a slender young woman who had introduced herself as Esperanza López Mateos.

"Have you ever climbed this volcano before?" Neill asked.

"Before I climbing Popo eight times. This is my nine times climbing him," said Esperanza. Popo, I had learned, was the warrior god watching over his princess. When they talked about Iztaccíhuatl, they always said "her."

Neill turned forward and studied the rutted gravel road the caravan was following. It was getting rougher with each passing kilometer, and she could see in the grey dawn light that it would soon dwindle to a rubble-strewn track. Turning to the young men sitting with me in back Neill said, "I suppose y'all have been up before?"

They glanced briefly at one another. "*Claro, sí*, yes," they answered. They chatted to each other rapidly in Spanish, and then one said, "We climb him five, six, twelve . . . all twenty-three times climb him."

Moisés Abrigo said, "One member of our club has been to the caldera one hundred and thirty-five times."

Neill said, "Oh my," and fell silent.

The grey light of dawn seemed to glow in the canyons, even though the sun was still well below the saddle between the two peaks. Drivers switched off headlights as the cars entered an open lot at tree-line. The Explorers packed up four tents and stakes, rope ladders, blankets, bundles of fire wood and provisions for three days and two nights on the mountain. Following the advice of famed mountaineer Otis McAllister, Neill had brought trekking food—raisins and other dried fruits, nuts, chocolate bars, some turkey and chicken sandwiches, two canteens of tomato juice, cubes of hard cheese. She looked apprehensively at the scarce supplies the Explorers had packed, mostly canteens of water, packets of tortillas, coffee and chocolate.

Esperanza spied the critical expression on Neill's face. "Friends think I crazy climbing mountains," she said, "but I go up him on spirit and eat nothing."

Moisés Abrigo explained. "Many climbers cannot eat on Popo. It is the altitude. Food stays in the throat. We think liquids are better."

From out of nowhere, it seemed, fifteen Indian porters appeared. The Indians wore cotton pajamas and rough sandals, and each had a serape draped over his shoulders. They quickly squatted in front of the large packs, strapped on *mecapales* over their head scarves and hoisted the packs off the ground. Leaning forward into the trumplines, they moved silently up the stony grade. At over 13,000 feet it was cold enough for Neill to wear her expedition parka, and she wondered how the porters could possibly summit in such scant clothing. But a few hours later, after a labored climb to 15,500 feet, where the track was entirely on snow and ice, she would exchange the parka for a light balloon-silk windbreaker. By then the Indians had wrapped their sandaled feet in rags.

I was really not feeling well at the altitude, taking in deep breaths one after another just sitting still, with seemingly no effect. It's a terrifying feeling that I am in no hurry to experience again. I waited at the car park, eyes closed and panting, until a driver gave me a lift back to Coyoacán, and from there I got a jitney to the San Ángel. I heard nothing more from Neill until her return to Mexico City three days later, and it would be another week before she could tell me in detail what happened on Popo.

That was an event that would affect her for the rest of her life. When she did tell me what happened, over several days of my visits at the hospital, she related it almost as she later wrote about it in her final book.

———

As she set out, Neill knew her two days at the capital's elevation hadn't been enough for her to become properly acclimated to altitude. But up she went, toward the rear of the line of climbers. By the time she exchanged her parka for the windbreaker, she was breathless from the effort. She doggedly pushed on, panting and aching. She counted her slow-motion steps, one-two-three-four-five, and then she knelt forward on her ice axe to regain her breath. One foot placed in front of the other, count to five, kneel and rest, then move again. From time to time she looked ahead at the receding dots farther up the steep slope. They too were moving at a half-frozen pace, and when they stopped they too had to kneel forward into the icy slope, as it was too steep to stand up straight to rest.

She forced herself to move on: Count to five, kneel for a few seconds, then rise and step ahead, one foot in front of the other, again and again. Whenever she stopped for rest she had to fight the urge to sleep—wouldn't it be so sweet, she thought, just the ticket, a little nap to restore the energy, here in the cold, blinding sun. But if Neill had no other resource, she had determination. She resisted the impulse to lie down and drove herself to get up and put one foot ahead of the other. One-two-three-four-five, kneel, lurch forward and step again, one foot in front of the other.

She wanted to wipe her nose and clean her goggles, so she removed her mittens and tucked them under one arm while she searched her pockets for a handkerchief. A mitten slipped away from her and skittered down the icy slope until it faded out of sight. A porter above her, seeing her lose the mitten, dropped his pack from its *mecapale* and staked it with his ice axe. He stair-stepped back down to her, somberly pulled out a gauntlet from his pocket and handed it to her. Then he headed back up the mountain.

By late afternoon, exhausted, dehydrated and nauseated from the lack of oxygen, Neill slowly approached the summit. She crawled like a dazed prizefighter the last dozen yards until hands reached down and pulled her up by her windbreaker and over the rim. The explorers already were preparing for the descent into the caldera. The view into the volcano was partially obscured by swirling yellow smoke and steam, and the fumes, she said, smelled like chlorine and sulfur. A lake of boiling milky-green water seethed a thousand feet below. Moisés Abrigo was busy with his ice axe, notching steps into the frozen slope. He built a short stairway to a ledge where rope ladders would be attached for the climb down to the main gallery. The porters were resting next to their loads, all except for the one who was supposed to carry Neill's large pack of equipment, including her Laplander sleeping bag. He had failed to make the summit, and nobody went in search of him. Perhaps he had returned to his village with the expensive gear, they said, or perhaps he would find another climber in Puebla. The Explorers grinned but looked remorseful.

Under the fading sunshine Neill lay on her back in the snow until she stopped gasping for air. She began to feel euphoric, realizing she had won the fight after all. She gazed northward, down on Iztaccihuatl's three ice-covered humps topping out at over 17,000 feet. She felt like she was flying. In her giddiness she imagined soaring off the rim of Popo and down into the yellow fumes of the abyss. What fun it would be to sweep along the icy sides of the crater, to skim the boiling lake and rise upward to the hard blue sky.

Moisés Abrigo put his hand on her shoulder. Follow Esperanza down steps to the resting place," he said gently. "The *cargadores* will bring down the rope ladder. Then we all go down to the place to sleep." Neill stood and carefully climbed down the ice stairs, her crampons digging into the surface like claws.

It grew dark on the first ledge, and the air was frigid. Neill insisted that Esperanza, who was visibly shivering, take her parka. The *cargadores* came down with the rope ladders and began securing them at the rim of the ledge. Neill grew restless with waiting. She climbed back up the steps to the lip of the crater and gazed at the distant scenery in the growing dusk. A couple of men followed her. She identified Pico de Orizaba, looming far to the south and still sunlit at the top. In the opposite direction she again admired the glaciated torso of Iztaccíhuatl. She spied Puebla stretched out to the west, its lights just coming on. And farther northward lay the capital city, a twinkling furnace of hazy colors surrounded by dark mountains. Somebody called from down below, and she returned to the ledge and the rope ladder.

The party lined up for their turns at the descent. First down was Moisés Abrigo. He moved smoothly to keep the rope ladder from becoming a pendulum. The mechanism was just two ropes with wood slats every eighteen inches, swinging freely as it draped over the sloping surface inside the crater. It disappeared into the opaque haze below and ended at the main terrace more than two hundred feet down. It was a half hour of careful work to reach the bottom. When Moisés Abrigo pulled on the signal line, the second Explorer stepped over the edge and slowly descended the swinging ladder, now being held at the bottom. More quickly a third, a fourth, then Esperanza, another male Explorer, and an Indian went down, and then someone shouted "*Alto!*"

They had been at it for nearly three hours, and the evening had become night, completely dark and much colder. One of the men at the upper ledge said to Neill, "We sleep here, go again tomorrow." Then he briefed the others–23 Explorers, and 13 Indian porters–in Spanish. They all would spend the night on the narrow ledge. Neill's sleeping bag was gone and her parka and pack with her provisions had already been taken below. Roberto Munde, a short, heavy-set young man with a Pancho Villa mustache, handed her a wool sweater. She reckoned this was not going to be a pleasant night. She sat on the gauntlet, looked around and began to shiver.

At dawn the party rose and began the descent to the tents on the rubble-strewn terrace below. A belaying rope was fastened around the waist of each person for the climb down the rope ladder. Roberto Munde went first. Neill was number eight in line, and she did just as the others had done before her, backing over the rim of the ledge while holding onto the top slats of the ladder and blindly finding lower slats with her feet. Two hundred and twenty-five feet down and twenty minutes later, she was in the welcoming grasp of Abrigo and Munde.

Her feet at last on the gravel slopes of the gallery, she set off immediately to find her equipment and begin exploring the caldera. She was ravenous but couldn't eat her sandwiches, because food stuck in her throat. She drank tomato juice and ate some fruit.

The terrace surrounded the boiling lake, which lay hundreds more feet below. The caldera above the party was oval shaped and over half a kilometer across at its narrowest. All around them vents leaked sulfurous steam, and fissures with greenish water were percolating and fuming. The air reeked, and yellow clouds drifted up from the lake and swirled around in the intense midday sunlight. The party wore handkerchiefs over their faces as sunscreens and gasmasks, but still the smell was nauseating. Neill said she'd never been so excited. They took photographs and movies, drew diagrams, pocketed samples of ash and gravel.

The second night in the volcano was better than the first. The camp was on powdery gravel that the Explorers had leveled for pitching tents. Neill had her parka for warmth, and she could stretch out in clean clothes in a tent. It was crowded, with ten or more people in each tent, and the air stank of sulfur all night, but she had eaten and hydrated, and she had managed to borrow a blanket from one of the Explorers.

For an hour or more after the tent flaps were closed, Neill was entertained by the others' stories of sulfur mining in Popo's crater. Indian laborers, they said, once used dynamite to blast the nearly pure sulfur from the walls below the gallery. They would pulverize it and haul it in large cloth sacks to a hoist line. Hoisted above, the bags were stacked on sleds and slid down the icy slope to wagons waiting at tree line. A lot of Indians died on Popo, and they were paid one peso a day for their work. The use of dynamite for sulfur mining, the storytellers said, caused an unnatural eruption of the volcano in 1927. Popo was that sensitive.

The explorers' voices faded into the night rumblings of the volcano, and Neill slept soundly.

The next morning the Explorers and porters began packing up the camp and made ready to climb out of the crater and descend to the vehicles for the long trek back to Mexico City. Neill has half way up, at a spot where the ladder lay over a rough rock face, when her leg suddenly snagged on a sharp outcrop. The Indians pulling her from above couldn't hear her shouting "Stop! *Alto!* Stop!" Her pant leg gave way, split vertically and ripped off at the knee. The release sent her spinning and swaying on the ladder, and she tightened her grip and shut her eyes to avoid getting sick. She rallied and continued hand over hand, with the Indians hauling on the harness until she was grabbed by the wrists and pulled onto the ledge. Her leg was scraped, but other than feeling cold and embarrassment, she was fit to climb to the rim and prepare for the descent to the cars, over a mile down.

Roberto Munde reattached Neill's crampons to her boots. Moisés Abrigo warned her not to go too fast on the descent. "There always is a danger of feeling too good on the way down. When the ice is hard it is slippery like glass, and below are the rocks and ravines."

Neill tied handkerchiefs around her exposed leg and headed down the glacier with the second group of Explorers. Ahead of them were Indians, sliding with the heavy packs, and half a dozen of the Explorers. Abrigo had assigned Munde to guide Neill. Munde was an adherent of the sliding descent, sitting on the slope and controlling the downward slide by regulating his speed with the ice axe. He showed Neill, and she followed his example. With him just ahead of her, Neill slid and dug in her ice axe, stopping to walk on patches of bare rock where winds had scoured the surface of snow.

A few hundred feet below the summit they approached a large area of exposed rock and Neill dug in her ice axe, cautiously came to a stop and began to stand up. As she rose, her right crampon caught the left binding, and she stumbled and fell onto her side. She naturally rolled to ease the fall, but on the near-vertical grade she couldn't stop her movement and went downward, first rolling and then falling head over heels, whirling and tumbling at an accelerating speed that quickly turned her into a one-person avalanche. She desperately dug at the mountain with her ice axe, but it was no help. The last thing she heard before passing out was the snap of her shoulder as it left its socket. She went into free-fall.

The rest of the story I got from the Explorers. They carried her down in a sling they had made from a blanket. Neill opened her eyes and asked for water, and Abrigo tipped a canteen to her mouth. She lost consciousness again, but at least she was breathing. Her fall had been stopped by two

Explorers in the lead party. They had heard shouts, saw her plummeting like a boulder toward them and braced their feet on their ice axes. She smashed into a rock outcrop before ricocheting off and continued flying toward them. If they hadn't caught her, she would have tumbled nearly a mile to the parking area and her certain death.

They brought her down in the gathering darkness. The exhausted Explorers carefully slid the casualty onto the backseat of a sedan owned by a Dr. Ernesto Chavez. In a quirk of good luck for Neill, the physician happened to be completing a hike around the waist of Popo when the team arrived at the clearing. Dr. Chavez replaced some of the improvised bandages the Explorers had applied to her head and mangled eyelid, approvingly inspected the splint made of three ice axes and crampon bindings, and made sure she was immobilized and well hydrated. Then they set off slowly for Amecameca and Mexico City.

The doctor drove north all night and arrived at the emergency room entrance of the American-British Cowdray Hospital just as dawn began to glow on the eastern horizon. Neill was scrubbed and sewn up—she needed twenty-seven stitches to close wounds on her face. The doctors surgically repaired her pulverized clavicle and the three compound fractures of her right thigh. She was placed in a toe-to-hip plaster cast and a shoulder brace and wouldn't be able to walk or lift her arm for three months. That's how I found her the next morning.

———

It was a frustrating period for Neill. She longed to be out and about, and she complained often to the medical staff and me that she was not making progress fast enough, that she was stir-crazy, that she needed more social contact. I was there every visiting hour. The nurses would say, *"Bueno, pues, es normal, Señora Campbell. Tranquila. Quiere leer algo?"* But she had read all their *Life* and *Collier's* magazines, and her editor hadn't yet sent her the books she had asked for. They called her Mrs. Campbell, and it was Harold Campbell who had written to Mr. Perkins and requested books for Neill to read in hospital. It was Campbell who had asked the ambassador to look in on her, and it was Campbell who had said she was permitted to go on the Explorers Club expedition without me as a little holiday from work.

The package of books arrived, and Neill sampled the current novels with distracted attention. Maury and Lorna Stafford visited, bringing a potted orchid and some recent copies of the New York Times. "Can't talk about business right now, of course," the Consul General muttered, "but your Harold rang up and said all is safely on hold at home. Expressed his wishes that you'll be back in harness *tout de suite*. Nice of him."

"If he calls again please tell him I'm doing my damnedest to get on my feet and out of this asylum at the soonest possible moment. He needn't worry."

A tiny smile flickered for a second on one side of Maury's face.

During Neill's ninth week of recovery the attending physician decided she was healed enough to go outside by wheelchair to a sunny patio. The nursing aide left her on her own to enjoy the fresh air and views, but the leg cast was maddeningly heavy. Although it rested on a wooden paddle extending from the front of the wheelchair, Neill had to lean backward to the opposite side to keep the whole arrangement in balance. After a while she grew tired and shifted her position, and once the heavy cast started to move there was nothing she could do to stop it. She tipped over and tumbled out of the wheelchair onto the tile patio floor, re-breaking her collar bone.

Another surgery followed, and she was confined to her hospital room for an additional month before she was able to move about, by that time on two canes. Meanwhile, some members of the Explorers Club paid a visit. They brought the founder of their organization, Otis McAllister. He gave Neill a certificate attesting to her climb into the cone of Popocatépetl, and she was very pleased. The expedition members who visited brought with them a short film they had made during their time in Popo's caldera. They set up a screen and projector in Neill's room, and some of the hospital staff and I joined them in viewing their adventure. There was Neill photographing the steaming lake and the streaks of color on the caldera walls, and she could be seen emerging from one of the tents after a breakfast had been laid out for her. The film ended with scenes of the team standing at the summit not long before her catastrophic fall.

At some point more than four months after her arrival from Popo, Neill took her rehabilitation into her own hands. She left the hospital with her two canes and traveled by bus to a remote spa northwest of the capital. While we were packing her up at the hospital, Stafford dropped in for a chat.

"You seem determined, my dear, to put yourself out of commission. Please don't keep trying." He seemed amused by his own comment and made a nasally chuckling noise. "But I understand you intend to go to the baths at Ixtapan. First-rate idea. And you can do something for us while you're restoring your strength. There's some talk about a group of women, possible fellow travelers, could be headed to the hot springs. Shouldn't be difficult to meet up with them, school teacher on leave from Paramus named Linder and a young oil heiress from Houston, real socialite, Blaffer family. The other one is an East Coast editor of some sort. All I know about them. I'm told they're moving around in Blaffer's phaeton with her chauffer at the wheel. Perhaps you could check on them? Just a routine call back would suffice, if there's nothing urgent. If there is, Kokio should contact Campbell direct."

"Maury, I'm going to the baths to recover from these goddamned injuries. I'm not very ready to go to work." Then her stage look of consternation softened, and she smiled. Phaeton was a word that appealed to Neill. "But I'll see what I can do."

Campbell must have had no further need for me there, possibly assuming that Neill would be in rehab for too long to justify my expenses in Mexico. I was recalled to the San Francisco office and given other work to do. I learned about the rest of Neill's misadventure only after I was sent back to Mexico City, this time with a more disconsolate assignment. I would hear the dramatic description of events from Neill, again in leg casts.

———

In the early 1940s the village of Ixtapan de la Sal and the roads serving it were primitive. But there were fine thermal baths and a luxury retreat called Hotel Balneario, which was as much restorative clinic as it was hotel. Neill soaked in the thermal waters day after day and set up a rigorous training regimen that included walking as far as she could tolerate, increasing the distance with each outing and gradually decreasing her dependence on her canes. After six weeks she was walking unaided back to the hotel from the village, a distance of nearly two kilometers, on the rutted dirt road.

She kept a careful eye on her fellow inmates, as she called the guests at the hotel. For the first month all she saw were Mexican business tycoons and officials and their families enjoying the waters. A few small groups of privileged internationals—rich exiles and stateless persons—came and went periodically. To Neill they seemed like albatrosses, searching for a place to alight and rest for awhile. Almost all the guests would stay for a few days or a week and then head off toward the capital, often in the Balneario coach. She took notes.

One morning while she was having breakfast on the hotel's front patio, she saw a black late-model Buick sedan enter the cobbled driveway. It wasn't a phaeton, but it was a Series 80, smart enough, and despite the gravel and pot-holed road, it was clean and shiny. Leather-clad luggage was strapped to the trunk lid, and Neill heard laughter coming from inside the car. Three women exited from the rear doors, one very young and gaily dressed in a breezy floral print dress, and two middle-aged and wearing slacks and blouses. A trim man in chauffeur's livery already was busy unfastening the luggage and handing it to hotel staff.

At dinner Neill asked to be seated near their table and listened to their talk for awhile. The youngest of the three had charming speech, part British RP and part Texas drawl. The other two obviously were from the East Coast. Neill promptly struck up a conversation, and introductions were made all around. Within twenty-four hours the threesome of Cecile Blaffer, Rose Linder and Mary Charles Cole became a foursome. The others were riveted by Neill's tales of her injuries from Popo and her adventures and travels twice around the world.

For her part, Neill found Cecile Blaffer's social position alluring. Cecil had been a Houston debutante and was an heiress to a fantastic oil fortune. But in 1942 she was merely a highly polished, entirely pleasant young traveling companion. The school teacher, Rose Linder, was on leave, "a sort of sabbatical" she said. In conversation she made literary allusions with ease and seemed to have a vast store of information. She was Neill's height but delicate-looking, as if she had spent much of her life in a library.

Neill found Mary Charles Cole alluring for other reasons. She had a certain light in her eyes. Between jobs as feature writer and editor for news magazines, Mary Charles had been in Washington D.C. for years and called herself "an armchair adventurer." She said she was now determined to get out of the armchair and expand her inventory of countries visited and languages spoken, starting with Central America and ending, she hoped, in Asia. Neill wondered who among them was a fellow traveler, most likely, she decided, not Miss Blaffer.

Within a few days Neill had sized up Mary Charles and begun a seduction, happily reciprocated, according to Neill. The three tourists helped Neill with her baths, gave her massages and walked with her to the village and back. At night, after dinners, Neill and Mary Charles could be seen lying side by side on lounges by the pool, their fingers just touching. About the time Neill felt able to cover the distance without canes at all, the news broke about a new volcano that erupted in a cornfield in Colima, far to the west. Ash from the volcano was already darkening the daytime skies across Mexico, and the newspapers were full of stories about the growing "baby volcano," Paricutín. Neill recounted the following conversations to me in detail but barely alluded to them in her book.

———

Rose Linder was the first to suggest going. "I'd love to see what all the fuss is about over there around Uruápan," she said. "Could you make a trip of that distance, Neill?"

For Neill a chance for adventure always trumped a chance for indolence and romance. She already had decided she must see Paricutín up close. "I could be ready in fifteen minutes," she said. Cecile and Mary Rose agreed it would be a grand excursion. Perhaps after visiting Paricutín the four of them could motor up to Guadalajara.

That night at dinner Neill excused herself and quickly phoned Maury Stafford from the lobby. He was still in his office, as they eat later in the capital.

"Getting on okay, are you? Walking and all that?"

"I only need one cane and that one just for emergencies. Actually, Maury, I'm so fit I could ride a horse. I walk four kilometers every morning."

"And those three wandering Americans, ever come across them? Harold was wondering."

"They've been here over two weeks, and we've become fast friends, all of us. But really, Maury, I'm getting nothing. Nothing so far. They want to go to Michoacán to see the new volcano. Tomorrow. I'm going to go with them. Maybe I'll have something to send later on."

"For God's sake, Neill. Going to climb another volcano? Couldn't just read the papers, could you?"

"Maury, really. Shall I stay here and merely watch them drive off?"

"Mmm. Well, point taken. You'll just use extra caution near that smoker, won't you."

"Can you renew my travel papers and post them to me at Uruápan? That would be lovely. I'll contact you later."

She returned to the table, and the others asked if everything was alright. "Oh, I just had to let my editor know what I'm up to, now that we're going off on a great excursion." Rose admitted she was duly impressed that her new friend would be ringing up Maxwell Perkins in the middle of the night.

The chauffer drove them all day and into the night, stopping only in Morélia for lunch. After a night in Uruapan, they headed north to San Juan Parangaricutiro, an ancient village at the end of the road. A few kilometers further on, up an old cart track, lay the tiny indio settlement of Paricutín. They hired Tarascan Indian guides and horses and set off for an afternoon and evening of viewing the violent throes of a new volcanic mountain.

As the women and their guides approached the exploding cone, they could feel the ground shaking and hear its deep rumble. They decided to camp close to the ridge of hot ash and rocks that had formed a torus around the bottom of the rising cone. Other adventurers hiked to the site or came on horses. Two livestock huts made of logs and thatch served as visitors' shelters. Neill and her new friends took the nearer hut for the afternoon and evening to photograph the volcano, and their guides retreated some distance with the horses near the second shelter. After supper at their camp, Cecile heard the others say they wanted to stay overnight in the hut. She decided to return by horseback to Parangaricutiro and sleep in relative comfort and safety in the Buick.

Neill, Rose Linder and Mary Charles Cole lay on mats in their shelter and gazed at the spectacle of molten rock, churning smoke and steam, fiery belches from the cone and flashes of lightning. Neill took photos, and nobody could sleep. The volcanic debris began collecting on the roofs of the shelters, and around three a.m. without warning their hut suddenly collapsed, pinning Neill under a fallen roof beam. Mary Charles sprained an ankle but was otherwise uninjured. Rose hurt her back but crawled out of the rubble unaided. Neill was crushed under the log beam and was covered by ash and a gravel of small volcanic rocks. The only person to help Neill, besides Mary Charles and the chauffer, was an elderly Tarascan man. They frantically dug her out and managed to pull the log off her. It was apparent that Neill's hip was smashed and one leg was badly fractured.

Eventually three English speaking men came by in the dark and tended to the women. They said they heard cries for help. Two were from the capital–a German merchant named Gilberto Fink and a correspondent for *El Universal* simply called "Figaro." The third man was Nelson C. Steenland, a young research scientist for the U.S. Geological Survey. This odd party stayed the remainder of the night and, when Cecile Blaffer returned the next day with horses and more guides, Steenland trussed Neill onto a makeshift travois and they all returned to Parangaricutiro.

The chauffeur drove the women back to Mexico City, stopping only for fuel and snacks from a roadside vendor. The women passed the time talking about the astonishing things they had seen and speculating about why the three Samaritans were traveling together. They wondered how long Neill would be in recovery. None of them, least of all Neill, doubted that she would fully recover.

Again she was admitted to the Cowdray Hospital, this time to mend three fractures of her pelvis and a break in her left femur. She remained an inpatient for six weeks. A handwritten note soon arrived from Stafford:

> *Very bad luck on your accident. Ambassador Messersmith, General Walker and Captain Hickey all send best wishes for a speedy recovery. Awaiting any further reports on your travels and traveling companions, but attend first to your rehabilitation. Maury.*

The three traveling companions did not come to the hospital to see her, and she never again heard from them. Years later, she would read that Cecile Blaffer had married Prince Tassilo von Furstenberg of Austria, and she would tell people she traveled with a princess to see Paricutin being born.

Neill was discharged on August 17, 1943 and was quartered briefly in the capital with the del Rio family, friends of the U.S. Embassy. No word came from Campbell, the embassy was keeping distant, and Neill was happy to be resting in quiet isolation. She ate heartily, resumed her regimen of daily walks, baths and massages, and soon gained strength enough to travel once more. She delayed submitting a report on her recent assignment, wishing to "get away from the near-death horror of the accident," as she later told me, and to recover her composure.

Campbell contacted my boss and asked to have me go back down to Mexico. Neill needed to be debriefed, but more important to the agency, they wanted her to receive a delicate message, one that apparently was too awkward for them to deliver themselves: They directed me to "settle" Neill.

I rang up from my hotel near the *zócalo* and suggested that I go out to visit her. I told her I had come down from San Francisco for some much needed rest, which happened to be true. When she came to the door and greeted me, she looked worse than I had expected. We embraced, Neill none too steadily, and I said, "You've really banged yourself up good this time."

"They told me I might never play tennis again, but golf isn't out of the question." Neill had a determined grin. She sat down carefully in a large *equipale* chair.

"I know you, Neill James. I'm sure they never mentioned golf, and you might start thinking first about just walking again."

"Lots of limpers play golf. But we'll see." She paused and studied me for a few seconds. "You're just back here for R and R?"

"Neill, you need some time," I said, "to get over these injuries. You need a place where you can get away from all the expectations and distractions."

"That's exactly what I want, a time away, a good long time to get back on my feet."

I took Neill's hand. "When you do get back on your feet, Neill, you'll need something else to do, something of your own making. So you don't have to depend on this."

"I always have my writing career, Margie. And so we'll see how much I'll have to depend on these people in the future."

"I know of a place, and we can go there together. Just south of Guadalajara, a little fishing village where there's a group of interesting artists, oddballs like you and me. I have friends there, and we can stay for as long as you wish."

"What's it called?"

"Ajijic," I said.

Neill took the train to Guadalajara the very next day. I flew up a few days later, and we booked a room at the Hotel Morales. I had sent a note to the Heuers, my contacts at Ajijic, and they made a casita ready for our arrival.

After a week in noisy Guadalajara, Neill and I packed our suitcases and boarded a bus for the city of Chapala, the main commercial town on the north shore of Lake Chapala. From there we hired a skiff and set sail westward to Ajijic. Late that afternoon we settled in at the Heuers' casita, where we could finally relax and enjoy a quiet dinner overlooking the lake. It was wide and peaceful as a shimmering inland sea, and we watched the village lights coming on like strings of diamonds on the far shore a dozen miles away. The surrounding mountains shaded off in the dusk from deep greens to dark rose to purple.

Neill admired the cascading flowers and mango and Poinciana trees in the Heuers' *huerta*. She looked all around her and said pensively, "I could live here forever."

"This wouldn't be a bad place to start a new life."

"I don't see why, after I'm fully recovered, I couldn't do my travels from here and still get contracts for my other work. There's plenty of need for that right here in Mexico these days."

"You will need to find something else to keep you going, Neill. There won't be any assignments from the agency in the future."

"With the war and the SIS expanding all over the hemisphere, there must be plenty of opportunities. You just have to ask, Margie."

"We're both too old-school for them to make the investment. SIS is looking for lawyers, Neill, kids just out of college."

"Hard to imagine nobody would need an independent traveler like me."

"I'm sorry to tell you, but nobody's keeping you on, my dear, and this time it looks like it's for good."

Neill stared at me for a few seconds and then gazed out to the lake. "Good glory, to think I delay a report for a few weeks, a trivial little routine report, while I'm laid abed with broken hip and leg, and they just up and cut me loose! What a shameful cowardice. I feel so forsaken!"

"It's not the report, Neill. They say you take too many risks. You cost too much. And you're too"—and here I hesitated to find the right words for the message they wanted me to deliver—"you're not careful enough with your targets. An agent, probably SIS, named Steenland sent a caution to Captain Hickey. It was critical of your actions at Ixtapan and Paricutín. I'm afraid Campbell has washed his hands, too. I'm sorry."

Neill was quiet for a few moments. Then she lifted her chin and slapped the table. "I've earned my oats by my own wits many times before. And, as I say, I always have my writing career. I have a book to finish about Mexico, and I'm going to put Ajijic in it, too."

We closed out her files, she signed the exit papers and the clearance termination, and I gave her the final security briefing. Neill was nearing her 49th birthday, and she had just been abandoned by her employer of over two decades, set adrift without a future pension, without relocation expenses, without even a thank-you or civil handshake. I had been a good girl, not difficult like Neill, so I probably could expect the handshake and thanks. Maybe a glass paperweight.

I stayed on for a month while Neill continued to heal. We shopped in the village and had our morning coffee by the lake shore, we attended parties thrown by the handful of expatriates, we sunbathed nude on benches in the *huerta*, and some evenings we drank beer with the local

Mexicans at the cantina. When I was ready to return to San Francisco, she said goodbye at breakfast and didn't bother to see me off at the dock. She was busy evaluating the gardens at a house she thought she might rent.

XI

Katie Lawrence

"Now what about this place?"

"Ajijic," said the driver.

"I dare say," said E.

—Sybille Bedford, *A Visit to Don Otavio*

Neill told everybody that the blouse bodega was her idea. She even tried to convince me. Well, I knew better, and she had to know it. She told the same story in letters to her sister. In a newspaper article about it, the local gringo reporter called her the founder of Mexico's silk industry. Oh, she always got her way with the press. Decades later, when she was just beginning to get dementia and was aware of it, she said the idea came to her from cooperatives she had seen in Chinese villages just before World War II. I think she was trying to assure herself that she could still remember how things really happened. But she always insisted hers was the first apparel business in Ajijic and there was no silk production before she started it.

Well, what actually happened was three or four years before she opened her blouse making shop and store there in the front courtyard at Quinta Tzintzuntzan, another gringa already had a weaving room and clothing store, using the old-time Indio methods to make skirts and shirts and blouses. That was Helen Kirtland Goodridge, and she had a well established business when I moved here. I never got to know her very well, I don't know why, and by the time it occurred to me to ask her about it, Helen had already passed away. But her son John once told me Helen started up her hand-weaving shop at her house in the mid-Forties and the thing that made her business successful was the fact that she employed only Mexicans for the labor, almost all men, and so the people trusted her. She continued running her shop until she retired in 1974. John came up then from Mexico City and expanded the business and ran it until he retired for good.

Anyway, just a few years after Neill came here, about when I arrived, she was beginning to get the idea that Scribner's in New York wouldn't be publishing any more of her writing, for whatever reason, and she was trying to keep up with the A-Listers and was running out of money. She might have thought that because of her marketing skills Ajijic could become a production center of fine cotton clothing based on the traditional Indio designs, or maybe she just looked around for opportunities and saw Helen's successful business and figured she could hitch a ride on it. In either case, after a few years of living on her savings and trying to write a new novel, Neill decided to put writing aside in favor of going into the business of making and selling women's blouses. She would need a new angle, though, something Helen Kirtland didn't have.

Well, Neill's new angle was to hire only women for the shop and store, and she advertised it as an all-*mujer* cooperative that was going to free Mexican wives from bondage, you know, the economic dependence on their men. Now that's a noble idea. Being the brains behind the operation, naturally Neill would grab a big slice of the take as her commission, but she didn't realize that she was going against a native practice that was hundreds of years old. The true old way was that the whole family would be involved in making clothing, and the men did most of the weaving and design work. It was only after the *bracero* programs drew a lot of the men away to work north of the border that women began to do most of the weaving at home. So Neill was laying claim to something that already had happened as an unwelcomed side effect of a foreign labor policy. But in spite of that stigma her bodega did make beautiful blouses and scarves and aprons, and it was profitable and remained in operation for nearly a decade, always in competition with Helen Kirtland's.

Of course Neill was never satisfied with the status quo. She saw an advertisement in a magazine for silk worm eggs and thought it might offer her some added revenue and another advantage over Helen. Besides, she loved silk. She came to my casa all excited one morning and told me about her plan. I remember I was still having my first cup of coffee on my patio.

"Katie-Tee," she said—she called me that when we were getting along. She was almost breathless and, as usual when she had a scheme, grinning like a cat with a mouse. "I believe I have found a new gold mine."

"Your last one didn't pan out too well," I said.

She ignored that. "I'm going to transform the apparel industry of Jalisco. We're going to make blouses and rebozos out of silk."

I should have learned not to be surprised by anything she said. "They already do that down in Oaxaca," I said.

"But that's Oaxaca, half a world away. And they make silk mainly for the family and local sales. I'll do it for the tourist and international markets," she said.

I asked her where she was going to get the silk.

"I'm going to make it from my own silkworms," she said, as if she had run silk worm farms before, which I suspected she hadn't. "There's a supplier in San Luis Potosí who gets the graines from the Mexican government, and I can buy enough to start producing silk in the first year. It's not those Spanish *criollo* worms but the new *mejorados*, a hybrid Japanese they've come up with. They make stronger cocoons and more threads."

Neill seemed pleased with herself for learning about the worms, and when I asked her what she was going to feed them, she said she would have to plant mulberry trees and already had a section of her *huerta* set aside for her grove. I knew nothing about mulberry trees, except for the big black-fruit trees I had seen as a child in Canada, but Neill already had been looking into what grows best in Mexico, and she said she had some *moralos blancos* on order from down near Uruápan.

She put her energy into the idea—well, she always had more schemes and energy than common sense—and, sure enough, in a couple of years she got her silk production up and running and actually began weaving silk fabric for blouses and such. I believe that given enough time her business really would have transformed Ajijic and the apparel economy of Jalisco, if only it hadn't been for the malaria.

There had been an outbreak, and it became serious enough for the national government to step in. After her first year of silk production, once her trees were big enough to feed the worms, the government workers started spraying programs to control the malaria. Teams of sprayers would show up in Ajijic, and nobody was exempted. The workers marked the houses with numbers to keep count and make sure the spraying was done right. The trouble was, the poison killed not just mosquitoes but all the other insects and lots of small animals, too. The chickens and cats that used to roam around the village keeled over or disappeared and nobody had hens' eggs for a long time, unless they bought them up in Guad. I guess the wild chickens that lived on the ridges eventually came down to the villages around the lake, and that's why we have hens today. Unfortunately it also killed all the silkworms and graine, which is what Neill called the eggs. She couldn't get a new supply of graine, so she was out of luck.

"It's back to cotton and wool, Katie-Tee," she said, looking toward the future as usual. But when her bodega operated in direct competition with Helen Kirtland it didn't provide her enough income to keep up Quinta

Tzintzuntzan and live the way she wanted to live. So she turned the business over to the women's cooperative and began to invest in houses. Just like that. That's the real reason she got out of the clothing business.

But ever afterward she would tell newcomers she got the first silkworms in the history of Mexico by traveling to Japan herself and bringing the eggs back in steamer trunks filled with Japanese mulberry leaves. Then she hinted Amelia Earhart flew them back with her. I observed that as Neill got very old she seemed to forget the facts and just made up stories, as if the important thing was to entertain people and get them to believe whatever she said. I admit it occasionally irked me, but I couldn't help but admire her audacity.

I first became friendly with Neill because of the ice. By then I was divorced and teaching literature up in Guad at the international school, and I rented one of Neill's houses at Six Corners. In the early days, ice would come down to us every morning in big blocks on the bus from Chapala and then on a wagon over that awful road we called *calle baches* that eventually became the highway. By the time the ice arrived here in Ajijic the blocks were half their original size, and the iceman would just plunk yours on the street cobbles in front of your door. You had to leave the pesos in a box at your entrance, and if you didn't get out there right at delivery time, or if it was delivered late or early, you wouldn't have much ice by the time you did fetch it. Then you had to have a place to put it. A few rich gringos had iceboxes, but almost everybody else here put their ice in a cold hole in the kitchen floor. If it was kept covered with burlap and the lid was kept closed and the ice got in there in time, it might last until nearly bed time.

Well, as a woman of the world Neill wasn't having any of that. There was no electricity, and no phones and only primitive septic systems in Ajijic then. Our water in those days came from the big well near the plaza, and everybody would send their *mozo* to the cistern every morning to haul water in buckets. It was good, clean water, but it took hours to get that chore done.

One day I went next door to Neill's house for something, to borrow some oil or herbs or something, I don't remember. She asked me to stay for a while and join her for tea, and we sat on her patio and looked out on the lake sparkling in the sun, with the pelicans and ducks and those white cattle egrets, and we drank iced tea. She said to me, "Katie-Tee, do you know where this ice comes from?"

"Guadalajara, I suppose," I said. This was before ice was made from local water, and it was much safer than today's ice.

"Some of it comes from our Mexican glaciers and some comes in ships from either far down South America or New England and Alaska, depending on the season."

"Oh," I said. I didn't know what she was getting at, but she always had an angle.

"I used to sell ice, you know. There was a lot of competition, but I moved ice all across the Southeast of the United States and later in Central America. Before that in Hawaii. In Florida I had a crew of pretty girls working for me, and I trained them up. The company sent me to a school in Chicago to study refrigeration and the ice market. Something I learned on that job is that a person needs only three conditions to sell residential ice: a hot climate, a backward economy and slack labor. It's all dependent on labor, and the labor must be able to work hard and fast, because quick and efficient delivery to the ice box in a climate and economy like that is most important."

I remember her reclining there on her chaise longue, holding up her tea glass like it was a cocktail and saying, "We've got the climate and the primitive economy. No problem there. But we have peculiar labor conditions, Katie-Tee. Not that our Mexican friends are over-employed, they in fact are underused. And it's not that they can't work efficiently. But the problems are attitudinal."

Then she explained it would be impossible to change the attitudes of the ice man because it's part of his culture. He might or might not arrive on time. And it was too big a job for her to take over the entire ice industry. She said the only way to improve refrigeration in Ajijic was to bring in electricity, to hell with the lazy ice men. Her plan was to sell refrigerators to the gringos and commercial establishments—like the old posada and the Ajijic Hotel and the markets—and to the few wealthy Mexicans who came to the lake from Guad on weekends. She wanted me to help her, but it wasn't just to sell refrigerators.

The problem we would solve first, she said, was electricity. Ajijic didn't have any, and she would find a way to persuade the utility to bring it in from San Antonio on the east. Once we got electricity in, Neill could concentrate on opening her appliance store and we would become tycoons. She even owned the right building for it, on the other end of Ocampo. And because it's against Mexican law for gringos to bring in appliances across the border, she knew there would be a growing market as new people came down.

With me in tow, she started a campaign. She convinced the Ajijic *alcalde* to join her in pressuring the electric power board, and she met with Chapala business leaders and showed them how they would benefit from people having electricity in Ajijic. Together we designed handbills and wrote letters and used her contacts at the consulate in Guad to lobby the electric board. Since it was a nationalized monopoly, she thought she would also bring pressure from Mexico City, where she knew some important people. And I think she actually did, because within a few months workers began installing poles and lines along the *calle baches*, and it wasn't long before Ajijic wasn't a scruffy little fishing village without electricity anymore.

Of course, with the power poles it was easier to bring in the telephone too, and in a short time every block had a couple of houses with a phone. But Neill lost out on the refrigerator sales. No sooner had electricity arrived when a big retailer from the capitol came up and opened an appliances shop on Colón, and she figured she couldn't under-price them. Still, she got the credit for bringing electricity and telephones to Ajijic, and sure enough she soon began to make it sound like it was her charitable gift and that was her main intention in the first place.

Of course, Ajijic changed a lot after electricity came in. You started to hear radios inside houses all around town, instead of the usual singing or shouting and laughter. And with the streetlights the kids stayed out later at night, and I think that changed a lot about the way the Mexican families lived. Also, I noticed that shortly after electricity and the appliances store came in, not as many women would go down to the lake to do their laundry, especially the women who worked as maids for the gringos. I had loved to see them, all squatting at the water's edge in their bright-colored aprons and headscarves. It was as if some thief kept picking flowers from my garden and after a while there were no more blossoms left.

The big difference to me with the street lighting, though, was the turtles crossing up on the highway. For God knows how long, the turtle migration used to happen like clockwork every year at the first of June–thousands, maybe hundreds of thousands of little black turtles no bigger than your hand, crawling their way down after dark to the lake from the mountains. They used to cover the *calle baches* like a moving carpet, so that nothing else could pass for maybe eight or ten hours, almost all night. They needed a moonlit night for the migration. People from all around, and sometimes scientists and tourists from outside Mexico, everybody would come to Ajijic, set up chairs and benches and little cookers to grill fish and meat and tortillas for suppers and just sit there at dusk, waiting for dark and the turtles to come paddling across the road. Then, when the streetlights came, the turtles were scared off. They must have found some other way to get to the lake or somewhere else to migrate to, because we saw fewer and fewer of them, just like the ladies doing laundry, and eventually there were no more turtle crossings.

Neill used to say, "Well, that's progress, Katie-Tee. You have to give something up to get something you want." She loved and collected plants and animals, but that never got in her way. She was a bundle of contradictions.

When I lived next door and was just getting to know her, Neill had a trapeze installed in her upstairs bedroom. She was always concerned about her health and looks and took herbal remedies and exercised and went to the baths every week at Cosala or the spa over near Chapala at the Monte Carlo Hotel.

For Neill the trapeze was a way to have a little excitement along with her exercise. She had it rigged up from the ceiling in her front bedroom, but the room was too small to get a full swing on the contraption indoors. Her bedroom faced over the street with French doors and a little balcony out front, so early every morning she would open the balcony doors and swing out over the street like Tarzan's girlfriend, usually with next to nothing on. I even saw her swing naked on her trapeze one time. So when she said to me, "Come on over, Katie-Tee, and take a ride on my trapeze," I didn't have the nerve at first to do it. But she was persistent, and eventually I came over and took a swing on the thing, and I kind of enjoyed it. Nothing else ever happened, but I knew what she had on her mind.

Well, imagine her doing that, a woman of her age. Of course she never was honest about her age, and you couldn't tell then by her looks that she was as old as she was. She was a good looking woman, firm and vigorous even with her short leg, though she wasn't especially muscular, and she had beautiful, thick hair that she could style in any fashion, and that was true even when she was very elderly and there was a lot of salt in the pepper. There was something supple but firm and forceful about her character, too, and she had a way of looking at you that made you think she was interested in you but she might think she was more sophisticated or clever, smarter than you—something hard to pinpoint but you had the feeling you were always in a competition of some sort.

Yet you wanted to have conversations with her. She was very interesting and she did know a lot about everything, at least she sounded like she did, and she used to cause me to question myself. I welcomed her company, though, because she was full of stories, always intriguing stories, and people find it hard to resist a good story. Well, she obviously had traveled a lot, and she had been a writer, though she didn't write much after she settled here.

That's another odd thing about her being an author—she had no literary papers and very few books. There were no libraries then at Lakeside, not even for the Mexicans, and we gringos all swapped books. But Neill had a smaller collection than most of us, didn't read much besides magazines and her books on nutrition and gardening, and she almost never kept a diary. So it seemed very odd at first that she started the two libraries here. And she didn't have any writer friends or correspondents, though she did tell those stories about her famous visitors from the past.

In the early days she used to claim she knew most of the rich bohemians and artists, the famous eccentrics who came in the Thirties and during the War, a little before I arrived. Tennessee Williams once came down to play cards with her and they drank at the old posada, she said, and George Bernard Shaw had called on her when he came through this part of Mexico. She told me Sybille Bedford and Esther Murphy Arthur stayed at her house off and on, but I remember that they only visited once and it didn't go very well. On the other hand, *Life* magazine published a spread on Ajijic that made it look like living here was one continuous round of high society parties and she was the hub. But then, she did have a knack for dealing with the press.

The episode with Sybille Bedford caused quite a stir. Bedford and her companion Esther Murphy Arthur were touring Mexico after the war, and when they passed through Chapala somebody told them about an American writer who lived in Ajijic. They stayed at the west end of the lake at an ex-governor's family mansion—Bedford described it all in her first book—but it wasn't long before they grew restless and came back looking for the gringo author. The story I heard first, and it came from Neill's cook, was that an English writer and her American companion came calling one afternoon and there was a row and Neill kicked them out. Then someone from the ex-governor's household paddled over in his *piragua* and threatened Neill with some sort of legal action, and Neill kicked him out too.

Later I heard a more detailed and believable version from Peter Lilley, another expat writer. Peter had lived in San Antonio since about 1930 and talked to both Neill and Sybille Bedford right after their encounter. Peter wasn't particularly fond of Neill because he thought she had copied the ideas from his books for her *Dust on My Heart*, and besides he was English. But in his favor he was widely regarded as an honest and observant man, so I really had no reason to doubt his word.

Peter said Sybille Bedford was in the midst of growing pains as an author, really struggling to get free from the influence of Aldous Huxley, who was her mentor and something like a foster father to her. Anyway, she was trying to write in her own style and so she was critical of everything he was involved in at the time, all the movies work and his experiments with mystical writings and drugs. Well, Neill didn't know much about Huxley. She had heard rumors about his most famous books but had never read any of them. She knew from magazine articles, though, that he was a world-famous writer who had gotten involved in mysticism and vegetarianism, which she very much approved of. I doubt that Neill knew beforehand that Bedford and Arthur had had any personal connection with Huxley, but apparently during their visit his name came up.

The way Peter described the meeting, Neill dropped the name into the conversation, saying something like, "My Mexican diet has been inspired by Mr. Aldous Huxley, and as an author I admire his novels so much."

"Such imperfect ambiguity," Esther whispered.

"Just as I am not inspired by Spam and chutney," Sybille said, "I find nothing inspiring about Aldous Huxley."

Neill came to the defense of both Spam and Huxley, and Sybille accused her of knowing nothing about either.

If I had to guess, I'd say Neill found Sybille quite a threat to her shaky public image and sense of herself as an author, as both the visitors were much, much more worldly than she ever would be, in spite of her wide travels. They probably had ways to let her know they were more clever and weren't buying her pose. In any case, Neill and Sybille didn't hit it off, and according to Peter they soon were insulting each other.

Neill told her visitors they were as rude as Yankee peddlers. Sybille replied with something about rudeness being superior to false politesse, and Esther Murphy Arthur said the height of rudeness is to accuse others of it. And on it went until Neill demanded that the two immediately leave Quinta Tzintzuntzan.

According to Peter, on her way out Sybille was heard to say, "I wonder who could have written her books?" Neill grabbed a lacquered fish platter from the patio bar and hurled it in their direction. It was a near miss and smashed against the brick arch over the gate. Shards of crockery flew everywhere, and the two women scooted off hand in hand, laughing and apparently unhurt.

Peter didn't know anything about any legal action against Neill, and nothing ever would have been said about the encounter if I hadn't asked. Now it occurs to me that Neill's anger might have been fueled by seeing Sybille and Esther so happily together, when she was so terribly lonely. It's sad to think that Neill had such longings, and at that time her money was running out, and she was permanently scarred from her accidents, and she already was not popular with the upper crust gringos, what we still call the A-List.

She had a big luau one time, though, under the fig trees by her patio, and even some A-List people came. Everybody was supposed to come in costume—she gave the choice of Tarascan or Hawaiian or Asian—and we sat on rattan mats under her big fig tree and were fed roast pig and rum drinks while a wandering Mariachi band played a Mexican version of Hawaiian songs. I remember Neill in a very short grass skirt and not much on for a top, and her hair was pinned up so it tumbled over her forehead like a dark waterfall. I still have a photograph of that party, with Neill in the foreground in her costume and looking a little distracted or disappointed. It must have been taken during a lull in the fiesta. Most of the women came in white suits or blouses and slacks and had bright flower leis around their necks, but a few of the others were dressed like Neill, and after enough rum had been consumed Neill taught them how to hula. People came and went all day and night, and we all drank too much, and the party ended up at the lakeshore, where everyone but the retired ambassador went in for a midnight dip.

Still, she tried to entertain and do charitable work for the Mexicans. For decades Neill hosted a Christmas open house, and a lot of Mexican neighbors would bring their kids and some of the gringos would come by and everybody enjoyed her spread of fruitcakes and eggnog, the same thing every Christmas Eve. Fewer and fewer of the A-List people showed up as the years went by, but the Mexicans seemed to truly appreciate her parties, and maybe the difference was that they didn't disapprove of Jana, while the gringos thought she was a lunatic, despite the amusement she gave them.

Oh, Jana was a blessing for Neill. She came down on vacation from New York in 1962. She had been a spinster grade-school teacher in New Orleans all her life, and when she was fifty-five she met a man who promised her an exciting new life in New York. They married, but within two years Jana was off traveling in Mexico on her own while the divorce was pending. She heard about the offbeat life in Ajijic and, being an eccentric herself, must have felt right at home here, because she never went back to New York.

She truly was an original, and she enjoyed looking the part. She always wore bright colors, lime green or hot pink like bleeding hearts or orchid, her favorite, and it would be the same color from the top of her hat down to her shoes. She always wore a big hat with a tall feather or big flower sticking out of it, and sometimes, when she was much older, she'd wear two hats at a time. She had cloth shoes and sandals in all her bright colors, rows of them in her closet, together with matching handbags. Even her makeup and nail polish would be the same color, heaven knows where she got it, and she smeared the lipstick on so thick it made her mouth look bigger than it was.

I knew Neill was feeling lonely. She hadn't had a steady companion in Mexico, and the gringos had begun to drift away from her. She had often asked her sister Jane to come down for a visit, but to my knowledge Jane's first trip to Lakeside came only after Neill's illness in the mid 1980's. I sometimes thought that was why she was friendly toward me, even though we had little in common except we were two single women who loved Ajijic. And I think she was lonely because she had no other real friends and needed someone to talk with. She couldn't carry on a conversation in Spanish, and many of the Mexicans were shy with her, maybe because it appeared that she had so much, or she had offended them. So that left just a few gringos who, like me, found Neill interesting and stimulating, and of course the few Mexicans who were dependent on her.

Well anyway, into Neill's loneliness fluttered Jana Saskova like a bright-feathered angel. The two must have seen something special in one another, something others failed to recognize or just misunderstood. I thought they were both shrewd and daring, but they sure cut an odd figure around the village, Neill at first all dressed up in a suit as if it was 1928, then more and more often as she grew older she would be in scruffy dungarees with her shirt tails out and sandals, and next to her would be willowy Jana in one of those florid outfits looking like an oversized peony, the two of them driving around in Neill's battered old Chevy or, after that one fell apart, her little Volkswagen with the bumper hanging off.

Jana had her own house, and she kept it running even when she lived with Neill at Quinta Tzintzuntzan. They loved each other dearly but they fought like alley cats, and sometimes at night if you walked past their patio gate on your way to the lake you could hear the crash of dishes being thrown. But I worried less about Neill after Jana arrived, because she seemed less desperate to visit with me or be accepted by the other expats, even the A-Listers, which I took to be a sign of contentment.

They remained together until Jana left Mexico in a huff after a series of quarrels. Some people said Jana traveled and lived here and there in Europe, but she later told me she had gone back to Louisiana to take care of her parents until they passed away. She was gone for nearly five years, and in that time Neill briefly entertained a number of companions. But she fought with all of them and clearly nobody held her fascination and heart the way Jana did. When Jana returned to Ajijic in 1970, she moved in again with Neill. Together they could afford full-time help, and they had a cook and housekeeper and a live-in gardener called Ramon, who also worked for them as a watchman. Neill despised cooking and housework and always had someone who took care of her kitchen.

Then they decided to take their great round-the-world trip together. They both loved to travel, and even though by then Jana was at least sixty-five and Neill was seventy-five and lame, they were determined to face the challenges of months on the go. They went by train to Mexico City and flew from there to Panama, where they boarded a steamship bound for New Zealand. Their plan was to travel the South Seas and Australia, then go on to Ceylon and India. They would decide which route to take from India, but they intended to circle the globe, together making a gigantic ring for themselves.

The next thing I knew, Jana showed up back here a month later without Neill. She took her things from Quinta Tzintzuntzan and moved back to her house, and for several weeks we didn't see her at the post office or the butcher's or on her strolls along the lake shore. After Neill returned, the two of them began to be seen together again on their afternoon walks with their dogs and parrots, going sometimes slowly and sometimes at a march along the shore from the pier at Ajijic all the way to the chapel at San Antonio. I puzzled over that until my housekeeper told me Miss James and Mrs. Saskova had had *una pelea pequeña*, a little falling out, in *Nueva Zelandia*, but now there had been *una reconciliación*. She had heard the story from Mrs. Saskova's cook, who was her sister-in-law.

From that time on Neill and Jana kept separate housekeeping. But they were constant companions and went traveling overseas at least twice again, once in the late Seventies and again around 1980. As Neill became more forgetful, and especially after her stroke, or whatever it was, she spent more time alone at home and less with Jana. It wasn't that they had another *pelea pequeña* or had turned to someone else for companionship, but Neill became inward in her late years and got all wrapped up in things like improving her health by nutritional tonics and herbal teas and Eastern spiritual exercises, and I suspect Jana was not interested in all that.

Neill grew fearful, too, although she had always feared being buried alive. That was something that we both were afraid of, being put into the ground before we were really dead. So we made a pact that whichever one of us who died first, the other one would be responsible for making sure she was really and truly dead before the burial. Hah! It was so silly. We promised to inject some poison into the body, just to be sure.

But while my fear about being buried alive didn't bother me much and I hardly ever thought about it, Neill worked hard to get rid of hers, like a phobia. She bought books about exposing your fears and overcoming nightmares, and for a while she kept a dream diary because one of her books convinced her that her secret phobias could be understood if she analyzed her dreams correctly. The dream analysis eventually turned into a preoccupation with her spiritual advancement. She had it linked to knowledge of spiritual truth, as if there is an encyclopedia of information that would lead her to enlightenment. Oddly, considering the inner sorts of things she was wishing for, she also connected it to her prosperity. She wanted to remove from her life all negative thoughts, her quick temper and ego, her phobias and certain "problems"–including, she told me, the problems of financial insecurity.

Neill was approaching 80 years of age then, and maybe she was trying to make things right. It was about that time that she started the first library. She's now most fondly remembered in Ajijic because of the *bibliotecas*, but even there it's mostly based on myths instead the true history. Even before she opened her bodega in the late Forties Neill had the idea of creating a library for the Mexicans. She saw herself as a force for literacy in the village, and her belief was that illiteracy was responsible for holding back the Mexicans from being economically successful. Well, she always thought of literacy in terms of commerce. I think at the time it was part of her search to find some noteworthy charitable work to do, and as an idea it was wonderful, but nothing came of it for nearly thirty years.

There was no library anywhere between the lake and Guadalajara, for either Mexicans or gringos. The Mexicans for the most part couldn't read and had no books. The kids would learn to read in the first four grades and then would always leave school and forget their reading. Shortly after Neill settled at Ajijic she had donated some children's books to a teacher in Chapala. People later said that that was her first library, but it wasn't that at all. Her real efforts to create libraries for both the kids and Mexican adults began only after she had control over a lot of real estate and had regained some personal influence in the Mexican community.

She persuaded the owner of the building on Ocampo next to Serna's grocery to donate a room for a small library. Then she went to Chapala and pressured the *alcalde* to earmark some money from the city budget for books. She had help from two Mexican women who shared her views on literacy and who spoke for her when they went to shame the local government into supporting them. One of those women, Angelita Camara, actually ran the library on Ocampo and was the teacher of the kids who came to the library, and Neill took the credit for being its founder. Well, it never would have happened without Neill's ideas and talent for public relations, so why shouldn't she be the face of the charity?

It also was her idea to give the Mexican kids art lessons at the library and to teach them etiquette so they would be able to do well later in society beyond Ajijic. Angelita Camara made that a reality, too. She hired the art teachers, and some of those were gringos you never heard of. Neill just came by from time to time to observe and evaluate, like an Army commander inspecting the troops. Many of those kids went on to school in Guadalajara and sometimes to art college at San Miguel, and a few became famous artists and now live in Mexico City or Hollywood or have their own galleries around here. So there is some truth to the stories about Neill's legacy of giving to the community.

Anyway, the first *biblioteca publica* became so popular that Neill eventually dedicated a couple of rooms in one of her own buildings at six corners, on the west end of town, for a branch library. They used the same strategy to get the books, and she donated the space. She would walk over there early every morning with her dog—it was Bronco, one of her big German shepherds—and inspect the library and make sure the teacher and librarian, Josefina Cuadilla, was ready for the day. For a while after the Colmena was added Jana helped with the libraries, but she basically hung around and sometimes cleaned up after school, because Jana had no talent for actually running things. I lived in that *seis esquinas* neighborhood and became very familiar with the library and the clinic that replaced it after the branches were consolidated and moved to the Society because of the vandalism.

Neill wanted the title and recognition, but she didn't care to do the work. When it came to running the Colmena branch—it was called that because of the double boveda ceiling and at first the place was always buzzing like a beehive with all the little kids—she couldn't find another person like Angelina or Josefina, so she turned it over to a group of older students and just dusted off her hands. The students apparently thought they would remodel the little building, and some of the workers basically tore the place apart and ruined everything, including the books. The shelving and tables, file cabinets, lamps, all the painting supplies, everything was either taken or broken, and the roof was left off into the rainy season so the books got wet. I saw it almost every day, because by then, as I say, I was living here, scarcely two blocks away from La Colmena and had to pass it every time I walked to the post office or the plaza. I kept warning her that it was going badly.

The library had to close and the *policia* kicked out the students. Neill said they were art students at the University of Guadalajara who came in and took over the place, as if they were a motorcycle gang and she couldn't do anything about it. She took the loss very personally and complained about it for years afterward, but she solved the problem by getting the Society to take over the entire library operation. That was when she transferred one of the long buildings at Quinta Tzintzuntzan to the Society for the English language library and their offices, and she insisted the *biblioteca publica* would have to be there too as a condition of the deal. She thought she was a millionaire at the time, so she began to give away the empty buildings at *seis esquinas* to Jalisco for the mothers and infants clinic and the social services offices.

That's where the greatest publicity came from, the Society loudly and publicly praising her for her sponsorship and donation of the libraries, and she loved it. It was her pattern. Over and over she could pull a rabbit out of the hat, and I came to admire her skill at doing it and then calling it just good luck. In her nineties she was honored by most of the expatriate groups in Jalisco as the great benefactress of Ajijic. The gringo newspapers gave her awards and published articles about her, complete with the usual errors, like saying she started the libraries in 1944. And the Society honored her with a fiesta. They even named their annual art fair and their library for her. When she was ninety-five the local weekly gave her their Lifetime Achievement Award.

I don't know how much the honors late in her life were influenced by the Who's Who volumes, but there were a lot of them, and Neill showed them to anyone she could corner. Way back during the war, when she was still writing, she was put in the real one, the *Who's Who in America*, but forty years later she was taken in by those imitators. Cheated is a better word for it. I thought it was pitiful, because some of those books are as phony as paste jewelry, and they take advantage of people's insecurities and give them nothing but a title to brag about.

I'm sure Neill came across them in some magazine. She used to read the sort of magazines that had advertisements for products that look expensive and glamorous but actually are little more than junk, like those soapstone museum sculptures and watches that look like the best European ones but are made in Hong Kong or Mexico City. All the same, by the time Neill was in her late eighties she was beginning to get a little forgetful, and she was easily confused about things. I guess when it came to her reputation it didn't matter how old or confused she was, she always would be very naïve about come-ons that appealed to her vanity.

In 1983 she applied to be in the *Universal Who's Who of Female Intellectuals*, and to nobody's surprise, she was immediately accepted. They published out of Cambridge, England, which sounds grand but they had nothing to do with Cambridge University. She was required to write her brief biography as part of the application, and that was the bit they put in their book. Word-for-word: No work for them. Neill was the least likely person to be called an intellectual, but she loved the sound of it. She was encouraged to buy some volumes at a special low price which was actually a special high price, and before I knew it she had ordered a dozen of them. The deal was that the more books you bought the lower the price of each book, but even if you bought a hundred it still would cost you more than it cost them. And they were supposed to be honoring you. Neill was so proud of herself for being in Who's Who that she gave some of those books to people she hardly knew. I'm sure she didn't understand it wasn't the real *Who's Who* and had probably forgotten she already was in it.

The next year she went through the same thing when the same publisher invited her to appear in *The World's Who's Who of Women Artists* and *The International Registry of Literary Personalities*, and in 1985 she was contacted by the National Biographical Association to be in their *Profiles of America's Leaders Hall of Fame*. That one included a plaque and press kit to go along with the books. The Association also got her to buy her listing in their *Index of Outstanding American Women*. Then she was approached by those Cambridge people again and offered to be promoted to something called Honored Member, which meant she would be featured with other Honored Members at the front of the book, with a half page photograph and a list of her accomplishments. She had to pay extra for that honor, and she bought another dozen volumes.

It wasn't long before her house was cluttered with these expensive but basically worthless books. They looked good on the surface, but the things were poorly edited, one was even bound upside-down, and they were full of undistinguished people. It was a shame, and nobody could convince her that she was being cheated. I tried. She got so angry at me I thought she was going to throw a fit.

I said to her one day, "You know, those books cost a lot of money, Neill. With the devaluation and the freeze on dollars, you can't be too careful with your money."

She had come over to my casa, and while we were having a glass of tea she grabbed my *Universal Who's Who of Female Intellectuals* she had given me. She commented about how proud she was to be in such a prestigious volume. When I cautioned her about the cost, she said, "I deserve to be in those books, Katie-Tee, and I like to give them to my friends and acquaintances, so there's no harm in that. Besides, these are beautiful books, and they're fun to just look through—so many important people with interesting backgrounds." She sounded a little wistful.

"Neill," I said, "all those biographies are written by the people themselves, same as yours. They could be anybody, and they could have done anything. I bet I could apply to be in the next edition and they would welcome me, too."

"You are dreadfully wrong, Katie. Just as it says in the Preface, these people all have been professionally successful and they have improved their communities. I am proud to be associated with them and with the publisher."

"Well," I said, "I'll bet they come after you again to get you to become a sponsor or patron or something. They list them at the back."

Neill was silent for a few moments and I figured she had already paid to be listed as a financial supporter. I observed that the cover was put on upside down, or maybe the text was printed upside down.

She brushed that aside. "It's a privilege, Katie, to be able to contribute to such a distinguished publication. And that's all I'm going to say on the subject to someone like you, who don't understand this sort of things."

"Neill, I don't want to see you go broke or become the laughing stock of Lakeside because of these books. That's all."

"Laughing stock? If y'all don't want that book you can just give it back to me and I'll find somebody who can appreciate it." And with that she put down her glass and my book and went home without saying another word.

I've often thought about Neill's biographies in those vanity Who's Whos. They listed mainly the books she wrote for Scribner's and her work for the State Department and of course her travels before she came to Mexico. She once included something about advanced study at the University of Chicago, but far as I know the only schooling she had in Chicago was a training seminar some Ice marketing group paid her to attend. The odd thing is she never included much about her bodega or the libraries or the art scholarships, never anything about the houses she fixed up and gave away or the fireplace she invented.

It was like she had lived two disconnected lives, but the one she lived before coming to Ajijic–the one that nobody down here could verify and many doubted–became an evolving tale that she used for building up her second life, the one that started after she arrived. It was like she created a mythical figure of herself so that she would be sure to have admirers here in Mexico, as if her legacy among us expats mattered that much. Or maybe she was trying to give herself something to admire. Some people here who don't believe her think it's shameful, her trying to cash in for glory on a made up past life like that. But I think we all do a little of it, remaking the past over and over, because we have to and if we didn't we wouldn't have a past.

XII

Damon Byrd James

La esperanza le pertenece a la vida, es la vida misma defendiéndose .
—Julio Cortázar, *Rayuela* [*Hopscotch*]

Scant evidence remains of Aunt Neill's life in Mexico, not much more than can be recovered of her life before she settled there at Lake Chapala, although the municipal government maintained essential records of her real estate transactions and there were some odds and ends still held at the Society. I encountered many stories about her during my two sojourns to that idyllic region, stories both favorable and unsavory, none clearly reliable. Most of them were from people who had scarcely known her, some even from people who moved to Mexico after she had passed. What became clear, however, is that controversy remains and feelings still run high among a small group of old-timers regarding what happened to her property and savings and the arrangements for her personal care in the several years before she died.

She seems to speak to me from beyond the grave, still working to confuse the record to enhance her mystery and elevate her reputation. She won't even be clear about the timing of her death. I am in possession of two documents that provide conflicting dates, one in exact agreement with the October 8, 1994 that is inscribed on the blue tile tablet marking her burial site beneath an enormous tree in the backyard of her rehabilitated estate in Ajijic and in agreement as well with the obituary published in the English language newspaper of Chapala. The other is a U.S. Department of State death certificate, issued at Guadalajara and signed by the Vice Consul General, a Mr. Frederick J. Williamson. It says she died at 12:02, a.m. or p.m. not specified, on September 15, 1994. I suspect the latter document is in error, because the last residential address for Neill given on it is incorrect, and her age and year of birth are incorrect. Moreover, it indicates the death was recorded at the Civil Registry Office of Chapala, Book 1, account number 96, on October 10, 1994.

If that date is to be credited and the municipality of Chapala was conforming to Mexican law, which is not always the case among Mexican municipalities, my great-aunt once removed must have died within the previous 48 hours, which places her death at October 8 or 9 of that year, just as the marker says. On the other hand, that tile plaque by the big fig tree in Ajijic also has inscribed on it an incorrect date for her birth, off by three days, which could render the entire memorial somewhat suspect. So it remains less than completely clear to me precisely when she gave up the ghost and went to her final rest.

What became increasingly apparent to me over the years of my investigations into her history, however, is that the final period of her life was not passed in comfort and security. She seemed always to have sought comfort and ease but never required or courted security, until her dementia began. Quite the opposite, it would appear, as the meager records and credible stories available all suggest that she pursued risks and dangers for stimulation nearly to the end of her life. The archives reveal that she was still traipsing around South Asia when she was in her middle eighties, a crone with two canes apparently away on a government paid espionage assignment from Indonesia to Burma and back. And then another.

She must have called in an old debt. No intelligence agency with a sense of its own mission and honor would have put an elderly, lame woman in harm's way unless she had been guaranteed protection from the apparent danger of the assignment and the agency officers believed they could make good on their promise. My surmise, based on the dispatches and travel records, is that it was a gift of some sort made to look like her old work, a late payment for earlier services rendered or possibly the equivalent of hush money, for she knew a lot about the agency's precursors and their activities during the World Wars and the twenty-odd years between them, and she might have maintained some bitterness about the way she and other women had been treated.

Whatever the impetus might have been, Neill departed Mexico on October 21, 1977, at age eighty-two and in the company of a girlfriend, most likely her usual companion Jana Fick Saskova. They were bound initially for Shanghai, where they landed on the 27th following a stopover in Tokyo. Her visas tell the tale. They traveled in China for a few days and ended up in Hong Kong on the 30th. From there they went to Bangkok for three days, then to Manila until November 7. They returned on that date to Tokyo and spent most of November in Japan, but by November 26 they were back in the Philippines and by the 29th they were in Malaysia, city unspecified. This itinerary would exhaust any decathlete, and thus I find it difficult to imagine how strong she must have been as a cane-toting octogenarian. The pattern of stops is one typical of the courier, and it appears most likely that Neill was carrying a secure mail bag for the government. It might be relevant that the Philippines were in great turmoil in 1977 and remained under martial law, and the government had just entered a cease-fire with the Moro rebels.

Neill undertook a similar sojourn about two years later, again accompanied by her friend Jana Saskova. They were gone from Ajijic from mid-September until the third week of December. That travel took them to Indonesia, Shanghai, Bangkok, The Socialist Republic of the Union of Burma–probably Rangoon–Bangkok again and upcountry Thailand, Hong Kong and return through Neill's beloved Honolulu. She was eighty-four years old, and her letters that year to her sister Jane, who of course also is my great aunt once-removed, revealed that she had failing eyesight and hearing, though the following year she claimed both were much improved through the rigorous administration of her self-prescribed diet of herbal remedies and the daily use of a slant-board.

Three documents in the file released to me by the government suggest that she relished her last periods of travel as a contract intelligence agent. One was an internal memorandum that commented on a field report submitted by an agent whose cover name was "Kokio." Kokio being a species of hibiscus native to Hawaii, and flower names not ordinarily being assigned to males, the code name suggests the agent would have been female and most likely Great Aunt Neill. Moreover, the timing of the information contained in the memorandum exactly fit her itinerary for her 1977 sojourn to Asia. Although much of the text was redacted, it appears to have alleged that the agent Kokio had exceeded authority and scope of the assignment and had traveled further afield in the Philippines than the supervising field officer wished, such that the agency lost track of Kokio for a few days.

The report Kokio submitted, however, proved of such high value that no corrective action was taken. That illegitimate report of hers, submitted from the field like perfume over the transom, had accurately predicted the elevation of Rodolfo Salas to CPP Chairman at such time as Jose Maria Sison would be captured or killed, and the report estimated the capture to happen within a few days and Sison's replacement within a month. It's now well known that Mr. Sison was arrested on November 10, 1977 in La Union, and Mr. Salas became head of the Communist Party by the end of December. The supervisor's memorandum concluded with a recommendation that the agency should revise policy to consider returning to a pre-World War II practice by employing more "nontraditional contractors."

The second document was a four page letter dated June 1980 in response to a complaint of age-based discrimination. It transmitted an agency finding of no discrimination because the complainant, being a temporary contract employee and identified only as T-79-44, lacked standing to submit a discrimination suit. It also offered a veiled apology without admitting any culpability. Like the earlier document, the letter was littered with redactions, but I noticed clues in the recapitulation of the complaint statement that strongly suggested T-79-44 was our Neill.

As I could make it out, the alleged discrimination was based on age and gender. The letter referenced the accusation that the agency gave the agent no substantive work to do and attempted to keep her under twenty-four hour surveillance throughout her travels, despite the generous salary and travel expenses for her and a companion. The agency letter said these were "regrettable perceived lapses."

The third document was a memorandum for the file, presumably the personnel record, which simply stated "Do not rehire." It was signed by the Director for South and Southeast Asia.

Neill traveled outside of Mexico two more times, to Ecuador and the Galapagos in November of 1981 and on a cruise through the Panama Canal and the Caribbean in 1985. Those apparently were pleasure travels taken as part of commercially guided tours in the company of strangers, other elderly folks. By then she had declined opportunities to travel with Jane.

In fact, it's unclear if she ever visited Jane and Frank in California. They seemed determined to help her get out of Mexico, so much so that they built a full housekeeping cottage on their Vista property and offered it as a home for her dotage, but there is no evidence to suggest that she ever came to see it. Neill wished to keep something private, hidden even from her closest and clearly most beloved sibling. I believe the private matter was her financial condition, which appeared always to be on the brink of disaster, like a flimsy mansion constructed on the edge of an eroding cliff. It is half the story of why she remained in that remote village by the lake and why in the end she kept herself so detached from her Mississippi family.

Her career as an author, it seems clear, had been a professional pretense. While she could write a well constructed and lively sentence, she had no real talent for anything more challenging than advertising copy or the personal letter. With a grand literary life foreclosed, she embarked initially on the kinds of work she had done earlier in her life—publicity, the manufacture and sale of clothing, and refrigeration. For a while she scraped by. Strapped for money and hobbled by her old injuries, she found herself confined to rural Mexico until she could create a way to finance her exit. She had always maintained that her stay in Mexico was temporary. Sadly for her, only in old age did she finally and grudgingly admit to Jane that she believed she would live out the rest of her days in Ajijic. What was unsaid is that she could not afford to leave.

In her early business enterprises, she tried to exploit both the buying power of the growing expatriate population and the low cost of Mexican labor. Unlike her competitor in the weaving and apparel trade, she aimed to sell not to the poorer local population but to the wealthier newcomers. That idea was rational, if a bit cold-hearted, but it was incomplete as a business plan. From what little records I could find, it appears that her apparel business was moderately successful, excepting that she diverted for her personal use too much from the earnings, rather than reinvesting in the operation. In that sense she continuously undercapitalized her enterprise, and ultimately it went under.

She also misunderstood the large scale economics that affected her, and that misunderstanding greatly influenced what happened to her more successful later efforts in the real estate development business. She chanced on the common insight that her opportunities for financial gain would be enhanced if she bought something very cheap and sold it very dear, and the increased gain would be all the greater to the extent that the smallest investment possible be made to improve the commodity between buying and selling it.

Real estate in Ajijic, unlike blouses or ice, could be bought from Mexicans for almost nothing and sold to foreigners at astronomically higher multiples of the purchase price, if certain improvements were made and the costs of the necessary improvements could be kept very low. Neill saw that the newly arrived expatriates would pay handsomely for authentic village homes, and she knew local building materials and labor could be purchased for mere pennies. There were no building codes. This scheme too was rational, and because of magnitudes of scale, and because she created what today we would call a vertically integrated business, controlling everything from getting the raw materials to selling the finished product, her real estate enterprise was successful enough to sustain her for a long period, covering more than three decades of her life in Ajijic. For a time she even seemed to believe, magically, that she had become wealthy.

But here is the crack in the magic mirror. All her transactions, naturally, were in Mexican pesos. And the surplus capital she took as profit from the sales and rentals of her properties she either spent directly or invested in time-share certificates of deposit, initially at two or three local banks. Because of the volatility of the Mexican currency and economy, two calculations are necessary to sustain true security of investments there.

First, it's necessary to track the rate of return on the certificates of deposit in comparison to the inflation rate. Second, tracking the exchange rate of Mexican currency to international currencies, in particular the U.S. dollar, is necessary for knowing if the investment has value outside the borders of Mexico. Neill appears to have done neither of these calculations but instead got lured into a frame of mind that was purely local, as if she had lost sight of the horizon and could focus only on what was near her feet.

She managed her time deposits like a slush fund. Instead of paying her household staff wages from her personal budget, she sometimes would get them to agree instead to receive a gift certificate of deposit that guaranteed a certain percentage return, the interest from which they could then draw upon to meet their personal needs. When I calculate the pesos and dollars, it appears that Neill was both saving herself money in the short run and circumventing the Mexican employment laws that require employers to pay taxes on wages and a hefty severance fee based on wages when someone left employment.

Neill insisted on keeping a full staff of housekeeper, cook, maid, and gardener, at first part-time and later full-time, as she repeatedly said she detested domestic work herself and especially loathed kitchen work. In the context of the rest of her pretensions and self-delusions, I would venture the additional reason that she believed it only fitting and proper that she should live out her days in a manorial arrangement, complete with adequate numbers of people under her command to serve her.

Neill's capital holdings fluctuated, so that sometimes she held considerable property around Ajijic, renting some houses, renovating others for sale and devoting still others to civic uses, and at other times holding several houses for pending sales when the market was right. Eventually she was undercut in real estate by new entrepreneurs. By the 1980s, Canadian developers were building entire gated neighborhoods and flying in prospects from Quebec and Toronto and Vancouver for short vacations and sales tours. That cut into the upper end of the market. Other people who had an eye to the more modest segment of the market came to Ajijic and started up realty sales businesses whose trade they primed by buying up the remaining available Mexican houses and small commercial buildings. In a short time, the supply of dirt-cheap raw materials that had made Neill's operation so profitable dried up, and she perforce turned to managing rentals instead of selling her properties.

The bigger threat to her financial stability was the currency devaluation. At least three times the peso was allowed to float, because of runaway inflation and fiscal irresponsibility in Mexico City, and probably in the state capitals as well. In her early years as a real estate developer, Neill would write to Jane with assurances that she was doing well, buying this and that property and putting her money into time-deposits. By the 1970s, Neill was writing that she was confident she would have enough to live on for the rest of her days because her banks paid such handsome dividends. As time went on Neill told Jane she was a "peso millionaire," and in mock-protest complained that she was "drowning in pesos." In a July 1982 letter to Jane she said, "By the way, if you find the special cooking equipment recommended in the new cook book, don't hesitate to buy it whatever the price! and keep the address of the place where you find it for me I will HOARD MY MOUNTAIN OF pesos and buy the complete set for Neill."

Shortly after her 88th birthday she wrote to Jane, on January 31, 1983, "to tell you the exciting news that you have a MULTI MILLIONAIRE in the family. It's ME! And my fortune's going to double in two years." She said she had checked with her local bank to see if she owned any funds in untapped time deposits. The banker told her she had three and a third million pesos that were idling in a special account because she hadn't instructed the banks about what she wished to do with the money. They would exchange it for dollars, if she wished, but she would lose over half of her investment. She decided to leave it in pesos and reinvest it at the proffered 59% interest. She wrote that she also had "two or three million" in two local banks which had been expropriated by the government and the fate of those funds was unknown.

The previous year the first great devaluation was declared, and Neill appeared to be only vaguely aware of its implications for her investments. All dollar assets were frozen, which meant Neill was quarantined unless she could establish a fund in dollars outside Mexico. For a time she had an account in San Francisco at the Bank of Nova Scotia. I suspect she had expatriate clients of her real estate business pay her by dollar transfers in the United States. I eventually discovered that Jane suggested the payment scheme and set up the account for her after learning that dollars were embargoed in Mexico.

I wish not to be too harsh in my judgments of Neill, because by this time she was nearing ninety years of age, and her crisis had occurred earlier that same year. Her fortunes thereafter took a precipitous fall, as inflation in Mexico was rising geometrically. She already had been pinching pesos. She stopped servicing her Volkswagen, which she had paid her handyman to drive for her—when he drove she called him her chauffeur. She declined to keep a telephone, telling Jane she would take calls at a neighbor's house and pay the neighbor one hundred pesos "for the molestation." One hundred pesos then was worth about a tenth of an American dollar. The neighbor apparently didn't cotton to the arrangement, because in the next letter Neill instructed Jane to telephone her at the house of Mexican-American friends Rafael and Luisa Murillo, whose response to the offer of a hundred pesos for the "molestation" she described as, "They haw hawed me." She stopped sending gifts but instructed Jane she should buy this or that for herself and then tell how much it cost so Neill could reimburse her. Of course Jane did not follow that fanciful plan. Perhaps it's too stern a judgment, but it seems Neill's devotion was as deep as her efforts to please.

She promised to visit Jane and Frank for Thanksgiving 1984 because Rafael and Luisa Murillo offered to drive her to California and back, but she canceled her plan and apologized afterward. The Murillo couple planned another trip for Neill to visit Jane and Frank the following March, and again Neill alternated between rapt enthusiasm and rejection of the plan. That trip too was cancelled. That was the year Neill stopped writing sensible letters to her sister.

It's understandable that Neill withdrew, if my theory about her crisis holds true, which is that things changed for Neill forever around the end of 1984, her ninetieth. Following a dozen typically normal letters she wrote and sent to Jane between January 7 and November 13 of that year, she wrote on November 14 a wildly incoherent message in pencil, and one of her staff mailed it to Jane, possibly to alert her.

The letter was fifteen pages of fragmented ravings interspersed with sentences and short paragraphs that were perfectly sensible but seemingly unaware of the rest of the words surrounding them. Much of the interpretable part of the letter concerned her finances and "bad men" who are out to get her because they think she is a "rich Americana," images reminiscent of a dream diary she had kept a decade earlier. She wrote pleasantly for a bit about her library in Ajijic, saying: "Some estudents come from Jocolopec [i.e., Jocotepec] and Chajalas [i.e., Chapala] to do research. AJIJIC is probably the only Puelage [i.e., pueblo or village] in Mexico with a reference shelf & also books for all ages . . . ." Thereupon, however, she embarked on a new direction:

> *One year the Government gave me police protection for 365 nights until I told them things were better & I did not need the two soldiers who spent the night policing my garden & watching my house. Yesterday I appealed to the local authorities in AJIJIC–But they were r--- and*

negative!–I went to Chapala which bosses AJIJIC & the new man there said he could do nothing for me! My gardener jose Carlenada [i.e., Candelaria] night watches for me! I may be wrong but I fear he has been 'bought' by the men who want to kidnap me & hold me for a huge ransom, mistakenly thinking I am a 'Rich American' (see footnote).

The footnote refers to a comment she appended about having been in two vanity Who's Who volumes. She ended that section of her letter, after closing "best love to you both," with the following painful observation: "This letter is the worst and saddest I have ever written. My intuition about my night gardener was 100% correct. Love Neill."

But that was not the end. There was much more in that hand-scrawled letter, after the foregoing. I reproduce some of it here to illustrate the basis for my conclusion about her condition.

7:30 A.M. Still fireworks bright as day!

Did not dare to go to bed Murillo will doubtless cal the villains.

Murillo has called the villain & received his orders. Gorgeous colored fireworks in my garden which are visible thru the two small steel doors. The exhibit is on my small back patio.

Murillo trying to earn his money!

Sitting at my desk in my studio I can see my entire garden is light gorgeous as for Xmas They want me to open my. . .

I planned to type this letter but was unable to get the machine's cover unrolled! I only hope they do not set my house on fire!

I imagine, 150 feet high fireworks in my garden bright as daylight in colors–Hoping I will unlock my steel door. I am not that dumb–

This could be end of my life made certain if I opened the door to see the beauty!

Wills Murillo appointed executive. My life is very probable in great danger. He needs the money! Love, Neill

Murillo needs money he will get from. . .

FIREWORKS –50 meters high

Higher than my tallest trees
In gorgeous colors
Beautiful

They are trying to get me
Out so they can
Kidnap me and
Kill me as to make
My will ineffective because

It is not registered yet

Plans to get it from the lawyer today and have to register it with official Chapala, Jalisco Mexico will write you jus how and where you to go get the money & Property

I have money with Banamex Chapala Jalisco

DREAM STATE

I praised them and they responded with rapidly graceful motions—I thanked them in Spanish & English & the whole company showed their appreciation by rapid movements.

I had been sitting on a large equtall on my tiled corridor replete with plants. I walked out across the tiled area to get a closer view—That was when I realized that my rose bushes, tiger lilies, even the ferns were moving gracefully and rapidly. Even close up they group of bealirines [i.e., ballerinas?]

Make list of plants involved.

The letter goes on for several more pages in that manner, concluding this way:

I remembered my two dogs barking like mad protecting my casa in the patio—

The padrones wanted light for their nefarious business and had climbed the stair and bring the out of doors ----------- created enough light for their work in the patio. I slipped my pistol from its

P.S.
Jane, please give a bonus to my two servants

This mixture of what the psychologists call word-salad and bits of coherency suggests a neurological event that is like a short-circuit in an old house, the lights flickering on and off, sparking at some junctions and going dark in some rooms. It most surely is a sign that Neill was undergoing an ischemic stroke, possibly a series of small strokes, through the nighttime hours of November 14, 1984, and she was fortunate only in that she lived and the house didn't catch fire. Nobody in the letter's chain seemed to care about the fact that Neill actually kept a loaded .38 caliber revolver at her bedside.

She appeared to have recovered somewhat in due time, and she celebrated her ninetieth birthday, January 3, 1985, aboard the Sagafjord, where a photo was taken of her blowing out a candle on a large sheet cake and with many of the ship's passengers gathered around her. She sent the photo to Jane and commented in the accompanying letter that she was home again "and everything well taken care of by Jose who acts as gardener and night watchman in my house and garden." Had she forgotten, or was she averting her eyes to the night of terror a mere two months earlier? My conclusion is that Neill recognized that she was losing her mind, and this was the other secret she wished to keep from her family.

Neill's subsequent letters to Jane–and by that time Jane was her only correspondent–became increasingly sad, deranged and infrequent. She repeated things, made up stories about her past, sent the same faux-Who's Who pages again and again, and completely lost track of her money. Jane notified her that her Nova Scotia Bank account had been overdrawn, and Neill claimed she knew nothing about any such account and furthermore had no money in any bank. Yet she had consolidated her accounts in the Lloyd's bank in Chapala in 1986, and Rafael Murillo had managed to get most of her funds, some $35,000, to California for Jane to place in the Nova Scotia Bank of San Francisco. Neill's penultimate letter, sent in June of 1988, was faintly reminiscent of the one about her night of terrors nearly four years earlier. In it she typed:

> I do not have a centavo in the Bank. I am completely out of money . . . . I have nothing I can sell (except my house and I have to live in it. This situation has crept upon me without my noticing it.
>
> I planned to will my property to you. But you said NO.
>
> I could not realize that this situation was creeping upon me.
>
> I still do not realize how it happened,
>
> I could sell my house. But I would have no place to live.
>
> Don't think I have been extravagant about my affairs. I have actually been chinchy.
>
> ACCEPT THE PROPERTY AND SELL IT, PLEASE. But le let me live on it for a few more years. I cannot explain how this has happened to me. I certainly have lived economically and have n not given away or loaned anything to anybody.
>
> Uou wont be able to believe it, but I have to borrow money for a stamp for this letter from the maid! Which embarasses me no end.
>
> > [signed]
> > Love Neill

In fact she had funds at three banks in two countries. By 1989 Neill ceased writing entirely.

Great Aunt Jane's husband, General Loomis, died in 1989. The same year, the Jalisco International Society acquired a hard-driving and ambitious new president. Marcus J. Hardy had been a government agent during and after World War II and spent most of the next twenty years in Honduras as owner of a factory that manufactured timepieces and calculators. I heard some rumors in Ajijic that he also worked during the post war decades for the CIA. During that time he and his wife Charlene lived a comfortable life in northern California, punctuated by frequent trips to and extended stays in Central America. That went on until he retired to Malta, which they found a bit tame and too English for their tastes.

The following year, 1986, they moved to Ajijic. Just then the expatriate population was growing dramatically, with each season bringing in ever larger hordes of new retirees from Canada and the rust belt of the United States to occupy the glut of new houses. When Hardy was named president of the Jalisco International Society there were no other serious contenders, and he took office with vigor and an assumed mandate. Aside from the American Legion in Chapala, the Society was the only full-service social support organization for internationals in the region, so it wielded considerable influence in the expatriate community.

On my two research trips to Lake Chapala I repeatedly heard reports that Neill had been one of the founders of the Society in 1955 and had remained a member and a power behind the scenes for the rest of her life. It piqued my curiosity, because she and Jana were known to be shunned by many of the Society leaders. I therefore examined the documents establishing the Society and all the membership records, and I discovered that Neill not only was not a founder and never a member of the Society, but also she was not even listed as a member of the expatriate residential community in the late 1950's. I am tempted to conclude that even from the start she was more sidelined by the non-Mexican establishment than popular history would indicate.

Marcus Hardy knew the Society would need new quarters, as it had vastly outgrown its rented offices and had no places to store records and hold meetings and offer the sorts of services the new generation of executives envisioned and new residents desired. Neill already had turned over control of her libraries to the Society and had made the bodega building available rent-free for that use, so Hardy had an incentive for looking more closely at Neill's compound at Quinta Tzintzuntzan to solve his space problems. It consisted of four and a half thousand square meters enclosed by adobe walls, with two iron gated entrances from a main east-west road and another on the side street half a block off the lake front. There were two sturdy, spacious brick houses, an immense patio of Saltillo tiles, and workshops, fish ponds, gardens, and lawns surrounded by hundreds of semitropical trees. It was a lovely mess, an Eden in chaos because for at least the preceding decade Neill had not been able to keep it up as it should have been maintained, even though she employed a full-time gardener.

Neill's so-called last will and testament was transcribed on October 1, 1986, by Linda Bishop, a woman who had been in Ajijic for nearly forty years but only recently had been befriended by Neill. Linda took dictation from Neill for the will and created some of Neill's local letters. The will was meant to replace all her earlier ones, going back to the first, which Neill hand-wrote in 1950. The 1986 document gave all her property and Mexican accounts to her then-living nieces and nephews and gave the library collection and its building and the ground beneath it to the Society, on condition that they maintain the library in perpetuity for Ajijic's children. Actually, two versions of the same will were drawn up, the first with Linda's husband Lester and Rafael Murillo as co-executors, and the second one with only Linda listed as executor. A month later, on October 31, Mr. Hardy, as JIS Secretary, wrote Neill a note conveying his happy belief that she was giving to the Society all her property within the compound. The next day Neill replied through her new friend Linda Bishop, who probably was coaching her, to say in unequivocal terms that she did not intend to give the entire property to the Society but was turning over only the library.

Apparently that clarification did the trick, for all was quiet on the subject for a few years as the Society struggled with ever more inadequate facilities. In the meantime, however, Jane had come down to see Neill and help manage her financial affairs. That was when the plan was hatched for transferring some of Neill's funds out of Mexico, and Jane promised to pay a monthly stipend to Neill from the interest, which she arranged to be wire-deposited at the Lloyd's Bank in Chapala. During that 1986 visit Jane made clear to Murillo, the Bishops, and Neill that she did not want possession of Neill's property in Mexico, had no desire to manage it and thought it would be better placed with descendants, nieces, and nephews. She gave the relevant names and addresses to Neill to use in writing up a new will, which she did, in the two versions transcribed by Linda Bishop.

Then news of Jane's widowhood in 1989 reached Ajijic through Rafael and Luisa Murillo. Mr. Hardy, by then JIS President, persuaded one of the Society Directors to contact Jane with the suggestion that she consider authorizing an exchange of lifetime in-home tenancy for Neill in return for Neill's grant of the entire property to the Society. The Society said they would look after Neill for the rest of her days. I suspect they believed that a woman already ninety-four years old would not be under their care for much longer. I also suspect this solved a number of vexing problems for Great Aunt Jane. She did not like Ajijic and had already declared she had no interest in holding property there. She now believed the nieces and nephews would likewise find the inheritance to be more nuisance than blessing. Perhaps she had canvassed them.

Neill had long been troublesome, so much so that with two exceptions there had been continuous turnover of her domestic help, and her friendships among the expatriates were fraught, short-lived, and sometimes embarrassing to the community. Two Mexicans worked for Neill for over thirty years, but there were interregnums because of quarrels and misunderstandings even with those loyal servants. Jana Saskova had been a steadfast friend and companion, but ultimately she was not up to the attentions and periods of solitude Neill required as they both declined in mental health and advanced in bodily infirmity. Jane would turn eighty-six that year and could not imagine herself assuring Neill's care on a day to day basis, even if doing so remotely from Vista. And yet she generously financed Neill's support and wanted something to happen that would secure Neill's reputation as a great woman in her community.

The obvious way was to have her formally honored as a benefactress, but to secure that honor would need the enthusiastic support of the power brokers in the Lake Chapala area. Pages from vanity press Who's Who books and charitable deeds for Mexican children would be insufficient. Besides, Jane could well afford to pay for Neill's domestic support, as she was the General's sole beneficiary, and by the time of his death they were comfortably wealthy.

Jane negotiated an agreement with Hardy and the Society board of directors, without telling the Bishops. It seems she may not even have told Neill, letting the directors think she was updating Neill about their negotiations. In any event, the arrangement they came to called for the annulment of Neill's will, the transfer of all Neill's property to the Society, a guarantee that Neill could live out her life at Quinta Tzintzuntzan, the designation of trustees to oversee Neill's care for the rest of her life, and a financial arrangement whereby Jane would continue to provide a monthly stipend to cover Neill's expenses for routine and extraordinary needs.

All parties benefited, and the Society faithfully kept to their agreement. Neill's bank accounts were reconsolidated in a trust fund at Banamex in Chapala, and when that was done it was discovered that her time deposit accounts at Caja Seguridad de Chapala had been pilfered, by whom I never could figure out. But whoever it was, Neill lost almost every peso she had invested. She hadn't been entirely irrational about threats to her finances after all.

Linda Bishop had concerns about the arrangement, but Hardy told her and others that Neill knowingly agreed to it. She had done so in person, he said, asking questions until satisfied and then signing the papers of her own free will. But the Bishops and a few other old-timers told me they knew that Neill already was suffering from some form of dementia. With a flash of the Neill from bygone years, she told Linda her "forgettery was taking over."

It wasn't long after the agreement was legalized and implemented that Neill began receiving highly publicized honors for her contributions to the community and the arts. She was declared the International Patroness of Ajijic and had suddenly become the Jalisco International Society's Woman of the Century. Jane came to visit in late April 1990 and personally guided Neill through an afternoon of teas with Society officers and directors and a handful of old expatriate friends and Mexican families.

At a celebration called "Homenaje a Sra Neill James" put on by her former Mexican student-artists, Neill was called the godmother of Mexican artists. A mariachi encircled the two elderly sisters seated on the stage and played loud, passionate songs while people milled about eating frijoles and taking photos. The local Spanish and English language newspapers published the photos, and Neill insisted that the clippings be sent to every business and charitable organization along the lake's north shore. That year she received the Lifetime Achievement Award created by the expatriate magazine *Las Orejas del Lago*.

A trust was created, funded mostly by Jane. The Society was committed to use the trust for Neill's care and maintenance until her death, but they also did considerable renovation and improvement of the property, which was badly needed and which they funded on their own. Jane suggested that a television set and satellite feed service might be good for Neill, and she sent a check to cover the costs. The trustees vetoed that idea as impractical, and the check was returned.

A few Ajijic residents kept Jane informed by letter about Neill's health and activities. They always reported that Neill was doing well and felt happy. Neill still took daily walks by the lake, they said, although she needed an assistant, and she occasionally went out for lunch at the Nuevo Posada restaurant, where she would sit on the broad patio overlooking the lake and receive the greetings of old-time expatriates who knew her. She was moved from her upstairs bedroom to the *sala* downstairs, where her bed was set up near the big fireplace of her own design. The letters said she was warmer and happier living downstairs, and it was easier for her to go outdoors.

Her last outing took place when Jane and a Mississippi niece visited Ajijic the summer of 1994. A July 4th party was held at the Society compound, and Neill and her sister and niece attended the picnic on Neill's tiled patio under the great fig tree. Neill did not know what the event was and did not recognize anybody but Jane, but she smiled merrily and clapped her hands when the mariachis played.

That was the last time any of her kin saw Neill, for on the rainy morning of October 8, 1994, Socorro the house maid came to wake her around ten o'clock and saw that she had passed away overnight, still smiling as if she were at last having a pleasant dream. In line with Mexican law, Neill's body was cremated two days later, and on October 17 the Society held a memorial service on the lawn behind the tile patio. Her ashes were buried there beneath the big fig tree, where a tile plaque was laid to commemorate her dates.

Nobody from the family attended.

Author's Note

All is mystery; but he is a slave who will not struggle to penetrate
the dark veil.

—Benjamin Disaeli

"Once upon a time, to a tiny fishing village on the shores of a lovely lake in
Western Mexico, there came a fairy godmother. Well, not exactly . . . . Neill
James was an actual person and a talented writer and her magic wand was
nothing more than an abiding love for the Mexican people, especially the
women and children, and the financial means to do something
to help them."

———

Thus begins a praiseful reminiscence by Mildred Boyd, published in the
October 2004 issue of the expatriate magazine *El Ojo del Lago*. When I
interviewed the cigarillo puffing journalist in Ajijic, the tiny fishing village
of her feature article, Boyd told me she couldn't answer questions about
Neill James because she had never known her. Miss James, she said, was
gone to Alzheimer's disease by the time she had arrived on the scene. The
information she used in her story was based on testimonials from people
who said they had been touched by Neill James and recollections by others
in the international community at Lake Chapala.

I later learned that for a quarter century James had been a dedicated
world traveler, a self described nomad at heart. She wrote, "I am, by
instinct, a global vagabond. I cannot rest from travel." Her books describe
exotic sojourns to places even the most intrepid adventurers and war
correspondents rarely saw. If that were true, I thought, how did it happen
that she stopped traveling in midlife and remained for the next fifty years in
a remote Mexican pueblo?

The actual Neill James did write the five books described in this
narrative, and Maxwell Perkins was her editor at Charles Scribner's Sons.
Yet after she settled at Ajijic and finished *Dust on My Heart*, she stopped
writing, and today she is all but forgotten as an author. Why would a
successful travel writer give up her career so suddenly? She left no papers,
no diaries, and only a few letters and photos. Did she lead two distinctively
different lives in tandem, and if so what was the hinge-pin?

I became further intrigued when her admirers in Mexico told me she
had received visits from such luminaries as D.H. Lawrence, Amelia Earhart,

George Bernard Shaw and the publishers of *Time* and *Life*. Yet no evidence has surfaced that any literary celebrities came to see her, and I knew Lawrence and Earhart had died long before Neill James first arrived in Mexico. Mildred Boyd's description of her as a person of means and the expatriates' belief that she had come from an aristocratic family of Dixie plantation owners was a conclusion that was not held by Neill's descendants in Mississippi. The longer I sought to satisfy my curiosity about who she was, the more mysteries and contradictions I uncovered.

Two persons, complete strangers to each other and living a continent apart, told me they believed Neill James had been a spy. That theory, if true, would solve many of the problems of missing information, bizarre patterns of travel, and contradictory stories about her character and actions. But it implied a further puzzle: Why would an intelligence agent in mid-career come to land for good in rural Mexico? My quest to find out who she really was would last a decade and would end in frustration.

Yet I could not let her just go into the dustbin of history. Something about both the available remnants of her life and the critical missing parts insisted that I reconstruct a plausible life for her, as if she were part of my own heritage. It might have been the passion of her elderly admirers in Ajijic that drew me on and demanded a mediating story; equally it might have been the haughty way her critics, some of whom clearly weren't old enough to have known her, dismissed her. It might have been the tales I heard in Mexico about Neill almost singlehandedly bringing her village into the 20th Century, or the tiny margin notes I found scribbled in her 1972 kitchen calendar, reminding her of massages and medicines and appointments with her lawyer or bankers. It might have been the pervasive sense of her already having been lost to history, evident in the faded magazine articles about her from the 1950s, the mildewed copies of her books rotting on the bookshelves of her house, the new conference table occupying what had been her bedroom and castoff furniture and tools stored in her bathroom. But what most indelibly haunted my mind are the stories I heard describing Neill, an ancient woman hobbled by ancient injuries, on her daily walks to the lake.

———

This book is the result of my imagination's encounter with the available facts about the real Neill James. While it is a work of fiction, the story nonetheless is inspired by and is as faithful, within the constraints of fiction, as I could make it to her actual life history. Biographer and scholar Hermione Lee wrote that "different kinds of narrative may fit different kinds of biographical subjects." [1] In the case of Neill James—a self-mythologizing and secretive subject who left a legacy of contradictory tales, missing documents, and major gaps in the historical record—the kind of biographical narrative that fit best for my telling of her life was fiction.

At first I tried to write Neill's life story as a conventional biography. Ultimately I decided I would never know enough about her to succeed in that way. The difficulties I faced led me to question whether any biographer ever knows enough about his or her subject. Most biographers, as Nicholas Tolstoy observed, frame their work as if relating everything significant about a subject's life and telling it factually. But most biographies are about already famous people—literary celebrities, popular entertainers, political leaders—nearly all of whom self-consciously have left substantial documentary archives. It is as if ordinary lives aren't worth telling about—don't have the moral gravitas or the interest value of the lives of the well-known—or are too poorly documented for the biographer's work. Yet, in every person's life, including the life of a great general or Hollywood star or corporate bigwig, something is hidden, sometimes intentionally but also almost always inadvertently: There are too many moments, people and events in our lives for anyone to gain access to every detail. Every biographer must choose among all the knowable details the ones that seem to be important to tell about. The unknowable details—the bits that remain below consciousness or remain unrecorded—can have powerful influences on what comprises a life.

It's also evident that every biography contains artistic fictions and necessary misrepresentations: imagined conversations; actions not supported by indisputable records; gaps in time and space filled in like cracks in a narrative seam by the caulk of guesswork; and conclusions implicitly based on intuition or on what a reasonable person would have concluded, given the missing bits of evidence, those unknowable details among them. Jeanne W. Halpern wrote, "As the biographer becomes involved in gathering, selecting, organizing, and finally writing, he or she cannot help but become the re-creator of a life." [2] Arguing furthermore that biography always contains fictional aspects, Ira Bruce Nadel observed that "fictive form rather than historical content dominates as the events of a life become the elements of a story." [3] Michael Lackey points out that the reverse also is true, especially in postmodern fiction: Fiction writers expropriate biography and historical facts to create works of art that are increasingly becoming recognized by the literary establishment as legitimate members.[4]

More important, it seems to me that much of what is interesting about any person's life is what it means to that person to be her or him. Creative nonfiction theorist Robert Root said, "To recover an individual life you must recover the individual's world. They are inseparable; they dwell in one another." [5] Such a recovery in every case must be inferential, relying on the cultural knowledge, analytic imagination and intuition of the biographer.

In these ways all biographies are more or less fictional, and yet readers often assume that, unless told otherwise, the biography in their hands is factual. There is a break-point, and I do not know precisely where it lies in the biographical research for any other writer, beyond which a biographer must embrace and admit to writing fiction. In recovering Neill James's life, the case for my explicit embrace of fiction was strong and clear.

———

Throughout the ten years of my research I continuously came up with information that showed Neill had lied about or exaggerated or hidden her own story. She reframed her identity again and again. She wrote and published wedding announcements for her marriage to Harold Charles Knilands Scott-McGregor Campbell, but no evidence of the marriage has been found, not by me and not by James family members or other researchers. It didn't help my work that she used different names for the putative husband in letters and several public documents and that she attributed to him an apparently phony college degree from Carnegie Tech.

My belief is that her travel books papered over a second, secret career. Again, scant evidence is available about her intelligence work, and my conclusion that she had been a spy is based on patterns of her activities, suggestive government documents and interviews with persons who had come to the same judgment as mine. With her dissembling she divided people: I interviewed expatriates in Mexico who adored her, others who merely tolerated her and still others who had nothing good to say about her. Most of them, like Mildred Boyd, had never met her.

Yet Neill James was a bold, passionate and accomplished woman, and she lived an exceptionally long and adventure-filled life. Most of the broader events depicted in this book I believe are true, though I have embellished them with details, fictional characters, and subplots to tell a story. I followed Neill's exact itinerary, from birth to her final rest. I placed her in actual historical settings and activities–labor unrest and U.S. Army negative intelligence around World War I in the Pacific Northwest and espionage elsewhere in the United States during the interwar period;

intelligence operations targeting Japanese nationals in Hawaii, Japan and the Chinese mainland; all the details on the Third Asiatic Expedition and J. Mckenzie Young, the movements of Agnes Smedley with the Indian independence group and the Eastern Comintern in China, and the Institute of Pacific Relations material–these and more align generally with the historical record.

My coverage of events that happened on the world stage during Neill's life is not intended to be history. Moreover, I know of no hard evidence that would prove that Neill actually met up with Smedley or Hu Shih or Ernest Hemingway. On the other hand, it is at least plausible, because she was in the right neighborhoods at the right times and it is unlikely that she would have passed up the opportunity.

The same plausibility approach holds for the story's other characters. Thus, while all the military agency heads and top government officials from around the world actually existed as named, Vernon Shaw is my creation. There must have been, however, an officer like Shaw who supervised and mentored the underlying espionage career I believe Neill had. Other purely fictional characters are Mae Foster and Bhuma Singh Sharma, but Neill must have had a first love like Mae–nearly all my interviewees said that Neill loved women and that she famously accounted for the Campbell husband by saying, "He was Campbell the second, and that's about how long the marriage should've lasted." Bhuma Singh Sharma is a composite of two actual double-agents of that era.

Damon Byrd James is the fictional character who gets closest to the role of nonfiction narrator speaking for me and my research. The family saga he tells of in the first chapter reflects the true genealogy and history of the James clan as I could determine it. Katie Lawrence, Geraldine Sartain, Marguerite Cowlpitz Miller and Jana Saskova all were real people, as were most of the other persons portrayed in the narrative, but they appear in this book solely as fictional characters. The few people who I thought might be still living are likewise fictionalized and given different names. I also have created places and organizations that are merely inspired by actual ones; thus, for example, all the vanity *Who's Who* volumes are my inventions and the Lovejoy Ave Atelier never existed as such.

The letters between Neill and Maxwell Perkins are inspired by the editorial correspondence files in the Charles Scribner archive at Princeton. Neill did in fact wire Maxwell Perkins with a request for a reindeer "or anything with four legs and antlers." Most, but not all, of the letters from Neill to Jane reflect the way she wrote the actual ones. Most of the telegrams and all the intelligence reports and government documents are fictional creations.

Without the assistance of countless people I would not have been able to write this book. I am indebted to Anna Lee Pauls of Princeton University's Libraries for help in obtaining Neill's editorial files and production records. I am grateful also for professional assistance given by Prof. Susan Armitage, Allison Botelho, Laura Cappell, Anika Mitchell Perkins, Prof. Rick Spence, Marilyn Von Seggern, Andrew Shaindlin, and Cathy Young. I was fortunate to be given access to the University of Miami Otto G. Richter Special Collections Library, the Fant Memorial Library at the Mississippi University for Women, the New Haven Free Public Library, Washington State University's Holland and Terrell Libraries, the Mississippi Department of Archives and History, and the Grenada County Chancery Office in Grenada, Mississippi. Thanks also to Mary Redfern, Assistant Curator at the National Museums of Scotland.

For information, hospitality and access to the Neill James memorabilia collection in Ajijic I am thankful to the officers and staff of the Lake Chapala Society: Tod Jonson, Nancy Kreevan, Alan Maley, Jim Penton, Mary Alice Sargent, Charlie Smith, and former LCS librarian Ann Heath. My thanks are owed to Ajijic area residents who provided personal insights in interviews: Mildred Boyd, Ektor Carranza, Judy Eager, Michael Eager, Lila Kawananakoa, Judy King, Katie Lawrence, Doris Molinari and John Molinari. Sadly, some of these witnesses no longer are living. I received personal encouragement, information and technical help from Toni Beatty, A. Scott Berg, Printer Bowler, Dr. Neil James Campbell, Clive Coy, Dr. Chisato Dubreuil, Dayle Duffy-Cavaliere, David Gero, Sean Godfrey, Pamela Greenwood, Edward Grossman, Matthew Hogan, Prof. Paul Hooper, Carina Larson, Helen McLeod, Robert Nihiru, Kevin Riddle, Gene Smethers, Christine Smith, Herbert A. Thomas, Dr. David Truly, Patricia Walker, and Sandy Ward. I am grateful to all of them.

Neill James's descendants were graciously generous when I asked for access to their personal materials and their memories. My appreciation goes to Emma Connolly, Robert W. Neill, Jr., June and Thomas Snowden, and Nancy van Doren. I am particularly indebted to one descendant who was of inestimable help in shaping the story: Elizabeth Tomlinson not only provided much vital information from her own research files but she also put my interpretations and sources of data to the test and directed me to new lines of potential inquiry. My research assistant, librarian and friend Ann Warrington deserves special praise–she happily guided me through the most perplexing searches for documents and missing persons, and she has been a first-rate sounding board and early reader as I tried out new ideas and voices. Ed Suominen, editor, publisher and intrepid computer programmer, had the curiosity and flexibility to take on this arcane subject matter when few others, if any, would. The story, however, is my interpretation and mine alone. Any historical errors, infelicities of writing, or misjudgments of character also are solely mine.

In the preface to his autobiography Mark Twain remarked that a person's actions and words are but a tiny part of his life; most of his life is lived inside his head. I never will know how Neill James made sense of her own life and identities, because all of that remained inside her head. But it will not be for want of trying: Like Julia Blackburn's engagement with her subject Daisy Bates, I have held Neill James inside "a small corner of my mind for so long that it can sometimes seem as if I must have met her, but have simply forgotten the circumstances of our meeting." [6] For tolerating my decade-long obsession with the life of another woman—my quest to get Neill out of a corner of my mind by learning what might have been going on in hers—I owe my most profound thanks to my wife, Anna.

–Stephen Preston Banks

Notes

1. Lee, Hermione (2009). *Biography: A very Short Introduction*. New York: Oxford University Press, p. 123.

2. Halpern, Jeanne W. (1978). "Biographical images: Effects of formal features on the way we see a life," *The New Criterion*, Fall, Vol. 1, Number 4, pp. 1-14.

3. Nadel, Ira Bruce (1984). *Biography: Fiction, Fact and Form*. New York: St. Martin's Press.

4. Lackey, Michael (2014). *Truthful Fictions: Conversations with American Biographical Novelists*. New York: Bloomsbury Academic.

5. Root, Robert (2003). *Recovering Ruth: A Biographer's Tale*. Lincoln NE: University of Nebraska Press, p. xvi.

6. Blackburn, Julia (1994). *Daisy Bates in the Desert*. New York: Pantheon books, p. 13.

Bibliography

Aaron, Daniel (Ed.) (1978). *Studies in biography.* Cambridge: Harvard University Press.

Anhalt, Diana (2001). *A gathering of fugitives: American political expatriates in Mexico, 1948-1965.* Santa Maria CA: Archer Books.

Armitage, Careyn Patricia (2008). *Silk Production and its Impact on Families and Communities in Oaxaca, Mexico.* PhD Dissertation, Iowa State University.

Batvinis, Raymond J. (2007). *The origins of FBI counterintelligence.* Lawrence: University Press of Kansas.

Bedford, Sybille (1986). *A visit to Don Otavio: A traveller's tale from Mexico.* New York: Counterpoint.

Berberova, Nina (1988). *Moura: The dangerous life of the Baroness Budberg.* New York: New York Review of Books.

Borg, Dorothy (1947). *American policy and the Chinese Revolution, 1925-1928.* New York: American Institute of Pacific Relations and The Macmillan Company.

Cohen, Lisa (2012). *All We Know: Three Lives.* New York: Farrar, Straus and Giroux.

Hamilton, Nigel (2007). *Biography: A brief history.* Cambridge: Harvard University Press.

Harris, Charles H. III & Louis R. Sadler (2003). *The archaeologist was a spy: Sylvanus G. Morley and the Office of Naval Intelligence.* Albuquerque NM: University of New Mexico Press.

Harrison, Marguerite (1935). *There's always tomorrow: The story of a checkered life.* New York: Farrar & Rinehart.

James, Neill (1937). *Petticoat vagabond up and down the world.* New York: Charles Scribner's Sons.

James, Neill (1939). *Petticoat vagabond among the nomads.* New York: Charles Scribner's Sons.

James, Neill (1940). *White reindeer.* New York: Charles Scribner's Sons.

James, Neill (1942). *Petticoat vagabond in Ainu land and up and down East Asia.* New York: Charles Scribner's Sons.

James, Neill (1946). *Dust on my heart.* New York: Charles Scribner's Sons;

reissued 1997 as a second edition by Lake Chapala Society, Ajijic, Jalisco, Mexico.

Jeffreys-Jones, Rhodri (2007). *The FBI: A history.* New Haven CT: Yale University Press.

Jensen, Joan M. (1991). *Army surveillance in America, 1775-1980.* New Haven CT: Yale University Press.

Lackey, Michael (2014). *Truthful Fictions: Conversations with American Biographical Novelists.* New York: Bloomsbury Academic.

Lary, Diana (2007). *China's Republic.* Cambridge UK: Cambridge University Press.

Lee, Hermione (2009). *Biography: A very short introduction.* Oxford UK: Oxford University Press.

Mahoney, M.H. (1993). *Women in espionage: A biographical dictionary.* Santa Barbara CA: ABC-CLIO, Inc.

MacKinnon, Janice R. and MacKinnon, Stephen R. (1988). *Agnes Smedley: The life and times of an American radical.* Berkeley, CA: University of California Press.

May, Ernest R. (ed.) (1984). *Knowing one's enemies: Intelligence assessment before the two world wars.* Princeton NJ: Princeton University Press.

McGee, Micki (ed.) (2008). *Yaddo: Making an American culture.* New York: The New York Public Library and Columbia University Press.

Meier, Andrew (2008). *The lost spy: An American in Stalin's secret service.* New York: W.W. Norton & Company.

Moreira, Peter (2006). *Hemingway on the China Front: His WWII spy mission with Martha Gellhorn.* Washington D.C., Potomac Books, Inc.

Nadel, Ira Bruce (1984). *Biography: Fiction, Fact and Form.* New York: St. Martin's Press.

O'Toole, G.J.A. (1991). *Honorable treachery: A history of U.S. intelligence, espionage, and covert action from the American Revolution to the CIA.* New York: Morgan Entrekin/The Atlantic Monthly Press.

Pachter, Marc (Ed.) (1978). *Telling lives: The biographer's art.* Washington, D.C., New Republic Books/National Portrait Gallery.

Price, David H. (2008). *Anthropological intelligence: The deployment and neglect of American anthropology in the Second World War.*

Durham and London: Duke University Press.

Prange, Gordon W. (1984). *Target Tokyo: The story of the Sorge spy ring*. New York: McGraw-Hill.

Price, Ruth (2005). *The lives of Agnes Smedley*. Oxford UK: Oxford University Press.

Proctor, Tammy M. (2003). *Female intelligence: Women and espionage in the First World War*. New York and London: New York University Press.

Richelson, Jeffrey T. (1995). *A century of spies: Intelligence in the twentieth century*. New York: Oxford University Press.

Root, Robert (2003). *Recovering Ruth: A biographer's tale*. Lincoln: University of Nebraska Press.

Snow, Edgar (1939). *Red star over China* (revised edition). New York: Garden City Publishing Co., Inc.

Stevenson, William (2007). *Spymistress: The life of Vera Atkins, the greatest female secret agent of World War II*. New York: Arcade Publishing, Inc.

Talbert, Roy (1991). *Negative intelligence: The Army and the American Left, 1917-1941*. Oxford: University Press of Mississippi.

Volkman, Ernest, and Blaine Baggett (1989). *Secret intelligence: The inside story of American's espionage empire*. New York: Doubleday.

Winters, Kathleen C. (2010). *Amelia Earhart: The turbulent life of an American icon*. New York: Palgrave Macmillan.